Acclaim for *The Traveller*:

'The pace is fast, the characters intriguing and memorable, the evil dark and palpable, and the genre-bending between fantasy and thriller seamless . . . He could be a force to reckon with'
Kirkus Reviews

'Twelve Hawks' much anticipated novel is powerful, mainstream fiction built on a foundation of cutting-edge technology laced with fantasy and the chilling specter of an all-too-possible social and political reality'
Publishers Weekly

'The book they say is the new *Da Vinci Code*. Take some Orwellian undertones, add a dash of Philip Pullman and sprinkle with a few lines of Dan Brown'
Metro

'Compelling. Picture *The Matrix* crossed with William Gibson and you'll have a sense of *The Traveller*'
Newsday

'A cyber *1984*. Page-turningly swift, with a cliffhanger ending'
New York Times

Also by John Twelve Hawks

THE TRAVELLER

and published by Corgi Books

JOHN TWELVE HAWKS

THE

Dark River

Book Two of
The Fourth Realm Trilogy

CORGI BOOKS

TRANSWORLD PUBLISHERS
61–63 Uxbridge Road, London W5 5SA
A Random House Group Company
www.rbooks.co.uk

THE DARK RIVER
A CORGI BOOK: 9780552153355

First published in Great Britain
in 2007 by Bantam Press
a division of Transworld Publishers
Corgi edition published 2008

Addresses for Random House Group Ltd companies outside the UK
can be found at: www.randomhouse.co.uk
The Random House Group Ltd Reg. No. 954009

The Random House Group Limited supports The Forest Stewardship
Council (FSC), the leading international forest certification
organisation. All our titles that are printed on Greenpeace approved
FSC certified paper carry the FSC logo.
Our paper procurement policy can be found at
www.rbooks.co.uk/environment

Typeset in 11/13pt Fairfield by
Falcon Oast Graphic Art Ltd.

Printed in the UK by CPI Cox & Wyman, Reading, RG1 8EX.

2 4 6 8 10 9 7 5 3

for my children

AUTHOR'S NOTE

The Dark River is a work of fiction inspired by the real world.

An adventurous reader can touch the sundial hidden beneath the streets of Rome, travel to Ethiopia and stand outside the holy sanctuary in Axum, or walk through Grand Central Terminal in New York and look up at the mystery on the concourse ceiling.

The aspects of the Vast Machine described in the novel are also real or under development. In the near future, both private and governmental total information systems will monitor every aspect of our lives. A central computer will remember where we go and what we buy, the e-mail we write, and the books we read.

Each attack on privacy is justified by the pervasive culture of fear that seems to surround us and grow stronger every day. The ultimate consequences of that fear are expressed in my vision of the First Realm. Its darkness will exist forever and it will be opposed—forever—by compassion, bravery, and love.

—John Twelve Hawks

DRAMATIS PERSONAE

In *The Traveller*, John Twelve Hawks introduced readers to an ancient conflict going on beneath the surface of our day-to-day world. This conflict involves three groups of people: the Brethren, the Travellers, and the Harlequins.

Kennard Nash is the leader of the Brethren, a group of powerful individuals who oppose any change in the established social structure. *Nathan Boone* is the secret organization's head of security. The Brethren are called the "Tabula" by their enemies because they see both humanity and human consciousness as a tabula rasa—a blank slate on which they can scrawl their own message of intolerance and fear. In the eighteenth century, the British philosopher Jeremy Bentham designed the Panopticon: a model prison where one observer could monitor hundreds of prisoners and remain unseen. Both Nash and Boone believe that the computerized surveillance system being created in the industrial world will allow them to establish a Virtual Panopticon.

For centuries, the Brethren have tried to exterminate the Travellers: men and women who have the power to send their energy into one of six realms. The realms are parallel realities that have been described by visionaries from every faith. Travellers return to this world with new insights and revelations that challenge the established order and the Brethren believe that they are the primary source of social instability. One of the last surviving Travellers was *Matthew Corrigan*, but he disappeared when the Brethren's mercenaries attacked his home. His two surviving sons, *Michael and Gabriel Corrigan*, lived off the Grid until they discovered that they also had the power to become Travellers.

The Travellers could have been exterminated many years ago, but they've been protected by a small group of dedicated fighters called Harlequins. Matthew Corrigan was once protected by a German-born Harlequin named *Thorn* who was killed in Prague by Nathan Boone. Thorn's daughter, *Maya*, was sent to America to find the two Corrigan brothers. Maya is supported by a French Harlequin named *Linden*, and she often thinks about the legendary Harlequin *Mother Blessing*, who has disappeared. When Maya visited Los Angeles, she found two allies: a martial arts teacher named *Hollis Wilson* and a young woman named *Vicki Fraser*.

As the story continues, Michael Corrigan has gone over to the Brethren while his younger brother, Gabriel, is hiding with Maya, Hollis, and Vicki. At New Harmony, the Arizona community started by Matthew Corrigan, storm clouds cover the sky and snow begins to fall . . .

THE
Dark River

PRELUDE

Snowflakes began drifting down from the darkening sky as the members of New Harmony returned to their homes for dinner. The adults working on a retaining wall near the community center blew on their hands and talked about storm fronts, while the children cocked their heads backward, opened their mouths, and spun around trying to catch the ice crystals on their tongues.

Alice Chen was a small, serious girl in jeans, work boots, and a blue nylon parka. She had just turned eleven, but her best friends, Helen and Melissa, were both twelve going on thirteen. Lately, the two older girls had been having long conversations about childish behavior and which boys at New Harmony were stupid and immature.

Although Alice wanted to taste the snowflakes, she decided that it wasn't very mature of her to twirl around with her tongue out like the Lower School babies. Pulling on her knit cap, she followed her friends down one of the paths that crisscrossed through the canyon. It was difficult to be grown-up. She was relieved when Melissa tagged Helen, shouted, "You're it!" and darted away.

The three friends dashed down the canyon, laughing and chasing one another. The night air was cold and smelled of pine and wet soil and the faint odor of a wood fire down by the greenhouse. As they passed through a clearing, the snowflakes stopped falling for a moment and swirled around in a circle—as if a family of ghosts had lingered to play among the trees.

There was a distant mechanical sound, growing louder, and the girls stopped running. Seconds later, a helicopter with Arizona Forest Service markings roared above them and continued up the canyon. They had seen helicopters like that, but always in the summer. It was strange to see one in February.

"They're probably searching for someone," Melissa said. "Bet a tourist went looking for the Indian ruins and got lost."

"And now it's getting dark," Alice said. It would be terrible to be alone like that, she thought—getting tired and scared as you trudged through the snow.

Helen leaned forward and slapped Alice on the shoulder. "Now you're it!" she said. And they started running.

* * *

A NIGHT-VISION device and a thermal imaging sensor were mounted on the underside of the helicopter. The NVD collected visible light as well as the lower portion of the infrared spectrum, while the thermal sensor detected the heat emitted from different objects. The two devices sent their data to a computer that combined everything into a single video image.

Eighteen miles from New Harmony, Nathan Boone sat in the back of a bread delivery truck that had been converted to a surveillance vehicle. He sipped some coffee—no sugar, no cream—and watched as a black-and-white vision of New Harmony appeared on a monitor.

The head of security for the Brethren was a neatly dressed man with short gray hair and steel-rimmed glasses. There was something severe, almost judgmental in his manner. Policemen and border guards said, "Yes, sir," when they first met him, and civilians usually lowered their eyes when he asked them a question.

Boone had used night-vision devices when he was in the military, but the new dual camera was a significant advance. Now he could see targets both inside and outside at the same time: one person strolling beneath the trees and another washing the dishes in the kitchen. Even more helpful was that the computer was capable of evaluating each source of light and making an informed guess whether the object was a human being or a hot frying pan. Boone saw the new camera as evidence that science and technology—indeed, the future itself—were on his side.

George Cossette, the other person sitting in the truck, was a surveillance expert who had been flown in from Geneva. He was a pale young man with a great many food allergies. During the eight days of surveillance, he had occasionally used the computer's Internet uplink to bid on plastic figurines of comic book heroes.

"Give me a count," Boone said, watching the live feed from the helicopter.

Concentrating on the monitor, Cossette began to type commands. "All sources of heat or just the humans?"

"Just the humans. Thank you."

Click. Click. Fingers moving on a keyboard. A few seconds later, the sixty-eight people living at New Harmony were outlined on the screen.

"How accurate is that?"

"Ninety-eight to ninety-nine percent. We might have missed one or two people who were on the edge of the scan zone."

Boone took off his glasses, polished them with a small flannel cloth, and watched the video a second time. Over the years, Travellers and their Pathfinder teachers had preached about the so-called Light that existed inside every person. But real light—not the spiritual kind—had become a new method of detection. It was impossible to hide, even in the darkness.

* * *

SNOWFLAKES CLUNG TO Alice's hair as she entered the kitchen, but they melted before she pulled off her jacket. Her family's house was built in the Southwest style, with a flat roof, small windows, and little exterior decoration. Like all the other buildings in the canyon, the house was made of straw—bales had been stacked into walls, skewered with steel rods, and then covered with waterproof plaster. The ground floor was dominated by one large area with a kitchen, living room, and open staircase that led to a sleeping loft. A doorway led to Alice's bedroom, a home office, and a bathroom. Because of the thick walls, there was an alcove around each window frame; the one in the kitchen was filled with a basket of ripening avocados and some old bones found out in the desert.

A pot boiling on the electric stove gave off steam and fogged up the window glass. On a cold night like this, Alice felt as if she were living in a space capsule dropped to the bottom of a tropical lagoon. If she wiped the moisture away from the window, she would probably see a pilot fish gliding past white coral.

As usual, her mother had left a mess in the kitchen—dirty bowls and spoons, stems from cut basil, and an open flour container just waiting for the mice. Alice's black braid swung back and forth as she moved about the kitchen, putting away food and wiping up crumbs. She washed the mixing bowls and spoons, and then placed them on a clean towel as if they were scalpels on a surgical table. When she was putting away the flour, her mother came downstairs from the sleeping loft carrying a stack of medical magazines.

Dr. Joan Chen was a petite woman with short black hair. She was a physician who had moved to New Harmony with her daughter after her husband died in a car accident. Every evening before dinner, Joan changed from jeans and a flannel shirt to a long skirt and a silk blouse.

"Thanks, honey. But you didn't have to clean up. I would have done all that . . ." Joan sat in a carved chair near the fireplace and placed the magazines on her lap.

"Who's coming for dinner?" Alice asked. The people at New Harmony were always sharing meals with each other.

"Martin and Antonio. The budget committee has to make a decision about something."

"Did you get bread at the bakery?"

"Well, of course I did," Joan said. Then she fluttered her right hand as if she were searching for a memory. "That is, maybe I did. I think so."

Alice searched the kitchen and found a loaf of bread that appeared to be about three days old. Turning on the oven, she split the loaf in half, rubbed both sides with fresh garlic, and drizzled on some olive oil. As the bread roasted on a steel tray, she set the table and got out the serving platter for pasta. When she was finally done, she intended to walk silently past her mother to protest all the work she had to do. But when she approached the chair, Joan reached out and touched her daughter's hand.

"Thank you, dear. I'm lucky to have such a wonderful daughter."

* * *

SCOUTS WERE IN position at the perimeter of New Harmony, and the rest of the mercenaries had just left a motel in San Lucas. Boone e-mailed a message to Kennard Nash, the current head of the Brethren. A few minutes later, he received a response: *The previously discussed action is now confirmed.*

Boone called the driver of the SUV carrying the first team. "Proceed to Point Delta. Employees should now take their PTS medication."

Each mercenary was carrying a plastic packet containing two pretraumatic stress pills. Boone's employees had nicknamed them "pits pills," and swallowing them before an action was called "taking your pits." The medication temporarily immunized anyone entering a violent situation against strong feelings of guilt or regret.

The original research concerning PTS was done at Harvard University when neurologists found out that accident victims taking a cardiac drug called propranolol had decreased amounts of physiological trauma. Scientists working for the Brethren's research group, the Evergreen Foundation, realized the implications of this discovery. They obtained a grant from the U.S. Defense Department to study the drug when used by soldiers in combat. The PTS medication inhibited the brain's hormonal reactions to shock, disgust, and fear. This lessened the formation of traumatic memories.

Nathan Boone had never taken a PTS pill or any other kind of trauma medication. If you believed in what you were doing, if you knew you were right, then there was no such thing as guilt.

* * *

ALICE STAYED IN her bedroom until the rest of the budget committee showed up for dinner. Martin Greenwald arrived first, knocking softly on the kitchen door and waiting for Joan to greet him. Martin was an older man with stubby legs and thick eyeglasses. He had been a successful businessman in Houston until his car broke down on the freeway one afternoon and a man named Matthew Corrigan stopped to help him. Matthew turned out to be a Traveller, a spiritual teacher with the power to leave his body and travel to other realities. He had spent several weeks talking to the Greenwald family and their friends, then had embraced them all at one final meeting and walked away. New Harmony was a reflection of the Traveller's ideas—an attempt to create a new way of living that was apart from the Vast Machine.

Alice had learned about Travellers from other kids, but was uncertain how it all worked. She knew that there were six different worlds, called realms. This world—with its fresh bread and dirty dishes—was the Fourth Realm. The Third Realm was a forest with friendly animals, and that sounded great. But there was also a Realm of hungry ghosts, and another place where people were always fighting.

Matthew's son, Gabriel, was a young man in his twenties who was also a Traveller. In October, he had spent a night at New Harmony with a Harlequin bodyguard named Maya. Now it was early February, and the adults were still talking about Gabriel while the kids argued about the Harlequin. Ricky Cutler said Maya had probably killed dozens of people and that she knew something called the Tiger Claw Variation: one punch to the heart, and the other guy was dead. Alice decided that the Tiger Claw Variation was a big fake invented on the Internet. Maya was very much a real person, a young woman with thick black hair and ghostly blue eyes who carried her sword in a tube hanging from her shoulder.

A few minutes after Martin arrived, Antonio Cardenas thumped on the door and walked in without asking. Antonio was a swaggering, athletic man who had once been a contractor in Houston. When the first group moved into the canyon, he had built the three windmills up on the mesa that provided the community's electric power. Everyone at New Harmony liked Antonio; some of the younger boys even wore their tool belts in the same low-slung way he did.

The two men smiled at Alice and asked her about her cello lessons. Everyone sat down at the oak wood table—like most of the furniture in the house, it had been built in Mexico. The pasta was served and the adults began to discuss the issue before the budget committee. New Harmony had now saved enough money to buy a sophisticated battery system to store electric power. The current system allowed every family to have a stove, a refrigerator, and two space heaters. More batteries would mean more appliances, but perhaps that wasn't a good idea.

"I think it's more efficient to keep the washing machines up at the community center," Martin said. "And I don't think we need espresso machines and microwave ovens."

"I disagree," Joan said. "Microwaves actually use less power."

Antonio nodded. "And I'd like some cappuccino in the morning."

* * *

AS ALICE CLEARED the table of dirty dishes, she glanced at the wall clock over the sink. It was late Wednesday night in Arizona, which meant Thursday afternoon in Australia. She had about ten minutes to get ready for her music lesson. The adults ignored her while she quickly pulled on her long winter coat, got her cello case, and went outside.

It was still snowing. The rubber soles of her work boots made a crunching sound as she walked from the front door to the gate. A six-foot-high adobe wall surrounded the house and vegetable garden; it kept out the deer in the summertime. Last year, Antonio had installed a large gate with carvings of scenes from the Garden of Eden. If you stood close enough to the dark oak wood you could see Adam and Eve, a flowering tree, and a serpent.

Alice pushed the gate open and passed beneath the archway. The path up the canyon to the community center was covered with snow, but that didn't bother her. The kerosene lantern she carried swung back and forth as the snowflakes kept falling. Snow covered the pine trees and mountain mahogany; it transformed a pile of firewood into a mound that looked like a sleeping bear.

The community center was made up of four large buildings around a courtyard. One of the buildings was the Upper School for older students, eight rooms that were designed for online learning. A router in the storage room was connected to a cable that led to a satellite dish on the mesa above them. There were no telephone lines at New Harmony, and cell phones didn't work in the canyon. People either used the Internet or the satellite phone kept at the community center.

Alice turned on the computer, removed her cello from its carrying case, and positioned a straight-backed chair in front of the Web cam. She connected with the Internet and a moment later her cello teacher appeared on the large monitor screen. Miss Harwick was an older woman who had once played for the Sydney Opera.

"Have you practiced, Alice?"

"Yes, ma'am."

"Let's start with 'Greensleeves' today."

Alice drew the bow back and her body absorbed the deep vibration from the first note. Playing the cello made her feel bigger, more substantial, and she could hold on to that power for a few hours after she stopped playing.

"Very good," said Miss Harwick. "Now let me hear section B again. This time focus on your pitch in the third measure and—"

The monitor screen went black. At first, Alice thought that something was wrong with the generator. But the electric lights were working and she could hear the faint hum of the computer fan.

While she was checking the cables, a door squeaked open and Brian Bates walked into the room. Brian was a fifteen-year-old boy with dark brown eyes and blond hair down to his shoulders.

Helen and Melissa thought he was cute, but Alice didn't like to talk about things like that. She and Brian were music friends; he played the trumpet and worked with teachers in London and New Orleans.

"Hey, Celloissima. Didn't know you were practicing tonight."

"I'm supposed to be having a lesson, but the computer just went off."

"Did you change anything?"

"Of course not. I went online and contacted Miss Harwick. Everything was okay until a few seconds ago."

"Don't worry. I'll fix it. I've got a lesson in forty minutes with a new teacher in London. He plays for the Jazz Tribe."

Brian put down his trumpet case and pulled off his parka. "How are the lessons going, Celloissima? I heard you practicing on Thursday. It sounded pretty good."

"I've got to come up with a nickname for you," Alice said. "What about Brianissima?"

Brian smiled as he sat down at the computer. "Issima is a feminine ending. It's got to be something different."

Pulling on her coat, Alice decided to leave her cello at the community center and go back to the house. A door from the performance room led to a storage closet. She stepped around a potter's wheel and left the cello leaning against the wall in a corner, protected by two plastic bags of ceramic clay. That was when she heard a man's voice coming from the performance room.

Alice returned to the partially opened door, peered through the gap, and stopped breathing. A big man with a beard was pointing a rifle at Brian. The stranger wore brown-and-green camouflage clothing like the deer hunters Alice had seen on the road to San Lucas. Dark green camouflage grease was smeared on his cheeks, and he had special goggles with a rubber strap. The goggles were pushed upward on his forehead, the two eyepieces combining into a single lens that reminded her of a monster's horn.

"What's your name?" the man asked Brian. His voice was flat and neutral.

Brian didn't answer. He pushed back the chair and got up slowly.

"I asked you a question, pal."

"I'm Brian Bates."

"Anybody else here in this building?"

"No. Just me."

"So what are you doing?"

"Trying to go online."

The bearded man laughed softly. "You're wasting your time. We just cut the cable to the mesa."

"And who are you?"

"I wouldn't worry about that, pal. If you want to grow up and get laid, own a car, stuff like that—then you better answer my questions. Where's the Traveller?"

"What traveller? Nobody has visited this place since the first snowfall."

The man motioned with his rifle. "Don't be cute. You know what I'm talking about. A Traveller stayed here with a Harlequin named Maya. Where'd they go?"

Brian shifted his weight slightly, as if he were going to sprint for the door.

"I'm waiting for an answer, pal."

"Go to hell . . ."

Brian jumped forward and the bearded man fired his rifle. The gunshots were so loud that Alice jerked away from the door. She stood in the shadows for a full minute, the sound still vibrating through her body, and then returned to the light. The man with the rifle was gone, but Brian lay on his side, as if he had fallen asleep on the floor, curled around a bright pool of blood.

Her body was the same, but her Alice-self—the girl who had laughed with her friends and played the cello—had suddenly become much smaller. It felt as if she were living inside a hollow statue, looking out at the world.

Voices. Alice stepped back into the shadows as Brian's killer returned with six other men. They all wore camouflage clothing and radio headsets with little microphones that curved around to their mouths.

Each man carried a different kind of rifle, but all the weapons had a laser-sighting device attached to the barrel. The leader—an older man with short hair and wire-rimmed glasses—was talking softly into his headset. He nodded and switched off the transmitter clipped to his belt.

"Okay, Summerfield and Gleason are in position with the thermal sensors. They'll stop anyone trying to escape, but I don't want that to happen."

A few of the men nodded. One of them was testing his laser sight, and a little red dot danced across the white wall.

"Remember—the weapons you've been given have been registered under the names of people who live here. If for some reason you have to use an unregistered weapon, please keep track of location, target, and number of shots fired." The leader waited until his men nodded. "Okay. You know what to do. Let's go."

The six men went away, fitting the goggles over their eyes, but the leader remained in the room. Pacing back and forth, he spoke occasionally on the headset. *Yes. Confirmed. Next objective.* The leader ignored Brian's dead body—almost as if he hadn't noticed it—but when a thin line of blood trickled across the floor, he gracefully stepped over it and kept moving.

Alice sat down in a corner of the storage room, drew her knees up to her chest, and closed her eyes. She had to do something—find her mother, warn the others—but her body wouldn't move. Alice's brain kept producing thoughts, and she watched them passively as if they were fuzzy images on a television screen. Someone was crying, talking loudly—and then she recognized a familiar voice.

"Where are my children? I want to see my children . . ."

Returning quietly to the door, Alice saw that the leader had brought Janet Wilkins into the room. The Wilkins family came from England; they had just joined New Harmony a few months ago. Mrs. Wilkins was a plump, fussy woman who seemed to be afraid of everything—rattlesnakes, rockslides, and lightning.

The leader held Mrs. Wilkins's arm tightly. He guided her across the room and made her sit down on the straight-backed chair. "There you go, Janet. Make yourself comfortable. Can I get you a glass of water?"

"No. That's not necessary." Mrs. Wilkins saw the dead body, and then she turned her head away. "I-I want to see my children."

"Don't worry, Janet. They're safe. I'll take you to them in a few minutes, but there's one thing I need you to do first." The leader reached into his pocket, pulled out a piece of paper, and handed it to Mrs. Wilkins. "Here. Read this."

A video camera on a tripod had been placed in the room. The leader set the camera five feet away from Mrs. Wilkins and made sure that she was in the viewfinder. "Okay," he told her, "go ahead."

Mrs. Wilkins's hands were shaking as she began to read: "'In the last few weeks, members of New Harmony have received messages from God. We cannot doubt these messages. We know they are true . . .'"

She stopped reading and shook her head. *No. Can't do this.* Standing behind the video camera, the leader drew a handgun from his shoulder holster.

"'But there are disbelievers among us,'" Mrs. Wilkins continued. "'People who have followed the teachings of the Evil One. It's important that we perform a cleansing act so that all of us can enter the Kingdom of Heaven.'"

The leader lowered his gun and switched off the camera. "Thank you, Janet. That was a good first step, but it's still not enough. You know why we're here and what we're looking for. I want information about the Traveller."

Mrs. Wilkins started crying, her face contorted into a mask of sadness and fear. "I don't know anything. I swear . . ."

"Everybody knows something."

"The young man isn't here anymore. He's gone. But my husband said Martin Greenwald got a letter from a Traveller a few weeks ago."

"And where is this letter?"

"It's probably in Martin's house. He has a little office there."

The leader spoke into his headset. "Go to the

Greenwald house in sector five. Search the office for a letter from the Traveller. This is level-one priority." Switching off his radio, he took a step toward Mrs. Wilkins. "Anything else you can tell me?"

"I don't support the Travellers or the Harlequins. I'm not on anybody's side. I just want my children."

"Of course. I understand." Once again, the leader's voice was soft and comforting. "Why don't you join them?"

He raised the handgun and shot her. Mrs. Wilkins's body fell backward with a thump. The leader looked down at the dead woman as if she were a piece of trash left on the floor, then slid his gun back in its holster and left the room.

Alice felt like time had stopped and restarted in a herky-jerky manner. It seemed to take a very long time to push the closet door open and walk through the rehearsal room. When she reached the hallway, time went so fast that she was conscious of only a few things: the concrete walls, the beckoning doorway, the man with the steel glasses at the other end of the corridor who raised his gun and shouted at her.

Alice went the other way, pushing the door open and running out into the night. It was still snowing and very cold, but the darkness surrounded her like a magic cloak. Her face and bare hands felt like they were burning when she emerged from the grove of juniper trees and approached the house. The lights were still on inside; that had to be a good sign. When she passed beneath the archway she reached out and touched the flowering tree that Antonio had carved into the gate.

The front door was unlocked. Alice entered the house and saw that the dinner dishes were still on the table. "Hello," she said softly. No one answered. Moving as quietly as possible, she inspected the kitchen and then entered the living room. Where was she supposed to go? Where were the adults hiding?

Alice stood still and listened for voices, anything that would tell her what to do. The wind blew snowflakes against the windows while the space heater hummed softly. She took a step forward and heard a faint dripping sound, as if water were leaking out of a kitchen pipe. The sound came again—a little louder—then she circled around the couch and saw a pool of blood. A drop of blood trickled down from the loft and splattered on the floor.

Her body began moving again and she slowly climbed the staircase to the loft. There were only fourteen steps, but it felt like the longest journey of her life. Step. Another step. She wanted to stop, but her legs kept moving. "Please, Mommy," she whispered as if she were begging for a special favor. "Please . . ." And then she was up in the loft and standing next to her mother's body.

The front door slammed open. Alice crouched down in the shadows, a few inches away from the bed.

A man had entered the house. He was talking loudly into his headset microphone.

"Yes, sir. I'm back at sector nine . . ."

There was a splashing sound and Alice peered over the edge of the loft. A man wearing camouflage clothing was pouring a clear liquid over the furniture. The sharp smell of gasoline filled the air.

"No kids here—only the targets in my sector. Raymond caught two people running for the trees, but they were both adults. Affirmative. We took the bodies inside."

The man tossed the empty fuel can onto the floor, returned to the entryway, and lit a wooden match. He held it in front of his face for an instant and Alice saw, not cruelty or hatred, but simple obedience. The man tossed the match on the floor and the gasoline immediately caught fire. Satisfied, the man walked out the door, closing it behind him.

Black smoke filled the room as Alice stumbled down the staircase. There was a single window on the north side of the house, about six feet above the floor. She pushed her mother's desk against the wall, clicked the latch open, and crawled outside, falling onto the snow.

All she wanted to do was hide like a small animal curled up in a burrow. Coughing and crying from the smoke, she passed through the carved gate one last time. A chemical odor filled the air; it smelled like a garbage fire at the dump. Alice followed the adobe wall to a patch of bear grass and began scrambling up the rocky slope that led to the ridge above the canyon. As she climbed higher, she saw that all the houses were burning now, the flames flowing like a luminous river. The canyon got steeper and she had to grab at branches and clumps of grass, pulling herself upward.

Near the top of the ridge, she heard a cracking sound and a bullet hit the snow-covered dirt in front of her. She threw herself sideways and rolled back down the hill, covering her face with her hands. Her body went about twenty feet, then hit a thornbush and stopped. As she began to get up, she remembered what the leader had said at the community center. *Summerfield and Gleason are in position. Thermal sensors.* And what did the word *thermal* mean? Heat. The gunman could see her because her body was warm.

Lying on her back, Alice began to scoop up snow with her bare hands. She covered her legs with snow, then lay flat and pushed snow over her stomach and chest. Finally, she buried her left arm and used the right arm to cover her neck and face, leaving a little opening around her mouth. Her bare skin began to tingle and burn, but she stayed beside the thornbush and tried not to move. As the cold penetrated her body, the last particle of her Alice-self flickered and faded and died.

$\mathcal{M}$ichael Corrigan sat in a windowless room at the Evergreen Foundation's Research Center, north of New York City. He was watching a young Frenchwoman as she wandered through the Printemps Department Store in Paris. The surveillance cameras in the store reduced everything to black and white and shades of gray, but he could see that she was a brunette, fairly tall, and quite attractive. He liked her short skirt, black leather jacket, and her shoes—high heels with thin straps tied around her ankles.

The scanner room resembled a private facility for showing movies. It had a large flat-panel video screen and speakers built into the walls. But there was only one place to sit—a butternut-brown leather lounge chair with a computer monitor and keyboard on a pivoting steel arm. Whoever was using the room could type directions into the system or slip on a

phone headset and talk to the staff at the new
computer center in Berlin. The first time Michael sat
in the chair, he had to be guided through the use of
scanning programs and backdoor access channels to
surveillance systems. Now he could do simple tracking operations on his own.

The young brunette was walking through the
beauty-care section. Michael had checked out
the store a few days earlier and was hoping that his
target would take the escalator upstairs to the
Printemps de la Mode section. Although surveillance
cameras weren't allowed in the individual changing
rooms, there was a hidden camera in the public area
at the end of the hallway. Occasionally the
Frenchwomen would come out wearing lingerie so
they could study themselves in a full-length mirror.

* * *

MICHAEL'S PRESENCE IN the scanner room was just
another indication of his growing influence among
the Brethren. He was a Traveller like his father,
Matthew, and younger brother, Gabriel. In the past,
Travellers had been seen as prophets or mystics, mad-
men or liberators. They had the power to break free
of their bodies and send their conscious energy—
their "Light"—to other realities. When they returned,
they had visions and insights that transformed the
world.

Travellers had always encountered resistance from the authorities, but in the modern era a group of men called the Brethren began to identify Travellers and kill them before they could challenge the established order. Inspired by the ideas of Jeremy Bentham, an eighteenth-century British philosopher, the Brethren wanted to establish a Virtual Panopticon, an invisible prison that would contain everyone in the industrial world. The Brethren believed that once the population assumed they were being watched at all times, they would automatically follow the rules.

The true symbol of the age was a closed-circuit surveillance camera. Computerized information systems had formed a Vast Machine that could link images and information to monitor large populations. For thousands of years, those in power had tried to ensure the permanency of their particular system. Finally, this dream of social control had become a real possibility.

The Brethren had entered Michael's and Gabriel's lives when they were growing up on a farm in South Dakota. A team of mercenaries looking for their father had attacked their home and set fire to the buildings. The two Corrigan brothers had survived, but their father had disappeared. Years later, after being raised by their mother off the Grid, the Corrigans ended up in Los Angeles. Nathan Boone and his men first captured Michael, and then Gabriel. They transported both brothers to the Evergreen Foundation's Research Center.

The Brethren's scientists had built a powerful quantum computer, and the subatomic particles at the heart of the machine had enabled communication with the other realms that only Travellers had been able to explore. The new quantum computer was supposed to track a Traveller's passage across the four barriers to other worlds, but a young Harlequin named Maya had destroyed it when she rescued Gabriel.

Whenever Michael evaluated his new change in status, he had to admit that Maya's attack on the Research Center was the crucial step in his personal transformation. He had shown his loyalty—not to his brother—but to the Brethren. Once the wreckage was cleaned up and a new security perimeter was established, Michael had returned to the center. He was still a prisoner, but eventually everyone in the world was going to be part of an enormous prison. The only real distinction was your level of awareness. There was going to be a new alignment of power in the world, and he planned to be on the winning side.

* * *

IT HAD TAKEN only a few sessions in the room for Michael to be seduced by the power of the Vast Machine. There was something about sitting in the chair that made you feel like God looking down from heaven. Right now, the young woman wearing the leather jacket had just stopped at a makeup counter and was chatting with the salesclerk. Michael slipped on the headset and pressed a switch. Immediately, he was talking to the Brethren's new computer center in Berlin.

"This is Michael. I want to speak to Lars."

"Just a minute, please," said a woman with a German accent. A few seconds later, Lars came on the line. He was always helpful, and never asked impertinent questions.

"Okay. I'm at Printemps in Paris," Michael said. "The target is at the makeup counter. So how do I get her personal information?"

"Let me take a look," Lars said.

A small red light appeared on the lower right corner of the screen. That meant Lars had access to the same image. Often several technicians were watching the same surveillance system or you attached yourself to the activities of a bored security guard sitting in a monitoring room somewhere. The guards—who were supposedly the first line of defense against terrorists and criminals—spent a great deal of their time stalking women through malls and then out into the parking lot. If you switched on the audio, you could hear them chatting to one another and laughing when a woman wearing a tight skirt was about to get into a sports car.

"We can reduce her face to an algorithm and

compare it to the photographs in the French passport database," Lars explained. "But it's much easier if we just pick up her credit card number. Look at your personal monitor and click the dedicated tele-communications option. Type in as much information as possible: location of the phone, date, time—which is right now, of course. The Carnivore program will skim her number the moment it's transmitted."

The store clerk slid the young woman's card through a scanner and numbers flashed onto the screen. "And there it is," Lars said as if he were a magician who had taught his apprentice a new trick. "Now double-click . . ."

"I know what to do." Michael moved the cursor to the cross-reference button and, almost instantly, additional information began to appear. The woman's name was Clarisse Marie du Portail. Twenty-three years old. No credit problems. This is her phone number. This is her home address. The program translated from French into English a list of items she had bought with her credit card during the last three months.

"Watch this," Lars said. A box on the top right-hand corner of the screen displayed a grainy image from a street surveillance camera. "See that building? That's where she lives. Third floor."

"Thanks, Lars. I can handle the rest."

"If you scroll down the credit card bill, you'll see that she paid for a visit to a women's health clinic. Do you want to see if she got birth control pills or had an abortion?"

"Thank you, but that's not necessary," Michael said.

The little red light disappeared from the screen, and once again he was alone with Clarisse. Carrying a little plastic bag with the makeup, the young woman continued through the store and stepped onto the escalator. Michael typed in a few directions and switched over to a new camera. A lock of brown hair rested on Clarisse's forehead and almost touched her eyes. She brushed it back with one hand, and then gazed around at a new display of merchandise. Michael wondered if she was looking for a dress to wear to a special event. With a little more help from Lars, he could access her e-mail.

The electronically activated door glided open and Kennard Nash entered the room. Nash was a former army general and national security adviser who was currently the head of the Brethren's executive board. There was something about his stocky build and brusque manner that reminded Michael of a football coach.

Michael switched to another surveillance camera—goodbye, Clarisse—but the general had already seen the young woman. He smiled like an uncle who had just found his nephew perusing a men's magazine.

"What location?" he asked.

"Paris."

"Is she cute?"

"Definitely."

As Nash approached Michael, his tone became more serious. "I've got some news that might interest you. Mr. Boone and his associates just concluded a successful field assessment of the New Harmony community in Arizona. Apparently your brother and the Harlequin visited this place a few months ago."

"So where are they now?"

"We don't know exactly, but we're getting closer. An analysis of e-mail messages stored on a laptop computer indicates that Gabriel is probably a few miles away from here—in New York City. We still don't have the computing power to search the entire world, but now we can focus on this particular location."

Becoming a Traveller had given Michael certain abilities that helped him survive. If he relaxed in a certain way—didn't think, just observed—he could slow his perceptions so that he could see split-second changes in someone's facial expressions. Michael could tell when someone was lying, could detect the thoughts and emotions that everyone concealed in their day-to-day lives.

"How long will it take to find my brother?" he asked.

"I can't say. But this is a very positive step. Up until now, we've been searching for them in Canada and Mexico. I never thought they'd go to New York."

Nash chuckled softly. "This young Harlequin is crazy."

And now the world began to slow within Michael's mind. He could see a hesitation in Nash's smile. A quick look to the left. And then a split-second twisting of the lips into a sneer. Perhaps the general wasn't lying, but he was definitely hiding some fact that made him feel superior.

"Let someone else finish the work in Arizona," Michael said. "I think Boone should fly to New York immediately."

Once again, Nash smiled as if he had the high cards in a poker game. "Mr. Boone will stay there for one more day evaluating some additional information. His team found a letter during a search of the compound." General Nash paused and let the statement linger in the air.

Michael watched Nash's eyes. "And why is that important?"

"The letter is from your father. He's been hiding from us for quite a long time, but it appears that he's still alive."

"What? Are you sure?" Michael jumped out of the chair and almost ran across the room. Was Nash telling him the truth, or was this just another test of loyalty? He examined the general's face and the movements of his eyes. Nash looked superior and proud—as if he enjoyed this demonstration of his authority.

"So where is he? How can we find him?"

"I can't tell you at this time. We don't know when the letter was written. Boone couldn't find an envelope with a postmark or a return address."

"But what did the letter say?"

"Your father inspired the formation of New Harmony. He wanted to encourage his friends and warn them about the Brethren." Nash watched Michael pace around the room. "You don't look very happy about this news."

"After your men burned down our house, Gabe and I kept this fantasy going. We convinced each other that our father had survived and was looking for us as we drove around the country. When I got older, I realized that my father wasn't going to help me at all. I was on my own."

"So you decided he was dead?"

"Wherever my father went, he was never coming back. He might as well have been dead."

"Who knows? Maybe we can arrange a family reunion."

Michael wanted to slam Nash against the wall and slap the smile off his face. But he turned away from the older man and regained his composure. He was still a prisoner, but there were ways around that. He had to assert himself and guide the Brethren in a certain direction.

"You killed everyone at New Harmony. Correct?"

Nash seemed annoyed by Michael's blunt language. "Boone's team achieved its objectives."

"Do the police know what happened? Has it become news?"

"Why should you be concerned with that?"

"I'm telling you how to find Gabriel. If the media doesn't know about this, then Boone should make sure they find out."

Nash nodded. "That's definitely part of the plan."

"I know my brother. Gabriel visited New Harmony and met the people who lived there. This event is really going to affect him. He'll have to react, do something on impulse. We need to be ready."

2

Gabriel and his friends were living in New York City. A minister from Vicki's church named Oscar Hernandez had arranged for them to stay in an empty industrial loft in Chinatown. The grocery store on the ground floor took sports bets, so the store had five phone lines—all registered in different names—plus a fax machine, a scanner, and a high-speed Internet connection. For a small payment, the grocer allowed them to use these electronic resources to substantiate their new identities. Chinatown was a good place for these transactions because all the shopkeepers preferred cash to the credit cards and ATM cards that were monitored by the Vast Machine.

The rest of the building was occupied by different businesses that used undocumented immigrants as workers. A garment sweatshop was on the first floor, and the man on the second floor manufactured pirated DVDs. Strangers walked in and out of the building during the daytime, but at night everyone was gone.

The fourth-floor loft was a long, narrow room with a polished wood floor and windows at both ends. It had once been used as a factory for fake designer handbags, and an industrial sewing machine was still bolted to the floor near the bathroom. A few days after they arrived, Vicki hung painter's tarps on clotheslines, creating a men's bedroom for Gabriel and Hollis, and a women's bedroom for herself and Maya.

Maya had been wounded during the attack on the Evergreen Research Center, and her recovery was a series of small victories. Gabriel could still remember the first night she was able to sit up in a chair to eat dinner, and the first morning she took a shower without Vicki's help. Two months after they arrived, Maya was able to leave the building with the others, limping up Mosco Street to the Hong Kong Cake Company. She waited outside the street stall—wobbly, but determined to stand on her own—while an elderly Chinese woman made cookies like crepes on a black iron griddle.

Money wasn't a problem; they had already received two shipments of hundred-dollar bills sent by Linden, a Harlequin who lived in Paris. Following Maya's instructions, they created false identities that included birth certificates, passports, driver's licenses, and credit cards. Hollis and Vicki found a backup apartment in Brooklyn and rented mail drops and postal boxes. When everyone in the group had the necessary documents for two false identities, they would leave New York and travel to a safe house in Canada or Europe.

Sometimes Hollis would laugh and call their group "the four fugitives," and Gabriel felt as if they had become friends. On some nights, the four residents of the loft each cooked a dish for one big meal, then sat around the table playing cards and joking about who was going to wash the dishes. Even Maya smiled occasionally and became part of the group. Gabriel could lose his self-consciousness during those moments, forget that he was a Traveller and that Maya was a Harlequin—and that his ordinary life was gone forever.

* * *

ON WEDNESDAY NIGHT, everything changed. The group had spent two hours at a jazz club in the West Village. As they strolled back to Chinatown, a truck driver tossed bound stacks of a tabloid newspaper onto the sidewalk. Gabriel glanced down at the headline and stopped moving.

THEY KILLED THEIR KIDS!
67 Die in Arizona Cult Suicide

The front-page article was about New Harmony, where Gabriel had gone only a few months earlier to visit the Pathfinder Sophia Briggs.

They bought three different newspapers and hurried back to the loft. According to Arizona police, the killing was motivated by religious mania. Reporters had already interviewed the former neighbors of the dead families. Everyone agreed—the people living at New Harmony had to be crazy. They had left good jobs and beautiful homes to live in the desert.

Hollis skimmed through the article in the *New York Times*. "According to this, the guns were registered to the people who lived there."

"That doesn't prove anything," Maya said.

"The police found a video made by a British woman," Hollis said. "Apparently, she gave some kind of speech about destroying evil."

"Martin Greenwald sent an e-mail to me a few weeks ago," Maya said. "He gave no indication of any problems."

"I didn't know you heard from Martin," Gabriel said with surprise, and he watched Maya's face change. He knew instantly that she was hiding something important from them.

"Yes, well, I did." Trying to avoid Gabriel's eyes, she walked over to the kitchen area.

"What did he tell you, Maya?"

"I made a decision. I thought it was best—"

Gabriel stood up and took a step toward her. "Tell me what he said!"

Maya was close to the door that led to the stairway. Gabriel wondered if she was going to run away rather than answer his questions.

"Martin received a letter from your father," Maya said. "He asked about the people at New Harmony."

For a few seconds, Gabriel felt as if the loft, the building, the city itself had vanished; he was a boy, standing in the snow, watching an owl fly in circles above the smoldering ruins of his family's home. His father was gone, vanished forever.

Then he blinked and returned to this moment: Hollis was furious, Vicki looked hurt, and Maya seemed defiant about her decision.

"My father's alive?"

"Yes."

"So what happened? Where is he?"

"I don't know," Maya said. "Martin was careful not to send that information over the Internet."

"But why didn't you tell me—"

Maya interrupted him, the words spilling out of her mouth. "Because I knew you'd want to go back to New Harmony and that was dangerous. I planned to return to Arizona myself once we left New York and you were at a safe house."

"I thought we were in this together," Hollis said. "No secrets. Everybody on the same team."

As usual, Vicki stepped forward in her role as

peacemaker. "I'm sure Maya realizes that she made a mistake."

"You think Maya is going to apologize?" Hollis asked. "We're not Harlequins, which means—in her mind—we're not on her level. She's been treating us like a bunch of children."

"It was *not* a mistake!" Maya said. "All those people at New Harmony are dead. If Gabriel had been there, he would have been killed, too."

"I think I have the right to make my own decisions," Gabriel said. "Now Martin is gone and we don't have any information."

"You're still alive, Gabriel. One way or the other, I've protected you. That's my obligation as a Harlequin. My *only* responsibility."

Maya turned, snapped the lock open, and stormed out of the apartment, slamming the door behind her.

3

The word *zombie* lingered
in Nathan Boone's mind like a whisper. It seemed out
of place in the hospitality lounge of the private airport
terminal near Phoenix, Arizona. The room was
decorated with pastel-colored furniture and framed
photographs of Hopi dancers. A cheerful young
woman named Cheryl had just baked chocolate chip
cookies and brewed fresh coffee for the small group
of corporate passengers.

Boone sat down at a workstation and switched on
his laptop computer. Outside the terminal it was an
overcast, blustery day, and the wind sock on the
tarmac kept snapping back and forth. His men had
already loaded sealed bins containing weapons and
body armor onto the chartered jet. Once the local
ground crew finished fueling the plane, Boone and
his team would fly east.

It had been easy to manipulate the police and

media perception of what had happened at New Harmony. Technicians working for the Brethren had already hacked into government computers and registered a list of firearms to the names of Martin Greenwald and other members of the community. The ballistics evidence and Janet Wilkins's video statement about messages from God convinced the authorities that New Harmony was a religious cult that had destroyed itself. The tragedy was tailor-made for the evening news, and none of the reporters were inspired to look any deeper. The story was over.

There was a report from one of the mercenaries about a child running near the containment perimeter, and Boone wondered if it was the same Asian girl he had seen at the community center. This could have been a problem, but the police hadn't found anyone alive. If the girl had escaped the initial attack, she had either died of exposure out in the desert or had been hiding in one of the houses that burned to the ground.

He activated a coding system, went on the Internet, and began to check his e-mail. There was promising news about the search for Gabriel Corrigan in New York City, and Boone answered that immediately. As he scrolled through the other messages he also found three e-mails from Michael asking about the search for his father. *Please send a progress report*, Michael wrote. *The Brethren would like immediate action on this matter.*

"Pushy son of a bitch," Boone muttered, and then glanced over his shoulder to see if anyone had heard him. The Brethren's head of security found it disturbing that a Traveller was giving him orders. Michael was now on their side, but as far as Boone was concerned he was still the enemy.

The only biometric data available for the father was a driver's license photo taken twenty-six years ago and a single thumbprint placed next to a notarized signature. That meant it was a waste of time to check the usual government data banks. The Brethren's search programs would have to monitor e-mail and phone calls for any kind of communication that mentioned Matthew Corrigan's name or statements about Travellers.

In the last few months, the Brethren had finished building a new computer center in Berlin, but Boone wasn't allowed to use it for his security operations. General Nash had been very mysterious about the executive board's plans for the Berlin center, but it was clear that it was a major breakthrough in the Brethren's goals. Apparently they were testing something called the Shadow Program, which was going to be the first step in the establishment of the Virtual Panopticon. When Boone complained about his lack of resources, the staff in Berlin had suggested a temporary solution: instead of using the computer center, they would bring in zombies to help with the search.

A zombie was the nickname for any computer infected by a virus or Trojan horse that allowed it to be secretly controlled by an outside user. Zombie masters directed the actions of computers all over the world, using them to send out spam or extort money from vulnerable Web sites. If the site owners refused to pay, their servers were overwhelmed by thousands of requests sent out at the same moment.

Networks of zombies called "bot nets" could be bought, stolen, or traded on the Internet black market. During the last year, the Brethren's technical staff had purchased bot nets from different criminal groups and had developed new software that forced the captive computers to perform more elaborate tasks. Although this system wasn't powerful enough to monitor all the computers in the world, it could handle a search for a specific target.

Boone began typing a command to the computer center in Berlin. *If the auxiliary system is operational begin searching for Matthew Corrigan.*

"Excuse me, Mr. Boone . . ."

Startled, he looked up from his work. The charter pilot—a clean-cut young man in a navy blue uniform—was standing a few feet away from the workstation.

"What's the problem?"

"No problem. We're fueled up and ready to go."

"I've just received some new information," Boone said. "Change our destination to Westchester County

Airport and contact the transportation desk. Tell them I want enough vehicles to take my staff into New York City."

"Yes, sir. I'll call them right now."

Boone waited until the pilot walked away, then resumed typing. *Let the computers chase this ghost,* he thought. *I'll find Gabriel in the next two days.*

He finished his message a minute later and sent it off to Berlin. By the time he reached the tarmac, hidden software programs awoke within captured computers all over the world. Fragments of computer consciousness began to assemble like an army of zombies sitting quietly in an enormous room. They waited without resistance, without consciousness of time, until a command forced them to start searching.

In the suburbs of Madrid, a fourteen-year-old boy played an online fantasy game. In Toronto, a retired building inspector posted comments about his favorite team in a hockey forum. A few seconds later, both of their computers worked a little bit slower, but neither noticed the change. On the surface, everything was the same, but now the electronic servants obeyed a new master with a new command.

Find the Traveller.

Gabriel pressed a button on his cell phone and checked the time. It was one o'clock in the morning, but noises still rose up from the street. He could hear a car horn and a distant police siren. A vehicle with a loud stereo was cruising down the block, and the thumping bass of a rap song sounded like the beat of a muffled heart.

The Traveller unzipped the top half of his sleeping bag and sat up. Illumination from a streetlight leaked in through the whitewashed windows, and he could see Hollis Wilson lying on a folding cot six feet away from him. The former martial-arts teacher was breathing steadily, and Gabriel decided that he was asleep.

It had been twenty-four hours since he had learned that the people of New Harmony were dead and his father was still alive. Gabriel wondered how he was supposed to find someone who had disappeared from his life fifteen years ago. Was his father in this world or had he crossed over to another realm? Gabriel lay back down on the cot and raised his left hand. Late at night, he felt receptive to the attractions—and dangers—of his new power.

For a few minutes he focused on the Light inside his body. Then came the difficult moment: still concentrating on the Light, he attempted to move his hand without consciously thinking about it. Sometimes this seemed impossible; how could you choose to move your body and then ignore that choice? Gabriel breathed deeply and the fingers of his hand twitched forward. Little points of Light—like the stars of a constellation—floated in the shadowy darkness while his physical hand was limp and lifeless.

He moved his arm and the Light was reabsorbed by his body. Gabriel was shivering and breathing hard. He sat up again, pulled his legs out of the sleeping bag, and placed his bare feet on the cold wood floor. *You're acting like an idiot*, he told himself. *This isn't a party trick. Either cross over or stay in this world.*

Wearing a T-shirt and cotton sweatpants, Gabriel slipped through a gap in the tarps and entered the main part of the loft. He used the bathroom, then walked over to the kitchen area to get some water from the sink. Maya was sitting on the couch near the women's sleeping area. When the Harlequin was recovering from her bullet wound, she had spent most of her time sleeping. Now that Maya was able to walk around the city, she was filled with restless energy.

"Everything okay?" she whispered.

"Yeah. I'm just thirsty."

He turned on the cold-water tap and drank directly from the faucet. One of the things he liked about New York City was the water. When he'd lived in Los Angeles with Michael, the public water always had a faint chemical taste.

Gabriel walked back across the loft and sat beside Maya. Even after the argument about his father, he still enjoyed looking at her. Maya had her Sikh mother's black hair and her German father's strong features. Her eyes were a distinctive pale blue, like two faint dots of watercolor floating on a white background. Out on the street she concealed her eyes beneath sunglasses, and a wig covered her hair. But the Harlequin couldn't disguise how she moved her body. She walked into a grocery store and stood in a subway car with the balanced posture of a fighter who could take the first punch and not be knocked off her feet.

When they first encountered each other in Los Angeles, he thought Maya was the most unusual person he had ever met in his life. The Harlequin was a modern woman in many ways—an expert in all aspects of surveillance technology. But she also had carried the weight of hundreds of years of tradition on her shoulders. Maya's father, Thorn, had taught his

little girl that Harlequins were *Damned by the flesh.*
Saved by the blood. Maya seemed to believe that she
was guilty of some fundamental error that could only
be corrected by risking her life.

Maya saw the world clearly—any foolishness and
clutter in her perceptions had been destroyed years
ago. Gabriel knew that she would never break the
rules and fall in love with a Traveller. And right now,
his own future was so unclear that he felt that it was
equally irresponsible for him to change their
relationship.

He and Maya had their defined roles as Traveller
and Harlequin, and yet he was drawn to her
physically. When she was recovering from the bullet
wound, he had picked her up and carried her from
the cot to the couch, feeling the weight of her body
and smelling her skin and hair. Sometimes the tarp
wasn't fully closed and he saw her talking to Vicki as
she pulled on her clothes. There was nothing
between them—but there was everything. Even
sitting beside her on the couch felt both pleasant and
uncomfortable.

"You should get some sleep," he said gently.

"I can't close my eyes." When Maya was tired, her
British accent became stronger. "The brain won't
stop."

"I can understand that. Sometimes it feels like I've
got too many thoughts and not enough places to put
them."

There was another moment of silence and he listened to her breathing. Gabriel reminded himself that Maya had lied about his father. Were there other secrets? What else did he need to know? The Harlequin moved a few inches away from Gabriel so they weren't so close. Maya's body tensed and he heard her take a deep breath, as if she were about to do something dangerous.

"I've also been thinking about the argument we had last night."

"You should have told me about my father," Gabriel said.

"I was trying to protect you. Don't you believe that?"

"I'm still not satisfied." Gabriel leaned toward her. "Okay—so my father sent a letter to the people at New Harmony. Are you sure you don't know where the letter came from?"

"I told you about Carnivore. The government is constantly monitoring e-mail. Martin would never have sent crucial information through the Internet."

"How do I know you're telling me the truth?"

"You're a Traveller, Gabriel. You can look at my face and see that I'm not lying."

"I didn't think I needed to do that. Not with you." Gabriel got up from the couch and walked back to his cot. He lay down, but it was difficult to sleep. Gabriel knew Maya cared about him, but she didn't seem to understand how much he wanted to find his father.

Only his father could tell him what he was supposed to do now that he was a Traveller. He knew that he was changing, becoming a different person, but he didn't know why.

Closing his eyes, he dreamed of his father walking down a dark street in New York City. Gabriel shouted and ran after him, but his father was too far away to hear. Matthew Corrigan turned a corner, and when Gabriel reached it his father had disappeared.

Within the dream, Gabriel stood beneath a streetlight on pavement dark and glistening from the rain. He glanced around him and saw a surveillance camera mounted on the roof of a building. There was another camera on the lamppost and a half dozen others at various points on the empty street. That was when he knew that Michael was also searching, but his brother had the cameras and the scanners and all the other devices of the Vast Machine. It was like a race—a terrible competition between them—and there was no way he could win.

Although Harlequins sometimes saw themselves as the last defenders of history, their historical knowledge was based more on tradition than on the facts found in textbooks. Growing up in London, Maya had memorized the location of the traditional execution sites scattered around the city. Her father had shown her each place during their daily lessons on weapons and street fighting. Tyburn was for felons, the Tower of London was for traitors, the shriveled bodies of dead pirates hung for years from the Execution Dock at Wapping. At various times, the authorities had killed Jews, Catholics, and a long list of dissenters who worshipped a different god or preached a different vision of the world. A certain spot in West Smithfield was used for the execution of heretics, witches, and women who had killed their husbands—as well as the anonymous Harlequins who had died protecting Travellers.

Maya felt the same sense of accumulated misery the moment she entered the Criminal Court building in lower Manhattan. Standing just inside the main entrance, she gazed upward at the clock that hung from the two-story ceiling. The building's white marble walls, the Art Deco lighting fixtures, and the ornate railing on the stairways suggested the grand sensibility of an earlier era. Then she lowered her eyes and studied the world that surrounded her: the police and the criminals, the bailiffs and lawyers, the victims and witnesses—everyone shuffling across the dirty floor to the gateway metal detector that awaited them.

Dimitri Aronov was a plump older man with three strands of greasy black hair plastered across the top of his bald head. Carrying a battered leather briefcase, the Russian émigré approached the metal detector. When he entered the gateway, he stopped for a second and glanced over his shoulder at Maya.

"What's the problem?" the guard asked. "Keep moving . . ."

"Of course, Officer. Of course."

Aronov stepped through the gateway, then sighed and rolled his eyes as if he just remembered that he left an important file in his car. He passed back through the checkpoint and followed Maya out the revolving door. For a moment, they stood at the top of the broad stairway and looked out at the skyline of lower Manhattan. It was about four o'clock in the afternoon. Thick gray clouds hung over the city, and the sun was a blurred patch of light on the western horizon.

"So? What do you think, Miss Strand?"

"I don't think anything—yet."

"You saw it yourself. No alarm. No arrest."

"Let's take a look at your product."

Together, they came down the steps, zig-zagged through the sluggish traffic clogging Centre Street, and walked into the small park at the middle of the square. The Collect Pond Park had once been the site of a massive pool of raw sewage during the early days of New York. It was still a dark place, overshadowed by the tall buildings that surrounded the patch of ground. While several signs commanded New Yorkers not to feed pigeons, a flock of the birds fluttered back and forth and pecked at the dirt.

They sat down on a wooden bench just beyond the range of the park's two surveillance cameras. Aronov placed the briefcase on the bench and wiggled his fingers. "Please inspect the merchandise."

Maya snapped open the top of the briefcase. She peered inside and found a handgun that looked like a 9mm automatic. The weapon had over-and-under barrels and a textured grip. When she picked it up, she discovered that it was very light—almost like a child's toy.

Aronov began to speak in the cadence of a salesman. "The frame, the grip, and the trigger are high-density plastic. The barrels, the slides, and firing pin are super-hard ceramic—as strong as steel. As you just witnessed, the assembled weapon will pass through any standard metal detector. Airports are not as easy. Most of them have back scanners or millimeter wave machines. But you can break the weapon into two or three pieces and hide them in a laptop computer."

"What does it fire?"

"The bullets were always the problem. The CIA has designed the same kind of gun using a caseless system. Amusing, yes? They are supposed to be fighting terrorism, so they created the perfect terrorist weapon. But my friends in Moscow went for a less sophisticated solution. May I?"

Aronov reached into the briefcase. He pushed back the slide and revealed what looked like a stubby brown cigarette with a black tip. "This is a paper cartridge with a ceramic bullet. Think of it as the modern equivalent of the system used by an eighteenth-century musket. The propellant ignites in two stages and pushes the bullet out the barrel. It's slow to reload, so . . ." Aronov wrapped his left hand around the gun and snapped the second barrel into place. "You get two quick shots, but that's all you're going to need. The bullet cuts through your target like a piece of shrapnel."

Maya leaned away from the briefcase and looked around to see if anyone was watching. The gray facade of the Criminal Courts building loomed above them. Police cars and the white-and-blue buses used to transport prisoners were double-parked on the street. She could hear the traffic circling the little park, smell

Aronov's floral cologne mixed with the slippery scent of wet leaves.

"Impressive, yes? You must agree."

"How much?"

"Twelve thousand dollars. Cash."

"For a handgun? That's nonsense."

"My dear Miss Strand . . ." The Russian smiled and shook his head. "It would be difficult, if not impossible, to find anyone else selling this weapon. Besides, we've done business together. You realize that my merchandise is of the best quality."

"I don't even know if the gun can fire."

Aronov shut the briefcase and placed it on the pavement beside his feet. "If you wish, we can drive out to a garage owned by a friend of mine in New Jersey. No neighbors. Thick walls. The cartridges are expensive, but I'll let you shoot two of them before you give me the money."

"Let me think it over."

"I'll drive past the street entrance to Lincoln Center at seven o'clock this evening. If you're there, you get a special deal for one night only—ten thousand dollars and six cartridges."

"A special deal is eight thousand."

"Nine."

Maya nodded. "I'll pay you that if everything works as promised."

As she left the park and cut across Centre Street, Maya called Hollis on her cell phone. He answered his phone immediately, but didn't speak.

"Where are you?" she asked.

"Columbus Park."

"I'll be there in five minutes." She dropped the phone into her shoulder bag and took out a random number generator—an electronic device about the size of a matchbox that hung from a cord around her neck.

Maya and the other Harlequins called their enemies the Tabula because this group saw human consciousness as a tabula rasa—a blank slate that could be scrawled with slogans of hatred and fear. While the Tabula believed that everything could be controlled, Harlequins cultivated a philosophy of randomness. Sometimes they made their choices with dice or the number generator.

An odd number means turn left, Maya thought. *Even means go right.* She pressed a button on the device, and when 365 flashed on the display screen, she headed left down Hogan Place.

* * *

IT TOOK HER about ten minutes to walk to Columbus Park—a rectangular patch of asphalt and woeful-looking trees a few blocks east of Chinatown. Gabriel liked to visit the park in the afternoon, when it was filled with elderly Chinese men and women. The old people formed complex alliances based on who came from the same province or village. They gossiped and nibbled on snacks brought in plastic containers as they played mah-jongg and an occasional game of chess.

Hollis Wilson sat on a park bench wearing a black leather jacket that concealed a .45-caliber automatic purchased from Dimitri Aronov. When Maya first met Hollis in Los Angeles, he had shoulder-length dread-locks and wore stylish clothes. In New York, Vicki had cut his hair short and he had learned the Harlequin rule of concealment: always wear or carry something that conveys a false identity. That afternoon he had pinned two buttons to his jacket that announced: WANT TO LOSE WEIGHT? TRY THE HERBAL SOLUTION! The moment New Yorkers saw the lapel buttons, they turned their eyes away.

As Hollis guarded Gabriel, he studied a loose-leaf copy of *The Way of the Sword*, the meditation on com-bat written by Sparrow, the legendary Japanese Harlequin. Maya had grown up with the book, and her father was constantly repeating Sparrow's famous statement that Harlequins should "cultivate random-ness." It annoyed her that Hollis was trying to take possession of this key part of her training.

"So how long have you been here?" she asked.

"About two hours."

They looked across the park to another row of benches where Gabriel was playing chess at a park table with an elderly Chinese man. The Traveller had also changed his looks during their time in New York. Vicki had given him a very short haircut, and he usually wore a knit cap and sunglasses. When they first met in Los Angeles, Gabriel had long brown hair and the casual manner of a young man who spent his time skiing in the winter and surfing in the summer. He had lost weight in the last few months and now had the drained appearance of someone who had just recovered from a long illness.

Hollis had picked a good defensive position with clear sightlines to almost every area of the park. Maya gave herself permission to relax for a moment and enjoy the fact that they were still alive. When she was a little girl, she had called these moments her "jewels." The jewels were those rare times when she felt safe enough to appreciate something pleasant or beautiful—a sky pink from a sunset or the nights her mother cooked a special meal like lamb *rogan josh*.

"Did anything happen this afternoon?" she asked.

"Gabe read a book in the sleeping area, then we talked for a while about his father."

"What did he say?"

"He still wants to find him," Hollis said. "I understand how he feels."

Maya watched carefully as three elderly women approached Gabriel. The women were fortune-tellers who sat at the edge of the park and offered to predict your future for ten dollars. Whenever Gabriel walked past them, they would extend their hands slightly—palms facing upward, the right hand beneath the left—like beggars asking for alms. This afternoon, the fortune-tellers were merely showing their respect. One of them placed a cardboard cup of tea on the folding table used for the chess game.

"Don't worry," Hollis said. "They've done this before."

"People are going to talk about it."

"So what? Nobody knows who he is. The fortune-tellers just sense he has some kind of power."

The Traveller thanked the women for the tea. They bowed to him, and then walked back to their post near the fence. Gabriel returned to his chess game.

"Did Aronov show up for the meeting?" Hollis asked. "His text message said he was offering a new piece of equipment."

"He tried to sell me a ceramic handgun that we could carry through metal detectors. It was probably manufactured by a Russian security agency."

"What did you tell him?"

"I haven't made up my mind. I'm supposed to meet him at seven o'clock tonight. We'll drive to New Jersey so I can fire it a few times."

"A weapon like that could be useful. How much does he want for it?"

"Nine thousand dollars."

Hollis laughed. "I guess we don't get a 'good customer' discount."

"Should we buy it?"

"Nine thousand in cash is a lot of money. You should talk to Vicki. She knows how much we've got and how much we're spending."

"Is she at the loft?"

"Yeah. She's organizing dinner. We'll go back there when Gabriel's done with this game."

Maya got up from the bench and cut across the dead grass to where Gabriel was playing chess. When she wasn't alert to her own emotions, she found herself wanting to be near him. They weren't friends—that was impossible. But she felt as if he looked into her heart and saw her clearly.

Gabriel glanced up at her and smiled. It was just a brief moment between them, but it made her feel both happy and angry at the same time. *Don't be a fool*, Maya told herself. *Always remember: you're here to take care of him, not to care about him.*

She passed through Chatham Square and headed down East Broadway. The sidewalk was crowded with tourists and Chinese people buying food for dinner. Roast duck and scallion chicken hung from hooks just inside the steamed-up windows, and she almost bumped into a young man carrying a suckling pig wrapped in clear plastic. When no one was watching Maya unlocked the door and entered the building on Catherine Street. More keys. More locks. And then she was inside the loft.

"Vicki?"

"I'm here."

Maya pulled back one of the tarps and found Victory From Sin Fraser sitting on a cot, counting currency from several different countries. In Los Angeles, Vicki had been a modestly dressed member of the Divine Church of Isaac T. Jones. Now she was wearing what she called her artist costume—embroidered blue jeans, a black T-shirt, and a Balinese necklace. Her hair was braided and there was a bead at the end of each strand.

Vicki glanced up from the stacks of money and smiled. "Another shipment arrived at the Brooklyn apartment. I wanted to check our current total."

The women's clothes were stored in cardboard boxes or hung from a dress rack that Hollis had bought on Seventh Avenue. Maya pulled off her overcoat and slipped it onto a plastic hanger.

"What happened when you met the Russian? Hollis said he probably wanted to sell you another handgun."

"He offered me a special weapon, but it's expensive." Maya sat down on her folding cot and briefly described the ceramic gun.

"Seed to sapling," Vicki said as she slipped a rubber band on a packet of hundred-dollar bills.

By now, Maya was familiar with a variety of phrases from the collected letters of Isaac Jones, the founder of Vicki's church. *Seed to sapling, sapling to tree* meant that you should always consider the possible consequences of your actions.

"We have the money, but it's a dangerous weapon," Vicki continued. "If criminals got control of it, they could use it to hurt innocent people."

"It's the same with any weapon."

"Will you promise to destroy it when we're finally in a safe place?"

Harlekine versprechen nichts, Maya thought in German. *Harlequins don't promise*. It was like hearing her father's voice. "I will consider destroying it," she told Vicki. "That's all I can say."

As Vicki continued counting the money, Maya changed her clothes. If she was meeting Aronov near the concert halls at Lincoln Center, then she had to look as if she were going out for a social evening. That meant ankle boots, black dress pants, a blue sweater, and a wool peacoat. Because of the money involved, she decided to carry a handgun: a short-barreled .357 Magnum revolver with an aluminum frame. The pants were loose enough to conceal an ankle holster.

Maya's throwing knife was held with an elastic bandage on her right arm while a push knife was worn on her left arm, close to the wrist. The push knife had a sharp triangular blade with a T-shaped handle. Holding the handle in your fist, you punched at your target with all your strength.

Vicki had stopped counting the money. She looked shy and a little embarrassed. "I have a problem, Maya. I thought—maybe—we could talk about it."

"Go on . . ."

"I'm getting close to Hollis. And I don't know what to do about it. He's had a lot of girlfriends, and I'm not very experienced." She shook her head. "In fact, I'm not experienced at all."

Maya had watched the growing attraction between Hollis and Vicki. It was the first time she had ever noticed the evolution of two people who were falling in love. At first, their eyes followed each other when one of them got up from the table. Then they leaned forward slightly when the other person was talking. When they were apart, they spoke about the other person in a bubbly, foolish manner. The whole experience made Maya realize that her father and her mother had never been in love. They respected each other and had a strong commitment to the alliance of their marriage. But that wasn't love. Harlequins weren't interested in that emotion.

Maya slipped the revolver into the ankle holster. She made sure that the Velcro safety strap was fastened, and then pulled her pant leg down so that the cuff touched the top of her boot. "You're talking to the wrong person," she said to Vicki. "I can't give you any advice."

The Harlequin took nine thousand dollars off the cot and headed for the door. She felt strong at that moment—ready for combat—but the familiar surroundings reminded her of Vicki's help during her recovery. Vicki had fed Maya, changed her bandages, and sat on the couch beside her when she was in pain. She was a friend.

Damn friends, Maya thought. Harlequins acknowledged obligations to one another, but friendship with citizens was regarded as a waste of time. During her brief attempt to live a normal life in London, Maya had dated men and socialized with the women who worked with her at a design studio. But none of these people were her friends. They could never understand the peculiar way she saw the world; that she was always hunted—always ready to attack.

Her hand touched the latch, but she didn't open the door. *Look at the facts*, she told herself. *Cut your heart open and dissect your feelings. You're jealous of Vicki. That's all. Jealous of someone else's happiness.*

She returned to the sleeping area. "I'm sorry I said that, Vicki. There are a lot of things going on right now."

"I know. It was wrong of me to bring this up."

"I respect you and Hollis. I want you both to be happy. Let's talk about it when I get back tonight."

"Okay." Vicki relaxed and smiled. "We can do that."

Maya felt better when she finally got out of the building. Her favorite hour was approaching: the transition between day and night. Before the streetlights went on, the air seemed to be filled with little black specks of darkness. Shadows lost their sharp edges and boundaries faded away. Like a knife blade, sharp and clean, she passed through the gaps in the crowd and cut through the city.

6

Maya walked north from the alleyways of Chinatown to the broad avenues of Midtown Manhattan. This was the visible city, where the Vast Machine asserted its control. But Maya knew there was an intricate world beneath the pavement, a labyrinth of subway lines, railroad tracks, forgotten passageways, and utility tunnels lined with electric cables. Half of New York was hidden from sight, burrowed deep within the bedrock that supported the tenements in Spanish Harlem as well as the glass towers on Park Avenue. And there was a parallel world of humanity that was hidden as well, different groups of heretics and true believers, illegal immigrants with false papers and respectable citizens with secret lives.

An hour later she was standing on the marble steps that led to the Lincoln Center for the Performing Arts. The theater and concert buildings were on the perimeter of a large plaza with a lighted fountain at the center. Most of the performances hadn't started yet, but musicians wearing black clothes and carrying instrument cases hurried up the steps and cut across the plaza to different concert halls. Maya shifted the money to a zippered pocket inside her jacket, then glanced over her shoulder. There were two surveillance cameras in clear view, but they were aimed at crowds near the fountain.

A taxi pulled up to the arrival area. Aronov was sitting in the back. When he gestured with his hand, Maya came down the steps and got in beside the Russian.

"Good evening, Miss Strand. How pleasant to see you again."

"The gun has to work or no sale."

"Of course." Aronov gave directions to the driver, a young man with a spiky haircut, and they pulled back onto the street. Within a few blocks, they were on Ninth Avenue, heading south.

"You brought the money?" he asked.

"No more than we discussed."

"You are a very suspicious person, Miss Strand. Perhaps I should hire you as an assistant."

As they crossed Forty-second Street, Aronov took a ballpoint pen and a leather-bound notebook out of his pocket as if he were about to write a memo. The Russian began to talk about his favorite nightclub in Staten Island and the exotic dancer there who had

once been a member of the Moscow Ballet. It was
meaningless chatter, something a car salesman would
say as he guided you around the lot. Maya wondered
if the ceramic gun was a fake and if Aronov was
planning to steal the money. Or maybe it was nothing.
He knows I'm carrying a handgun, Maya thought. *He
sold it to me.*

The driver turned right on Thirty-eighth Street and
followed signs to the Lincoln Tunnel. Rush-hour
traffic converged upon the entrance, and then sorted
itself into different lanes. Three separate tunnels—
each with two lanes—led under the river to New
Jersey. Traffic was heavy, but the cars were traveling
about thirty miles an hour. Peering out the side
window, she watched a power cable move up and
down on the white tile facade that lined the tunnel.

Maya turned as the Russian shifted his weight on
the seat beside her. He clicked the ballpoint pen and
a needle emerged from the tip. Within that instant,
Maya saw each detail with total clarity. Her hand
grabbed Aronov's wrist. Instead of fighting his attack,
she went with its force, guiding him halfway downward, and then jerking his arm to the left.

Aronov stabbed himself in the leg. He screamed
with pain, and now Maya used all her strength,
punching him in the face while holding the needle in
his flesh. The Russian sucked in air like a drowning
man, then went limp and slumped against the car
door. Maya touched his neck—still alive. Whatever

chemical was in the fake pen was just a tranquilizer. She searched the outside pocket of Aronov's raincoat, found the ceramic gun, and transferred it to her shoulder bag.

A clear Plexiglas barrier separated the front seat from the back, and she could see that the taxi driver was talking into a headset. Both doors were locked. She tried to roll down the side windows, but they were locked as well. Glancing over her shoulder, she realized that a dark SUV was directly behind the cab. Two men sat in front, and the mercenary in the passenger seat was also using a headset.

Maya drew her revolver and tapped the barrel on the Plexiglas barrier. "Unlock the doors!" she shouted. "Hurry up!"

The driver saw the gun, but didn't obey her. There was a calm center within her mind, like a chalk circle drawn on the pavement, and Maya stayed within its boundaries. The barrier between the seats would be bulletproof. She could smash the side window, but it would be difficult to crawl out through the small opening. The safest exit was through the locked door.

She pushed her revolver into her waistband, drew her throwing knife, and forced the sharp point between the window frame and the plastic trim panel. The panel wouldn't move more than half an inch, so she took out the push knife and jabbed it into the small opening. Forcing downward with both blades, she pried open the plastic, exposing an interior steel panel. The panel was thick enough to resist bullets, but the holding brackets looked fragile.

Maya knelt on the floor of the cab, pointed her revolver at the top bracket, and fired. The gunshot was painfully loud. Her ears were ringing as she pulled down on the steel panel—exposing the latch, a steel rod, and the power-lock actuator. Now it was easy. She pushed her knife onto the point where the rod and the actuator connected and pulled upward. The lock popped open.

She had overcome the first obstacle, but still wasn't free. The taxi was moving too fast for her to jump safely. Maya took a deep breath and tried to push the fear out through her lungs. They were about fifty feet away from the tunnel exit. When the traffic emerged, the cars would slow momentarily while changing lanes. Maya estimated she had about two or three seconds to get out before the taxi picked up speed.

The driver knew that the side door was open. He glanced up into the rearview mirror and said something into his telephone headset. The instant the cab came out of the tunnel, Maya grabbed the door and jumped. The door swung outward. She held on tightly as the cab went over a bump and she was slammed back against the door frame. Cars swerved and brakes screeched as the taxi driver began to cut across the lanes. He looked back at her for an instant and the cab smashed into the side of a blue commuter bus. Maya was flung from the door and landed on the road.

She scrambled to her feet and glanced around her. The entrance to the tunnel on the New Jersey side looked like a man-made canyon. A high concrete wall was on her right, with houses perched on a steep slope farther up. To her left were the tollbooths for vehicles entering the tunnel. The SUV had stopped about twenty feet away from the cab, and a man wearing a suit and tie got out and stared at her. He didn't draw a gun; there were too many witnesses, and three police cars were parked near the tollbooths. Maya started running toward an exit ramp.

* * *

FIVE MINUTES LATER, she was in Weehawken, a shabby commuter town with dirt alleyways separating three-story clapboard houses. When she was sure no one was looking, she scrambled over the stone wall that formed the back courtyard of a deserted Catholic church and pulled out her cell phone. Hollis's phone rang five or six times before he answered.

"Exit high! Purest children!" During the last three months, she had come up with three escape plans. "Exit high" meant whoever was in the loft should use the fire escape to climb onto the roof. "Purest children" meant they should rendezvous at Tompkins Square Park on the Lower East Side.

"What happened?" Hollis asked.

"Just do what I say! Get out of there!"

"We can't do that, Maya."

"What are you—"

"Some visitors have arrived. Come home as soon as you can."

Maya found a taxi and raced back to Manhattan. Sitting low in the backseat, she told the driver to cruise down Catherine Street. A group of teenagers was playing basketball at the public housing project, but no one appeared to be watching the loft building. She jumped out of the cab, hurried across the street, and unlocked the green door.

Maya drew her handgun as soon as she stood on the ground-floor landing. She could hear the sounds of cars passing down the street and a faint creaking noise when she climbed the wooden staircase. The moment she reached the door, she knocked once, and then raised the revolver.

Looking frightened, Vicki opened the door and Maya slipped into the room. Hollis stood a few feet away holding the shotgun.

"What happened?" he asked.

"It was a trap," Maya said. "The Tabula know we're in New York. Why are you still here?"

"As I said, we have visitors."

Hollis motioned to the right. Someone had pulled back the painter's tarps that defined the men's sleeping area. Oscar Hernandez, the Jonesie minister who had rented the loft, sat on a folding cot with a young Latino wearing a red sweatshirt.

"Maya! Thank God you're all right!" Hernandez stood up and gave her a big smile. He was a city bus driver who always wore his clerical collar when conducting church business. "Welcome back. We were starting to worry about you."

An older woman's voice came from the women's sleeping area. Maya hurried across the loft and pulled back one of the tarps. Sophia Briggs, the Pathfinder who lived in an abandoned missile silo near New Harmony, sat on a cot talking to Gabriel. Sophia was the teacher who had taught Gabriel how to use his ability to cross over to different realms.

"Ah, the Harlequin returns." Sophia studied Maya as if she were a rare species of reptile. "Good evening, my dear. I didn't think I'd see you again."

Something moved in the shadows over by the radiator. Was it a dog? Had Sophia brought a pet with her? No, it was a little girl sitting on the floor, her knees up, her arms wrapped around her legs. When Maya took a step closer, a face came up, a small face that displayed no emotion. It was the Asian girl from New Harmony. Someone had survived.

7

Gabriel watched Maya's eyes as she glanced at the little girl and then turned to Sophia. "I thought everyone was killed . . ."

"Everyone but Alice Chen—Joan's daughter. I found her down in the missile silo protected by my lovely king snakes. The Tabula mercenaries came searching for us, but they only explored the main level."

"How did you get to New York?"

"Dr. Briggs drove to Austin, Texas, and contacted a member of our church," Hernandez explained. "A few of us still believe in 'Debt Not Paid.' We will protect Travellers, Harlequins, and their friends."

"But why are they *here*?"

"Alice and I are both witnesses," Sophia said. "We were passed from church to church until someone contacted Reverend Hernandez."

"Well, you've come to the wrong place. I won't

accept an obligation for you or this child." Maya walked over to Alice Chen. "Do you have grand-parents? An aunt or uncle?"

"Alice has stopped talking," Sophia said. "It's clear that she's been through a traumatic experience."

"I heard her talk at New Harmony." Maya stood over Alice and spoke slowly. "Give me a name. I need the name of someone who can take care of you."

"Leave her alone, Maya." Gabriel got up from the cot and crouched down beside the little girl. "Alice . . ." he whispered, and then he felt the aura of grief that enveloped her. The feeling was so powerful and so dark that he almost fell to his knees. For a moment he wished he had never become a Traveller. How had his father endured such pain from others?

Gabriel stood up and faced Maya. "She stays with us."

"These two people will slow us down. We have to get out of here *now*."

"She stays with us," Gabriel repeated. "Or I'm not leaving this loft."

"We won't have to take care of them for long," Vicki said. "Reverend Hernandez has some friends who live on a farm up in Vermont."

"They live completely off the Grid—no credit cards, no phones, no attachments at all," Hernandez said. "You can stay there as long as you want."

"And how are we supposed to make this journey?" Maya asked.

"Take the subway to Grand Central Terminal. A train leaves on the Harlem Line at eleven twenty-two tonight. Get off at a town called Ten Mile River and wait on the platform. A church member with a car will pick you up and take you north."

Maya shook her head. "The whole situation has changed now that the Tabula realize we're in New York. They'll be monitoring everywhere—it will be dangerous to move around. There are surveillance cameras on the street and in each subway station, and the computers will scan for our images and target our exact location."

"I know all about the cameras," Hernandez said. "That's why I brought a guide."

Hernandez raised his hand slightly and the young Latino sauntered to the middle of the room. He was wearing a baseball cap and loose athletic clothing that advertised various sports teams. Although he tried to swagger, he looked nervous and eager to please.

"This is my nephew, Nazarene Romero. He works in the maintenance division of the New York Transit Authority."

Nazarene adjusted his extra-large pants as if that were part of the introduction. "Most people call me Naz."

"Good to meet you, Naz. I'm Hollis. So how are you going to get us to Grand Central?"

"First things first," Naz said. "I'm not in my uncle's church. Understand? I'll get you out of the city, but I wanna be paid. It's a thousand for me plus another thousand for my friend Devon."

"Just to travel to a train station?"

"You won't be tracked." Naz raised his right hand as if he were swearing an oath in court. "I guarantee it."

"That's not possible," Maya said.

"We're going to a station with no cameras and traveling on a train with no passengers. All you gotta do is follow my directions and pay me when it's done."

Hollis stood up and approached Naz. Although he held the shotgun with his left hand, he didn't need the weapon to be intimidating. "I'm not a church member these days, but I still remember a lot of the sermons. In his Third Letter from Mississippi, Isaac Jones said that anyone who takes the wrong path would cross a dark river to a city of endless night. Doesn't sound like the kind of place you'd like to spend eternity . . ."

"I'm not selling anybody out, man. I'm just gonna be your guide."

Everyone looked at Maya and waited for her to make a decision. "We'll take you and the child up to the farm in Vermont," she told Sophia. "After that point, you're on your own."

"As you wish."

"We leave in five minutes," Maya said. "Each person can bring a knapsack or one piece of luggage. Vicki, distribute the money so that you're not carrying all of it."

Alice remained on the floor, silent but watching as

they quickly sorted through their belongings. Gabriel stuffed two T-shirts and some underwear into a canvas shoulder bag along with his new passport and a packet of hundred-dollar bills. He didn't know what to do with the Japanese sword that Thorn had given to his father, but Maya took the weapon from him. Carefully, she placed the talisman in the black metal tube she used to carry her Harlequin sword.

While the others continued to get ready, Gabriel brought a cup of tea over to Sophia Briggs. The Pathfinder was a tough old lady who had spent most of her life alone, but she looked exhausted from the cross-country trip to New York.

"Thank you." Sophia reached out and touched his hand. Gabriel felt like they were back in the abandoned missile silo in Arizona and she was teaching him how to free his Light from his body.

"I've thought about you a great deal in the last few months, Gabriel. What's been going on here in New York?"

"I'm all right. I guess . . ." Gabriel lowered his voice. "You taught me how to cross the barriers, but I still don't know how to *be* a Traveller. I see the world differently, but I don't know how I'm supposed to change things."

"Have you done any more exploring? Did you reach the other realms?"

"I met my brother in the Realm of the hungry ghosts."

"Was it dangerous?"

"I'll tell you about it later, Sophia. Right now, I want to know about my father. He sent a letter to New Harmony."

"Yes. Martin showed it to me when I went to his house for dinner. Your father wanted to know how the community was doing."

"Was there a return address? How did he expect Martin to contact him?"

"There was an address on the envelope, but Martin was going to destroy it. All it said was, 'Tyburn Convent. London.'"

Gabriel felt as if the shadowy loft was filled with light. *Tyburn Convent. London.* His father was probably living there. All they had to do was travel to Britain to find him.

"Did you hear that?" he told the others. "My father is in London. He wrote a letter from a place called Tyburn Convent."

Maya handed the .45 automatic to Hollis and took a handful of bullets for her revolver. She glanced at Gabriel and shook her head slightly. "Let's get to a safe place and then we'll talk about the future. Is everyone ready?"

Reverend Hernandez agreed to stay in the loft for one more hour, using the stove and the lights as if someone were home. The rest of the group crawled out the window to the fire escape and climbed up onto the roof. It felt like they were standing on a platform above the city. Clouds drifted over Manhattan, and the moon looked like a smudged chalk mark in the sky.

They passed over a series of low walls and reached the roof of a building farther up Catherine Street. The security door had a deadbolt lock, but Maya didn't see that as an obstacle. The Harlequin took out a thin piece of steel called a tension wrench, inserted it into the keyhole, and turned the plug slightly. Then she forced a locksmith's pick in above the wrench and used it to push the upper pins into the housing. When the last pin clicked into place, she pushed the door open and guided them downstairs to the ground floor of a storage building. Hollis opened the door and they stepped into an alleyway that led to Oliver Street.

It was about ten o'clock in the evening. The narrow streets were filled with young men and women who wanted to eat Peking duck and a few egg rolls before they spent the night dancing at clubs. People got out of taxis or stood on the sidewalk examining the menus displayed in restaurant windows. Although Gabriel and the others were concealed in the crowd, he felt as if every surveillance camera in the city were tracking their movements.

The feeling got stronger when they followed Worth Street to Broadway. Naz led the way, Hollis beside him. Vicki was next, followed by Sophia and Alice. Gabriel could hear Naz explaining how the subway system was being converted to a system that used computer-controlled trains. On some lines, the motorman spent his entire shift sitting in the cab of the front car, staring at the controls that worked without him.

"A computer in Brooklyn makes the train start and stop," Naz said. "All you gotta do is punch a button every few stops to show that you're not asleep."

Gabriel glanced over his shoulder and saw that Maya was about six feet behind him. The straps of her shoulder bag and the sword carrier crossed like a black X in the middle of her chest. Her eyes moved slightly back and forth like a camera that was continually scanning a danger zone.

They turned left onto Broadway and approached a triangular park. City Hall was a few blocks away—a large white building designed with a wide stairway leading up to Corinthian columns. This fake Greek temple was only a few hundred feet from the Woolworth Building, a Gothic cathedral of commerce with a spire that reached into the night.

"Maybe the cameras have been tracking us," Naz said. "But it don't make no difference. The next camera is down the street. See it? It's on the lamppost near the stoplight. They got us walkin' up Broadway, but now we disappear."

Stepping off the sidewalk, he led them through the deserted park. There were a few security lights on the asphalt pathways, glowing with a feeble energy, but their little group remained in the darkness.

"Where are we going?" Gabriel asked.

"There's a deserted subway station right beneath us. They built it a hundred years ago and closed it down right after World War Two. No cameras. No cops."

"How do we get up to Grand Central Terminal?"

"Don't worry about that. My friend is gonna show up in about fifteen minutes."

They passed through a cluster of scraggly pine trees and approached a brick maintenance building. A ventilation grate was on the west side of the building, and Maya smelled the dusty odor of the underground. Naz led them around the building to a steel security door. Ignoring the various warning signs—DANGER! AUTHORIZED ENTRY ONLY!—he pulled a key ring out of his knapsack.

"Where did you find that?" Hollis asked.

"In my supervisor's locker. I kind of borrowed the keys a couple of weeks ago and copied them."

Naz opened the door and led them into the building. They were standing on a steel floor surrounded by circuit boxes and electrical conduits; an opening in one corner led to a staircase. The door closed behind them and a loud boom echoed in the small space. Alice took two quick steps forward before controlling her fear. She looked like a half-wild animal that had just been returned to a cage.

The circular staircase went downward like an

enormous corkscrew to a landing where a single light bulb burned above a second security door. Naz sorted through his stolen keys, mumbling to himself as he tried to open the lock. Finally he found the right key, but the door still wouldn't move.

"Let me try." Hollis raised his left foot and aimed a front kick at the lock. The door popped open.

One by one, they entered the abandoned City Hall station. The original light fixtures were empty, but someone had attached an electrical cable to the wall and run it to a dozen bulbs. A token booth was at the center of the entrance lobby; it had a little dome-shaped copper roof and looked as if it belonged in the sort of old-fashioned movie theater that had ushers and a red velvet curtain. Beyond it were wooden turnstiles and a concrete platform by the subway tracks.

A layer of grayish-white dust covered the floor; the air was stale and smelled like machine oil. Gabriel felt as if he were locked inside a tomb until he gazed upward at the vaulted ceiling. It reminded him of a medieval church—an interior of high arches that rose from the ground and met at central points. The tunnel itself was another set of arches, illuminated by tarnished brass chandeliers that held frosted-glass globes. No advertisements. No surveillance cameras. The walls and ceilings were decorated with white, red, and dark green ceramic tiles that formed intricate geometric patterns. It made the underground environment feel like a sanctuary, a place of refuge from the disorder above them.

Gabriel felt warm air move across his skin, and then heard a distant rumble, growing in power. Seconds later, a subway train came around the curve and raced through the station without stopping.

"That's the number six local," Naz said. "It loops through here and heads back uptown."

"Is that how we get to Grand Central?" Sophia asked.

"We're not riding on the six. It's too public." Naz glanced at his watch. "You get a private train with nobody watching. Just wait. Devon should be here in a few minutes."

Naz paced in front of the booth, and then looked relieved when a pair of headlights appeared in the tunnel. "Here he comes. I need the first thousand—right now."

Vicki handed a wad of hundred-dollar bills to Naz, and their guide passed through a wooden turnstile to the platform. He waved his arms as a single subway car rolled into the station pulling a hopper car piled high with trash bags. A slender black man—well over six feet tall—was operating the controls in the front cab. He stopped the subway car and opened the double doors. Naz shook hands, exchanged a few words, and then handed the money to his friend.

"Hurry up!" he shouted. "Another train will be here in a minute."

Maya led the group into the subway car and told

them to sit at either end, away from the windows. Everyone obeyed her—even Alice. The little girl seemed completely aware of everything that was going on, but she never showed any expression.

Devon stood in the doorway of the closet-sized cab. "Welcome aboard the trash train," he said. "We got to change tracks a couple times, but we'll be up at Grand Central in about fifteen minutes. We'll stop at a maintenance platform because there aren't any TV cameras in that area."

Naz was grinning as if he'd just performed a magic trick. "See? What'd I tell you?"

Devon pushed the control lever down and the train jerked forward, picking up speed as it left the abandoned station. The car rocked back and forth, and then they were heading north beneath the streets of Manhattan. Devon stopped at the Spring Street station, but didn't open the doors. He waited until a green light flashed in the tunnel, then pushed the lever again.

Gabriel got up from his seat and stood next to Maya. The window in the door was open a few inches and warm air pushed into the car. As the train shifted onto a new track, it felt as if they were traveling through a secret part of the city. Light appeared in the distance, reflected on the tracks; there was a clattering sound and then they glided slowly through the Bleecker Street station. Gabriel had traveled on the east-side line several times before, but this experience was different. They were safe within a shadow land, one step beyond the scrutiny of the Vast Machine.

Astor Place. Union Square. And then the door to the control room popped open. The train was still moving, but Devon wasn't touching the controls.

"Something's going on . . ."

"What's the problem?" Maya asked.

"We're a maintenance train," Devon said. "I'm supposed to be running it. But the computer took over when we left the last station. I tried to contact the command center, but the radio's dead."

Naz jumped up and raised both hands as if he were trying to stop an argument. "It's no big deal. There's probably another train up the line."

"If that was true, then they would have stopped us at Bleecker." Devon stepped back into the control room and moved the lever again. The subway car ignored his efforts and passed through the Twenty-third Street station at the same moderate speed.

Maya drew the ceramic gun she had taken from Aronov. She kept the weapon pointed at the floor. "I want the train stopped at the next station."

"He can't do that," Naz said. "The computer is running everything."

Everyone was standing now—even Sophia Briggs and the girl. They held on to the poles in the middle of the car as lights flashed through the windows and the wheels clicked like a ticking watch.

"Is there an emergency brake?" Maya asked Devon.

"Yeah, but I don't know if it will work. The computer is telling the train to keep moving."

"Can you open the doors?"

"Not unless the car has stopped. I can release the safety lock and you can open them manually."

"Good. Do that right now."

Everyone looked out the window as they rolled through the Twenty-eighth Street station. The few New Yorkers standing on the platform looked as if they were frozen within that instant of time.

Maya turned to Hollis. "Push the door open. When we reach Forty-second Street, we're going to jump."

"I'm staying on the train," Naz said.

"You're coming with us."

"Forget that. I don't need your money."

"I wouldn't worry about the money right now." Maya raised the gun slightly, pointing it at Naz's kneecap. "I want to keep away from the cameras and get on that train at Grand Central Terminal."

Devon switched off the safety lock as they left the Thirty-third Street station. Hollis forced back two of the side doors and held them open. Every few yards they rattled past a steel I-beam holding up the tunnel ceiling. It felt like they were traveling down an endless passageway with no way out.

"Okay!" Devon shouted. "Get ready!" There was a red lever with a T-shaped handle mounted on the wall of the car's control room. Devon grabbed the handle, pulled down hard, and there was a screeching sound of steel scraping against steel. The subway car began to shiver but the wheels kept turning. As they approached Forty-second Street, the New Yorkers waiting in the station backed away from the edge of the platform.

Alice and Sophia jumped first, followed by Vicki, Hollis, and Gabriel. The train was going slowly enough that Gabriel managed to stay on his feet. Looking up the concrete platform, he saw Maya pull Naz out the open door. The wheels of the train kept screeching as it disappeared into the tunnel. People on the platform looked startled, and one man punched out a number on his cell phone.

"Come on!" Maya shouted, and they started running.

8

The van drove around the concrete security barrier and stopped at the Vanderbilt Avenue entrance to Grand Central Terminal. A National Guardsman standing in front of the train station approached them, but Nathan Boone motioned to one of his mercenaries, a New York City detective named Ray Mitchell. Ray lowered the passenger window and showed the soldier his badge. "Got a call about a couple of drug dealers doing business in the terminal," he said. "Someone said they had a little Chinese girl with them. Can you believe it? I mean—come on—if you're selling crack, get a babysitter."

The Guardsman grinned and lowered his rifle. "I've been in the city for six days," he said. "Everyone here is a little crazy."

The driver, a mercenary from South Africa named Vanderpoul, stayed behind the wheel as Boone got out of the van with Mitchell and his partner, Detective Krause. Ray Mitchell was a small, fast-talking man who liked to wear designer clothes. Krause was his opposite: a large, awkward cop with a flushed face who seemed to be permanently angry. Boone paid a monthly retainer to both police officers and gave them occasional bonuses for extra work.

"Now what?" Krause asked. "Where'd they go after they jumped?"

"Hold on," Boone said. His headset was relaying continual information from two teams of mercenaries as well as the Brethren's computer center in Berlin. The technicians had hacked into the New York transit system's surveillance network, and they were using their scanning programs to look for the fugitives.

"They're still in the subway station on a transit level," Boone said. "The cameras are getting a direct feed as they walk toward the shuttle train."

"So we go to the shuttle?" Mitchell asked.

"Not yet. Maya knows we're tracking her, and that's going to influence her behavior. The first thing she'll do is get away from the cameras."

Smiling, Mitchell glanced at his partner. "And that's why she's going to be caught."

Boone reached back into the van and took out the aluminum suitcase that contained the radio tracking equipment and three sets of infrared goggles.

"Let's go inside. I'm going to contact the response team parked on Fifth Avenue."

The three men entered the terminal and walked down one of the wide marble staircases built to resemble a part of the old Paris opera house. Mitchell caught up with Boone as they reached the main concourse. "I got to make things clear," he said. "We'll guide you around New York and run interference, but we're not taking anybody out."

"I'm not asking you to do that. Just deal with the authorities."

"No problem. I'll check in with the transit police and tell them we're at the terminal."

Mitchell took out his badge, clipped it to his jacket, then hurried down one of the corridors. Krause stayed with Boone like a giant bodyguard as they approached a central information booth with a four-faced clock mounted on the roof. The size of the main concourse, its arched windows, white marble floors, and stone walls, confirmed his belief that his side was going to win this secret war. Millions of people passed through the terminal every year, but only a few of them knew that the building itself was a subtle demonstration of the Brethren's power.

One of the Brethren's strongest supporters in America during the early twentieth century was William K. Vanderbilt, the railroad tycoon who had commissioned the construction of Grand Central Terminal. Vanderbilt requested that the main concourse's arched ceiling be decorated with the constellations of the zodiac, five stories above the marble floor of the station. The stars were supposed to be arranged as if they were in a Mediterranean sky during Christ's lifetime. But no one—not even the Egyptian astrologers of the first century—had ever seen such an arrangement: the zodiac on the ceiling was completely reversed.

It amused Boone to read the various theories as to why the stars were shown this way. The most popular idea was that the painter had duplicated a drawing found in a medieval manuscript and that the stars were shown from the point of view of someone outside our solar system. No one ever explained why Vanderbilt's architects had allowed this odd conceit to appear in such an important building.

The Brethren knew that the ceiling's design had nothing to do with a medieval concept of the heavens. The constellations were in the correct position for someone concealed inside the hollow ceiling, looking downward at travellers hurrying to their trains. Most of the stars were twinkling lightbulbs in a powder-blue sky, but there were a dozen sight holes as well. In the past, police officers and railroad security guards had used binoculars to follow the movements of suspicious-looking citizens. Now the entire population was being tracked with scanners and other electronic equipment. The reversed zodiac suggested that only the watchers from above saw the universe accurately. Everyone else assumed that the stars were in the right place.

A call came in on the sat phone, and a former British soldier named Summerfield whispered into Boone's ear. The response team had arrived at the Vanderbilt entrance and had parked behind the van. For this operation, the team was comprised of mostly the same men who had worked in Arizona. The New Harmony operation had been good for morale; the necessary violence had unified a group of mercenaries with different nationalities and back-grounds.

"Now what?" Summerfield asked.

"Break into small groups, and then enter from dif-ferent doors." Boone looked up at the schedule board. "We'll meet near track thirty—the train going to Stamford."

"I thought they were getting on the shuttle."

"All Maya wants to do is protect her Traveller. She'll hide as quickly as possible. That means going down a tunnel or finding a maintenance area."

"Is the objective still the same?"

"Everyone but Gabriel is now in the immediate-termination category."

Summerfield switched off his phone, and Boone picked up another call from the Internet team. Maya and the other fugitives had reached the shuttle area, but they were lingering on the platform. Boone had killed Maya's father, Thorn, in Prague last year, and he felt an odd personal connection to the young woman. She wasn't as tough as her father, perhaps because she had resisted becoming a Harlequin. Maya had already made one mistake—and the next choice would destroy her.

9

Naz had guided Maya and the rest of the group through a warren of stairs and passageways to the Times Square shuttle. The platform was a brightly lit area where a shuttle train departed from one of three parallel tracks. The gray concrete floor was dotted with blackened pieces of chewing gum that formed a random mosaic. A few hundred feet away, a group of West Indian men with steel drums pounded out a calypso tune.

So far, they had avoided the mercenaries, but Maya was sure they were being watched by the underground surveillance system. Now that their presence in New York had been discovered, she knew that the full resources of the Tabula would be used to find them. According to Naz, all they had to do was walk down the subway tunnel and take a staircase to the lower level of Grand Central Terminal. Unfortunately, a transit policeman was patrolling the area and, even if he disappeared, someone might tell the authorities that a group of people had jumped onto the tracks.

The only safe route into the tunnel was through a locked door labeled with the tarnished gold lettering KNICKERBOCKER. In a more convivial era, a passageway once led directly from the subway platform to the bar of the old Knickerbocker Hotel. Although the hotel was now an apartment building, the door remained—unnoticed by the tens of thousands of commuters who walked past it every day.

Maya stood on the platform feeling very conspicuous as commuters hurried to board the shuttle. When the train clattered out of the station, Hollis approached her and spoke in a quiet voice.

"You still want to get on the train going to Ten Mile River?"

"We'll evaluate the situation when we reach the platform. Naz says there aren't any cameras there."

Hollis nodded. "The Tabula scanners probably detected us when we left the loft and walked through Chinatown. Then somebody figured out we were using the old subway station and hacked into the transit computer."

"There's another explanation." Maya glanced over at Naz.

"Yeah, I thought about that, too. But I watched his face in the subway car. He really looked scared."

"Stay close to him, Hollis. If he starts running, stop him."

A new shuttle train arrived, took on a new crowd of passengers, and then rattled west toward Eighth Avenue. It felt like they would be standing there forever. Finally the transit policeman got a call on his radio and hurried away. Naz ran over to the Knickerbocker door and fumbled through the keys on his ring. When the lock clicked, he smiled and pulled the door open.

"Special subway tour goes this way," he announced, and a few commuters watched the group disappear through the doorway. When Naz shut the door, they stood close together in a short, dark passageway. He led them past a manhole cover and then down four concrete steps to the subway tunnel.

Everyone stood between one set of tracks as Naz pointed at a third rail filled with electric current. "Be careful with the wooden shield that covers that," he told them. "If it breaks and your body hits the rail, you're dead meat."

The tunnel was black with soot and smelled like sewage. Water trickled down the drainage channel; it oozed through the concrete wall and made the surface glisten like oil. The City Hall station had been dusty, but fairly clean; the tunnel to Times Square was littered with trash. Rats were everywhere—dark gray ones nearly a foot long. This was their world, and they weren't afraid of humans. When intruders appeared, the rats continued to rummage through the garbage, squeaking at one another or scurrying up the walls.

"They're not dangerous," Naz said. "Just watch where you're going. If you fall down, they crawl all over you."

Hollis stayed close to their guide. "Where's this doorway you were talking about?"

"It's right around here. Swear to God. Start looking for a yellow light."

They heard a low, rumbling sound, like distant thunder, and saw the headlights of the approaching shuttle. "Next track! Next track!" Naz shouted. Without waiting for the others, he leaped over the third rail to the adjacent track.

Everyone but Sophia Briggs followed Naz. The old woman looked exhausted and slightly confused. As the lights of the shuttle got closer, she took a risk and stepped directly on the wooden cover of the third rail. It held her weight. A moment later, she passed through the gloom and joined the others.

Naz darted up the track and then came back looking excited. "Okay. I think I found the door to the stairway. Just follow me and—"

The shuttle train on the next track absorbed the rest of his words. Maya saw quick flashes of different passengers framed within the windows—an old man with a knit cap, a young woman with braids—and then the train was gone. A candy wrapper flew up in the air and drifted downward like a dead leaf.

They kept walking to a juncture that led off in three different directions. Naz took the track on the right and then led them to an open doorway illuminated by a single lightbulb. He climbed up three metal steps and entered a maintenance tunnel, followed by Alice and Vicki. Hollis reached the top of the steps and shook his head. "We need to slow down. Sophia is getting tired."

"Find a safe place and wait for us," Maya said. "Gabriel and I will bring her along."

Maya knew that her father would have betrayed the rest of the group to save the Traveller, but she couldn't fall back on this strategy. Gabriel wasn't going to leave anyone behind in the tunnels—least of all the woman who had been his Pathfinder. She looked down the tunnel and saw that Gabriel had taken Sophia's knapsack and placed it on his own shoulders. When he offered his arm to Sophia, the old lady shook her head vigorously, as if to say, *I don't need anyone's help*. Sophia took a few steps forward and then a red laser beam cut through the gloom. "Get down!" Maya shouted. "Get—"

There was a sharp cracking sound and a bullet hit Sophia in the back. The Pathfinder fell forward, tried to get up, and then collapsed. Maya drew her revolver and fired down the tunnel as Gabriel scooped up Sophia and ran toward the steps. Maya followed him, pausing in the open doorway to fire again. The laser beam vanished as four dark shapes retreated into the shadows.

Maya broke open the revolver and used the ejector

rod to push out the empty cases. She was reloading as she entered a maintenance tunnel with brick walls, and found Gabriel on his knees embracing Sophia's limp body. His brown leather jacket was covered with blood.

"Is she breathing?"

"She's dead," Gabriel told her. "I held her and she was dying and I felt the Light leave her body."

"Gabriel . . ."

"I felt her die," Gabriel said again. "It was like water flowing between your fingers. I couldn't hold it back . . . couldn't stop it . . ." He shivered violently.

"The Tabula are very close," Maya said. "We can't stay here. You're going to have to leave her."

She touched Gabriel's shoulder and watched as he gently lowered Sophia's body onto the floor. A few seconds later, they hurried down the tunnel to a stairway landing where the others were waiting. Vicki gasped when she saw the blood on Gabriel's jacket, and Alice looked as if she were about to run away. The child's head moved back and forth. Maya sensed what Alice was thinking: *Who will protect me now?*

"What happened?" Vicki asked. "Where's Sophia?"

"The Tabula killed her. They're right behind us."

Vicki put her hands to her mouth and Naz looked shocked. "That's all," he said. "I quit. I'm not part of this."

"You don't have a choice. As far as the Tabula are concerned, you're just another target. Right now we're directly under the train station. You've got to get us out of this area and back on the street." She turned to the others. "This is going to be difficult, but we need to stay together. If we get separated, meet at Purest Children at seven o'clock tomorrow morning."

Looking frightened, Naz led the group downstairs to a tunnel with electrical conduit on the ceiling. It felt as if the weight of the terminal were pushing them deeper into the earth. Another staircase appeared—a very narrow one—and Naz followed it. The air in this new tunnel was warm and moist. Two white pipes, each two feet in diameter, were fastened to the walls.

"Steam pipes," Naz muttered. "Don't touch."

Following the pipes, they passed through a pair of steel safety doors and entered a maintenance room with a thirty-foot ceiling. Four large steam pipes from different parts of the underground were joined together in the room; the pressure was monitored with stainless-steel gauges and diverted with regulator valves. Stagnant water dribbled out of a crack in the ceiling and dripped downward. The room had the fetid, moldy smell of a hothouse for tropical plants.

Maya shut the safety door behind her and looked around. Her father would have called this a "box canyon"—a place with one way in and no way out. "Now what?" she asked.

"I don't know," Naz said. "I'm just trying to get away."

"That's not true," Maya said. "You led us here."

She drew the push knife and held the T-shaped handle in her fist. Before Naz could react, she grabbed his jacket and slammed him against the wall. Maya held the tip of her knife against the slight indentation just above Naz's breastbone.

"How much did they pay you?"

"Nothing! Nobody paid me nothing!"

"There aren't any surveillance cameras in these tunnels. But they followed us anyway. And now you've led us into another trap."

Gabriel stepped beside her. "Let go of him, Maya."

"This was all planned. The Tabula didn't want to attack a building in Chinatown. It was too public and there were too many police in the area. But down here, they can do whatever they want."

A drop of water hit one of the steam pipes and there was a faint hissing sound. Gabriel leaned forward and watched Naz's face with a focused intensity.

"Are you working for the Tabula, Naz?"

"No. Swear to God. I just wanted to make some money."

"Maybe they tracked us in a different way," Vicki said. "Remember back in Los Angeles? They put a tracer bead in one of my shoes."

Tracer beads were small radio devices that broadcast the location of a target. Maya had been careful about any object taken into the loft during the last few months. She had inspected each piece of furniture and article of clothing like a suspicious customs agent. As she concentrated on the knife, a feeling of doubt and hesitation came to her; it felt like a ghost had entered her body. There was one object that she hadn't examined, a golden apple thrown in her path so tempting, so irresistible, that the Tabula knew she would grab it.

Maya stepped away from Naz, slid the knife back into its sheath, and pulled the ceramic gun from her shoulder bag. The struggle with Aronov came back to her, and she analyzed each moment. Why hadn't they killed her when she entered the taxi? Because it was planned, Maya thought. Because they knew she would lead them back to Gabriel.

No one spoke as she checked the ceramic handgun. The barrel and the frame weren't thick enough to conceal a tracer bead, but the plastic pistol grip was perfect. Maya shoved the grip into the narrow gap between two pipes on the wall and then used the gun barrel as a lever. She forced the barrel down hard, and the grip cracked open with a loud snap. A pearl-gray tracer bead fell onto the floor. When she picked up the bead it felt warm, like a spark from a fire glowing in her hand.

"What the hell is that?" Naz asked. "What's going on?"

"That's how they tracked us in the tunnel," Hollis said. "They're following the radio transmitter."

Maya set the tracer bead on a narrow concrete

ledge and crushed it with her revolver. She felt as if her father were in the room, looking at her with contempt. He would have spoken to her in German, something cutting and harsh. When she was a little girl, he had tried to teach her the Harlequin way of looking at the world—always suspicious, always on your guard—but she had resisted. And now, because of her thoughtless impulse to take this weapon, she had destroyed Sophia and led Gabriel into a trap.

Maya looked around the room for an exit. The only possible way out was a maintenance ladder attached to the wall that ran parallel to a vertical steam pipe. The pipe went up through a hole in the ceiling, and the narrow gap might be wide enough to push through.

"Climb that ladder and get to the next floor," she told the others. "We'll find a way out through the train station."

Naz hurried up the ladder and squeezed through the gap to the upper level. Gabriel was next, followed by Hollis and Vicki. Ever since they had left the loft in Chinatown, Alice Chen had been at the front of the group—trying to escape the Tabula. This time, she climbed up the ladder and hesitated. Maya watched as the child tried to figure out the best way to protect herself.

"Hurry up," Maya told her. "You've got to follow them."

Maya heard a thump as one of the steel doors in

the tunnel was slammed shut. The men who had killed Sophia were in the tunnel, getting closer. Alice slid back down the ladder and disappeared beneath one of the steam pipes. Maya knew it was useless to go after the girl; she would stay hidden until the Tabula left the area.

Standing in the middle of the maintenance room, Maya analyzed her choices with the ruthless clarity of a Harlequin. The Tabula were moving quickly and probably weren't expecting a counterattack. So far, she had failed to protect Gabriel, but there was a way to make up for her mistakes. Harlequins were damned by their actions, but redeemed by their sacrifice.

Maya removed her shoulder bag and tossed it on the floor. Using the pressure gauges and valves as handholds, she climbed onto a steam pipe and then lifted herself up onto the one above it. Now she was fifteen feet above the floor, directly opposite the entrance to the room. The air was warm and it was hard to breathe. A faint noise came from the tunnel. She drew the revolver from the holster and waited. Her legs trembled with the strain. Her face was covered with sweat.

The door slammed open and a big man with a beard crouched in the opening. The mercenary was holding a gun with a laser sight mounted below the barrel. He glanced quickly around the room and took a few steps forward. Maya dropped through the air and began firing. A bullet hit the mercenary at the base of his throat and he collapsed.

Maya fell on the floor, rolled forward, and jumped to her feet. She saw that the dead man's body was keeping the door open. Red laser beams flashed from the dark hallway and she ran for cover. A bullet ricocheted off the walls and struck one of the gauges. Steam spurted into the air. She ducked down, wondering where to hide, and Alice's hand emerged from beneath one of the pipes.

When another bullet hit the wall, Maya lay flat on the concrete and pushed herself sideways beneath the pipe. Now she was lying directly behind Alice, and the little girl gazed back at the Harlequin. Alice didn't look frightened or angry—more like a zoo animal studying a new addition to her cage. The shooting stopped and the laser beams vanished. Silence. Maya held her revolver with two hands, the right hand cradled in the left. She got ready to stand up, extend her arms, and fire.

"Maya?" A man's voice came from somewhere in the dark tunnel. An American voice. Calm, not frightened. "This is Nathan Boone. I'm head of security for the Evergreen Foundation."

She knew who Boone was—the Tabula mercenary who had killed her father in Prague. Maya wondered why Boone was talking. Perhaps he was trying to make her angry so that she would decide to attack.

"I'm sure you're there," Boone said. "You just killed one of my best employees."

The Harlequin rule was never to speak to an enemy unless it gave you some kind of advantage. She wanted to remain silent, but then she remembered Gabriel: if she distracted Boone, then the Traveller would have more time to escape.

"What do you want?" she asked.

"Gabriel is going to be killed if you don't let him walk out of this room. I promise not to hurt Gabriel, Vicki, or your guide."

Maya wondered if Boone knew about Alice. He would kill her also if he realized the child had survived the destruction of New Harmony. "What about Hollis?" she asked.

"Both of you made a decision to fight the Brethren. Now you have to deal with the consequences."

"Why should I trust you? You killed my father."

"That was his choice." Boone sounded annoyed. "I gave him an alternative, but he was too stubborn to take it."

"We need to talk this over. Give us a few minutes."

"You don't have a few minutes. There's no alternative. No negotiations. If you're a true Harlequin, then you'll want to save the Traveller. Send the others down the tunnel or everyone in the room is going to die. We have a technical advantage."

What was he talking about? Maya thought. What technical advantage? Alice Chen was still staring at her. The little girl touched the warm steam pipe above them with her palm and then extended her hand—trying to communicate some message. "What are you telling me?" Maya whispered.

"Have you made your decision?" Boone shouted.

Silence.

A bullet hit one of the two fluorescent light fixtures hanging from the ceiling. A second burst of gunfire and the fixture was blown away with a shower of sparks; it bounced off one of the steam pipes and hit the floor.

Now that the room was darker, Maya understood what the child was trying to convey. Boone and his mercenaries had night-vision devices. Once the second light fixture was destroyed, she would be blind while Boone and his men could see their targets. The only way to hide from infrared devices was to become very cold or to push your body next to a warm object. Alice knew this; that was why she had stayed behind and hidden beneath the steam pipe.

The shooting started again; two laser beams were aimed at the second light fixture. Alice rolled away from the steam pipe and stared at the dead body lying in the doorway. "Stay here!" Maya shouted. But the girl jumped up and ran over to the doorway. She crouched down when she reached the dead mercenary, making herself as small as possible, then grabbed some equipment that had been clipped to the man's belt. When Alice scurried back, Maya saw that the girl was carrying night-vision goggles attached to a head strap, and a hand-size battery pack. Alice tossed the goggles to Maya and returned to her hiding place beneath the steam pipe.

A bullet hit the second light fixture and the room was absorbed by darkness. It felt like they were in a cavern deep within the earth. Maya pulled the night-vision goggles over her eyes. She pressed the illuminator button and immediately the room was transformed into different shades of green. Anything warm—the steam pipes, the pressure gauges, the skin of her left hand—glowed with bright emerald color, as if these objects were radioactive. The concrete walls and floors showed a light green color that reminded her of new leaves.

Maya peered around the top edge of a steam pipe and saw a green light growing brighter as someone walked slowly down the tunnel to the open doorway. The light wavered slightly, then a mercenary wearing goggles appeared in the doorway. Carrying a sawed-off shotgun, he carefully stepped over the dead man's body.

She moved behind the pipe and pressed her back against the warm metal. It was impossible to predict the mercenary's position as he moved around the room; she could only plan the general direction of her attack. Maya felt as if all her energy were flowing from her shoulders and down her arms to the gun held in her hands. She breathed in, held her breath, and moved around the pipe.

A third mercenary holding a submachine gun had appeared in the doorway. The Harlequin shot him in the chest. There was a flash of light as the force of the bullet pushed him backward. Even before the dead mercenary hit the floor, Maya spun around and killed the man holding the shotgun. Silence. The faint scent of cordite mingled with the rotting smell of the room. The steam pipes glowed green around her.

Maya shoved the night-vision goggles in her shoulder bag, found Alice, and grabbed her hand. "Climb," she whispered. "Just climb." They hurried up the maintenance ladder, passed through the gap, and reached an area just below an open manhole. Maya stopped for few seconds and then decided: it was too dangerous to enter the track area. Still holding the little girl's hand, she pulled her down a tunnel that led away from the station.

10

Holding on to the rungs of the ladder with his left hand, Naz used his right to push on a cast-iron manhole cover. After much grunting and swearing, he finally maneuvered the cover over the lip of the holding bracket and shoved it to one side. Gabriel followed Naz through the opening to the lower level of Grand Central Terminal. They were standing between a soot-covered concrete wall and one of the tracks of the railroad line.

Naz looked as if he were ready to take off in any direction. "What's going on?" he asked. "Where are Vicki and Hollis?"

Gabriel peered down into the manhole and saw the top of Vicki's head. She was twenty feet below him, moving cautiously up the ladder.

"They're right behind me. It might take a minute."

"We don't have a minute." Naz heard a distant clattering sound, spun around, and saw the twin lights of an approaching train. "We got to get out of here!"

"Let's wait for the others."

"They'll catch up with us in the terminal. If the motorman sees us on the tracks he'll radio the transit police."

Gabriel and Naz sprinted across the tracks, vaulted onto the passenger platform, and walked up a concrete ramp toward the lights. Quickly, Gabriel removed his bloodstained jacket and turned it inside out. The lower concourse of the train station had been turned into a food court ringed with fast-food outlets. Only a coffee bar was open, and a handful of commuters dozed on benches while they waited for late-night trains. The two men sat down at a café table and waited for the others to emerge from the track area.

"What happened?" Naz asked. "You saw them, right?"

"Vicki was climbing the ladder. Hollis was just a few feet below her."

Naz jumped up and began to pace back and forth. "We can't stay here."

"Sit down. It's only been a couple minutes. We need to wait a little longer."

"Good luck, man. I'm gone."

Naz hurried over to the escalator and disappeared into the upper level of the terminal. Gabriel tried to imagine what had happened to the others. Were they trapped below? Had the Tabula caught up with them? The fact that a tracer bead was hidden in the ceramic gun had changed everything. He wondered if Maya would take an unnecessary risk to punish herself for what had happened.

Gabriel left the eating area and stood in the open doorway that led to the tracks. A surveillance camera was focused on the platform, and Gabriel had already noticed four other cameras mounted on the ceiling of the concourse. The Tabula had probably hacked into the terminal's security system and their computers were scanning the live feeds for his image. *Stay together.* That was what Maya had told them, but she had also provided a backup plan: if there was a problem, they would meet up tomorrow morning on the Lower East Side of Manhattan.

Gabriel returned to the dining area and concealed himself behind a concrete pillar. A few seconds later, four tough-looking men wearing phone headsets came down the escalator and ran through the doorway to the track area. The moment they were gone, Gabriel went the other way, climbing a staircase to the main concourse and passing through a doorway to the street. The cold winter air made his eyes water and his face sting. The Traveller put his head down and stepped into the night.

* * *

DURING THEIR TIME in New York, Maya had insisted that everyone memorize safe routes through the city and a list of single-residency hotels that were off the Grid. One of these places was the Efficiency Hotel on Tenth Avenue in Manhattan. For twenty dollars in cash you got twelve hours in a window-less fiberglass pod that was eight feet long and five feet high. The forty-eight pods lined both sides of a corridor and made the hotel look like a mausoleum.

Before Gabriel entered the hotel, he took off his leather jacket again and folded it so that the blood-stains weren't visible. The hotel clerk was an elderly Chinese man who sat behind a bulletproof barrier and waited for customers to slip their cash into a narrow slot. Gabriel paid him twenty dollars for the use of the pod and an extra five dollars for a foam rubber pad and a cotton blanket.

He received a key and walked down the hallway to the communal bathroom. Two Latino restaurant workers were standing bare-chested in front of the sinks, chattering to each other in Spanish as they washed the cooking grease off their faces and arms. Gabriel hid in a toilet stall until the two men were gone, then came out and washed his jacket in the sink. When he was done, he climbed a ladder to his rented space and crawled inside. Each pod had a fluorescent light and a small fan to keep the air circulating. There was a single peg to hold his jacket, and the wet leather began to drip softly, as if it were still sodden with blood.

Lying on the foam pad, Gabriel couldn't stop thinking about Sophia Briggs. He had felt the Light within her, surging and moving like a powerful wave of water, and then it had flowed through his hands. He could hear muffled voices through the thin walls of the pod and it felt like he was drifting through shadows, surrounded by ghosts.

* * *

MAYA HAD TAUGHT Gabriel that the Grid was not absolute; there were still gaps and shadow areas where you could move safely through the city. The next morning, it took him about an hour to avoid the surveillance cameras and walk over to Tompkins Square Park. In the financial district and in the Midtown area, the gray bedrock of Manhattan was close to the surface, providing a foundation for the skyscrapers that dominated the city. On the Lower East Side, the bedrock was hundreds of feet below the surface, and the buildings that lined the streets were only four or five stories high.

Tompkins Square Park had been the traditional site for political protests for more than a hundred years. A generation earlier, a group of homeless people had established a camp there until the police had closed the park and surrounded it with a massive circle of officers. The police then walked toward the center, ripping apart improvised shelters and beating anyone

who refused to leave. These days, huge elm trees
shaded the park in the summer, and black iron railings
surrounded every patch of ground. There were only two
surveillance cameras in the park; both were aimed at
the children's playgrounds and easily avoided.

Gabriel walked cautiously through the park and
approached the small redbrick building occupied by
the gardening staff. He passed through some open
gates and stopped in front of a white marble stela
with a small lion's-head fountain at the center. Faintly
visible in the marble were the outline of some
children's faces and the words THEY WERE THE EARTH'S
PUREST CHILDREN, YOUNG AND FAIR. This was the
memorial to a 1904 disaster when a ferry ship called
the *General Slocum* left New York Harbor carrying a
group of German immigrants to a Sunday school
picnic. The boat caught fire and sank without
lifeboats, and over a thousand women and children
died.

Maya used the memorial as one of three message
boards around Manhattan. The boards gave their
small group a communications alternative to the
easily monitored cell phones. On the backside of
the stela, at the marble base, Gabriel found some
graffiti that Maya had left a few weeks ago. It was a
Harlequin sign: an oval with three lines that symbol-
ized a lute. He looked around at the nearby basketball
court and the small garden. It was seven o'clock in
the morning and no one was there. All the negative

possibilities he had pushed out of his mind this morning returned with a dreadful power. Everyone was dead. And somehow, he was the cause of it.

Gabriel knelt down like a man about to pray. He took a felt-tip pen out of his jacket and wrote on the monument G. *here*. *Where you?*

He left the park immediately, walking across Avenue A to a small coffeehouse filled with old tables, rickety chairs, and a pair of school desks that looked as though they had been found on the street. Gabriel bought a cup of coffee and sat in the back room with his eyes on the doorway. His feeling of hopelessness was almost unbearable. Sophia and the families at New Harmony had been murdered. And now there was a strong possibility that the Tabula had killed Maya and his friends.

He stared down at the scratched surface of the table and tried to quiet the angry voice in his brain. Why was he a Traveller? And why had he caused all this pain? Only his father could answer these questions—and Matthew Corrigan was apparently living in London. Gabriel knew there were more surveillance cameras in London than in any other city in the world. It was a dangerous place, but his father must have gone there for some important reason.

No one paid attention as Gabriel opened his shoulder bag and counted the money in the packet Vicki had given him last night. There seemed to be enough cash to buy a plane ticket to Great Britain.

Since Gabriel had spent his entire life off the Grid, the biometric data on his passport chip couldn't be compared against any previous identity. Maya had seemed sure that he wouldn't have problems traveling to another country. As far as the authorities were concerned, he was a citizen named Tim Bentley who worked as a commercial real estate agent in Tucson, Arizona.

He finished his coffee and returned to the memorial in Tompkins Square Park. Using a scrap of newspaper he wiped out his previous message and wrote *G2LONDON*. He felt like the survivor of a shipwreck who had just carved a few words on a scrap of wood. If his friends were still alive, then they would know what had happened. They would follow him to London and find him at Tyburn Convent. If everyone was dead, then it was a message to no one.

Gabriel left the park without looking back and walked south on Avenue B. The morning air was still cold, but the sky was clear—almost painfully blue. He was on his way.

11

Michael finished his second cup of coffee, got up from the oak table, and walked over to the Gothic windows at one end of the morning room. The lead frames of the windows imposed a black grid upon the outer world. He was west of Montreal on an island in the middle of the Saint Lawrence River. Rain had fallen the night before, and a thick layer of clouds still lingered in the sky.

A meeting of the Brethren's executive board was supposed to begin at eleven o'clock in the morning, but the boat carrying the board members still hadn't arrived. The journey from Chippewa Bay to Dark Island took about forty minutes. If the waves were choppy, people stepped onto the dock looking pale. A helicopter ride from any city in New York State would have been much more efficient, but Kennard Nash had rejected a proposal to construct a helicopter pad near the boathouse.

"The trip across the river is a good experience for the Brethren," Nash explained. "It makes them feel like they're getting away from the ordinary world. I think that it encourages a certain kind of respect for the unique nature of our organization."

Michael found himself agreeing with Nash; Dark Island was a special place. A wealthy American industrialist who manufactured sewing machines constructed the castle on the island in the early twentieth century. Blocks of granite were dragged across the winter ice to build a four-story clock tower, a boathouse, and a castle. The castle had turrets and towers and fireplaces big enough to roast an entire steer.

These days a group of wealthy Germans owned Dark Island. Tourists were allowed to visit for a few months in autumn, but the Brethren used the castle during the rest of the year. Michael and General Nash had arrived three days ago with a technical crew from the Evergreen Foundation. The men installed microphones and television cameras so that members all over the world could participate in the executive board meeting.

The first day on the island, Michael was allowed to leave the castle and walk alone to the cliffs. Dark Island got its name from the massive fir trees that extended their branches over the pathways, filtering the light and creating shadowy tunnels of green. Michael found a marble bench at the edge of the cliff, and he spent several hours there, smelling the sharp pine scent and looking out at the river.

That night he ate dinner with General Nash, followed by whiskey in the oak-paneled drawing room. Everything at the castle was massive—the hand-carved furniture, framed paintings, and liquor cabinets. Animal heads were mounted on the wall of the drawing room, and Michael felt as if a dead elk were staring at him.

Nash and the rest of the Brethren viewed Michael as their source of information about the different realms. Michael knew that his position was still tenuous. The Brethren usually killed Travellers, but he had survived. He tried to make himself as indispensable as possible without showing the extent of his ambition. If the world was going to become an invisible prison, that meant one person had to be in control of both the guards and the prisoners. And why couldn't that person be a Traveller?

The Brethren had originally attached Michael to their quantum computer and attempted to contact more advanced civilizations in the other realms. Although the computer was destroyed, Michael had assured General Nash that he could eventually get any information they required. He thought it wise not to mention his own goals. If he found his father and gained any special knowledge, he intended to use it to his own advantage. Michael felt like a man who had escaped a firing squad.

During the last month, Michael had left his body on two different occasions. It was the same each time—at first, a few sparks of Light emerged from his body, and then all his energy seemed to flow out into a cold darkness. To find his way to any Realm, he had to pass through all four barriers: a blue sky, a desert plain, a town on fire, and an endless sea. These barriers had once seemed like insurmountable obstacles, but now he was able to cross them almost instantly—discovering the small black passageways that led him onward.

Michael opened his eyes and found himself in a town square with trees and benches and an outdoor bandstand. It was early in the evening, and men and women wearing dark suits and overcoats wandered down the sidewalk, restlessly entering the brightly lit shops, then emerging a few minutes later with nothing in their hands.

He had been here before; this was the Second Realm of the hungry ghosts. It looked like a real world, but everything in this place was an empty promise to those who could never be satisfied. All the packages in the grocery store were empty. The apples on the corner stand and the slabs of meat in the butcher shop were painted pieces of wood or pottery. Even the leather-bound books in the town library appeared real, but when Michael tried to read them he discovered there were no words on the pages.

It was dangerous to be here; he felt like the only

living creature in a town of phantoms. The people living in this realm seemed to recognize that he was different; they wanted to talk to him, touch him, feel his muscles and the warm blood that moved beneath his skin. Michael had tried to hide in the shadows while he peered through windows and searched the back streets for his father. Eventually, he found the passageway that led back to his world. When he crossed over a few days later, he ended up in the same town square, as if his Light had refused to go in any other direction.

* * *

THE GRANDFATHER CLOCK in the morning room began to chime, and Michael returned to the window. A powerboat had just arrived from Chippewa Bay, and the members of the Brethren executive board were stepping onto the dock. It was cold and blustery, but General Nash stood on the dock like a politician, saying hello and shaking hands.

"Has the boat arrived?" asked a woman's voice.

Michael turned and saw Mrs. Brewster, a board member who had arrived last night. "Yes. I counted eight people."

"Good. That means that Dr. Jensen's flight wasn't delayed."

Mrs. Brewster walked over to the sideboard and poured herself a cup of tea. She was in her fifties—a brisk Englishwoman who wore a tweed skirt, a sweater, and the kind of thick-soled practical shoes you'd need for a hike across a muddy pasture. Although Mrs. Brewster didn't seem to have a job title, the other board members deferred to the force of her personality, and no one used her first name. She acted as if the world were a chaotic school and she were the new headmistress. Everything needed to be organized. Slipshod work and bad habits would not be tolerated. No matter what the consequences, she was going to tidy up.

Mrs. Brewster poured some cream into her teacup and smiled pleasantly. "Looking forward to the board meeting, Michael?"

"Yes, ma'am. I'm sure it's going to be very interesting."

"You're quite right about that. Did General Nash tell you what was going to happen?"

"Not really."

"The man in charge of our computer center in Berlin is going to present a major technical innovation that will help us establish the Panopticon. We need the unanimous consent of the board to move forward."

"I'm sure you'll get it."

Mrs. Brewster sipped her tea, and then placed the china cup in its saucer. "The executive board has a few peculiarities. Members usually vote yes at a meeting and then put the knife in later. That's why you're here, Michael. Did anyone tell you that your participation was my idea?"

"I thought it was because of General Nash."

"I've read all about Travellers," Mrs. Brewster said. "Apparently some of them can look at a person's face and see what he or she is thinking. Do you have that particular skill?"

Michael shrugged. He was wary of revealing too much about his abilities. "I know if a person is lying."

"Good. That's what I want you to do during this meeting. It would be most helpful if you could notice who is voting yes, but thinking no."

* * *

MICHAEL FOLLOWED MRS. Brewster to the banquet room, where General Nash gave a short speech welcoming everyone to Dark Island. Three flat-panel video screens had been placed at one end of the room, faced by a semicircle of leather club chairs. The middle television screen was white, but a grid of boxes appeared on the screens of the two side monitors. Members of the Brethren from all over the world sat down at their computers and joined the meeting. A few members had video cameras, so their faces appeared on the screen, but usually the box described only a member's geographical location: Barcelona, Mexico City, Dubai.

"Ah, here he is," Nash said when Michael entered

the room. "Ladies and gentlemen, this is Michael Corrigan."

With his hand on Michael's right shoulder, Nash guided him around to meet the others. Michael felt like a rebellious teenager who had finally been allowed to attend the adults' party.

After everyone took their seats, Lars Reichhardt, the director of the Berlin computer center, walked up to the podium. He was a big man with red hair, flushed cheeks, and a booming laugh that filled the room.

"It's an honor to be speaking to all of you," Reichhardt said. "As you know, our quantum computer was damaged during last year's attack on our research center in New York. At this time, it's still not operational. Our new computer center in Berlin uses conventional technology, but it's still quite powerful. We've also created bot nets of cooperating computers around the world that obey our commands without the owner's knowledge . . ."

Lines of computer code appeared on the middle monitor behind the podium. As Reichhardt spoke, the computer code became smaller and smaller until it was condensed into a black square.

"We're also expanding our use of computational immunology. We have created self-sustaining, self-replicating computer programs that move through the Internet like white blood cells in the human body. Instead of looking for viruses and infections, these programs search for infectious ideas that will delay the establishment of the Panopticon."

On the screen, the tiny square of code entered a computer. It reproduced itself and then was transmitted to a second computer. Rapidly, it began to take over an entire system.

"Initially, we used computational immunology as a tool for discovering our enemies. Because of the problems with the quantum computer, we turned our cyber leukocytes into active viruses that damage computers filled with information that is determined to be antisocial. The program requires no maintenance once it is released into the system.

"But now I will turn to the *Hauptgericht*—the 'main course' of our banquet. We call it the Shadow Program . . ."

The monitor went dark and then showed the computer-generated image of a living room. Looking like one of the mannequins used to test car safety, a figure sat on a straight-backed chair. His face and body were comprised of geometric shapes, but he was recognizably human—a man.

"The use of electronic surveillance and monitoring has reached a crucial fusion point. Using both government and corporate sources, we have all the data necessary to track an individual during his entire day. We've simply combined it into one system—the Shadow Program. Shadow creates a parallel cyberreality that constantly changes to reflect the actions of each individual. For those members of the Brethren who would like more information after this talk, I'm warning you—the Shadow Program is . . ." Reichhardt paused, searching for a word. "I would call it *verführerisch*."

"Which means beguiling," Mrs. Brewster explained. "Seductive."

"Seductive. An excellent word.

"In order to show what the Shadow Program can do, I've chosen one member of the Brethren as our subject. Without his knowledge, I have established his duplicated self within our system. Photographs from passport and driver's license databases are converted into a three-dimensional image. Using medical records and other personal data, we can establish weight and height."

Michael had briefly meet Dr. Anders Jensen before the meeting started. He was a slight man with thinning blond hair who had some kind of position in the Danish government. Jensen looked surprised when his face appeared on the computer-generated man. Medical information flashed on the screen, and that data transformed the shape of the body. Information taken from a clothing store computer became a gray business suit and a blue necktie. When the figure was dressed, it stood up from the computer chair and waved.

"And here we are!" Reichhardt announced. "Dr. Jensen, meet your shadow self!"

Michael and the rest of the group applauded the achievement while Jensen forced a smile. The Dane didn't seem happy that his image was now held within the system.

"From housing records we can recreate Professor Jensen's apartment on Vogel Street. From credit card information, especially from mail-order companies, we can even place selected pieces of furniture in different rooms."

While the computer-generated professor paced back and forth, a couch, chair, and coffee table appeared in the room. Michael glanced at the others. Mrs. Brewster nodded at him and smiled knowingly.

"This is not exactly correct," Jensen said. "The couch is pushed against the wall near the door."

"I beg your pardon, Professor." Reichhardt spoke briefly into the thin microphone attached to his headset. The shadow couch melted away and appeared in the proper location.

"Now I'd like to show you the edited record of a few hours in Professor Jensen's life. The Shadow Program watched him nine days ago during a successful test of the system. Because the professor has a home security system, we know exactly when he leaves his apartment. Professor Jensen's mobile phone and his car's GPS system allow us to track his trip to a local shopping area. Two surveillance cameras are in the parking lot. The professor is photographed and a facial algorithm confirms his identity. The discount shopping card in Jensen's wallet comes with an embedded RFID chip. It informs a computer when he's entered a particular store. Here it's a business selling books, films, and computer games . . ."

On the screen, the shadow Anders Jensen began to walk down the aisle of a store, passing other shadow individuals. "Please understand—what you're seeing on the screen is not hypothetical. It corresponds to Professor Jensen's physical experience. We know what the store looks like because most modern businesses have been transformed into electronic environments to monitor shopping behavior. We know what the other customers look like because we've scanned their ID cards and found images of their faces in various databanks.

"Most products now have RFID chips to guard against theft. They also allow stores to track their shipments. Businesses in Denmark, France, and Germany have chip sensors in the shelves so they know if customers are attracted to promotions and packaging. This will become standard on everything in the next few years. Now watch. Professor Jensen goes to this particular shelf and—"

"That's enough," Jensen murmured.

"He picks up the product, returns it to the shelf. He hesitates and then decides to make a purchase of a DVD entitled *Tropical Sin III*."

General Nash laughed and the others joined him.

Some of the Brethren on the computer monitors were laughing as well. Looking crushed, Jensen stared down at the floor and shook his head. "I-I bought it for a friend," he said.

"I apologize, Professor, for any embarrassment this may have caused you."

"But you know the rules," Mrs. Brewster snapped. "All of us are equal within the Panopticon."

"Exactly," Reichhardt said. "Because of our limited resources at the moment, we have enough computing power to establish the Shadow Program in only one city—Berlin. The program will become fully active in fifteen days. Once we get the system running, then the authorities will face—"

"A terrorist threat," Nash said.

"Or something of that sort. At this point, the Evergreen Foundation will offer the Shadow Program to our friends in the German government. The moment it becomes established, our political allies will make sure that it becomes a worldwide system. This is not just a tool against crime and terrorism. Companies will like the idea of a system that can exactly determine an employee's location and actions. Is the employee drinking during lunch? Is he going to the library at night and taking inappropriate books from the shelves? The Shadow Program will allow a certain number of controversial books and films to exist in the marketplace. The public reaction to these commodities gives us more information to create our duplicate reality."

There was a brief silence, and Michael seized the opportunity. "I would like to say something."

General Nash looked surprised. "This is not the time or place, Michael. You can give me your notes after the meeting."

"I disagree," Mrs. Brewster said. "I would like to hear the views of our Traveller."

Jensen nodded rapidly. He was eager to move on to any topic of conversation that didn't involve the duplicate professor on the television screen. "Sometimes it's good to get a different perspective."

Michael stood up and faced the Brethren. Each person sitting in front of him was wearing a mask created by a lifetime of deceit, the adult face concealing the emotions once expressed as a child. As the Traveller watched, these masks dissolved into little fragments of reality.

"The Shadow Program is a brilliant achievement," Michael said. "Once it's successful in Berlin, it can easily be extended to other countries. But there is one threat that could destroy the whole system." He paused and looked around the room. "You have an active Traveller out in the world. A person who can cause resistance to your plans."

"Your brother is not a significant problem," Nash said. "He's a fugitive without any support."

"I'm not talking about Gabriel. I'm talking about my father."

Michael saw surprise in their faces and then

Kennard Nash's anger. The general hadn't told them about Matthew Corrigan. Perhaps he didn't want to look weak and unprepared.

"I beg your pardon." Mrs. Brewster sounded as if she had just found an error in a restaurant bill. "Didn't your father disappear years ago?"

"He's still alive. Right now, he could be anywhere in the world, organizing resistance to the Panopticon."

"We're investigating," Nash sputtered. "Mr. Boone is dealing with the problem and he assures me that—"

Michael interrupted. "The Shadow Program will fail—all of your programs will fail—unless you find my father. You know that he started the New Harmony community in Arizona. Who knows what other centers of resistance he has started—or is organizing right now?"

A tense silence engulfed the room. Looking at the faces of the Brethren, Michael knew that he had managed to manipulate their fear.

"So what are we supposed to do?" Jensen asked. "Do you have any ideas?"

Michael bowed his head like a humble servant. "Only a Traveller can find another Traveller. Let me help you."

12

On Flatbush Avenue in Brooklyn, Gabriel found a storefront travel agency with a dusty collection of beach toys displayed in the front window. The agency was run by Mrs. Garcia, an older Dominican woman who weighed at least three hundred pounds. Chattering in a mixture of English and Spanish, she pushed at the floor with her feet and scooted around the room in an office chair with squeaky wheels. When Gabriel said that he wanted to buy a one-way ticket to London—paying in cash—Mrs. Garcia stopped moving and studied her new customer.

"You have a passport?"

Gabriel placed his new passport on the desk. Mrs. Garcia inspected it like a customs official and decided that it was acceptable. "A one-way ticket makes questions with *inmigración y la policía*. Maybe questions no good. *Sí*?"

Gabriel remembered Maya's explanation of air travel. The people who got searched were grandmothers carrying fingernail scissors and other passengers who violated simple rules. While Mrs. Garcia rolled over to her desk, he checked the money in his wallet. Buying a round-trip ticket would leave him about a hundred and twenty dollars. "All right," he told her. "Sell me a round-trip ticket. On the first flight out."

Mrs. Garcia used her personal credit card to buy the ticket, and she gave Gabriel information about a hotel in London. "You don't stay there," she explained. "But you must give *el oficial del pasaporte* an address and phone number." When Gabriel admitted that he didn't have any luggage other than his shoulder bag, the travel agent sold him a canvas suitcase for twenty dollars and stuffed it with some old clothes. "Now you are a tourist. So what do you want to see in England? They might ask you that question."

Tyburn Convent, Gabriel thought. *That's where my father is.* But he shrugged his shoulders and looked down at the scuffed linoleum. "London Bridge, I guess. Buckingham Palace . . ."

"*Bueno*, Mr. Bentley. Say hello to the queen."

Gabriel had never flown overseas before, but he had seen the experience in movies and television commercials. Well-dressed people were shown lounging in comfortable seats, where they had conversations with other attractive passengers. The actual experience reminded him of the summer he and Michael had spent working at a cattle feed lot outside of Dallas, Texas. The cattle had bar-coded tags stapled to their ears, and a great deal of time was spent picking out the steers that had been there too long, inspecting them, weighing them, sorting them into pens, driving them down narrow chutes, and forcing them into trucks.

Eleven hours later, he stood in the customs line at Heathrow Airport. When it was his turn, he approached the passport officer, a Sikh with a full beard. The officer took Gabriel's passport and studied him for a moment.

"Have you ever visited the United Kingdom?"

Gabriel offered the man his most relaxed smile. "No. This is my first time."

The officer ran the passport through a scanner and studied the screen before him. The biometric information on the RFID chip matched the photograph and the information already placed within the system. Like most citizens in a dull job, the officer trusted the machine more than his own instincts. "Welcome to Britain," he said, and suddenly Gabriel was in a new country.

It was almost eleven o'clock at night when he changed his money, left the terminal, and took the Tube into London. Gabriel got off at King's Cross station and wandered around the area until he found a hotel. The single room was as big as a closet and frost crystals were on the inside of the window, but he kept his clothes on, wrapped himself in the thin coverlet, and tried to sleep.

Gabriel had turned twenty-seven a few months before he left Los Angeles. It had been fifteen years since he had seen his father. His strongest memories came from the period in which his family lived without electricity or telephones on a farm in South Dakota. He could still recall his father teaching him how to change the oil in the pickup truck, and the night that his parents danced with each other beside the firelight in the parlor. He remembered sneaking downstairs at night when he was supposed to be in bed, peering through the doorway, and seeing his father sitting alone at the kitchen table. Matthew Corrigan looked thoughtful and sad at those moments—as if an immense weight had been placed on his shoulders.

But most of all, he remembered when he was twelve and Michael was sixteen. During a heavy snowstorm, Tabula mercenaries attacked the farmhouse. The boys and their mother hid in the root cellar while the wind howled outside. The next morning, the Corrigan brothers found four bodies lying in the snow. But their father was gone, vanished from their lives. Gabriel felt as if someone had reached into his chest and removed some part of his body. There was an emptiness there, a hollow feeling that had never quite gone away.

* * *

WHEN HE WOKE up, Gabriel got directions from the hotel clerk and began to walk south, to the Hyde Park area. He felt nervous and out of place in this new city. Someone had painted LOOK LEFT or LOOK RIGHT at the intersections, as if the foreigners who filled London were about to be crushed by the black cabs and white delivery vans. Gabriel tried to walk a straight line, but he kept getting lost on narrow cobblestone streets that went off at odd angles. In America, you carried dollar bills in your wallet, but now his pocket was heavy with coins.

Back in New York, Maya had talked about the vision of London that she had learned from her father. Apparently, there was a patch of ground near Goswell Road where thousands of plague victims had been dumped into a pit. Perhaps a few bones were left, a coin or two, a metal cross once worn around a dead woman's neck, but this burial ground was now a car park decorated with billboards. There were similar places scattered around the city, sites of death and life, great wealth and even greater poverty.

The ghosts still remained, but a fundamental change was taking place. Surveillance cameras were everywhere—at traffic intersections and inside shops. There were face scanners, vehicle readers, and doorway sensors for the radiofrequency ID cards carried by most adults. The Londoners streamed out of the Tube stations and walked quickly to work while the Vast Machine absorbed their digital images.

Gabriel had assumed that Tyburn Convent would be a gray stone church with ivy on the outer walls. Instead, he found a pair of nineteenth-century row houses with leaded windows and a black slate roof. The convent was on Bayswater Road, directly across the street from Hyde Park. The traffic grumbled toward Marble Arch.

A short metal staircase led to an oak door with a brass handle. Gabriel rang the doorbell, and an elderly Benedictine nun wearing a spotless white habit and a black veil answered the door.

"You're too early," the nun announced. She had a strong Irish accent.

"Early for what?"

"Oh. You're an American." Gabriel's nationality appeared to be all the explanation that was necessary. "Tours of the shrine start at ten o'clock, but I suppose a few minutes don't matter."

She led him into an anteroom that resembled a small cage. One door of the cage permitted access to a staircase that went down to the cellar. Another door led to the convent's chapel and living quarters.

"I'm Sister Ann." The nun wore old-fashioned gold-rimmed spectacles. Her face, framed by the black wimple, was smooth and strong and almost ageless.

"I've got relatives in Chicago," she said. "Are you from Chicago?"

"No. Sorry." Gabriel touched the iron bars that surrounded them.

"We are cloistered Benedictines," Sister Ann explained. "That means we spend our time in prayer and contemplation. There are always two sisters who deal with the public. I'm the permanent one, and then we rotate in another every month or so."

Gabriel nodded politely, as if this were useful information. He wondered how he was going to ask about his father.

"I'd take you down to the crypt, but I've got to balance the accounts." Sister Ann pulled a large key ring out of her pocket and unlocked one of the gates. "Wait here. I'll get Sister Bridget."

The nun vanished down a corridor, leaving Gabriel alone within the cage. There was a rack of religious pamphlets on the wall and an appeal for money on the bulletin board. Apparently, some bureaucrat working for the City of London had decided that the nuns had to spend three hundred thousand pounds to make the convent wheelchair accessible.

Gabriel heard the rustle of fabric and then Sister Bridget appeared to float down the hallway to the iron bars. She was much younger than Sister Ann. The Benedictine habit concealed everything but her plump cheeks and dark brown eyes.

"You're an American." Sister Bridget had a light,

almost breathless way of speaking. "We get a lot of Americans here. They usually make very nice donations."

Sister Bridget entered the cage and unlocked the second door. As Gabriel followed the nun down a winding metal staircase, he learned that hundreds of Catholics had been hung or beheaded at Tyburn gallows right up the street. During Elizabethan times there seemed to be some form of diplomatic immunity, because the Spanish ambassador was allowed to attend these executions and carry away locks of hair from the dead. More relics had appeared in modern times, when the gallows area was dug up to create a roundabout.

The crypt resembled a large basement in an industrial building. It had a black concrete floor and a white vaulted ceiling. Someone had built glass cases to display bone fragments and pieces of bloodstained clothing. There was even a framed prison letter scrawled by one of the martyrs.

"So they were all Catholics?" Gabriel asked. He stared at a yellowed leg bone and two ribs.

"Yes. Catholic."

Gabriel glanced at the nun's face and realized that she was lying. Disturbed by this sin, she struggled with her conscience for a moment, and then said cautiously, "Catholics and . . . a few others."

"You mean Travellers?"

She looked startled. "I don't know what you're talking about."

"I'm looking for my father."

The nun gave him a sympathetic smile. "Is he in London?"

"My father is Matthew Corrigan. I think he sent a letter from this place."

Sister Bridget's right hand came up to her breast as if to ward off a blow. "Men aren't allowed in this convent."

"My father is hiding from people who want to hurt him."

The nun's anxiety was transformed into panic. She stumbled backward, moving toward the staircase. "Matthew told us he was going to leave a sign here in the crypt. That's all I can tell you."

"I've got to find him," Gabriel said. "Please tell me where he is."

"I'm sorry, I can't say more," the nun whispered. And then she was gone, her heavy shoes clomping up the metal stairs.

Gabriel circled the crypt like a man trapped in a building about to collapse. Bones. Saints. A blood-stained shirt. How would this lead him to his father?

Footsteps on the staircase. He expected to see Sister Bridget return, but it was Sister Ann. The Irish nun looked angry. Reflected light flashed on the surface of her glasses.

"May I help you, young man?"

"Yes. I'm looking for my father, Matthew Corrigan. And the other nun, Sister Bridget, told me—"

"That's enough. You have to leave."

"She said he left a sign—"

"Leave immediately. Or I will call the police."

The expression on the elderly nun's face allowed no objection. The keys on her iron ring made a bright jingling sound as she followed Gabriel up the staircase and then out of the convent. He stood in the cold as Sister Ann began to shut the door.

"Sister, please. You have to understand—"

"We know what happened in America. I read in the newspaper how those people were killed. Children, too. They didn't even spare the little ones. We won't have such things here!"

She shut the door—hard—and Gabriel heard the sounds of locks being snapped shut. He felt like shouting and pounding on the door, but that would just bring the police. Not knowing what to do, the Traveller gazed out at the traffic and the bare trees of Hyde Park. He was in a strange city without money or friends, and no one was going to defend him from the Tabula. He was alone, truly alone, within the invisible prison.

13

After wandering aimlessly for a few hours, Gabriel found his way to an Internet café on Goodge Street near the University of London. The café was run by a group of amiable Koreans who spoke only a few words of English. Gabriel got a payment card and walked by a row of computers. Some people were looking at pornography, while others were buying cheap plane tickets. The blond teenager sitting at the computer next to him was playing an online game where his avatar would hide in a building and kill any stranger who showed up alone.

Gabriel sat at a computer and entered different chat rooms trying to find Linden, the French Harlequin who had sent money to New York. After two hours of failure, he left a message on a Web site for collectors of antique swords. *G. in London. Needs financing*. He paid the Koreans for his computer time and spent the rest of the day in the library reading room at the University of London. When the library closed at seven o'clock, he returned to the Internet café and discovered that no one had responded to his message. Back out on the street, it was cold enough to see his breath. A group of students brushed past him, laughing about something. He had less than ten pounds in his pocket.

It was too cold to sleep outside, and there were surveillance cameras on the underground. As he drifted down Tottenham Court Road past brightly lit shops selling televisions and computers, he remembered Maya telling him about a location in West Smithfield where heretics, rebels, and Harlequins were executed by authorities. Once she used her father's language when she mentioned the area, calling it *Blutacker*. The German word originally denoted the cemetery near Jerusalem bought with the silver given to Judas, and then it acquired a more general meaning. It was any accursed place—blood ground. If this really was a Harlequin site, then perhaps there was a message board in the area or some indication of where he could find help.

He headed toward East London, asking for directions from people who all seemed to be either drunk or lost. One man who could barely walk straight started waving his arms around as if he were swatting flies. Finally, Gabriel walked up Giltspur Street past St. Bartholomew's Hospital and found two memorials that were only a few feet apart. One was in memory of the Scottish rebel William Wallace, while the other plaque was placed a few feet away from where the Crown had burned Catholics at the stake. *Blutacker*, thought Gabriel. But there were no Harlequin signs anywhere.

Turning his back to the memorials, he approached St. Bartholomew the Great, a small Norman church. The stone walls of the church had been chipped and darkened over the years, and the brick walkway was smeared with mud. Gabriel passed through an archway and found himself in a burial ground. Directly in front of him was a heavy wooden door with iron hinges that led into the church. Something was scrawled on the lower edge of the door, and, as he came closer, he saw four words written with a black felt pen: *HOPE FOR A TRAVELLER*.

Was the church a place of refuge? Gabriel knocked on the door, and then pounded on it with his fists, but no one answered. Maybe people were hoping for a Traveller, but he was cold and tired and needed help. Standing in the burial ground, he felt a strong desire to break free of his body and abandon this world forever. Michael was right. The battle was over and the Tabula had won.

As he turned away, he remembered how Maya had used the message boards she set up in New York City. What she wrote looked like graffiti, but every letter and stroke of the pen conveyed information. He knelt in front of the door and realized that *HOPE* was underlined. Perhaps it was just an accident, but the black line had a slight barb at the end, almost like an arrow.

When Gabriel came back out through the archway, he saw that the arrow—if it was an arrow—was pointing toward Smithfield Market. A big man wearing a white butcher's apron walked by carrying a shopping bag stuffed with beer cans. "Excuse me," Gabriel said. "Where's . . . Hope? Is that a location?"

The butcher didn't laugh or call him a fool. He jerked his head in the general direction of the market. "Just up the road, mate. Not far from here."

Crossing Long Lane, Gabriel approached the Smithfield meat market. For hundreds of years, the district had been one of the most dangerous areas of London. Beggars, harlots, and pickpockets mingled with the surging crowds while herds of cattle were whipped through the narrow streets to the slaughterhouse. Warm blood flowed through the gutters, giving off a faint white steam in the winter air. Flocks of ravens circled above the butchery, dropping down to fight over scraps of flesh.

Those times were gone, and now the central square was lined with restaurants and bookstores. But at night, when everyone had gone home, the spirit of the old Smithfield returned. It was a dark place, a shadowy place, dedicated to killing.

The main square between Long Lane and Charterhouse Street was dominated by the two-story building used to distribute meat throughout London. This huge market was the length of several city blocks and divided into sections by four streets. A modern Plexiglas awning ran around the circumference of the building to protect truck drivers loading supplies in the rain, but the market itself was a renovated example of Victorian confidence. The walls of the market were constructed with white stone arches, the gaps filled in with London brick. Massive iron gates painted purple and green were at each end of the building.

He circled the building once, then twice, looking for graffiti. It seemed absurd to search for "hope" in such a place. Why had the man in the butcher's apron told him to walk up the street? Exhausted, Gabriel sat down on a concrete bench in a little square across the street from the market. He cupped his hands in front of his mouth and tried to warm his fingers with his breath, then gazed around the square. He was at the junction of Cowcross Street and St. John's. The only business still open was a pub with a wooden facade about twenty feet away.

Gabriel read the name on the sign and laughed for the first time in several days. Hope. It was the Hope Pub. Leaving the bench, he approached the warm lights that glowed through the beveled glass and studied the sign swinging over the entrance. It was a crude painting of two shipwrecked sailors clinging to a raft in a turbulent sea. A sailing ship had appeared in the distance and both men were waving desperately. Another smaller sign indicated that a restaurant called the Sirloin was upstairs, but it had stopped serving an hour ago.

He entered the place half expecting a grand moment. *You've solved the puzzle, Gabriel. Welcome home.* Instead, he found the landlord scratching himself while a sullen barmaid wiped the counter with a rag. Little black tables were at the front, and benches were in the back. A glass case displaying some stuffed pheasants sat on an upper shelf beside four dusty bottles of champagne.

There were only three customers: a middle-aged married couple having a whispered argument and a weary old man who was staring at his empty glass. Gabriel bought a pint of beer with a few of his remaining coins and retreated to an alcove with cushioned benches and dark wood paneling. The alcohol was absorbed by his empty stomach and dulled his hunger. Gabriel closed his eyes. *Just for a minute,* he told himself. That's all. But he gave in to his weariness and fell asleep.

His body felt the change. An hour ago, the room was cold and static. Now it was filled with energy. As Gabriel began to wake up, he heard the sound of laughter and voices, felt a draft of cold air as the door squeaked back and forth.

He opened his eyes. The pub was crowded with men and women about his age greeting one another as if they hadn't met for several weeks. Occasionally one person would argue in a good-natured way with someone else, and then both of them would hand money to a tall man who wore wraparound sunglasses.

Were they football fans? Gabriel thought. He knew that the English were passionate about football. The men in the pub wore hooded sweatshirts and jeans. A few had tattoos—elaborate designs that emerged from their T-shirts and curled around their necks. None of the women wore a dress or a skirt; their hair was cut very short or tied back as if they were Amazon warriors.

He studied several people standing near the bar and realized that they had only one specific thing in common—their shoes. The athletic shoes weren't the conventional styles designed for basketball or jogging through the park; they had flashy colors, elaborate lacing, and the kind of treaded sole you'd need for all-terrain running.

Another blast of cold air and a new customer entered. He was louder, friendlier, and definitely fatter than the rest of the people there. His greasy black hair was partially covered by a wool cap with a ridiculous white pom-pom on the top. His nylon jacket was open, revealing a prominent belly and T-shirt with a silk-screen drawing of a surveillance camera with a red bar slashed across it.

The man with the cap bought a pint and made a

quick circuit of the bar, slapping backs and shaking hands like an alderman running for office. Watching closely, Gabriel could see a hint of tension in his eyes. After he had greeted a few people, the man entered the snug, sat down on the bench, and punched out a number on a mobile phone. When the recipient of the call didn't answer, he left a message.

"Dogsboy! It's Jugger! We're at the Hope and Sirloin. All the crews are in. So where are you, mate? Call me."

The man with the cap closed his cell phone and noticed Gabriel beside him. "You from Manchester?"

Gabriel shook his head.

"So what crew you with?"

"What's a crew?"

"Ah, you're from the States. I'm Jugger. What's your name?"

"Gabriel."

Jugger motioned to the crowd. "All these people are Free Runners. There are three London crews here tonight plus one down from Manchester."

"And what are Free Runners?"

"Come on! I know they got 'em in the States. It started up in France with a couple of lads just having fun on the rooftops. It's a way of seeing the city as a big obstacle course. You climb over walls and jump between buildings. You break free. It's all about breaking free. Understand?"

"So it's a sport?"

"For some. But the crews here tonight are hard-core underground. That means we run where we want. No boundaries. No rules." Jugger glanced to the left and right as if he were about to tell a secret. "Ever hear of the Vast Machine?"

Gabriel resisted the impulse to nod. "What's that?"

"It's the computer system that watches us with scanner programs and surveillance cameras. The Free Runners refuse to be part of the Vast Machine. We run above it all."

Gabriel watched the door as another group of Free Runners entered the pub. "So is this some kind of a weekly meeting?"

"No meetings, mate. We're here for a straight-line race. Dogsboy is our man, but he hasn't shown up yet."

Jugger held his seat as his crew began to gather in the snug. Ice was a fifteen- or sixteen-year-old girl, small and severe-looking with painted eyebrows that made her look like an underage geisha. Roland was a man from Yorkshire who talked slowly. Sebastian was a part-time college student with paperback books stuffed into the pockets of his frayed raincoat.

Gabriel had never been to England, and he found it difficult to understand everything they were saying. Jugger had once driven a "juggernaut"—which was what the British called a certain kind of truck, only it wasn't a truck—it was a "lorry." Potato chips were "crisps," and a glass of beer was "a bitter." Jugger was the informal leader of the crew, but he was endlessly teased about his weight and his "bobble hat."

Along with the British words, there was also a Free Runner vocabulary. The four members of the crew chatted casually about monkey vaults, cat leaps, and wall runs. They didn't just climb up the side of a building; they "murdered it" or "wolfed it down."

People kept talking about their best runner— Dogsboy—but he still hadn't arrived. Finally, Jugger's mobile phone began beeping and he motioned for everyone to be quiet.

"So where are you?" Jugger asked. As the conversation developed, he began to look annoyed and then angry. "You promised, mate. This is your crew. You're letting the crew down . . . Sod this for a game of soldiers . . . You can't just . . . Damn it!"

Jugger closed the phone and began to swear. Gabriel could barely understand half of what he was saying.

"I assume Dogsboy will not be in attendance," Sebastian said.

"Bastard says he's got a bad leg. I bet a tenner he's in bed with a bit of fluff."

The rest of the crew began complaining about their friend's betrayal, but they quieted down when the man with the wraparound glasses approached them. "That's Mash," Roland whispered to Gabriel. "He's holding all the side bets for tonight."

"Where's your runner?"

"I just talked to him," Jugger said. "He's . . . he's try-ing to find a taxi."

Mash sneered at Jugger's crew as if he already knew the truth. "If he doesn't show up in ten min-utes, you lose your side bets plus the hundred quid forfeit money."

"He might—maybe, perhaps—have a bad leg."

"You know the rule. No runner and you lose the forfeit."

"Gormless bastard," Jugger muttered. He looked up at his crew after Mash had returned to the bar. "Okay. Who's the runner? Somebody volunteer."

"I do technicals, not straight lines," Ice said. "You know that."

"Got me a bad cold," Roland said.

"You've had it for three years!"

"So why don't *you* do the race, Jugger?"

Gabriel had always enjoyed climbing up trees and running across the rafters of the family's barn. He continued to challenge himself in California with motorcycle racing and parachute jumps. But his strength and agility had been taken to a new level in New York when Maya recovered from her injury. In the evening, they would run through kendo exercises. Instead of wielding bamboo sticks, Maya would use her Harlequin sword while he fought with the talisman sword. This was the only time they both looked freely at each other's bodies. Their intense relationship seemed to express itself in a relentless combat. At the end of the kendo workout, both of them were breathing hard and drenched with sweat.

Gabriel leaned forward and nodded to Jugger. "I'll do it," he said. "I'll run for your crew."

"And who the hell are you?" Ice asked.

"This is Gabriel," Jugger announced quickly. "An American Free Runner. Expert class."

"If you don't have a runner you lose a hundred pounds," Gabriel said. "So pay me the forfeit money. Either way, it's the same. And I just might win your bets."

"You know what you got to do?" Sebastian asked.

Gabriel nodded. "Run a race. Climb some walls."

"You got to run the roof of Smithfield Market, cross over to the old slaughterhouse, get down to the street, and make it to the churchyard at St. Sepulchre-without-Newgate," Ice said. "If you fall, it's a twenty-meter drop to the street."

This was the moment—he could still change his mind. But Gabriel felt as if he had been drowning in a river and suddenly a boat had appeared. He had just a few seconds to grab for a rope.

"When do we start?"

* * *

THE MOMENT THE decision was made, Gabriel felt as if he were surrounded by a new group of best friends. When he admitted that he was hungry, Sebastian hurried off to the bar and returned with a chocolate bar and several bags of salt-and-vinegar crisps. Gabriel ate the food quickly and felt a surge of energy. He decided to stay away from alcohol, although Roland offered to buy him a pint of beer.

Jugger appeared to regain his confidence now that his crew had a runner. He circled the bar a second time, and Gabriel heard his swaggering voice rise above the general noise. Within a few minutes, half the crowd believed that Gabriel was a well-known Free Runner from the States who had flown over to London because of his friendship with Jugger's crew.

Gabriel ate another chocolate bar, and then went to the men's room to splash some water on his face. When he came out, Jugger was waiting for him. He pushed open a door and led Gabriel to an outside courtyard that was used by the pub during the summer.

"It's just us now," Jugger said. All his bluster had disappeared and he acted shy and unsure of himself—the fat boy who had been teased in school. "Tell me straight, Gabriel. Have you ever done this before?"

"No."

"A thing like this is not for the ordinary citizen. It's a right fast way to get killed. If you want, we can sneak out the back."

"I'm not going to run away," Gabriel said. "I can do it . . ."

The door burst open. Sebastian and three other

Free Runners appeared in the courtyard. "Here he is!" someone shouted. "Hurry up! Time to go!"

As they left the pub Jugger was absorbed by the crowd, but Ice fell in beside Gabriel. Gripping his arm tightly, she spoke in a low voice: "Watch your feet, but don't look farther down."

"Okay."

"If you're climbing up a wall, don't try to hug it. Push your body out a bit. It helps your center of gravity."

"Anything else?"

"If you get frightened, don't go any farther. Just stop and we'll get you off the roof. When people are scared, they fall."

No one was on the street except for the Free Runners, and some of them began showing off—jumping onto the edge of concrete traffic barriers and doing backflips through the air. Lit up by security lights, Smithfield Market looked like a massive temple of stone and brick dumped into the center of London. There were plastic sheets hanging over the steel doors that covered the loading docks, and the night wind made them sway.

Mash led them around the market and explained the route for the straight run. Once they made it up onto the roof, they would run the entire length of the building and use a metal awning to cross the street to an abandoned slaughterhouse. Some-how they would get down to the street and run up

Snow Hill to St. Sepulchre-without-Newgate. The first runner to reach the fenced-in churchyard was the winner.

As the crowd strolled back up the street, Ice pointed out the other men who had volunteered for the race. Cutter was a well-known crew leader from Manchester. He wore expensive-looking shoes and a red tracksuit made out of a satiny fabric that shimmered beneath the lights. Ganji was one of the London runners—a Persian immigrant in his early twenties with a slender, athletic build. Malloy was the fourth runner, short and muscular with a broken nose. According to Ice, he worked as a part-time bartender in dance clubs around London.

They reached the north end of the market and stood across the street near a butcher's shop that specialized in organ meats. Gabriel's hunger had vanished and he felt highly aware of his new surroundings. He heard laughter and people talking, smelled a faint garlic odor that came from the Thai restaurant down the street. The cobblestones were wet and looked like pieces of shiny black obsidian.

"No fear," Ice whispered like an incantation. "No fear . . . No fear . . ."

The market building rose up in front of the Free Runners like a massive wall. Gabriel realized that he would have to climb up the wrought-iron gate to the clear Plexiglas awning that was about thirty feet above the cobblestones. The awning was held in place by steel poles that came out of the wall at a forty-five-degree angle. He would have to shimmy up one of the poles to reach the roof.

Suddenly, it was quiet and everyone was watching the four runners. Jugger stepped in front of Gabriel and handed him a pair of fingerless climbing gloves. "Put these on," he said. "The steel gets damn cold at night."

"I want the money when I'm done."

"No worries, mate. I promise." Jugger slapped Gabriel on the shoulder. "You're a scrappy one. You are indeed."

Cutter's red tracksuit appeared to glow under the security lights. He wandered over to Gabriel and nodded. "You're from the States?"

"That's right."

"You know what a 'splat' is?"

Jugger looked flustered. "Come on now. We're just about to start."

"Just helping out," Cutter said. "Bit of education for our American cousin. A 'splat' is when you don't know what you're doing and you fall off a roof."

Gabriel stood still and peered into Cutter's eyes. "There's always a chance you'll fall. The question is— do you think about it? Or are you able to keep it out of your mind?"

Cutter's cheek twitched near the corner of his mouth, but he controlled his fear and spit on the ground.

"All bets in," a voice said. "All bets in." And then the crowd parted and Mash stood before them.

"This is happening because Manchester threw down a challenge to the London crews. May the best runner win and all that crap. But what we do is more than one race. Most of you know that. Walls and fences won't stop us. The Vast Machine can't track us. We make our own map of this city."

Mash raised his right hand and counted. "One, two . . ."

Cutter darted across the street and the rest of them followed. The wrought-iron gates were designed to resemble flowers and vines. Using these gaps as footholds, Gabriel began to climb.

When they reached the top of the gate, the slender Ganji slipped between the awning and the wall. Cutter followed, then Gabriel and Malloy. Their shoes made a thumping sound on the clear plastic, and the awning trembled. Gabriel grabbed one of the poles that jutted out from the top of the wall. The steel pole was as narrow as a rope and difficult to hold.

Hand over hand, his body hanging from the pole, he pulled himself up. When he reached the end of the pole, Gabriel found a three-foot space between the holding bracket and the top of the white stone facade that ran around the edge of the roof. *How am I supposed to get up?* he thought. *Can't be done.*

Gabriel glanced left and watched the three other

men trying to manage the dangerous transition to the roof. Malloy had the strongest arms and shoulders. He swung himself around so that he was on the top of the pole, his eyes looking downward. Still holding on tightly, he tried to shift his weight to the lower part of his body. When his feet were in the right position, he let go of the pole, grabbed for the top of the facade, and fell. Malloy hit the Plexiglas awning and began to roll off, but he grabbed the edge and stopped. Still alive.

Gabriel forgot about the others and concentrated on his own movements. Imitating Malloy's strategy, he swung himself around so that his feet were on the top edge of the slanted pole, his hands just a few inches higher. He hunched up like a man squeezed into a box, put the full weight of his body on his feet, and then threw himself upward. Gabriel grabbed the white stone facade; it was like a little wall around the border of the roof. Using all his arm strength, he pulled himself up and over the top.

The slate roof of Smithfield Market lay before him like a dark gray road. The night sky was clear; the stars were precise points of bluish-white light. Gabriel's mind was beginning to glide into the consciousness of a Traveller. He observed the reality around him as if it were an image on a screen.

Cutter and Ganji darted past him, and Gabriel returned to the moment. The loose slates on the roof made a clicking sound as he chased after his two opponents. A few seconds later he reached the first gap in the roof: a thirty-foot section where an intersecting road divided the building. Concrete arches holding sheets of ivory-colored fiberglass passed over the gap, but the fiberglass looked too fragile to support his weight. Moving like a tightrope walker, he stepped on an arch and crossed over to the other side of the roof. Cutter and Ganji were pulling away from him. His eyes moved past them to the stars, and it seemed like all of them were running toward the dark expanse of space.

At the second gap, the fiberglass sheets had been ripped away and only the concrete arches spanned the roof. Remembering what Ice had told him, Gabriel concentrated on his feet and tried not to look beyond them to the road, where a handful of curious Free Runners gazed upward at their progress.

Gabriel was relaxed and moving easily, but he was losing the race. He had to stop and traverse a third set of arches. Halfway across, he watched Cutter and Ganji jump onto a steeply angled metal awning that passed across Long Lane to the boarded-up brick building that had once been the market's slaughterhouse.

Cutter had sprinted down the length of the roof. Now he was cautious, straddling the top of the awning and walking slowly. Ganji was about five yards away and decided to take the lead. He stepped onto the left side of the awning, ran three steps, and lost his footing. He was falling, rolling, screaming as his legs went over the edge and his hands grabbed onto the rain gutter.

Ganji dangled in the air. His crew was on the street below him, yelling at him to hold on—just hold on!—they would come up and save him. But Ganji didn't need their assistance. He pulled himself up slightly and got one leg onto the slippery metal awning, followed by his entire body. By the time Gabriel reached the area, the Free Runner was lying face-down. Pushing with his toes and extending his hands, he moved toward safety.

"You all right?" Gabriel shouted.

"Don't worry about me. Keep going! London pride!"

Cutter had been far ahead of Gabriel, but the advantage disappeared on the flat roof of the slaughterhouse. The Free Runner darted back and forth looking for a fire escape or a security ladder that would get him down to the road. Moving to the south-west corner of the building, Cutter crawled over a low wall, grabbed a drainpipe, and swung himself out into space. Gabriel ran to the corner and looked down. Cutter was sliding down the pole, inch by inch, con-trolling his movement with the sides of his climbing shoes. When he saw Gabriel, Cutter stopped for second and nodded to his opponent.

"Sorry for what I said before we started. Just wanted to make you nervous . . ."

"I understand."

"Ganji took a close one there. Is he okay?"

"Yeah. He's fine."

"London did all right, mate. But Manchester wins this time."

Gabriel imitated Cutter's movements and swung himself out onto the corner drainpipe. Below him, Cutter was maneuvering around some evergreen shrubbery, pushing the branches away with his arms until he finally reached the ground.

The moment Cutter stepped into the street, Gabriel decided to take a risk. He pushed himself away from the wall, let go of the drainpipe, and fell twenty feet into the bushes. The branches cracked and snapped, but he went with the momentum, rolling to one side and then landing on his feet.

A few Free Runners had appeared in the area, like bystanders watching a citywide marathon. Cutter was showing his skill, running down a line of parked cars. One leap would take him onto a car hood; two steps and he was across the roof, leading to a one-step jump from the trunk that would propel him onto the next vehicle. Car alarms began to go off because of the impact of his feet, and the sharp, wavering sound echoed off the walls. Cutter shouted—"Up Manchester!"—and raised both arms in triumph.

Gabriel ran silently across the cobblestones. Cutter didn't see his opponent, and Gabriel began to narrow the space between them. They were at the bottom of Snow Hill, the narrow street that led up to

St. Sepulchre and the looming silhouette of the Old Bailey criminal court building. Cutter vaulted over a car, spun around, and saw Gabriel. Surprised, he took off and sprinted up the hill. When they were about two hundred yards from the church, Cutter couldn't resist his own fear. He began glancing over his shoulder again and again, forgetting everything but his opponent.

A black London cab emerged from the shadows and turned onto the street. The cabdriver saw the red tracksuit and slammed on the brakes. Cutter leaped up into the air, but his legs hit the cab's windshield and he bounced off like a straw effigy of a man tossed into the street.

The cab screeched to a stop. The Manchester crew came running, but Gabriel continued up the hill and climbed over the spike fence to the empty garden of St. Sepulchre. Bending over, he placed his hands on his knees and tried to catch his breath. A Free Runner in the city.

Maya walked down East
Tremont and turned onto Puritan Avenue. Directly
across the street was her current hiding place—the
Bronx Tabernacle of the Divine Church of Isaac T.
Jones. Vicki Fraser had contacted the local minister
and he had allowed the fugitives to stay at the church
until they figured out a new plan.

Although Maya would have preferred to leave New
York, the East Tremont section of the Bronx was
much safer than Manhattan. It was a frayed-at-the-
edges, working-class area—the kind of neighborhood
that had no large department stores and only a few
banks. There were surveillance cameras in East
Tremont, but they were easily avoided. The government cameras protected parks and schools. The
privately owned cameras were inside bodegas and
liquor stores—conspicuously pointed at the front
counter.

* * *

THREE DAYS EARLIER, she and Alice had escaped from the underground world beneath Grand Central Terminal. In the daytime, they might have encountered city workers, but it was very early in the morning and the tunnels were cold, dark, and empty. The dead-bolt locks and padlocks on the doors were standard models—not difficult to open with Maya's small collection of picks and tension wrenches. Her only other tool was the random number generator that dangled from the cord around her neck. At different junctions, she pressed the button and chose a direction based on the number that flashed on the screen.

They passed beneath the streets of the Midtown area and followed the railroad tunnel that ran up the west side of Manhattan. When they emerged from the tunnel, it was a new day. Alice hadn't gotten any food—or sleep—since they left the loft, but the little girl remained beside her. Maya flagged down a gypsy cab and told the driver to take them downtown to Tompkins Square Park.

Approaching the message board on the Purest Children memorial, she saw that no one was waiting for her. An unpleasant sensation—something close to fear—passed through her. Was Gabriel dead? Had the Tabula captured him? Maya knelt down on the cold pavement and read the message: *G2LONDON*. She knew Gabriel needed to find his father, but at that moment his decision felt like a betrayal. Her father was right—a Harlequin should never form an attachment with a Traveller.

When she came out of the park, she saw Alice standing beside the gypsy cab, waving frantically at her. Maya felt annoyed at this act of disobedience until she saw that Hollis and Vicki had just arrived in another taxi. They asked where Gabriel was and explained that they had been separated from him as well, eventually emerging from the underground and checking into an off-the-Grid hotel in Spanish Harlem. Neither of them discussed what had happened at the hotel, but Maya sensed that the warrior and the virgin had finally become lovers. Vicki's uneasiness around Hollis had completely disappeared. When she touched him at the Chinatown loft, it had always been a quick, fluttery gesture. Now she took the palm of her hand and held it against his arm or his shoulder, as if reaffirming the connection there.

* * *

THE BRONX TABERNACLE of the Divine Church was an impressive-sounding name for two rented rooms above the Happy Chicken restaurant. Crossing the street, Maya peered through the fogged-up window of

Happy Chicken and saw two bored cooks standing guard behind a steam table. She had purchased dinner there last night and discovered that the meat wasn't just cooked at the take-out restaurant; it was frozen, thawed, sliced, pounded with mallets, and then deep-fried until covered with a rock-hard crust.

A few feet down from the restaurant was a door that led to the tabernacle. Maya unlocked the door and climbed up the steep staircase. A framed photograph of the Prophet, Isaac Jones, hung over the entrance to the tabernacle, and Maya used a second key to get in. She walked into a long room filled with wooden benches. A pulpit for the minister and a small platform for the church musicians were at the front of the room. Directly behind the pulpit was a set of windows facing the street.

Hollis had stacked some of the benches up against the wall. His bare feet squeaked on the polished wooden floor as he ran through his "forms"—a graceful series of moves that displayed the basic elements of martial arts. Meanwhile Vicki sat on a bench with a leather-bound copy of *The Collected Letters of Isaac T. Jones*. She pretended to read the book, but kept watching Hollis kick and punch at the air.

"How'd it go?" Vicki asked. "Did you find an Internet café?"

"I ended up at a Tasti D-Lite ice cream shop on Arthur Avenue. They've got four computers with Internet access."

"Were you able to contact Linden?" Hollis asked.

Maya looked around the tabernacle. "Where's Alice Chen?"

"In the children's room," Vicki said.

"What's she doing?"

"I don't know. I made her a peanut-butter-and-jelly sandwich about an hour ago."

Church services went on for most of Sunday morning, so the tabernacle had a carpeted side room with toys for younger children. Maya walked over to the door that led to the room and peered through a window. Alice had draped a church banner over a table, and then had surrounded the table with every piece of furniture in the room. Maya assumed that the little girl was sitting at the dark center of this improvised fort. If the Tabula broke into the church it would take an extra few seconds to reach her.

"Looks like she's been busy."

"She's trying to protect herself," Vicki said.

Maya returned to the center of the tabernacle. "If Gabriel boarded a plane to London on Saturday, then he's already been there for seventy-two hours. I'm sure he went straight to Tyburn Convent to ask about his father. Linden said that the Harlequins have never dealt with this group of nuns. He has no idea if Matthew Corrigan is staying there."

"So what's our next move?" Hollis asked.

"Linden thinks we should travel to England and help him look for Gabriel, but there are two problems involving identification. Because Gabriel grew up off the Grid, the false passport we obtained for him matches the facts we inserted into the Vast Machine. That means he has the 'cleanest' passport—the one that is the most likely to be accepted by the authorities."

Vicki nodded slowly. "But the Tabula probably have biometric information about Hollis and me."

"They also have information about Maya," Hollis said. "Remember—she spent a couple of years in London living on the Grid."

"Linden and I have the resources to obtain clean, nontraceable identification when we're in Europe, but it's too risky for everyone to use our current passports on a plane trip. The Tabula have supporters in the various government security agencies. If they know our false identities, they'll attach a terrorist alert to our files."

Hollis shook his head. "What's the second problem?"

"Alice Chen doesn't even have a passport. There's no way we could take her on a plane to Europe."

"So what are we supposed to do?" Hollis asked. "Leave her here?"

"No. We don't want the church involved. The easiest plan is to check into a hotel, wait until she falls asleep, and then walk away."

Vicki looked shocked. Hollis was angry. *They'll never understand you*, Maya thought. That was what Thorn had told her a thousand times. The average

citizen walking down the street could never compre-
hend the way a Harlequin saw the world.

"Are you out of your mind?" Hollis said. "Alice is
the only witness to what happened at New Harmony.
If the Tabula know she's still alive, they'll kill her."

"There is an alternative plan. But you need to
accept the fact that, from this point on, either Linden
or I will be making all the decisions."

Maya had deliberately made her voice harsh and
uncompromising, but Hollis didn't look intimidated.
He glanced at Vicki, and then chuckled. "I think
we're about to be given an answer to our problems."

"Linden has made arrangements for us to leave on
a merchant ship to Great Britain. The trip across the
Atlantic will take about a week, but it will allow us to
enter the country without a passport. I'll protect Alice
from the Tabula here in New York, but we can't keep
guarding her. When we reach London, she'll be given
new identification and placed in a safe environment."

"All right, Maya. You've made your point," Hollis
said. "The Harlequins want to be in charge. Now give
us a minute to talk it over."

As Hollis and Vicki sat next to each other on the
bench, Maya walked over to the windows and looked
across the street at St. Raymond's Cemetery. The
huge cemetery was as crowded and gray as the city
itself; the tombstones, pillars and sad angels were
packed together like a jumble sale.

The fact that Hollis and Vicki were in love changed

everything; it implied a life together. *If they're clever,* Maya thought, *they'll run away from both the Tabula and the Harlequins. There's no future in this endless war.*

"We've made a decision," Vicki said. Maya returned to the middle of the room and noticed that the two lovers were now sitting apart. "I'm going with you and Alice on the boat to England."

"And I'm going to stay in New York for a few weeks," Hollis said. "I'll make the Tabula think that Gabriel is still in the city. When I'm done, you can figure out another way to get me out of the country."

Maya nodded her approval. Hollis wasn't a Harlequin, but he was starting to think like one. "That's a good idea," she said. "Just be careful."

Hollis ignored her and looked into Vicki's eyes. "Of course I'll be careful. I promise."

15

Sitting in the back of a Mercedes, Michael gazed out the side window at the German countryside. This morning he had eaten breakfast in Hamburg, and now he was traveling on the Autobahn with Mrs. Brewster to see the new computer center in Berlin. A security guard wearing a black suit was in the front seat next to the Turkish chauffeur. The guard was supposed to watch the Traveller and keep him from escaping, but that wasn't going to happen. Michael had no desire to return to the ordinary world.

When they first got into the car, he discovered that a polished wooden box with little drawers had been placed on the seat. Michael had assumed that the box held top-secret information involving the Brethren, but it actually contained a gold-plated thimble, a pair of silver scissors, and the spectrum of silk thread used for needlework.

Mrs. Brewster slipped on a phone headset and took out a sheet of canvas printed with an image of a rose. She made several calls, speaking in soothing tones to members of the Brethren while her strong fingers thrust the needle through the canvas. Her favorite expression was "brilliant," but Michael was beginning to understand the different ways she used the word. Some members of the Brethren were worthy of praise. But if she said "brilliant" slowly or sharply or in a bored monotone, someone was going to be punished for failure.

* * *

HE HAD LEARNED a great deal about the Brethren during the weekend conference on Dark Island. All its members were eager to establish the Virtual Panopticon, but there were different internal groups based on nationality and personal relationships. Although Kennard Nash was head of the executive board and in charge of the Evergreen Foundation, some members saw him as being too American. Mrs. Brewster was in charge of an organization called the Young World Leaders Program and had become the head of the European faction.

On Dark Island, Michael had given Mrs. Brewster his private evaluation of each member of the executive board. When the conference was over, Mrs. Brewster announced that she wanted Michael to accompany her while she checked on the progress of the Shadow Program. General Nash seemed annoyed by this request and by the fact that Michael had mentioned his father at the meeting. "Go ahead and take him," Nash told Mrs. Brewster. "Just don't let him out of your sight."

The next day, they were in Toronto boarding a private jet to Germany. Traveling with Mrs. Brewster was a quick education in power. Michael began to think that the politicians who made speeches and proposed new laws were only actors in an elaborate play. Although these leaders appeared to be in charge, they had to follow a script written by others. While the media was distracted by the culture of celebrity, the Brethren avoided the spotlight. They owned the theater, counted the tickets, and decided what scenes would be performed for the audience.

* * *

"PLEASE FOLLOW UP and inform me of any change," Mrs. Brewster said to someone in Singapore. She took off her headset, put down her needlework, and pressed a switch in her armrest. A glass divider emerged from the back of the front seat and clicked into place. Now the driver couldn't hear their conversation.

"Would you like some tea, Michael?"

"Thank you."

There was a cabinet in front of them, and Mrs. Brewster took out cups and saucers, cream and sugar, and a thermos of hot tea.

"One lump or two?"

"No sugar. Just cream."

"Now that's interesting. I thought you had a sweet tooth." Mrs. Brewster served Michael a cup of tea and then gave herself two lumps of sugar.

The china jiggled slightly when the car went over a bump, but sipping tea gave the backseat an odd atmosphere of domesticity. Although Mrs. Brewster had never had children, she enjoyed acting like a wealthy aunt who might spoil a favorite nephew. Over the last few days, he had watched her charm and flatter men from a dozen different countries. Men talked too much around Mrs. Brewster, and that was one of the sources of her power. Michael was determined not to make that mistake.

"So, Michael—are you enjoying yourself?"

"I guess so. I've never been to Europe before."

"What's your evaluation of our three friends in Hamburg?"

"Albrecht and Stoltz are on your side. Gunter Hoffman is skeptical."

"I don't know how you can assume that. Dr. Hoffman didn't say more than six words during the entire meeting."

"The pupils of his eyes contracted slightly whenever you spoke about the Shadow Program. Hoffman is some kind of scientist, right? Maybe he doesn't understand the political and social implications of the program."

"Now, Michael. You need to be more charitable toward scientists." Mrs. Brewster resumed her stitching. "I got my degree in physics at Cambridge and considered science as a career."

"So what happened?"

"In my final year at university, I began to read about something called chaos theory—the study of erratic behavior in nonlinear dynamic systems. The chattering classes have gotten hold of this term and use it in complete ignorance to justify romantic anarchism. But scientists know that even mathematical chaos is deterministic—in other words, what occurs in the future is caused by a past sequence of events."

"And you wanted to influence those events?"

Mrs. Brewster looked up from her stitching. "You *are* a very clever young man. Let's just say that I realized that nature prefers structure. The world will still have to deal with hurricanes and airplane crashes and other unpredictable disasters. But if we establish our Virtual Panopticon, human society will evolve in the right direction."

They passed a sign for Berlin and the car seemed to go a little faster. There was no speed limit on this road. "Perhaps you could call Nathan Boone after the meeting at the computer center," Michael said. "I'd like to know if he's found out anything about my father."

"Of course." Mrs. Brewster wrote a memo to herself on her computer. "And let's say Mr. Boone is successful and we find your father. What do you intend to say to him?"

"The world is going through a major technological change. The Panopticon is inevitable. He needs to realize that fact and help the Brethren achieve its goals."

"Brilliant. That's brilliant." She looked up from the keyboard. "We don't need any new ideas from Travellers. We just need to follow the rules."

* * *

BY THE TIME Michael finished his second cup of tea, they were in Berlin, driving down the tree-lined boulevard of Unter den Linden. The few groups of tourists on the street looked overwhelmed by the baroque and neoclassical buildings. Mrs. Brewster pointed out a stack of enormous books with the names of German authors on the spines. The memorial had been set up in Bebelplatz, where the Nazis had emptied the libraries and burned books in the 1930s.

"Many more people live in Tokyo or New York," she explained. "Berlin always feels like a city too large for its population."

"I guess a lot of buildings were destroyed during World War Two."

"Quite right. And the Russians blew up much of what survived. But that unpleasant past has been swept away."

The Mercedes turned left at the Brandenburg Gate and followed the edge of a park toward Potsdamer Platz. The wall that had once divided the city had vanished, but its presence still lingered in the area. When the wall was torn down, the empty space created a real estate opportunity. The death zone was now a distinct strip of skyscrapers designed in a bland modern style.

A long avenue called Voss Strasse had once been the site of the Reich Chancellery during World War Two. Much of the area was fenced off and under construction, but the driver parked in front of a massive five-story building that looked like it came from an earlier era.

"This was originally an office building for the German Reich Railway," Mrs. Brewster explained. "When the wall came down, the Brethren gained control of the property."

They got out of the car and approached the computer center. The building's outer walls were defaced with graffiti, and most of the windows were covered with metal security shields, but Michael could see traces of a grand nineteenth-century facade. There were scrolled cornices and the faces of Greek gods carved above the large bay windows that faced the street. From the outside, the building was like an expensive limousine that had been stripped and dumped down a ravine.

"There are two sections to this building," Mrs. Brewster explained. "We're going to be in the public area first, so be discreet."

She approached a windowless steel door guarded by a surveillance camera. There was a small plastic sign to one side that announced that the building was the headquarters of a company called Personal Customer.

"Is this a British company?" Michael asked.

"No. It's quite German." Mrs. Brewster pushed the door buzzer. "Lars recommended that we give it an English name. It makes the staff think that they're involved with something modern and international."

The door clicked and they stepped into a brightly lit reception area. A young woman in her twenties with rings in her ears, lips, and nose looked up at them and smiled. "Welcome to Personal Customer. May I help you?"

"I'm Mrs. Brewster and this is Mr. Corrigan. We're technical consultants here to see the computer. I do believe Mr. Reichhardt knows we're coming today."

"Yes. Of course." The young woman handed Mrs. Brewster a sealed envelope. "You go to the—"

"I know, dear. I've been here before."

They walked over to an elevator next to a conference room with glass walls. A group of company employees—most of them in their thirties—were sitting around a large table eating lunch and talking.

Mrs. Brewster ripped open the envelope, took out a plastic card, and waved it at the elevator's sensor. The door glided open, they stepped into the elevator, and she waved the card a second time. "We're going down to the basement. That's the only entrance to the tower."

"Is it okay to ask a question?"

"Yes. We're out of the public area."

"What do the employees think they're doing?"

"Oh, it's all perfectly legitimate. They're told that Personal Customer is a cutting-edge marketing firm that is collecting demographic data. Of course, advertising to *groups* of people has become completely old-fashioned. In the future, all advertising will be directed toward each individual consumer. When you see a billboard in the street, it will sense the RFID chip on your key chain and flash your name. The energetic young people you just saw are busy finding every possible source of data about Berliners and feeding it into the computer."

The elevator door opened and they stepped into a large basement without interior walls. Michael thought that the massive room looked like a factory without workers. It was filled with machinery and communication equipment. "That's the backup power generator," Mrs. Brewster said, pointing to the left. "That's the air conditioner and filtration system because, apparently, our computer doesn't favor polluted air."

A white pathway had been painted on the floor, and they followed it to the other end of the room. Although the machinery was impressive, Michael was still curious about the people he had seen in the conference room. "So the employees don't know that they're helping establish the Shadow Program?"

"Of course not. When the time comes, Lars will tell them that their marketing data is going to help defeat terrorism. We'll pass out bonuses and promotions. I'm sure they'll be quite pleased."

The white pathway ended at a second reception desk—this one manned by a burly security guard wearing a coat and tie. The guard had been watching their progress on a small monitor. He looked up when they approached the desk.

"Good afternoon, Mrs. Brewster. They are expecting you."

A door without knobs and handles was directly behind the reception desk, but the guard didn't buzz it open. Instead Mrs. Brewster approached a small steel box with an opening at one end. It was mounted on a ledge a few feet from the door.

"What's that?" Michael asked.

"A palm vein scanner. You place your hand inside and a camera takes a photograph with infrared light. The hemoglobin in your blood absorbs the light so your veins appear black in a digital photograph. My pattern is matched against a template stored in the computer."

She inserted her hand in the slot, a light flashed, and the lock clicked. Mrs. Brewster pushed open the door and Michael followed her into the second wing of the building. He was surprised to see that the interior had been completely gutted, exposing the rafters and the brick walls. Inside this windowless shell was a large glass tower held within a steel frame. The tower contained three stories of interconnected storage devices, mainframe computers, and servers racked up on cabinets. The entire system was accessible by a steel staircase and elevated catwalks.

Two men sat at a control panel in one corner of the room. They were separate from the closed environment of the tower—like acolytes not permitted to enter a chapel. A large flat-screen monitor hung above them, showing four computer-generated figures in a shadow car, rolling down a tree-lined boulevard.

Lars Reichhardt stood up and spoke in a loud voice. "Welcome to Berlin! As you can see, the Shadow Program has been tracking you ever since you arrived in Germany."

Michael looked up at the screen and saw that yes, the car on the screen was a Mercedes and it contained computer-generated images that resembled himself and Mrs. Brewster as well as the guard and chauffeur.

"Keep watching," Reichhardt said, "and you'll see

yourself about ten minutes ago, driving down Unter den Linden."

"It's all very impressive," Mrs. Brewster said. "But the executive board would like to know when the system will be completely operational."

Reichhardt glanced at the technician sitting at the control panel. The young man touched his keyboard and the shadow images instantly disappeared from the screen.

"We'll be ready to go in ten days."

"Is that a promise, Herr Reichhardt?"

"You know my dedication to our work," Reichhardt said pleasantly. "I'll do everything possible to achieve this goal."

"The Shadow Program has to work perfectly before we can contact our friends in the German government," Mrs. Brewster said. "As we discussed on Dark Island, we're also going to need suggestions for a national advertising campaign similar to what we've been doing in Great Britain. The German people need to be convinced that the Shadow Program is necessary for their protection."

"Of course. We've already done some work on that." Reichhardt turned to his young assistant. "Erik, show them the ad prototype."

Erik typed some commands and a television ad appeared on the screen. A knight with a black cross on his white surcoat stood guard as cheerful young Germans traveled on a bus, worked in office cubicles, and kicked a soccer ball in a park. "We thought we'd bring back the legend of the Teutonic Order of Knights. Everywhere you go, the Shadow Program will be protecting you from danger."

Mrs. Brewster didn't look impressed with the television ad. "I see where you're going with this, Lars. But perhaps—"

"It doesn't work," Michael said. "You've got to present an image that's more emotional."

"This isn't about emotions," Reichhardt said. "It's about security."

"Can you create some images?" Michael asked the technician. "Show me a mother and father looking at their two sleeping children."

Slightly confused about who was in charge, Erik glanced up at his boss. Reichhardt nodded and the young man continued typing. At first only faceless computer figures appeared on the screen, but then they began to morph into recognizable images of a father holding a newspaper and a mother holding his hand. They were standing in a bedroom filled with toys as two little girls slept in matching beds.

"So you start with this picture—an emotional picture—and you say something like 'Protect the Children.'"

Erik kept typing and the words *Beschuetzen Sie die Kinder* floated across the screen.

"They're protecting their children and—"

Mrs. Brewster interrupted. "And we're protecting

them. Yes, it's all rather warm and comforting. What do you think, Herr Reichhardt?"

The head of the computer center watched the screen as little details appeared. The mother's kind face filled with love. A nightlight and a storybook. One of the sleeping girls hugged her toy lamb.

Reichhardt smiled thinly. "Mr. Corrigan understands our vision."

16

The *Prince William of Orange* was a cargo ship owned by a group of Chinese investors who lived in Canada, sent their children to British schools, and kept their money in Switzerland. The crew was from Suriname, but all three officers were Dutchmen who had trained with the Netherlands merchant navy.

During the journey from America to England, neither Maya nor Vicki ever found out what was being carried inside the sealed shipping containers packed in the hold. The two women ate their meals with the officers in the ship's galley and, one night, Vicki had given in to her curiosity.

"So what's your cargo for this trip?" she asked Captain Vandergau. "Is it something dangerous?"

Vandergau was a big, taciturn man with a blond beard. He lowered his fork and smiled pleasantly. "Ahhh, the cargo," he said, and considered this question as if it had never been asked before.

The first mate, a younger man with a waxed mustache, was sitting at the end of the table. "Cabbage," he suggested.

"Yes. That is correct," Captain Vandergau said. "We carry green cabbage, red cabbage, canned and pickled cabbage. The *Prince William of Orange* provides cabbage to a hungry world."

It was an early spring crossing with a raw wind and a drizzling rain. The exterior of the boat was gunmetal gray, almost matching the sky. The sea was a dark green, the waves rising up to slap the bow like an endless series of small confrontations. In this dull environment, Maya found herself thinking too much about Gabriel. Right now Linden was in London, searching for the Traveller, and there was nothing she could do to help him. After several restless nights, Maya found two rusty paint cans that had been filled with concrete. Holding these weights in each hand, she ran through a series of exercises that left her muscles sore and her skin covered with sweat.

Vicki spent most of her time in the galley, drinking tea and writing her thoughts in a journal. Occasionally, a look of great pleasure appeared on her face, and Maya knew that she was thinking about Hollis. Maya wanted to deliver her father's lecture about love—that it made you weak—but she knew Vicki wouldn't believe any of it. Love seemed to make Vicki stronger and more confident.

Once Alice realized that she was safe, she spent almost every hour of daylight roaming around the ship—a silent presence on the bridge and in the engine room. Most of the crew had families of their own, and they treated Alice with great kindness, making her toys and cooking her special meals for dinner.

* * *

AT SUNRISE ON the eighth day, the boat passed the Thames flood barrier and began its slow passage up the river. Maya stood near the bow and stared at the glimmering streetlights of the distant villages. This wasn't home—she didn't have a home—but she had finally returned to England.

The wind grew stronger, rattling the wire lines attached to the lifeboats. Seagulls screeched and glided above the angry waves as Captain Vandergau paced across the deck clutching a satellite phone. Apparently, it was important that his cargo arrive at a certain dock in East London when a particular customs inspector named Charlie was working. Vandergau cursed in English, Dutch, and a third language Maya didn't recognize, but Charlie refused to answer any of his phones.

"Our problem is not corruption," the captain informed Maya. "It's lazy, inefficient British corruption." Finally he talked to Charlie's girlfriend and got the necessary information. "Fourteen hundred hours. Yes, I understand."

Vandergau gave a command to the engine room and the twin propellers began turning. When Maya went below she felt a faint vibration in the steel walls. There was a constant thumping sound, as if a gigantic heart were beating somewhere in the ship.

Around one o'clock in the afternoon, the first mate knocked on the door of their cabin. He told them to pack their belongings and come to the galley for instructions. Maya, Vicki, and Alice sat at the narrow table and listened to the glasses and dishes rattle in their wooden holding racks. The ship was turning around in the river, maneuvering toward a dock.

"Now what happens?" Vicki asked.

"After they get through the inspection, we'll go ashore and meet Linden."

"But what about the surveillance cameras? Will we have to disguise our appearance?"

"I don't know what's going to happen, Vicki. Usually, if you want to avoid being tracked, there are two possible responses. You do something so old-fashioned—so primitive—that you can't be detected. Or you go the opposite direction and use technology that's one generation ahead of the standard. Either way, the Vast Machine finds it difficult to process the information."

The first mate returned to the galley and made a

grand gesture with his arm. "Captain Vandergau sends you his compliments and requests that you follow me to more secure accommodations."

Maya, Vicki, and Alice entered the ship's walk-in food locker. With some help from the Javanese cook, the first mate shifted the supplies so that the three stowaways were concealed behind a wall of cardboard boxes. Then the metal door was shut and they were alone.

The fluorescent fixture above them radiated a harsh metallic light. Maya was carrying her revolver in an ankle holster. Both her Harlequin sword and Gabriel's Japanese sword were out of the carrier and placed on a ledge beside her. Someone was walking quickly down a passageway on the level above them, and the sharp clicking sound leaked through the ceiling. Alice Chen moved closer to Maya, only a few inches from the Harlequin's leg.

What does she want? Maya thought. *I'm the last person in the world to show her any love or physical affection.* She remembered Thorn telling her about a trip he had taken through the southern Sudan. When her father spent the day with missionaries at a refugee camp, a little boy—an orphan of war—had followed him around like a lost dog. "All living things have a desire to survive," her father explained. "If children have lost their family, they search for the most powerful person, the one who can protect them . . ."

* * *

THE DOOR OPENED and she heard the first mate's voice. "Storage locker."

A man with a London accent said, "Right." It was just one word, but the way it was delivered reminded her of certain aspects of Britain. *I'm all right, Jack.* Backyard gardens with ceramic gnomes. Chips and peas. Almost immediately, the door was shut and that was it: inspection over.

They waited some more and then Captain Vandergau entered the locker and dismantled the wall of boxes. "It's been a pleasure to meet you three ladies, but now it's time to leave. Follow me, please. A boat has arrived."

A dense fog had rolled in while they were hiding below. The deck was wet, and little beads of water clung to the railing. The *Prince William of Orange* was moored within the East London docks, but Captain Vandergau quickly escorted them to the starboard side of the ship. Attached by two nylon ropes, a narrow boat rode on the waves. The wooden boat was forty feet long and built for shallow water. It had a large central cabin with porthole windows and an open back deck. Maya had seen other narrow boats in London whenever she crossed one of the canals. People lived on the boats and used them for holidays.

A bearded man wearing a black mackintosh was

standing on the stern of the boat, holding the tiller. A hood covered his head and made him look like a monk from the Inquisition. He gestured—*Come down*—and Maya saw that a rope ladder was now attached to the side of the ship.

It took Maya and Alice only a few seconds to climb to the deck of the narrow boat. Vicki was a good deal more cautious, gripping the wooden steps of the rope ladder, and then glancing down at the narrow boat as it rose up and down on the waves. Finally her feet touched the deck and she let go. The bearded man with the hood— whom Maya began to think of as Mr. Mackintosh—bent down and started the boat's engine.

"Where are we going?" Maya asked.

"Up the canal to Camden Town." The bearded man had a strong East London accent.

"Shall we stay in the cabin?"

"If you want to stay warm. No reason to worry about the cameras. No cameras where we're goin'."

Vicki retreated to the little cabin, where a coal fire was burning in a cast-iron stove. Alice went in and out of the cabin, inspecting the galley, the sunroof, and the walnut paneling.

Maya sat next to the tiller as Mackintosh turned the boat around and headed up the Thames. A rainstorm had surged through the city's drainage system, and the water had turned dark green. The dense fog made it difficult to see more than ten feet in any direction, but the bearded man was able to navigate without visible landmarks. They passed a clanging buoy in the middle of the river and Mackintosh nodded his head. "That one sounds like an old church bell on a cold day."

Fog drifted around them, and the damp coldness made her shiver. The splashing waves disappeared, and they passed a dock with yachts and other pleasure boats. Maya heard a car horn in the distance.

"We're in Limehouse Basin," Mackintosh explained. "They used to bring everything here and dump it on barges. Ice and timber. Coal from Northumberland. This was the mouth of London, swallowing everything up so the canals could take it to the rest of the body."

The fog parted slightly as the narrow boat entered the concrete channel that led to the first canal lock. Mackintosh climbed a ladder to shore, closed a pair of wooden gates behind the boat, then pushed a white lever. Water surged into the lock and the boat rose up from the level of the basin to the canal.

Weeds and scrubland were on the left side of the canal; a flagstone pathway and a brick building with barred windows were on the right. It felt as if they had entered the London of an earlier time, a place with carriages and chimney soot that lingered in the air. Passing beneath a railway bridge, they continued up the canal. The water was shallow, and a few times the bottom of the boat scraped across sand and gravel. They had to stop every twenty minutes to enter a lock and rise up to the next level. Waterweeds brushed against the bow of the slowly moving boat.

Around six o'clock, they passed through the last canal and approached Camden Town. This once run-down neighborhood had become a site for small restaurants, art galleries, and a weekend street fair. Mackintosh pulled over to one side of the canal and unloaded the canvas shoulder bags that contained the women's belongings. Vicki had bought clothes for Alice back in New York, and everything was stuffed into a pink knapsack that had a unicorn on the back.

"Go up to the road and look for an African bloke named Winston," Mackintosh said. "He'll take you where you want to go."

Maya led Vicki and Alice up the pathway to the road that cut through Camden. A Harlequin lute was scrawled on the sidewalk, and it had a small arrow pointing north.

They walked about a hundred yards on the side-walk to a white van with an interlocking diamond pattern painted on the side. A young Nigerian with a round, chubby face got out and opened the side door of the van. "Good evening, madams. I am Winston Abosa, your guide and driver. I am most pleased to welcome you to Britain."

They got into the back and sat on steel benches welded to the walls. A metal grate separated this cargo area from the two front seats. Winston made several turns down the narrow streets of Camden. The van stopped, and suddenly the side door was yanked open. A big man with a shaven head and blunt nose peered in.

Linden.

* * *

THE FRENCH HARLEQUIN wore a long black overcoat and dark clothing. A carrying case for his sword hung from his shoulder. Linden had always reminded Maya of a foreign legionnaire who had no allegiance to anything except his comrades and fighting.

"*Bonsoir*, Maya. You're still alive." He smiled as if her continued survival were a subtle joke. "A pleasure to see you again."

"Did you find Gabriel?"

"Nothing so far. But I don't believe the Tabula have found him either." Linden sat on a bench nearest the driver and slipped a piece of paper through the grate. "Good evening, Mr. Abosa. Please take us to this address."

Winston pulled back onto the street and headed north through London. Linden placed his broad hands on his legs and studied the other passengers.

"I assume you are Mademoiselle Fraser."

"Yes." Vicki looked intimidated.

Linden glanced at Alice Chen as if she were a plastic bag of trash retrieved from the narrow boat. "And this is the child from New Harmony?"

"Where are we going?" Maya asked.

"As your father used to tell me: 'Solve the first problem first.' These days, there are very few orphanages, but one of our Sikh friends found a foster home in Clapton where a woman takes in children."

"Will Alice be given a new identity?" Maya asked.

"I've obtained a birth certificate and passport. She's been renamed Jessica Moi. Parents killed in a plane crash."

Winston drove slowly through the rush-hour traffic, and forty minutes later he pulled over to the curb. "Here we are, sir," he said softly.

Linden opened the side door and everyone got out. They were in Clapton near Hackney in North-east London. The residential street was lined with two-story brick terrace houses that had probably been built in the early 1900s. For years the neighborhood had presented a respectable face to the world, but now it was tired of keeping up appearances. Pools of dirty rainwater filled potholes in the street and pavement. The patches of ground in front of each building were overgrown with weeds and cluttered with plastic bins stuffed with garbage. A wanted poster for a lost dog was stapled to a tree, and the rain had made each letter bleed wavery black lines.

Linden glanced up and down the street. No obvious danger. He jerked his head at Vicki. "Take the girl's hand."

"Her name is Alice." Vicki had a stubborn look on her face. "You should say her name, Mr.—Mr. Linden."

"Her name is not important, mademoiselle. In five minutes she will have a new one."

Vicki took Alice's hand. The girl's eyes were frightened, questioning. *What's going on? Why are you doing this to me?*

Maya turned away from her. The little group walked down the sidewalk to number seventeen, and Linden knocked on the door.

Rain had trickled down the side of the house and swollen the door frame. Now the door was stuck, and they could hear a woman cursing as the knob moved back and forth. Finally the door popped open, and Maya saw a sixtyish woman standing in the hallway. She had stocky legs and broad shoulders, dyed blond hair with gray roots. Not foolish, Maya thought. A false smile on a shrewd face.

"Welcome, ducks. I'm Janice Stillwell." She focused on Linden. "And you must be Mr. Carr. We've been waiting for you. Our friend Mr. Singh told me you were looking for a foster home."

"That's correct." Linden stared at her like a detective who had just encountered a new suspect. "May we come in?"

"Of course. Where *are* my manners? It's been a drab little day, hasn't it? Time for a cup of tea."

The house smelled like cigarette smoke and urine.

A skinny little red-haired boy wearing nothing but a man's T-shirt sat halfway up the staircase in front of them. He retreated to the second floor as they followed Mrs. Stillwell into a front room with a window that faced the street. On one side of the room was a large television set playing a cartoon about robots. The sound was off, but a Pakistani boy and a small black girl sat on the couch, staring at the garish images.

"Some of the children," Mrs. Stillwell explained. "Right now, we're taking care of six. Yours would be lucky number seven. We got Gloria here from the court system. Ahmed is a private arrangement." Looking annoyed, she clapped her hands. "That's enough, you two. Can't you see we've got guests?"

The two children glanced at each other and left the room. Mrs. Stillwell herded Vicki and Alice over to the couch, but Maya and Linden remained standing. "Tea, anyone?" Mrs. Stillwell asked. "Cup of tea?" Some animal part of her sensed that the two Harlequins were dangerous. Her face was flushed and she kept glancing at Linden's hands—the blunt fingers and scarred knuckles.

A shadow appeared in the doorway, and then an older man smoking a cigarette entered the room. An alcoholic's saggy face. Frayed trousers and a stained pullover. "This the new one?" the man asked, looking at Alice.

"My husband, Mr. Stillwell . . ."

"So we got two blacks, two whites, Ahmed and Gerald, who's a mixed-breed. She'll be our first Chinese." Mr. Stillwell made a wheezy little laugh. "Bloody United Nations around here."

"What's your name?" Mrs. Stillwell asked Alice.

Alice sat on the edge of the couch with her feet flat on the rug. Maya moved toward the doorway in case the child tried to run away.

"Is she deaf or retarded?" Mr. Stillwell asked.

"Maybe she only speaks Chinese." Mrs. Stillwell leaned over the child. "You speakee English? This is your new home."

"Alice doesn't talk at all," Vicki said. "She needs special help."

"We don't give special help, ducks. We just feed and water them."

"You've been offered five hundred pounds a month," Linden said. "I'll make that a thousand if you take her right now. Three months from now, Mr. Singh will check on the situation. If there's a problem, he'll take her away."

The Stillwells glanced at each other and nodded. "A thousand pounds is all right," Mr. Stillwell said. "I can't work anymore because of me back . . ."

Alice jumped off the couch and ran toward the door. Instead of trying to get away, she flung her arms around Maya.

Vicki was crying. "Don't," she whispered to Maya. "Don't let them do this."

Maya felt the child's body pressed against her, the slender arms holding tight. No one had ever touched her like this before. *Save me*.

"Let go, Alice." Maya's voice was deliberately harsh. "Let go of me right now."

The little girl sighed and then stepped away. For some reason, the act of obedience made everything worse. If Alice had fought to leave the house, Maya would have twisted the child's arms back and forced her onto the floor. But Alice obeyed, just like Maya had obeyed Thorn all those years ago. And the memories pushed into Maya's thoughts, almost overpowering her—the brutal slaps and shouting, the betrayal in the underground when her father had set her up to fight three grown men. Perhaps the Harlequins defended the Travellers, but they also defended their own arrogant pride.

Ignoring the others, she faced Linden. "Alice isn't staying here. She's going with me."

"That's not possible, Maya. I've already made the decision."

Linden's right hand touched his sword case and then dropped to his side. Maya was the only other person in the room who understood that gesture. Harlequins never made empty threats. If they ended up fighting, he would try to kill her.

"Do you think you can intimidate me?" Maya said. "I'm Thorn's daughter. Damned by the flesh. Saved by the blood."

"What the bloody hell is going on?" Mr. Stillwell asked.

"Be quiet," Linden said.

"I will not be quiet! You just made an agreement for a thousand quid a month. There might not be a written contract, but I know my rights as an Englishman!"

Without warning, Linden crossed the room, grabbed Stillwell's throat with one hand, and began to squeeze. Mrs. Stillwell didn't rush to help her husband. Her mouth opened and shut as if she were swallowing air.

"Now, ducks," she murmured. "Ducks . . . Ducks . . ."

"On certain occasions, I let a taint like you speak to me," Linden said. "That permission has been withdrawn. Do you understand? Show me you understand!"

Stillwell's face was bright red. He managed to nod slightly, his eyes jerking back and forth. Linden let go and the old man collapsed onto the floor.

"You know our obligation," Linden said to Maya. "There's no way you can fulfill that promise and keep this child."

"Alice saved me when I was in New York. I was in a dangerous place and she risked her life to grab a pair of night-vision goggles. I have an obligation to *her* as well."

Linden's face was frozen, and his entire body was

tense. His fingers touched the sword case a second time. Directly behind the Harlequin, a silent television showed images of happy children eating breakfast cereal.

"I'll watch Alice," Vicki said. "I promise. I'll do everything . . ."

Linden pulled a wallet out of his coat pocket, took out some fifty-pound notes, and tossed them onto the floor like pieces of trash.

"You have no idea what pain is—*real* pain," he told the Stillwells. "Mention this to anyone and you'll find out."

"Yes, sir," Mrs. Stillwell babbled. "We understand, sir."

Linden marched from the room. The Stillwells were on their hands and knees, scrambling for the money, when the rest of the group walked out.

Clutching a straight razor, Jugger scowled and slashed the air near Gabriel's head. "The Ripper has returned to London and he's hungry for blood!"

Sebastian was sitting in a lawn chair next to the portable electric heater. He looked up from his paperback copy of Dante's *Inferno* and frowned. "Stop playing the fool, Jugger. Just finish the job."

"I'm finishing. In fact, this is one of my better efforts."

Jugger squirted some shaving cream on the tips of his fingers, dabbed it on the skin near Gabriel's ears, and then used the razor to cut off the American's sideburns. When he was done, he wiped off the residue with his shirtsleeve and grinned. "There you go, mate. You're a new man."

Gabriel got up from the stool and walked over to the cast-off mirror hanging on the wall near the door.

The cracked glass cut a jagged line through his body, but he could see that Jugger had given him a very short military haircut. His new appearance wasn't on the level of Maya's special contact lenses and finger shields, but it was better than nothing.

"Isn't Roland supposed to be back by now?" Gabriel asked.

Jugger checked the time on his mobile phone. "It's his turn for dinner tonight, so he's buying food. You helping him cook?"

"I don't think so. Not after I burned the spaghetti sauce last night. I asked him to check something out for me. That's all."

"He'll handle it, mate. Roland's good at simple tasks."

"Unbelievable! Dante just fainted *again*." Disgusted, Sebastian threw the book onto the floor. "Virgil should have guided a Free Runner through hell."

Gabriel left what used to be a front parlor and climbed up the narrow wooden staircase to his room. Frost decorated the upper walls and he could see his breath. For the last ten days, he had been living with Jugger, Sebastian, and Roland in a squat called the Vine House on the south bank of the Thames. The ramshackle three-story building had once been a farmhouse in the middle of the vineyards and vegetable gardens that supplied London.

Gabriel had learned one thing about eighteenth-century Englishmen—they were smaller than the current inhabitants of London. When he reached the top floor, he ducked his head down to pass through the doorway and enter the garret. It was a tiny, bare room with a low ceiling and plaster walls. The floorboards creaked when he crossed the room and peered out through the bull's-eye window.

Gabriel's bed was a mattress placed on four plywood pallets taken from a loading dock. His few clothes were dumped into a cardboard box. The only decoration in the room was a framed photo of a young woman from New Zealand named "Our Trudy." Wearing a tool belt and holding a sledgehammer, she faced the camera with a cocky smile. A generation ago, Trudy and a small army of squatters had taken over the abandoned houses around Bonnington Square. That time had passed and now the Lambeth Council licensed most of the buildings. But Trudy still smiled in the photograph and the Vine House remained—illegal, collapsing, and free.

* * *

WHEN JUGGER AND his crew caught up with Gabriel after the race across Smithfield Market, they had immediately offered him food, friendship—and a new name.

"How did you do that?" Jugger asked as they walked south toward the river.

"I took a chance coming down the drainpipe."

"You ever done it before?" Jugger asked. "A move like that takes confidence."

Gabriel mentioned the HALO parachute jumps he had taken back in California. The high-altitude, low-opening jumps forced you to leap out of a plane and free-fall for over a minute without opening your chute.

Jugger nodded as if this experience explained everything. "Listen up," he told the others. "We got a new member of our crew. Halo, welcome to the Free Runners."

Gabriel woke up the next morning in Vine House and immediately returned to Tyburn Convent. This was the only way he knew to find his father; he needed to climb down the metal stairs to the crypt and figure out what sign his father had left among the bones and tarnished crosses.

For three hours, he sat on a bench across the street from the convent and watched who opened the door for the convent's few visitors. That morning the visitors were greeted either by Sister Ann, the elderly nun who had refused to answer his questions, or Sister Bridget, the younger nun who had looked frightened when he mentioned his father. Gabriel returned to the convent two more times, but the same two women were minding the door. His only option was to wait until Sister Bridget was replaced by some-one who didn't recognize him.

When Gabriel wasn't watching the convent, he spent his afternoons aimlessly searching for his father in the suburbs of outer London. There were thousands of surveillance cameras in the city, but he minimized his risk by avoiding public transportation and the busy streets north of the river.

Becoming a Traveller gradually transformed the way he perceived the world. Gabriel could glance at someone and sense the subtle changes in their emotions. It felt like his brain was being rewired and he couldn't quite control the process. One afternoon, when he was walking across Clapham Common, his vision widened out to a 180-degree panorama. He could see the entire world in front of him at the same moment: the beauty of a yellow dandelion, the smooth curve of a black iron railing. And there were faces, too—so many faces. People came out of shops and shuffled down the street with eyes that showed weariness and pain and occasional flashes of joy. This new vision of the world was overwhelming, but after an hour or so, the panorama gradually faded away.

As the days passed, he found himself drawn into the preparations for a gigantic party at the Vine House. Gabriel had always been wary of social gatherings, but it was a different life being "Halo"— the American Free Runner without a past or a future. It was easier to ignore his own power and go off with Jugger to buy some more beer.

* * *

THE DAY OF the party was cold, but sunny. The first guests started showing up at one in the afternoon and more kept arriving. The small rooms of Vine House were filled with people sharing food and alcohol. Children darted through the hallway. A baby slept in a sling around a father's neck. Out in the garden, experienced runners were showing one another a variety of graceful ways to vault over a garbage bin.

As Gabriel circulated through the house, he was surprised to find out how many people knew about the race at Smithfield Market. The Free Runners at the party were a loosely organized group of friends who tried to live off the Grid. This was one social movement that the chattering faces on television would never notice—because it refused to be seen. These days, rebellion in the industrial countries was not inspired by obsolete political philosophies. True rebellion was determined by your relationship to the Vast Machine.

Sebastian went to school occasionally, and Ice still lived with her parents, but most of the Free Runners had jobs in the underground economy. Some people worked at all-night dance clubs and others served beer at pubs during football matches. They repaired motorcycles, moved furniture, and sold souvenirs to tourists. Jugger had a friend who picked up dead dogs for the Lambeth Council.

The Free Runners bought their clothes at street fairs and their food at farmer's markets. They walked through the city or used odd-looking bicycles with cobbled-together parts. Everyone had a mobile phone, but they used prepaid phone numbers that were difficult to trace. They spent hours on the Internet, but never joined a service provider. Roland made improvised antennas out of empty coffee cans that allowed access to different WiFi networks. This was called "fishing," and the Free Runners circulated lists of coffee shops, office buildings, and hotel lobbies where the bandwidth was easily accessible.

By nine o'clock at night, everyone who planned to get drunk had achieved their goal. Malloy, the part-time bartender who had been in the race, was making a speech about the government's plan to fingerprint children under the age of sixteen who were applying for a passport. The fingerprints and other biometric information were going to be stored in a secret database.

"The Home Office says fingerprinting some eleven-year-old girl is going to defeat terrorism," Malloy announced. "Can't people see that it's all about control?"

"You better control your drinking," Jugger said.

"We're already prisoners!" Malloy shouted. "And now they're gonna throw away the key. So where's the Traveller? That's what I want to know. People keep tellin' me 'Hope for the Traveller,' but I haven't seen sign of him."

Gabriel felt as if everyone at the party had suddenly learned his true identity. He glanced around the crowded front room, expecting Roland or Sebastian to point him out. *That's the Traveller. Right over there. Worthless bastard. You're looking at him.*

Most of the Free Runners had no idea what Malloy was talking about, but a few people seemed eager to hush up the drunken man. Two members of Malloy's crew began coaxing him out the back door. No one paid much attention and the party returned to normal. More beer. Pass the crisps. Gabriel stopped Jugger in the ground-floor hallway. "What was he talking about?"

"It's kind of a secret, mate."

"Come on, Jugger. You can trust me."

Jugger hesitated for a moment, and then nodded slowly. "Yeah. I guess that's true." He led Gabriel into the empty kitchen and began stuffing trash into a shopping bag. "Remember when we first met at the pub and I told you about the Vast Machine? Some Free Runners say that a group called the Tabula is behind all this monitoring and control. They're trying to turn Britain into a prison without walls."

"But Malloy was talking about somebody called a Traveller."

Jugger tossed the trash bag into a corner and opened a can of lager. "Well, that's when the story gets a little crazy. There are rumors that people called Travellers might save us from becoming prisoners.

That's why people write 'Hope for a Traveller' on walls around London. I've done it myself a few times."

Gabriel tried to keep his voice relaxed and casual. "And how is the Traveller going to change things, Jugger?"

"Hell if I know. Sometimes I think all this talk about Travellers is just a fairy tale. What's real is that I walk around London and I see they've put up more surveillance cameras and I start to get desperate. In a thousand little ways freedom is melting away, and nobody gives a damn."

* * *

THE PARTY HAD ended around one o'clock in the morning and Gabriel had helped mop the floors and pick up the trash. Now it was Monday, and he was waiting for Roland to return from Tyburn Convent. About an hour after his new haircut, Gabriel heard boots clomping up the staircase. There was a light tap on the door, and Roland entered the garret. The Free Runner from Yorkshire always looked solemn and a little bit sad. Sebastian once said that Roland was a shepherd who had lost all his sheep.

"Did what you wanted, Halo. Went to that convent." Roland shook his head slowly. "Never went to a convent before. Me family was Presbyterian."

"So what happened, Roland?"

"Those two nuns you told me about—Sister Ann

and Sister Bridget—are both gone. There's a new one there. Sister Teresa. She said she was the 'public nun' this week. Kind of a daft thing to say . . ."

"A public nun means they're allowed to talk to strangers."

"Right. Well, she did speak to me. Nice girl. I had half a mind to ask her if she wanted to go to a pub and have a pint. Guess nuns don't do that."

"Probably not."

Standing near the doorway, Roland watched Gabriel pull on his leather jacket. "You okay, Halo? Want me to go back to Tyburn with you?"

"This is something I need to do alone. Don't worry. I'll be back. What's for dinner?"

"Leeks," Roland said slowly. "Sausage. Mash. Leeks."

* * *

ALL THE BICYCLES at Vine House had nicknames and were stored in the garden shed. Gabriel borrowed a bicycle called the Blue Monster and headed north to the river. The Blue Monster had motorcycle handle-bars, the rearview mirror from a delivery truck, and a rusty frame splattered with bright blue paint. Its back wheel made a constant squeaking sound as he pedaled over Westminster Bridge and made his way through the traffic to Tyburn Convent. A young nun with brown eyes and dark skin opened the door.

"I'm here to see the shrine," Gabriel told her.

"That's not possible," the nun said. "We're just about to close."

"Unfortunately, I'm flying home tomorrow morning to America. Do you think I could have a quick look around? I've wanted to come here for years."

"Oh, I see. In that case . . ." The nun opened the door and allowed him to enter the cage that served as the convent's anteroom. "I'm sorry, but you can only spend a few minutes in the shrine."

She took the key ring out of her pocket and unlocked the gate. Gabriel asked a few questions and discovered that the nun had been born in Spain and had joined the order when she was fourteen. Once again, he climbed down the metal staircase to the crypt. The nun switched on the lights and he stared at the bones, the bloody clothes, and the other relics of the English martyrs. Gabriel knew that it was dangerous to come back here again. He had only one chance to find the clue that would lead him to his father.

Sister Teresa gave a little speech about the Spanish ambassador and Tyburn gallows. Nodding his head as if he were listening to every word, Gabriel wandered around the different display cases. Bone fragments. A blood-covered wisp of lace. More bones. He began to realize that he knew very little about either the Catholic Church or English history. It felt like he had just arrived at a classroom for a major exam without reading any of the textbooks.

"When the Restoration occurred, some of the common graves at Tyburn were opened and . . ."

Over the years, the wooden display cases in the crypt had been darkened by age and the hands of the faithful. If there were clues left here concerning his father, then they would have to be concealed within something that was recent. As he circled the room, he noticed a photograph in a clean pinewood frame that was hanging on the wall. Attached to the lower edge was a brass plaque that reflected the light.

Gabriel stepped closer and studied the black-and-white image. It was a photograph of a small, rocky island created when two jagged mountain peaks had emerged from the sea. About a third of the way down from the summit of the highest peak was a cluster of gray stone buildings—each built in the shape of an inverted cone. From a distance, they looked like massive beehives. The brass plaque had some words written in Gothic letters. *SKELLIG COLUMBA. IRELAND.*

"What's in this photograph?"

Startled, Sister Teresa stopped giving her prepared speech. "That's Skellig Columba, an island on the west coast of Ireland. It has a convent run by the Poor Clares."

"Is that your order?"

"No. We're Benedictines."

"But I thought everything in this crypt was either about your order or the English martyrs."

Sister Teresa's eyes moved downward and her lips

tightened. "God doesn't care about countries. Just souls."

"I'm not questioning that idea, Sister. But it does seem strange to find a photograph of an Irish convent in this shrine."

"I suppose you're right. It doesn't quite fit in."

"Did someone from outside the convent leave it here?" Gabriel asked.

The nun reached into her pocket and pulled out the heavy metal ring. "I am sorry, sir. But it's time for you to go."

Gabriel tried to hide his excitement as he followed Sister Teresa back upstairs. A moment later he was standing on the sidewalk. The sun had fallen below the trees in Hyde Park and it was getting cold. He unlocked the Blue Monster and rode the bicycle up Bayswater Road toward the roundabout.

Glancing in the rearview mirror welded to the handlebars, he saw a motorcycle rider wearing a black leather jacket about a hundred yards behind him. The rider could have roared up the street and disappeared into the city, but he held back, staying close to the curb. The rider's tinted helmet concealed his face. His appearance reminded Gabriel of the Tabula mercenaries who had chased after him in Los Angeles three months ago.

Gabriel made a quick turn onto Edgware Road and checked the mirror. The rider stayed behind him. The road was clogged with rush-hour traffic. Buses and cabs were only a few inches from one another as they traveled east. He turned onto Blomfield Road, bumped onto a sidewalk, and began to zigzag through the crowd that was leaving office buildings and hurrying to the underground. An older woman stopped and scolded him. "On the street—please!" But he ignored the angry looks and headed around the corner to Warwick Avenue.

A butcher's shop. A pharmacy. A restaurant advertising Kurdish food. Gabriel skidded to a stop and tossed the Blue Monster behind some bales of discarded cardboard boxes. Moving quickly, he returned to the sidewalk and passed through the electric door of a supermarket.

A shelf stacker glanced at him as he grabbed a shopping basket and hurried down an aisle. Should he return to Vine House? No, the Tabula might be waiting for him. They would kill his new friends with the same cold efficiency they had used on the families at New Harmony.

Gabriel reached the end of the aisle, turned the corner, and saw that the motorcycle rider was waiting for him. The rider was a tough-looking man with massive shoulders and arms, a shaven head, and smoker's lines in his face. He held the tinted helmet in his left hand and a satellite phone in his right.

"Don't run, Monsieur Corrigan. Here. Take this."

The rider extended his hand, offering the satellite

phone. "Talk to your friend," the man said. "But don't forget to use soft language. No names."

Gabriel took the phone and heard a faint crackle of static. "Who is this?" he asked.

"I'm in London with one of our friends," Maya said. "The man who gave you the phone is my business associate."

The motorcycle rider smiled slightly, and Gabriel realized that he had been tracked down by Linden, the French Harlequin.

"Can you hear me?" Maya said. "Are you all right?"

"I'm okay," Gabriel said. "It's good to hear your voice. I just found out where my father is living. We have to go find him . . ."

Hollis ate breakfast at a coffee shop, then walked down Columbus Avenue to the Upper West Side. It had been four days since Vicki and the others had left for London. During that time, Hollis had moved into a shabby single-residency hotel and found a job as a bouncer at a downtown club. When Hollis wasn't working he had offered bits of information to surveillance programs that fed into the Vast Machine. Each clue was supposed to convince the Tabula that Gabriel was still hiding in the city. Maya had given him a Harlequin slang word for what he was doing. It was called chumming—a fisherman term for throwing bait into the water to attract sharks.

The Upper West Side was filled with restaurants, nail salons, and Starbucks coffee shops. Hollis had never been able to figure out why so many men and women spent the day at Starbucks sipping lattes as they stared at their computers. Most of them looked too old to be students and too young to be retired. Occasionally, he had glanced over someone's shoulder to see what project took so much effort. He began to believe that everyone in Manhattan was writing the same movie screenplay about the romantic problems of the urban middle class.

At the Starbucks at Eighty-sixth Street and Columbus, he found Kevin the Fisherman sitting at a table with his laptop computer. Kevin was a slender young man, very pale, who ate, slept, and occasionally washed his armpits at Starbucks around the city. He had no home but Starbucks and no reality other than the coffee shop's WiFi access. If Kevin wasn't taking a nap or pushing his shopping cart to a new Starbucks, he was online.

Hollis grabbed a chair and pulled it up to the table. The Fisherman raised his left hand and wiggled his fingers to acknowledge the presence of another human being. His eyes focused on the computer screen while his right hand continued to type. Kevin had hacked into the files of a casting agency and downloaded the digital photographs of handsome— but unknown—New York actors. Using these photographs, he created profiles on Web sites for singles. The actors were turned into physicians, lawyers, or investment bankers who wanted to take long walks on the beach and get married. All over the world, hundreds of women were typing away, desperately trying to get Kevin's attention.

"What's up, Kevin?"

"Rich lady in Dallas." Kevin had a high-pitched, nasal voice. "She wants me to fly to Paris and meet her for the first time beneath the Eiffel Tower."

"Sounds romantic."

"Actually, she's the eighth woman I've met on the Internet who wanted to meet in either Paris or Tuscany. They must all watch the same movies." Kevin glanced up from the screen. "Help me out here. What's a good astrological sign?"

"Sagittarius."

"Good. That's perfect." Kevin typed a message and hit the send button. "You got another job for me?"

The Vast Machine had created the need for an untraceable way to send and receive Internet communications. Whenever someone used a computer to send e-mail or access information, the signal was identified by the Internet protocol address unique to that particular machine. Every IP address received by the government or a large corporation was retained forever. Once the Tabula had an IP number, it gave them a powerful tool to track Internet activity.

For day-to-day anonymity, Harlequins could use Internet cafés or public libraries, but a Fisherman like Kevin provided a different level of security. Each of Kevin's three computers had been bought at a swap meet, and that made them difficult to trace. The Fisherman also used special software programs that bounced e-mails off routers all over the world. Kevin was occasionally hired by Russian gangsters who lived in Staten Island, but the majority of his clients were married men who were having affairs or who wanted to download specialized pornography.

"How would you like to make two hundred dollars?"

"Two hundred dollars is good. You want me to send out more information about Gabriel?"

"Go into chat rooms and put comments on blogs. Tell everyone that you heard Gabriel give a speech against the Brethren."

"Who are the Brethren?"

"You don't need to know." Hollis pulled out a pen and wrote some information on a paper napkin. "Say that Gabriel is going to meet his followers tonight at a dance club downtown called Mask. There's a private room upstairs and he'll use it to give a speech at one o'clock in the morning."

"No problem. I'll get on it right away."

Hollis handed Kevin the two hundred dollars and got up from the table. "Do a good job on this and I'll give you a bonus. Who knows? Maybe you'll make enough to fly to Paris."

"Why would I want to do that?"

"You could meet the woman at the Eiffel Tower."

"That's no fun." Kevin returned to his computer. "Real flesh is too much trouble."

* * *

HOLLIS LEFT STARBUCKS and flagged down a taxi. On the way to South Ferry, he studied his copy of *The Way of the Sword*. Sparrow's book of meditations was divided into three parts: Preparation, Combat, and After the Battle. In chapter six, the Japanese Harlequin analyzed two facts that seemed contradictory. An experienced warrior always developed a strategy before an attack, and yet, in the confusion of the battle, the warrior usually did something different. Sparrow believed that plans were helpful, but their true power was that they calmed the spirit and prepared it for fighting. Toward the end of the chapter Sparrow wrote: *Plan to jump left although you'll probably go right*.

Hollis felt conspicuous on the ferryboat ride out to one of the most guarded locations in America—the Statue of Liberty. The boat was filled with school groups, elderly tourists, and families on vacation. He was a solitary black male carrying a backpack. When the boat reached Ellis Island, Hollis tried to lose himself in the crowd that was herded toward a large temporary structure that had been erected at the base of the statue.

He stood in line for about twenty minutes. When he reached the front he was told to enter a walk-in machine that reminded him of an enormous CAT scan. A mechanical voice told him to stand on two green shoeprints, and then he felt a sudden blast of air. He was in a sniffer—a machine that could sense the chemical emissions that came from explosives and ammunition.

When a green light flicked on, he was directed to a large room filled with lockers. No backpacks were allowed near the statue, so everything had to be stored in a wire basket. When Hollis placed a dollar into the payment slot, a mechanical voice demanded that he place his right thumb on a scanner. A sign above the lockers read *YOUR FINGERPRINT IS YOUR KEY. USE YOUR FINGERPRINT TO OPEN YOUR LOCKER UPON RETURNING.*

Concealed within the knapsack was a mold of Gabriel's right hand. A few weeks earlier, Maya had melted modeling plastic in a cooking pot, and Gabriel had dipped his hand into the brown goop. The mold was a bio dupe—a physical reproduction of biometric information—and it could be used as a decoy to distract the Tabula. Hollis concealed the fake hand in his jacket sleeve, and then pressed the rubbery thumb against the scanner window. In less than a second, Gabriel's print was transformed into a packet of digital information and transmitted to the computers of the Vast Machine.

"This way for Liberty. This way for Liberty," a guard chanted in a bored voice. Hollis left his knapsack in the locker and followed the other citizens as they entered the stone base of the enormous statue.

Everyone but Hollis looked happy. They were in the Land of the Free.

* * *

HOLLIS RETURNED TO his hotel late in the afternoon and was able to sleep for a few hours. When he opened his eyes, he was looking at a strip of four black-and-white photographs that he and Vicki had created in a "pose yourself" booth. An enormous cockroach approached this private altar and started waving its antennae, but Hollis flicked the insect onto the floor.

He picked up the photographs, held the strip beneath the lamplight, and studied the last image. Vicki had turned to look at him and her face showed both love and understanding. She truly knew him—knew the violence and selfishness that had claimed his past—but accepted him anyway. Her love made Hollis want to march out and slay monsters; he would do anything to justify her faith.

Around eight o'clock in the evening, he got dressed and took a cab downtown to the meatpacking district—a twenty-block patch of industrial buildings west of Greenwich Village. Mask, the dance club, occupied what had formerly been a chicken processing plant on West Thirteenth Street. It had been operating for three years, a fairly long time in this peculiar world.

The large central room was divided into two parts.

Most of the building was occupied by an open space for dancing, two bars, and a cocktail area. Toward the end of the room, a staircase led upward to a separate VIP area that overlooked the main dance floor. Only the pretty people—those with beauty or money—were allowed upstairs. The ground floor was for the bridge-and-tunnel crowd, customers who had either driven a car or taken a crowded train to get to Manhattan. The men who owned the club were obsessed with the ratio between these two groups. Although the bridge-and-tunnels made Mask a profitable business, they were drawn to the club by the actors and models who drank for free upstairs.

Without flashing lights and thumping dance music, Mask felt like it could easily be converted back into a factory for plucking dead chickens. Hollis went into the tiny employees' locker room and changed into a black T-shirt and sports jacket. A hand-lettered sign over the mirror announced that any employee selling drugs to customers would be fired immediately. Hollis had already discovered that management didn't mind employees selling drugs to one another—usually various uppers that kept the security staff alert until the end of the evening.

Hollis slipped on a radio headset that connected him to the other bouncers. He returned to the main room and walked upstairs. The employees at Mask saw the club as an elaborate device to squeeze money out of the customers. One of the most lucrative jobs was guarding the VIP area, and a man named Boodah currently held this post. Boodah had an African-American father and a Chinese mother. His nickname came from his enormous stomach, which appeared to protect him from all the craziness in New York.

The bouncer was arranging the chairs and cocktail tables inside his kingdom when Hollis came upstairs. "What's up?" Boodah asked. "You look tired."

"I'm all right."

"Remember. If anyone wants to go through the rope, they gotta come to me."

"No problem. I know the rules."

Boodah guarded the main entrance to the VIP area while Hollis stood at an exit on the opposite side. This exit was only used by pretty people who wanted to go to the downstairs bathroom or if they decided to rub shoulders with the sweaty crowd on the dance floor. Hollis's job was to keep everyone else out. Being a bouncer was about saying no all night long—unless you got paid to say yes.

* * *

HOLLIS HAD PERFORMED his job like an obedient drone, but he felt that something different might happen tonight. A walkway protected by a railing ran from the VIP area to the private room. Inside the room were leather couches, cocktail tables, and an intercom to order from the bar. A mirrored window overlooked the dance floor below. Tonight the private room was going to be occupied by some hustlers from Brooklyn who liked to use drugs at nightclubs. If the Tabula came to the room looking for Gabriel, they were going to get an unpleasant surprise.

Hollis leaned against the railing, stretching his leg muscles. He returned to his post when Ricky Tolson, the club's assistant manager, climbed the back staircase. Ricky was one of the owners' distant relatives. He made sure there was toilet paper in the bathroom and spent most of his time trying to pick up drunken women.

"How you doing, my brother?" Ricky asked. Hollis was too low in the club hierarchy to have a name.

I'm not your brother, Hollis thought. But he smiled pleasantly. "The private room is booked, right? I heard that Mario and his friends were coming tonight."

Ricky looked annoyed. "No, they called up and canceled. But there will be someone else. There always is . . ."

A half hour later, the club deejay began the evening with a Sufi religious chant, and then gradually brought in the thumping beat of house music. The bridge-and-tunnel crowd arrived first and grabbed the few tables near the bar. From his vantage point above the dance floor, Hollis watched young women wearing short skirts and cheap shoes run to the bathroom to check makeup and tease hair. Their male counterparts strutted around and waved twenty-dollar bills like little flags at the bartender.

The voices of the other bouncers whispered into his right ear from the radio headset. The security team had a continual dialogue going on about which man looked like trouble and which woman was wearing the most revealing dress. As the hours went by, Hollis kept his eye on the private room. It was still empty—but maybe nothing would happen tonight.

Around midnight he escorted two fashion models to a special bathroom that required a passkey. When he returned to his post, he saw Ricky and a girl wearing a tight green dress heading down the walkway to the private room. Hollis walked over to Boodah and shouted over the noise, "What's Ricky doing in the room?"

The big man shrugged as if the question barely deserved an answer. "Just another little girly. He'll give her some coke and she'll give him the usual."

Hollis looked down at the dance floor and saw two men wearing athletic jackets entering the club. Instead of checking out the women or buying a drink at the bar, they both looked up at the private room. One mercenary was short and very muscular. His pants looked too long for his fireplug body. The other man was tall and his black hair was pulled back in a ponytail.

The two men walked upstairs to the VIP area and the short mercenary slipped several bills into Boodah's hand. It was enough money to buy immediate respect and entrance past the red velvet rope. Within a few seconds, the men were sitting at a table and staring at the narrow walkway that led to the private room. Ricky was still there with his girlfriend. Hollis swore beneath his breath and remembered Sparrow's advice: *Plan to jump left although you'll probably go right.*

A drunken woman started screaming at her boyfriend and Boodah hurried down the staircase to solve the problem. The moment he left the area, the two mercenaries got up from the table and headed for the private room. The tall man moved slowly down the walkway while his partner stood guard. Lights hanging over the dance floor grew brighter and began flashing in rhythm with the beat. The tall mercenary turned and a sliver of light was reflected off the blade of a knife held tightly in his hand.

Hollis doubted that they had a photograph of Gabriel. Their instructions would be to kill whoever was in the room. Up until that moment, Hollis had started to believe that he could act like Maya and the other Harlequins. But he wasn't like them. None of the Harlequins would have worried about Ricky and the young woman, but Hollis couldn't stand back and let it happen. *To hell with it,* he thought. *If those two fools die, their blood stains my hands.*

With a courteous smile on his face, he approached the shorter of the two men. "Excuse me, sir. But the private room is occupied."

"Yeah, it's a friend of ours. So get the hell out of here."

Hollis raised his arms as if he were going to embrace the intruder. Then his hands became fists and punched toward each other, striking both sides of the man's head at the same time. The force of the concussion staggered the little man and he fell backward. The lights and the booming dance music were so overwhelming that no one noticed what had just happened. Hollis stepped over the body and moved forward.

The tall mercenary had his hand on the door handle, but he reacted immediately when he saw Hollis. Hollis knew that anyone holding a knife concentrated too much on the weapon; every particle of death and malevolence was squeezed into the point of the blade.

He reached out as if he were about to grab the mercenary's hand, then jerked backward as the man slashed out with the knife. Hollis kicked the toe of his shoe into the man's stomach. When the mercenary bent forward, gasping for breath, Hollis punched upward with all his strength, knocking the man over the railing.

People screamed below, but the music continued playing. Hollis ran down the walkway and forced a passage through the tables. When he reached the back staircase he saw that three other mercenaries were now pushing through the crowd. One of them was an older man with wire-rimmed glasses. Was this

Nathan Boone—the man who killed Maya's father? Maya would have attacked immediately, but Hollis continued moving.

The crowd surged back and forth like a herd of animals terrified by the smell of death. Hollis stepped onto the dance floor and pushed forward, shoving people out of the way. He reached the back hallway that led to the kitchen and restrooms. A group of young women were laughing about something while their makeup mirrors reflected the light. Hollis got past them and pushed through a fire door.

Two mercenaries wearing headsets stood in the alleyway. Someone had told them about Hollis and they were waiting. The older man raised a canister and shot chemical spray into Hollis's eyes.

The pain was incredible. It felt like his eyes were on fire. Hollis couldn't see—couldn't defend himself—as someone's fist shattered his nose. Like a drowning man, he grabbed the attacker in front of him, and then jerked his upper body forward, giving the mercenary a head butt in the face.

The first man fell onto the pavement, but the second man had his arm around Hollis's neck and began choking him. Hollis bit the man's hand. When he heard a scream, he grabbed the mercenary's arm, forcing it downward, and then twisted it until it snapped.

Blind. He was blind. Touching the rough brick wall beside him, he ran through his own darkness.

19

round ten o'clock in the
morning, Maya and the others passed through
the city of Limerick. Gabriel drove slowly through the
central shopping area, trying not to break any traffic
laws. His cautiousness disappeared the moment they
reached the countryside, and he stomped on the gas
pedal. Their little blue car roared down a two-lane
road, heading toward the west coast and the island of
Skellig Columba.

Normally Maya would have sat beside Gabriel so
she could look down the road and anticipate any
problems. But she didn't want Gabriel glancing at her
and interpreting the different expressions that
passed across her face. During her brief attempt to
live a normal life in London, the women in her
office had often complained that their boyfriends
never seemed to recognize their changing moods.
Now she was dealing with a man who could

do just that—and she was cautious of his power.

For the trip across Ireland, Vicki sat in the front passenger seat. Alice and Maya were in back, separated by a shopping bag filled with crackers and bottled water. The bag was a necessary barrier. Ever since they had arrived in Ireland, Alice had wanted to sit close to Maya. Once she had extended her fingers and touched the outline of the throwing knife that Maya wore beneath her sweater. It was all too intimate, too close, and Maya preferred to keep her distance.

Linden had leased the car with a credit card from one of his shell corporations registered in Luxembourg. He had purchased a cheap digital camera and plastic travel bags that read MONARCH TOURS—WE SEE THE WORLD. All these objects were props to make them look like tourists, but Vicki enjoyed having the camera. She kept saying, "Hollis would like this," as she rolled down the window to take another picture.

After stopping for gasoline in the town of Adare, they left the green farmland and followed a narrow road over the mountains. The treeless landscape reminded Maya of the Scottish Highlands; they passed rocks and brush and heather, a dash of purple rhododendrons growing near a drainage pipe.

As they came over a ridge, they saw the Atlantic Ocean in the distance. "He's there," Gabriel whispered. "I know he's there." No one dared challenge him.

* * *

MAYA HAD BEEN guarding Gabriel for several days, but they had both avoided an intimate conversation. She was surprised by the short haircut Gabriel had received in London. His shaved head made him look intense—almost severe—and she wondered if he was beginning to increase his powers as a Traveller. From the start, Gabriel seemed obsessed by the framed photograph he had seen at Tyburn Convent. He had insisted on going to Skellig Columba as soon as possible, and Linden could barely conceal his annoyance. The French Harlequin kept glancing at Maya as if she were a mother who had raised an unruly child.

Gabriel had made a second demand once they began to organize a trip to Ireland. For the last two weeks, he had been living with some Free Runners on the South Bank, and he wanted to say goodbye to his new friends. "Maya can come in with me, but you stay away," he told Linden. "You look like you're going to kill somebody."

"If I have to," Linden said. But he remained in the van when they reached Bonnington Square.

The old house smelled like fried bacon and boiled potatoes. Three young men and a tough-looking teenage girl with short hair were eating supper in the front room. Gabriel introduced the Free Runners to Maya and she nodded to Jugger, Sebastian, Roland, and Ice. He told them that Maya was his friend and that they were both going to leave the city that evening.

"You okay?" Jugger asked. "Anything we can do to help?"

"Some people might come around asking about me. Tell them I met a girl and we're going to the South of France."

"Right. Got that. Remember, you always got friends here."

Carrying his belongings in a cardboard box, Gabriel followed Maya back out to the van. They spent two days at a safe house near Stratford while Linden tried to get information about Skellig Columba. All he could learn on the Internet was that the island was originally the site of a sixth-century monastery founded by Saint Columba. The Irish saint, also known as Colum Cille, was an apostle to the pagan tribes in Scotland. In the early 1900s, the ruined buildings had been restored by an order of nuns called the Poor Clares. There was no ferry service to the island and the nuns did not welcome visitors.

* * *

THEY CAME OUT of the mountains onto a coastal road that ran between a limestone cliff and the ocean. Gradually, the landscape widened out to a marshland. Peat cutters worked in a distant bog, digging out bricks of compressed grass and clover grown during the Ice Age.

There were ponds and streams everywhere, and the road followed a winding river that emptied into a little bay. Rolling hills were on the north side of the bay, but they turned south to Portmagee, a fishing village facing a wharf and a low seawall. Two dozen houses were on the other side of the narrow road, and each reminded Maya of a child's drawing of a face: gray slate hair, two upper windows for eyes, a central red door for a nose, and two lower windows with white flower boxes that resembled a toothy grin.

They stopped at a village pub, and the barman told them that a man named Thomas Foley was the only person who went out to Skellig Columba. Captain Foley rarely answered his telephone, but he was usually home in the evening. Vicki arranged for rooms at the pub while Gabriel and Maya walked down the road. This was the first time they had been alone together since meeting in London. It seemed natural to be with him again, and Maya found herself thinking about the first time they'd met in Los Angeles. Both of them had been wary of each other and uncertain about their new responsibilities as Traveller and Harlequin.

Near the outskirts of the village, they found a crudely drawn sign that announced CAPTAIN T. FOLEY—BOAT TOURS. They walked down a muddy driveway to a whitewashed cottage, and Maya knocked on the door.

"Come in or stop knocking!" a man shouted, and they entered a front room filled with Styrofoam floats, discarded lawn furniture, and an aluminum rowboat on a sawhorse. The cottage appeared to be a sinkhole for all the trash in West Ireland. Gabriel followed Maya down a short hallway lined with stacks of old newspapers and bags filled with aluminum cans. The walls squeezed inward as they reached a second door.

"If that's you, James Kelly, you can bugger off!" shouted the voice.

Maya pushed the door open and they entered a kitchen. There was an electric stove in one corner and a sink filled with dirty dishes. An old man sat at the center of the room repairing a tear in a fishing net. He smiled, revealing a crooked set of teeth, stained dark yellow by a lifetime of smoking and strong tea.

"And who might you be?"

"I'm Judith Strand and this is my friend Richard. We're looking for Captain Foley."

"Well, you found him. What do you want him for?"

"We'd like to charter a boat for four passengers."

"That's easy enough to do." Captain Foley gave Maya an appraising look, gauging the amount of money he could charge. "Half-day trip up the coast is three hundred euros. Full day is five hundred. And you need to pack your own bloody lunch."

"I've seen photographs of an island called Skellig Columba," Gabriel said. "Think we could go there?"

"I take supplies to the nuns every two weeks."

Foley rummaged through the clutter on the kitchen table until he found a briar pipe. "But you can't put your foot on that particular island."

"What's the problem?" Gabriel asked.

"No problem. Just no visitors." Captain Foley opened up a cracked sugar bowl, took out a pinch of black tobacco, and stuffed it into his pipe. "The island is owned by the Republic, leased to the Holy Church, and chartered to the Order of the Poor Sisters. One thing they all agree on—government, church, and nuns—is that they don't want strangers tromping around Skellig Columba. It's a protected area for seabirds. The Poor Clares don't bother them because they spend their time praying."

"Well, perhaps if I just spoke to them and asked for permission to—"

"No one gets on the island without a letter from the bishop, and I don't see you waving one." Foley lit the pipe and puffed some sugary smoke at Gabriel. "And that's the end of the story."

"Here's a new story," Maya said. "I'll pay you a thousand euros to take us out to the island so that we can talk to the nuns."

The captain considered her offer. "That might be possible . . ."

Maya touched Gabriel's hand and pulled him toward the doorway. "I think we're going to look for another boat."

"It's more than possible," Foley said quickly.

"See you on the wharf at ten tomorrow morning."

They left the house and walked outside. Maya felt like she'd been trapped in a badger's den. It was close to nightfall and patches of darkness had appeared—tangled in the bushes and spreading beneath the trees.

The villagers were safe within their homes, watching television and cooking dinner. Lights glowed through lace curtains, and smoke came up from some of the chimneys. Gabriel led Maya across the road to a rusty park bench that overlooked the bay. The tide was out, leaving a strip of dark sand covered with driftwood and dead seaweed. Maya sat on the bench as Gabriel walked to the tide line and gazed out at the western horizon. The setting sun touched the ocean and was transformed into a hazy blob of light that flowed across the water.

"My father's on that island," Gabriel said. "I know he's out there. I can almost hear him talking to me."

"Maybe that's true. But we still don't know why he came to Ireland. There has to be a reason."

Gabriel turned away from the water. He walked over to the bench and sat down beside her. They were alone in the gloom, close enough so that she could feel him breathing.

"It's getting dark," he said. "Why are you still wearing your sunglasses?"

"Just a habit."

"You once told me that Harlequins were against habits and predictable actions."

Gabriel reached out and removed her sunglasses. He folded them and placed them beside her leg. Now he was staring straight into her eyes. Maya felt naked and vulnerable, as if she had been stripped of all her weapons.

"I don't want you to look at me, Gabriel. It makes me uncomfortable."

"But we like each other. We're friends."

"That's not true. We can never be friends. I'm here to protect you—to die for you, if that's necessary."

Gabriel looked out at the ocean. "I don't want anyone dying for me."

"We all understand the risk."

"Maybe. But I'm connected to what happened. When we first met in Los Angeles and you told me I might be a Traveller, I didn't understand how it was going to change the lives of the people I met. I have all these questions that I want to ask my father . . ." Gabriel fell silent and shook his head. "I never accepted the idea that he was gone. Sometimes, when I was a kid, I would lie in bed at night and have these imaginary conversations with him. I thought I'd grow out of that when I got older, but now it's even more intense."

"Gabriel, your father might not be on the island."

"Then I'll keep looking for him."

"If the Tabula know you're searching for your father, they'll have power over you. They'll put out false clues—like bait for a trap."

"I'll take that chance. But that doesn't mean that you have to come along. It would destroy me if something happened to you, Maya. I couldn't live with that."

She felt as if Thorn were standing behind the bench, whispering all his threats and warnings. *Never trust anyone. Never fall in love.* Her father was always so strong, so sure of himself—the most important person in her life. *But damn him*, she thought. *He's stolen my voice. I can't speak.*

"Gabriel," she whispered. "Gabriel . . ." Her voice was very soft, like that of a lost child who had given up hope of ever being found.

"It's all right." He reached out and took her hand. Only a sliver of the sun remained on the horizon. Gabriel's skin was warm to the touch, and Maya felt as if she would be cold—Harlequin cold—for the rest of her life.

"I will stand beside you no matter what happens," she said. "I swear that to you."

He leaned forward to kiss her. But when Maya turned her head, she saw dark shapes moving toward them.

"Maya!" Vicki called out to them. "Is that you? Alice got worried. She wanted to find you guys . . ."

* * *

IT RAINED THAT night. In the morning, a thick bank of fog lay on the ocean just outside the bay. Maya put

on some of the clothes she had bought in London—
wool pants, a dark green cashmere sweater, and a
leather coat with winter lining. After eating breakfast
at the pub, they walked over to the wharf and found
Captain Foley loading sacks of peat and plastic
storage boxes onto his thirty-foot fishing boat. Foley
explained that the peat was for the convent's
stove, and the boxes contained food and clean
clothes. The only water on Skellig Columba came
from rain that trickled into rock catch basins. There
was enough water for the nuns to drink and wash
themselves, but not enough to wash their black
skirts and veils.

The boat had an open deck for pulling in fishing
nets and an enclosed cockpit near the bow that gave
protection from the wind. Alice seemed excited to be
back on a boat. She went in and out of the hold,
inspecting everything, as they began to leave the bay.
Captain Foley lit his pipe and puffed some smoke in
their direction. "Known world," he said, and jerked
his thumb toward the green hills to the east. "And
this . . ." He gestured toward the west.

"End of the world," Gabriel said.

"That's right, boyo. When Saint Columba and his
monks first came to this island, they were traveling to
the farthest place west on a map of Europe. Last stop
on the tramline."

They entered into the fog the moment they left the
protection of the bay. It was like being in the middle

of an enormous cloud. The decks glistened and drops of water clung to the steel cables attached to the radio antenna. The fishing boat glided down into the trough of each new wave, only to rise up again to splash through the whitecaps. Alice held on to the rail at the stern, then ran back to Maya. Looking excited, she pointed at a harbor seal floating near the boat. The seal stared back at them like a sleek dog that had just found some strangers in his backyard.

Gradually, the fog began to burn away and they could see patches of sky overhead. Seabirds were everywhere: shearwaters and storm petrels, pelicans and white gannets with black-tipped wings. After traveling for an hour or so, they passed an island called Little Skellig that was a nesting ground for the gannets. The bare rock was colored white, and thousands of the birds swirled through the air.

Another hour passed before Skellig Columba emerged from the waves. It looks exactly like the photograph Gabriel had seen at Tyburn Convent: two jagged peaks of a submerged mountain range. The island was covered with brush and heather, but Maya couldn't see the convent or any other structure.

"Where do we land?" she asked Captain Foley.

"Patience, miss. We're coming in from the east. There's a bit of a cove on the south side of the island."

Keeping wide of the rocks, Foley approached a twenty-foot dock attached to steel pilings. The dock led to a concrete slab that was surrounded by a chain-link fence. A prominent sign with red and black letters announced that the island was a protected ecological area off-limits to anyone who had not received written permission from the Kerry diocese. A locked gate had been installed at the edge of the slab. It guarded a stone stairway that led up the slope.

Captain Foley cut the engine. The waves pushed his boat up against the dock and he threw a loop around one of the pilings. Maya, Vicki, and Alice climbed up to the concrete slab while Gabriel helped Foley unload the storage boxes and sacks of peat. Vicki went over to the gate and touched the brass padlock that held the latch. "Now what?"

"No one's here," Maya said. "I think we should get around the fence and walk up the ridge to the convent."

"Captain Foley wouldn't like that idea."

"Foley brought us here. I gave him only half the money. Gabriel isn't going to leave until he learns about his father."

Alice ran across the platform and pointed up the slope. When Maya stepped back, she could see that four nuns were coming down steps that led to the dock. The Poor Clares wore black habits and veils with white wimples and neck collars. The knotted white cords around their waists had been inspired by the Franciscan history of their order. All four women were wrapped in black woolen shawls that covered their upper bodies. The wind whipped the ends of the shawls back and forth, but the women kept moving until they saw that strangers had appeared on their island. They stopped—the first three nuns grouping together on the steps while the tallest nun remained a few steps behind.

Captain Foley carried two bags of peat onto the platform and dumped them near the gate. "Don't look good," he said. "The tall one is the abbess. She runs the show."

One of the Poor Clares climbed up the staircase to the abbess, received an order, and then hurried down the steps to the gate.

"What's going on?" Gabriel asked.

"End of story, boyo. They don't want you here."

Foley removed the knit cap from his bald head as he approached the gate. He bowed slightly to the nun and spoke in a low voice to her, then hurried over to Maya with a surprised look on his face.

"Excuse me, miss. My apologies for all I said. The abbess requests your presence in the chapel."

* * *

THE ABBESS HAD disappeared, but each of the three nuns grabbed a sack of peat and started to climb up the staircase. Maya, Gabriel, and the others followed them while Captain Foley remained with his boat.

In the sixth century, the monks led by Saint

Columba had built a staircase that ran from the ocean up to the summit of the island. The gray limestone was veined with white slate and spotted with lichen. As Maya and the others followed the nuns up the slope, the hushing noise of waves disappeared and was replaced by the sound of the wind. Wind blew past conical pieces of stone and rippled through scurry grass, saw thistle, and sorrel. Skellig Columba resembled the ruins of a massive castle with fallen towers and shattered archways. All the seabirds had disappeared and were replaced by ravens, which circled above them, cawing to one another.

They reached the top of a ridge and descended to the north side of the island. Directly below them were three successive terraces, each about fifty feet wide. The first terrace was occupied by a small garden and two catch basins for the rainwater that flowed down the face of the rock. On the second terrace were four stone buildings built without mortar; they resembled enormous beehives with wooden doors and round windows. A chapel was on the third terrace. It was about sixty feet long and shaped like a boat placed upside down on the beach.

Alice and Vicki remained with the nuns as Maya and Gabriel climbed down the steps to the chapel and went inside. An oak floor led to an altar at one end: three windows behind a simple gold cross. Still wrapped in her cloak, the abbess stood in front of the altar—her back to the visitors, her hands clasped in prayer. The door squeaked shut and all they could hear was the wind whistling through gaps in the rock walls.

Gabriel took a few steps forward. "Excuse me, ma'am. We just arrived on the island and we need to talk to you."

The abbess unclasped her hands and slowly lowered her arms. There was something about the gesture that was both graceful and dangerous. Maya immediately reached for the knife strapped to her arm. *No*, she wanted to scream. *No*.

The nun turned toward them and flung a black-steel knife through the air, burying it in the wood paneling a foot above Gabriel's head.

Maya stepped in front of Gabriel as her own throwing knife appeared in her hand. Holding the blade flat on her palm, she raised her arm quickly, and then recognized the familiar face. An Irishwoman in her fifties. Green eyes that were savage, almost crazy. A wisp of red hair pushing beneath the edge of the starched white wimple. A large mouth sneering at them with complete disdain.

"It's clear that you're not very alert—or prepared," the woman said to Maya. "A few inches lower and your citizen friend would be dead."

"This is Gabriel Corrigan," Maya said. "He's a Traveller, like his father. And you almost killed him."

"I never kill anyone by accident."

Gabriel glanced at the knife. "And who the hell are you?"

"This is Mother Blessing. One of the last remaining Harlequins."

"Of course. Harlequins . . ." Gabriel said the word with contempt.

"I've known Maya since she was a little girl," Mother Blessing said. "I was the one who taught her how to break into buildings. She always wanted to be just like me, but apparently she has a lot to learn."

"What are you doing here?" Maya asked. "Linden thought you were dead."

"That's what I wanted." Mother Blessing removed the black shawl and folded it into a little square. "After Thorn was ambushed in Pakistan, I realized that there was a traitor among us. Your father didn't believe me. Who was it, Maya? Do you know?"

"It was Shepherd. I killed him."

"Good. I hope he suffered a great deal. I came to this island about fourteen months ago. When the abbess died, the nuns made me their temporary leader." She sneered again. "We Poor Clares live simple but pious lives."

"So you were a coward," Gabriel said. "And you came here to hide."

"What a foolish young man. I'm not impressed. Perhaps you need to cross the barriers a few more times." Mother Blessing walked the length of the chapel, pulled the knife from the wood, and slid it back into the sheath that was concealed beneath her robes. "See the altar near the window? It contains an illuminated manuscript supposedly written by Saint Columba. My Traveller wanted to read this book, so I had to follow him to this cold little chunk of rock."

Gabriel nodded eagerly and took a few steps forward. "And the Traveller was . . . ?"

"Your father, of course. He's here. I've been guarding him."

20

Gabriel felt a surge of anticipation as he looked around the chapel. "Where is he?"

"Don't worry. I'll take you to him." Mother Blessing removed some bobby pins and pulled off the nun's veil. She shook her head slightly to release her tangled mane of red hair.

"Why didn't you tell Maya that my father was here on the island?"

"I haven't been in contact with any Harlequins."

"My father should have asked you to find me."

"Well, he didn't." Mother Blessing placed the veil on a side table. She picked up a sword held in a leather scabbard and slung the strap over her shoulder. "Didn't Maya explain this to you? Harlequins just protect Travellers. We don't try to understand them."

Without further explanation, she led Gabriel and

Maya out of the chapel. One of the four nuns, a very small Irishwoman, was waiting on a stone bench. Clutching some wooden rosary beads, she silently recited her prayers.

"Is Captain Foley still down at the dock?" Mother Blessing asked.

"Yes, ma'am."

"Tell him that our guests will remain on the island until I contact him. The two women and the girl will sleep in the common room. The young man will sleep in the storage hut. Tell Sister Joan to double the food available for dinner."

The small nun nodded and hurried away, still holding the rosary beads. "These women can follow orders," Mother Blessing said. "But all this praying and singing business does get annoying. For a contemplative order, they talk a great deal."

Maya and Gabriel followed Mother Blessing back up a short staircase to the monastery's middle terrace. It was a long patch of flat ground where the medieval monks had built four beehive huts with blocks of limestone. Because of the constant wind, the huts had heavy oak doors and small round windows. Each was about the size of a double-decker London bus.

Vicki and Alice had disappeared, but Mother Blessing said they were in the cooking hut. A thin line of smoke came from a stovepipe and was blown south by the wind. Following a dirt path, they walked past the nuns' dormitory and a building that Mother

Blessing called the saint's cell. The storage hut was the final building at the end of the terrace. The Irish Harlequin stopped and scrutinized Gabriel as if he were an animal at the zoo.

"He's inside."

"Thank you for guarding my father."

Mother Blessing pushed a wisp of hair away from her eyes. "Your gratitude is an unnecessary emotion. I made a choice and accepted this obligation."

She opened a heavy door and led them into a storage hut. The building had an oak floor and a narrow staircase that led up to another level. The only light came from three round windows that were placed like irregular portholes in the rock walls. Storage lockers were everywhere, along with cans of food and a portable electric generator. Candles had been left on a red box of first-aid supplies. The Irish Harlequin took out a small box of wooden matches and tossed them to Maya.

"Light some candles."

Mother Blessing knelt on the floor, the skirts of her nun's habit spreading around her. She passed her hand across the smooth oak surface and pushed at a discolored wood panel. It popped open, revealing a rope handle.

"Here we go. Step back."

Still on her knees, she pulled on the handle and a trapdoor opened in the floor. Stone steps led downward into darkness.

"What's going on?" Gabriel asked. "Is he a prisoner here?"

"Of course not. Take a candle and see for yourself."

Gabriel accepted a candle from Maya. He stepped around Mother Blessing and climbed down a narrow staircase to a brick-lined cellar with a gravel floor. There was nothing in the room except for a stack of large plastic buckets with steel handles. Gabriel wondered if the nuns used these to water their vegetable garden in the summertime.

"Hello?" he called. But no one answered.

There was only one way to go—through another oak door. Holding the candle in his left hand, he pushed the door open and entered a much smaller room. Gabriel felt like he had come to a morgue to identify a loved one. A body lay on a stone slab, hidden under a sheet of cotton muslin. He stood beside the body for a few seconds, then reached out and pulled the muslin away. It was his father.

The door creaked on its hinges as Maya and Mother Blessing entered the room. Both Harlequins carried candles, and their shadows mingled on the walls.

"What happened?" Gabriel asked. "When did he die?"

Mother Blessing rolled her eyes as if she couldn't believe such ignorance. "He's not dead. Put your head on his chest. You can hear a heartbeat every ten minutes or so."

"Gabriel has never seen another Traveller," Maya said.

"Well, now you have. This is the way you look when you cross over to another realm. Your father has been this way for months. Something happened. Either he liked it there and remained, or he's trapped and can't get back to our world."

"How long can he stay this way?"

"If he perishes in another realm, his body will decay. If he survives but never returns to this world, his body will die of old age. It wouldn't be a bad thing if he died in another world." She paused for a moment. "Then I could leave this nasty little island."

Gabriel spun away from his father and took a step toward Mother Blessing. "You can leave the island right now. Get the hell out of here."

"I've guarded your father, Gabriel. I would have died for him. But don't expect me to act like his friend. It's my responsibility to be cold and completely rational." Mother Blessing glared at Maya and stalked out of the room.

* * *

GABRIEL HAD NO idea how long he remained in the cellar staring at his father. Traveling all this distance to find an empty shell was so disturbing that part of his mind refused to believe it had really happened. He had a childish impulse to do everything over again—entering the hut, pulling up the trapdoor, climbing down the steps to reach a different conclusion.

After some time had passed, Maya took the end of the muslin sheet and pulled it over Matthew Corrigan's body. "It's getting dark outside," she said gently. "We should probably find the others."

Gabriel remained beside his father. "Michael and I were always looking forward to the moment when we would see him again. It was what we talked about before we went to sleep at night."

"Don't worry. He'll come back." Maya took Gabriel's arm and coaxed him out of the room. It was cold outside and the sun was falling toward the horizon. They walked down the path together and entered the cooking hut. It was warm and friendly there—like someone's home. A plump Irish nun named Joan had just finished baking a dozen scones, and she placed them on a serving tray along with different kinds of homemade jam and marmalade. Sister Ruth, an older woman with thick eyeglasses, bustled around the room putting away the supplies they had just brought up from the dock. She opened the stove and tossed a few chunks of peat into the fire. The compressed vegetation glowed with a dark orange light.

Vicki hurried down the staircase from the upper floor. "So what happened, Gabriel?"

"We'll talk about it later," Maya said. "Right now, we'd like some tea."

Gabriel unzipped his jacket and sat down on a bench near the wall. The two nuns were staring at him.

"Matthew Corrigan is your father?" Sister Ruth asked.

"That's right."

"It was an honor to meet him."

"He's a great man," Sister Joan said. "A great—"

"Some tea," Maya snapped, and everyone stopped talking. A moment later, Gabriel was holding a cup of hot tea in his cold hands. There was a tense silence until the two other nuns entered the hut carrying one of the storage boxes. Sister Maura was the small nun who had been praying outside the chapel; Sister Faustina was from Poland and had a strong accent. As they unpacked the supplies and inspected the mail, the nuns forgot about Gabriel and chatted happily.

The Poor Clares owned nothing but the crosses dangling from their necks. They lived without modern plumbing, refrigeration, or electricity, but they seemed to find great joy in the small pleasures of life. On the way back from the dock Sister Faustina had gathered some pink heather. She put it on the edge of each blue china plate like a splash of beauty, along with a dollop of Irish butter and a hot scone. Everything looked perfectly arranged—as if in a gourmet restaurant—but there was nothing artificial about this gesture. The world was beautiful to the Poor Clares; to ignore that fact was to deny God.

Alice Chen came down from the sleeping room and ate three scones with a great deal of strawberry jam. Vicki and Maya sat in a corner, whispering to each other and occasionally glancing in Gabriel's direction. The nuns drank their tea and discussed the mail that had just arrived with Captain Foley. They were praying for dozens of people all over the world, and they talked about these strangers—the woman with leukemia, the man with the shattered legs—as if they were close friends. Bad news was received solemnly. Good news was cause for laughter and celebration; it felt like it had become someone's birthday.

Gabriel kept thinking about his father's body and the white muslin sheet that reminded him of cobwebs covering an ancient tomb. Why was his father still in another realm? There was no way he could answer this question, but he remembered Mother Blessing telling them why his father had first come to this particular island.

"Excuse me," Gabriel said. "I'd like to understand why my father decided to come here. Mother Blessing said something about a manuscript written by Saint Columba."

"The manuscript is in the chapel," Sister Ruth said. "It used to be in Scotland, but it was returned to the island about fifty years ago."

"And what did Columba write about?"

"It's a narrative of faith—a confession. The saint

gave a detailed description of his journey to hell."

"The First Realm."

"We don't believe in your particular system, and we certainly don't believe that Jesus was a Traveller."

"He's the Son of God," Sister Joan said.

Sister Ruth nodded. "Christ was conceived by the Holy Spirit and born of the Virgin Mary. He was crucified, died, and was buried—and then he rose from the dead." She glanced at the other nuns. "All that is the foundation of our faith as Christians. But we don't feel that this contradicts the idea that God has allowed some people to become Travellers and that these Travellers can become visionaries or prophets—or saints."

"So Columba was a Traveller?"

"I don't know the answer to that question. But his spirit went to a place of damnation, and then he came back and wrote about it. Your father spent a great deal of time translating the manuscript. And when he wasn't in the chapel—"

"He walked all over the island," Sister Faustina said with a strong Polish accent. "He climbed up the mountain and looked at the sea."

"Can I go to the chapel?" Gabriel asked. "I'd like to see the manuscript."

"There's no electricity," Sister Ruth said. "You'd have to use candles."

"I just want to see what my father was reading."

The four nuns glanced at one another and

appeared to make a common decision. Sister Maura stood up and walked over to a chest of drawers. "There are enough candles on the altar, but you'll need some matches. Keep the door closed or the wind will blow the flames out."

Gabriel zipped up his jacket and left the cooking hut. The only light came from the stars and a three-quarter moon. At night, the four beehive huts and the chapel looked like dark mounds of rock and dirt, tombs for Bronze Age kings. Trying not to trip on the uneven pathway, he walked past the nuns' dormitory and the hut called the saint's cell where Mother Blessing was living. A faint bluish light glowed from an upstairs window of this building, and Gabriel wondered if the Irish Harlequin had a computer attached to a sat phone.

He climbed down the steps to the lower terrace and opened the unlocked chapel door. It was hard to see until he lit three large beeswax candles that burned with a dark yellow flame.

The chapel's altar was a rectangular box about the size of a small chest of drawers. A large wooden cross was attached to the top, and the rest of the box was decorated with carvings of mermaids, sea monsters, and a man with ivy growing out of his mouth. Kneeling in front of the altar, Gabriel found a crack that outlined a central drawer, but couldn't find a latch or a handle. He pulled and pushed each carving, but none of these pagan decorations opened the drawer. He was about to give up and return to the cooking hut for instructions when he tugged the wooden cross an inch forward. Instantly, there was a clicking sound and the drawer slid open.

Inside was a large object wrapped in a black cloth, a small college notebook with a cardboard cover, and two books. Gabriel unwrapped the cloth and found a manuscript with a heavy calfskin cover and vellum pages. The first page had a painted illustration of Saint Columba standing on the bank of a river. Although the book was very old, the colors were still bright. On the page opposite the picture was the beginning of the Irish saint's confession written in Latin.

Returning to the drawer, Gabriel inspected the other books. One was a worn English/Latin dictionary; another was a battered textbook for first-year Latin students. He opened the notebook and discovered his father's translation of the manuscript. The meticulous handwriting reminded Gabriel of the shopping lists his father used to pin onto a bulletin board in the farmhouse kitchen. Both he and Michael would check the list every morning to see if their parents had decided to buy store candy or some other treat for supper.

Holding the notebook close to a candle, Gabriel began to read about the saint's experience in the First Realm.

Four days after our celebration of the Virgin's

ascension into heaven, my soul left my body and I descended into this cursed place.

Gabriel turned the page, reading as quickly as possible.

They are demons in the shape of men and live on an island in the middle of a dark river. Light comes from fire— And then his father crossed this last word out and tried other alternatives. *Light comes from flames and the sun is hidden.*

On the last page of the notebook, Matthew had underlined several passages.

No faith. No hope. No path revealed. But by God's grace, I found the black doorway and my soul returned to the chapel.

Returning to the twelfth-century manuscript, Gabriel began to turn the vellum pages and inspect the illustrations. Columba wore a white robe and had a gold halo behind his head to show that he was a saint. But there were no demons or devils in this version of hell, only men wearing medieval clothing and carrying swords or spears. While the saint watched from behind a shattered tower, the citizens of hell tortured and killed one another with an unrestrained savagery.

He heard the door squeak open and turned away from the altar. A figure passed through the shadows and entered his small circle of candlelight. Maya. She had one of the nuns' black shawls wrapped around her head and upper body. Following Mother

Blessing's example, she had discarded the black metal tube and carried her Harlequin sword openly. The scabbard strap crossed her chest and the sword handle rose behind her left shoulder.

"Did you find the book?"

"Yes. But there's more than that. My father didn't know Latin, but he worked out a translation and wrote it down in a notebook. It's all about Saint Columba crossing over to the First Realm. I guess my father wanted to learn about the place before he went there."

A flash of pain passed across Maya's face. As usual, she seemed to know what he was planning. "He could be anywhere, Gabriel."

"No. It's the First Realm."

"You don't need to cross over. Your father's body is still in this world. I'm sure he'll come back eventually."

Gabriel smiled. "I don't know if anyone would be eager to return to Mother Blessing."

Maya shook her head and began to pace. "I've known her since I was a little girl. She's become so negative, contemptuous of everyone . . ."

"Was she always so intense?"

"I used to be in awe of her bravery and her beauty. I still remember traveling with her on a train up to Glasgow. It was a sudden trip—we didn't have time to prepare—and Mother Blessing wasn't wearing a wig or any sort of disguise. I remember how men looked at her; they were drawn to her, but they also sensed something dangerous."

"And you admired that?"

"That was a long time ago, Gabriel. Now I'm trying to find my own path. I'm not a citizen or a drone, but I'm not a pure Harlequin either."

"And so what kind of person do you want to be?"

Maya stopped in front of him and made no attempt to hide her emotions. "I don't want to be alone, Gabriel. Harlequins can have children and families, but they're never really attached to them. Once my father held up my sword and told me: 'This is your family, your friend, and your lover.'"

"Remember when we sat on that bench and looked out at the ocean?" He reached out and placed his hands on her shoulders. "You said that you'd stand beside me no matter what happened. That meant a lot to me."

They were having a conversation—words floating through the cold air—but suddenly, almost like a magic spell, there was a transformation. The island and the chapel fell away and the world became the two of them. And Gabriel saw no concealment in Maya's eyes, nothing false. They were connected to each other in some deep way, far beyond their roles as Traveller and Harlequin.

The wind pushed at the chapel door, testing its strength, trying to force its way inside. Gabriel leaned forward and kissed Maya for a long time, but then she pulled back. A powerful tradition had just been destroyed like a scrap of paper tossed into a fire. The desire he had felt for so many months pushed all his other thoughts away. When he looked at her, it felt as if there were no barriers between them.

Gently, he took the sword from her shoulder and placed it on a wooden bench. Gabriel returned to her, brushed the hair from her face, and they kissed again. Maya pulled away, but this time very slowly. She whispered in his ear.

"Stay here, Gabriel. Please. Stay here . . ."

An hour later they lay together on the floor wrapped in the black wool shawl. The room was still cold and they were only half-dressed. Gabriel's shirt was draped over the bench, and Maya felt his warm skin touching her breasts. She wanted to stay here forever. His arms were around her; for the first time she could remember, it felt as if someone were protecting her.

She was a woman lying with her lover, but her Harlequin self had been waiting like a ghost in a dark house. Suddenly she pulled away from Gabriel and sat up.

"Open your eyes, Gabriel."

"Why?"

"You have to get out of here."

He gave her a sleepy smile. "Nothing's going to happen . . ."

"Get dressed and return to the storage hut. Harlequins can't be involved with Travellers."

"Maybe I could talk to Mother Blessing."

"Don't even think about that. You can't say anything to her and you can't act differently. Don't touch me when she's around. Don't look in my eyes. We'll talk about this later. I promise. But right now you have to get dressed and go."

"This doesn't make any sense, Maya. You're an adult. Mother Blessing can't tell you how to live your life."

"You don't realize how dangerous she is."

"All I know is that she walks around this island giving orders and insulting everybody."

"Do this for me. *Please*."

Gabriel sighed, but he obeyed her. Slowly, he pulled on his shirt, boots, and jacket. "This will happen again," he said.

"No. It won't."

"It's what we both want. You know that's true . . ."

Gabriel kissed her on the lips and walked out of the chapel. When the door creaked shut, Maya was able to relax. She would let him return to the storage hut, wait a few minutes, then get dressed. Pulling the wool shawl around her body, she lay back on the floor. If she curled up in a ball, she could preserve the warmth of the Traveller's body pressed against hers, that moment of intimacy and exaltation. A memory drifted through her mind of making a wish on the

Charles Bridge in Prague. *May someone love me and may I love him in return.*

She was gliding into a pleasant dream when the door creaked open and someone entered the chapel. She felt a moment of pleasure, believing that Gabriel had come back to see her again; then she heard that someone walking hard and fast across the wooden floor.

Strong fingers grabbed her hair and pulled her upward. A hand slapped her across the face, drew back, and slapped again.

Maya opened her eyes and saw Mother Blessing standing over her. The Irish Harlequin had abandoned her nun's skirt and was wearing black pants and a sweater.

"Get dressed," Mother Blessing said. She picked up Maya's shirt and tossed it in her direction.

Maya removed the shawl and pulled on her shirt, fumbling with the buttons. Her feet were still bare, her shoes and socks scattered across the floor.

"If you lie to me in any way, I'll kill you in front of this altar. Do you understand what I'm saying?"

"Yes."

Maya finished buttoning her shirt and scrambled to her feet. Her own sword was about eight feet away on the bench.

"Are you Gabriel's lover?"

"Yes."

"And when did this start?"

"Tonight."

"I told you not to lie to me!"

"I swear that's true."

Mother Blessing stepped forward and grabbed Maya's chin with her right hand. She studied the younger woman, looking for any sign of deceit or hesitation. Then she pushed Maya away.

"I had my disagreements with your father, but I always respected him. He was a true Harlequin, worthy of our tradition. But you're nothing. You've betrayed us."

"That's not true." Maya tried to sound strong and confident. "I found Gabriel in Los Angeles. I protected him from the Tabula—"

"Didn't your father teach you? Or did you just refuse to listen? We protect Travellers, but we have no attachments to them. And now you've indulged yourself with this weakness and sentimentality."

Maya's bare feet touched the cold floor as she took a few steps to the right and picked up her sword. She placed the strap over her head so that the scabbard touched her back. "You knew me when I was growing up," she said. "You helped my father destroy my life. Harlequins are supposed to believe in randomness. Well, there was nothing random about my childhood! I was slapped and kicked and ordered around by you and every other Harlequin who passed through London. I was trained to kill without doubt or hesitation. I killed those men in Paris when I was sixteen . . ."

Mother Blessing was laughing softly, mocking her. "Poor little girl. I'm *so* sorry. Is that what you want to hear? Do you want pity—from *me*? Do you think anything was different when I was a child? I killed my first Tabula merc with a sawed-off shotgun when I was twelve! And you know what I was wearing? A white communion dress. My mother made me put it on so I could get closer to the altar and pull the trigger."

For a few seconds, Maya saw a hint of pain in the older woman's eyes. And she had a vision of a child in a white dress, standing in the middle of a vast cathedral, splattered with blood. The moment passed, and Mother Blessing's anger appeared to grow even more intense.

"I'm a Harlequin, just like you," Maya said. "And that means you can't order me around . . ."

Mother Blessing drew her sword with two hands, spun it over her head, and finished with the point aimed at the floor. "You'll do whatever I tell you. Your relationship with Gabriel is over. You'll never see him again."

Maya raised her right hand slowly—to show that she was not planning an immediate attack. Then she pulled her sword out of its scabbard and held it with the point facing up and the flat of the blade against her chest. "Call Captain Foley tomorrow and he'll take us off this island. I'll continue to protect Gabriel and you can guard his father."

"There's no discussion about this. No compromise. You will submit to my authority."

"No."

"You've slept with a Traveller and now you're in love with him. That sort of emotion just puts him in danger." Mother Blessing raised her sword. "Because I've destroyed my own fear, I can create fear in others. Because I don't care about my own life, all my enemies die. Your father tried to tell you this, but you were too rebellious. Maybe I can make you listen . . ."

Mother Blessing extended her left leg. It was a graceful, practiced movement—like the beginning of a dance. And then the Irish Harlequin propelled herself forward, attacking with quick, sharp movements of the wrists and hands. She slashed and jabbed with unrestrained power as Maya gave ground and tried to defend herself. The candle flames fluttered and the sound of clashing swords cut through the silence.

A few feet from the altar, Maya threw herself across the room like a diver entering the water. She somersaulted away from the other Harlequin, got back up, and raised her sword again.

Mother Blessing renewed her attack, driving Maya toward the wall. The Irish Harlequin swung her sword to the right, and then twisted it around at the last moment, catching Maya's sword near the hilt and ripping the weapon out of the younger woman's hands. The sword spun through the air and landed across the room.

"You will submit to me," Mother Blessing said. "Submit, or accept the consequences."

Maya refused to speak.

Without warning, the point of Mother Blessing's sword cut across Maya's chest, pulled back, cut across her left arm, pulled back, and then slashed her left hand. The three wounds felt like someone had burned her flesh. Maya looked into the Harlequin's eyes and realized that the next movement of the sword would end her life. She remained silent until a thought came to her that was so powerful it pushed away her pride.

"Let me see Gabriel one last time."

"No."

"I'll obey you. But I need to say goodbye."

22

The Evergreen Foundation occupied an entire office building at Fifty-fourth Street and Madison Avenue in Manhattan. Most of the employees thought they worked for a nonprofit organization that gave out research grants and managed the endowment. Only a small staff of workers with offices on the top eight floors handled the Brethren's less public activities.

Nathan Boone passed through the revolving door and entered the atrium lobby. He glanced at the decorative waterfall and the small grove of artificial spruce trees placed near the windows. The architects had insisted on living evergreens, but each new transplant withered and died, leaving an unsightly carpet of brown needles. The eventual solution was a grove of manufactured trees with an elaborate air system that gave off a faint pine scent. Everyone preferred the imitation evergreens: they seemed more real than something that grew in the forest.

Boone approached the security desk, stood in a small yellow square, and allowed the guard to scan his eyes. Once Boone's identity had been verified, the guard checked a computer screen. "Good afternoon, Mr. Boone. You're authorized to go to the eighteenth floor."

"Any other information?"

"No, sir. That's all it says. Mr. Raymond here will escort you to the correct elevator."

Boone followed a second guard to the last elevator in the hallway. The man passed an ID card in front of a sensor and then stepped out just before the doors closed. As the elevator began to rise, a video camera inside the elevator scanned Boone's face and confirmed it with the biometric information in the Evergreen Foundation's computer.

That morning, Boone had received an e-mail that asked him to meet with members of the Brethren's executive board. This was highly unusual. In the past few years, Boone had met the board only when Nash was in charge of the meeting. As far as he knew, the general was still on Dark Island in the Saint Lawrence River.

The elevator doors opened and Boone stepped into an empty waiting room. No one was in the receptionist's chair, but there was a small speaker on the desk.

"Hello, Mr. Boone." The voice that came from the

speaker was computer generated, but it sounded like a real person—a young woman who was bright and efficient.

"Hello."

"Please wait here in the room. We'll let you know when the meeting begins."

Boone sat on a suede couch near a glass coffee table. He had never visited the eighteenth floor, and he had no idea what sort of equipment was evaluating his reactions. A highly sensitive microphone could be listening to his heartbeat while an infrared camera might be monitoring changes in his skin temperature—people who were angry or scared had flushed skin and a faster heart rate. The computer could analyze this data and predict the likelihood of a violent reaction.

There was a faint clicking sound and then a drawer in the receptionist's desk glided open. "Our sensors have informed us that you are carrying a handgun," said the computer voice. "Please place it in the drawer. It will be returned at the end of the meeting."

Boone walked over to the desk and stared at the open drawer. Although he had worked for the Brethren for almost eight years, he had never been asked to surrender his weapon. He had always been a reliable and obedient employee. Had they started to doubt his loyalty?

"This is our second request," the voice said. "A failure to comply will be considered a violation of security."

"I'm in charge of security," Boone announced, then realized that he was talking to a computer. He waited for a few seconds, just to assert his independence, and removed the handgun from his shoulder holster. When he placed it in the desk drawer, three lines of light surrounded the weapon in a precise triangle. The drawer glided shut, and Boone returned to the couch. Boone didn't mind being scanned by a machine, but it annoyed him to be treated like a criminal. Obviously, the program hadn't been calibrated to show different levels of respect.

He stared at the large painting on the wall in front of him. It was a pastel blotch with legs that resembled a squashed spider. Three doors, each painted a different color, were at the end of the room. There was no way out except for the elevator, and the computer also controlled that system.

"The meeting is about to begin," the voice said. "Please go through the blue door and walk to the end of the corridor."

Boone stood up slowly and tried not to show his irritation. "And you have a nice day," he said to the machine.

The blue door moved smoothly into the wall the moment the sensors detected his body. He walked down a hallway to a stainless-steel door without a visible lock or handle. When this door slid open, he entered a conference room with massive windows that gave a view of the Manhattan skyline. Two members of the Brethren's executive board sat behind a long black table—Dr. Anders Jensen and Mrs. Brewster, the British woman who was pushing for the new Shadow Program in Berlin.

"Good afternoon, Nathan." Mrs. Brewster acted as if he were some kind of servant who had just dropped by her flat in South Kensington. "I assume you know Dr. Jensen from Denmark."

Boone nodded to Jensen. "We met last year in Europe."

A third person was standing in front of the windows, surveying the city. Michael Corrigan. A few months ago, Boone had captured Michael in Los Angeles and transported him to the East Coast. He had seen the young man scared and confused, but now a transformation had taken place. The Traveller seemed to radiate confidence and authority.

"I'm the one who asked for this meeting," Michael said. "Thank you for joining us at such short notice."

"Michael has become part of our effort," Mrs. Brewster said. "He completely understands our new objectives."

But he's a Traveller, Boone thought. *We've been killing people like him for thousands of years*. He wanted to grab Mrs. Brewster and shake her as if she had just started a fire in her own house. *Why are you doing this? Can't you see the danger?*

"And what are our new objectives?" Boone asked. "The Brethren have done everything possible to establish the Panopticon. Has that goal changed in the last few weeks?"

"The goal is the same, but now it's becoming possible," Michael said. "If the Shadow Program works in Berlin, we can expand it throughout Europe and North America."

"That involves the computer center," Boone said. "My job is to protect the Brethren from attacks by its enemies."

"And you haven't done a very good job of that," Dr. Jensen said. "Our Westchester research center was infiltrated and nearly destroyed, the completion of the quantum computer has been delayed, and last night Hollis Wilson assaulted several of your men at a Manhattan dance club."

"We expect to have some attrition of our contract employees," Mrs. Brewster said. "What bothers us is that Hollis Wilson escaped."

"I need a larger staff."

"Gabriel and his friends are not the immediate problem," Michael said. "You need to concentrate on finding my father."

Boone hesitated, and then spoke carefully. "These days I'm receiving different instructions from different sources."

"My brother has never been capable of organizing anything. He was just a motorcycle messenger in Los Angeles when your men tracked us down. My father has spent his life as a Traveller, and we know he's inspired alternative communities. Matthew Corrigan is dangerous and that's why he's the objective. You have your orders, Mr. Boone."

Mrs. Brewster nodded slightly, giving her assent. Boone felt as if the massive window had just shattered and there were shards of glass everywhere. A Traveller, one of their enemies, was speaking for the Brethren.

"If that's what you want . . ."

Michael walked slowly across the room. He was staring at Boone as if he had just heard every disloyal thought. "Yes, Mr. Boone. I'm in charge of finding my father, and that's what I want."

Gabriel heard the door of the storage hut slam open and hard-soled boots clomping up the staircase. Still wrapped in a heavy quilt, he rolled onto his back and opened his eyes. Sister Faustina, the Polish nun, came in with a wooden tray. She placed his breakfast on the floor, then stood with her hands on her waist.

"You asleep?"

"Not now."

"Your friends are awake. After breakfast, please to enter the chapel."

"Thank you, Sister Faustina. I'll do that."

The big woman remained near the staircase, studying Gabriel as if he were a new species of sea mammal that had washed ashore on the island.

"We talk to your father. He is a man of faith." Sister Faustina continued staring at him and sniffed loudly. Gabriel felt like he had just failed an inspection. "We pray for your father every night. Perhaps he is in a dark place. Perhaps he cannot find a way home . . ."

"Thank you, Sister."

Sister Faustina nodded and then stomped back down the staircase. There was no heat in the storage hut, so Gabriel got dressed quickly. The nun had brought him a pot of tea, a loaf of brown bread, butter, apricot jam, and a thick slice of cheddar cheese. Gabriel was hungry and he ate quickly, pausing only when he poured a second cup of tea.

Had he really made love to Maya last night? In the cold storage room, with sunlight pushing through the round windows, the moment in the chapel was distant and dreamlike. He remembered the first long kiss, the candle flames trembling as their bodies came together and then parted. For the first time since they had met each other, he felt that all of Maya's defenses had melted away and he could see her clearly. She loved him and cared for him, and his own emotions flowed back to her. Both Harlequin and Traveller were already set apart from the ordinary world, and now these two puzzle pieces had somehow touched and locked together.

Pulling on his jacket, he left the storage hut and followed the stone pathway past the other buildings. The sky was clear, but it was a raw, cold day with a northwest wind that pushed through the scurvy grass and saw thistle. Peat smoke trailed out from the cooking hut's stovepipe chimney, but Gabriel avoided the comfort there and went directly to the chapel.

He found Maya sitting on a bench with her sheathed sword resting on her legs. Wearing a black turtleneck sweater and black wool pants, Mother Blessing paced back and forth in front of the altar. The conversation between the two Harlequins stopped immediately when he entered the room.

"Sister Faustina said I was supposed to come here."

"That's right," Mother Blessing said. "Maya has something to tell you."

Maya glanced up at Gabriel and he felt as if he had been jabbed with a knife. The young Harlequin's aggressive confidence had disappeared. She looked sad and defeated, and Gabriel realized that somehow Mother Blessing had found out about last night.

"It's dangerous to have two Travellers in the same location," Maya said. Her voice was flat and unemotional. "We've contacted Captain Foley on the satellite phone. You'll leave this morning with Mother Blessing and go back to the mainland. She'll take you to a safe house somewhere in Ireland. I'll stay here and guard your father."

"If I have to go, I want you to come with me."

"We've already made the decision," Mother Blessing said. "You don't have a choice. I've guarded your father for six months. Now that will be Maya's obligation."

"I don't see why Maya and I can't stay together."

"We know what's best for your survival."

Maya was gripping the scabbard of her sword as if the weapon could save her from this conversation. Her face was desperate, pleading, but she looked back down at the floor. "This is the most logical decision, Gabriel. And that's what Harlequins should do—make calm, logical decisions concerning the protection of Travellers. Mother Blessing is far more experienced than I. She has access to weapons and reliable mercenaries."

"And don't forget about Vicki Fraser and the little girl," Mother Blessing said. "They'll be safe here on the island. It's difficult to travel with a child."

"We've done all right so far."

"You've been lucky." Mother Blessing strolled over to the clear window behind the altar that looked out at the sea. Gabriel wanted to argue with the Harlequin, but there was something about this middle-aged Irishwoman that was very intimidating. Over the years, Gabriel had seen a variety of fights in bars and on the street where two drunken men insulted each other and worked their way up to aggression. Mother Blessing had stepped over that line many years ago. If you challenged her, she would attack immediately—without restraint.

"When will I see you again?" Gabriel asked Maya.

"In a year or so perhaps she can leave the island," Mother Blessing said. "It might happen earlier if your father returns to this world."

"A year? That's crazy."

"The boat will be here in twenty minutes, Gabriel. Get ready to leave."

The conversation was over. Dazed, Gabriel left the two women and walked out of the chapel. Gabriel could see that Vicki and Alice were up on the ridge. He climbed the stone stairway to the next ledge, circled the garden and the rainwater catch basins, then followed the path that led to the highest point on the island.

Sitting on a sandstone boulder, Vicki gazed out at the dark blue ocean that surrounded them in every direction. The island made Gabriel feel like nothing else existed—that they truly were alone at the center of the world. About thirty feet away from her, Alice scrambled around the rocks, pausing every few minutes to slash at tall weeds with a stick.

Vicki smiled when Gabriel approached her and motioned to the girl. "I think she's pretending to be a Harlequin."

"I'm not sure that's a good thing," Gabriel said, and sat down beside Vicki. Above them, the sky was dotted with gannets and shearwaters. The birds rode invisible currents of air up to the heavens and glided back down again. "I'm leaving the island," Gabriel said. As he described the discussion in the chapel, Mother Blessing's decision gained weight and sub-stance—like a distant city approached through the fog. The wind became stronger and the black-and-white shearwaters began calling with high-pitched cries that made Gabriel feel lonely.

"Don't worry about your father, Gabriel. Maya and I will guard him."

"What if he returns to this world and I'm not here?"

Vicki took his hand and squeezed it tightly. "Then we'll tell him that he has a loyal son who did everything possible to find him."

* * *

GABRIEL RETURNED TO the storage hut, lit a candle, and climbed down into the cellar. His father's body was still lying on the stone slab, still covered with the sheet of cotton muslin. Gabriel's shadow wavered on the wall as he pulled off the sheet. Matthew Corrigan's hair was long and gray, and he had deep lines etched into his forehead and at the corners of his mouth. When Gabriel was growing up everyone had said that he looked like his father, but it was only now that he could see the resemblance. Gabriel felt as if he were looking at his older self—weary from a lifetime of peering into the hearts of others.

Kneeling beside the body, Gabriel pressed his ear against his father's chest. He waited for several minutes, and then was startled to hear the faint thump of a single heartbeat. It felt as if his father were only a few feet away from him, calling from the shadows. Gabriel stood up, kissed his father's forehead, and climbed back up the stairs. As he was closing the trapdoor, Maya walked into the hut.

"Is your father all right?"

"No change." Gabriel walked over to the doorway and embraced her. For a brief moment, she gave in to her emotions, holding him tightly while he stroked her hair.

"Foley just arrived with his boat," she said. "Mother Blessing is walking down the pathway to the dock. You're supposed to follow her right away."

"And she knows about last night?"

"Of course she knows." The wind pushed against the half-open door. Maya stepped away from him and slammed it shut. "We made a mistake. I didn't honor my obligation."

"Stop talking like a Harlequin."

"I *am* a Harlequin, Gabriel. And I can't protect you unless I'm like Mother Blessing. Cold and rational."

"I don't believe that."

"I'm a Harlequin and you're a Traveller. It's time you started acting like one."

"What are you talking about?"

"Your father has crossed over and might not come back. Your brother is part of the Tabula. You're the one person everyone is hoping for. I know you have the power, Gabriel. Now you have to use it."

"I didn't ask for this."

"I didn't ask for my particular life either, but that's what I was given. Last night we were both trying to avoid our obligations. Mother Blessing is right. Love makes you foolish and weak."

Gabriel stepped forward and tried to embrace her. "Maya . . ."

"I accept who I am. And it's time you acknowledged your own responsibilities."

"So what am I supposed to do? Lead the Free Runners?"

"You could talk to them. That's a start. They admire you, Gabriel. When we went to Vine House, I could see that in their eyes."

"All right, I'll talk to them. But I want you with me."

Maya turned away from Gabriel so that he couldn't see her face. "Take care of yourself," she said in a strained voice, and then she was out the door and striding up the rocky slope, the wind whipping through her black hair.

* * *

GABRIEL GRABBED HIS shoulder bag and climbed down the rocky staircase to the dock area. Captain Foley was in his fishing boat, tinkering with the engine. Mother Blessing marched back and forth on the concrete slab.

"Maya gave me the keys to the car you left at Portmagee," she told Gabriel. "We'll drive north to a safe house in County Cavan. I need to call some of my contacts and see if—"

Gabriel interrupted her. "You can do what you want, but I'm returning to London."

Mother Blessing made sure that Captain Foley was still on his boat—too far away to hear the conversation. "You've accepted my protection, Gabriel. That means I make the choices."

"I have some friends in the city—Free Runners—and I want to talk to them."

"And what if I don't agree?"

"Are you afraid of the Tabula, Mother Blessing? Is that the problem?"

The Irish Harlequin frowned as she touched her black metal sword case. She looked like a pagan queen who had just been insulted by a commoner. "It's quite clear that they're afraid of me."

"Good. Because I'm going back to London. If you want to protect me, then you'll have to come along."

24

Sitting near a top-floor window in Vine House, Gabriel looked out at the small public park in the middle of Bonnington Square. It was about nine o'clock in the evening. After nightfall, a cold layer of fog had drifted off the Thames River and pushed its way through the narrow streets of South London. The streetlights around the square burned with a feeble light, like little bits of fire overcome by a colder, more pervasive power. No one was in the park, but every few minutes another small group of young men and women approached the house and knocked on the door.

Gabriel had been back in London for three days, staying at Winston Abosa's drum shop in Camden Market. He had asked Jugger and his friends for help, and they had responded immediately. The word was out, and Free Runners from every part of the country were coming to Vine House.

Jugger knocked twice on the door before poking his head in. The Free Runner looked excited and a little nervous. Gabriel could hear the sound of voices coming from the crowd downstairs.

"A lot of people are showing up," Jugger said. "We got crews coming in from Glasgow and Liverpool. Even your old pal Cutter came down from Manchester with his friends. Don't know how they found out about this."

"Is there going to be enough room?"

"Ice is acting like a games director at a holiday camp—telling people where to sit. Roland and Sebastian are stringing cable down the hallway. There're going to be speakers all over the house."

"Thanks, Jugger.".

The Free Runner adjusted his knit cap and gave Gabriel an embarrassed smile. "Listen, mate. We're friends, right? We can talk about anything."

"What's the problem?"

"It's that Irishwoman who's your bodyguard. The front door was crowded with people, so Roland went around the house and climbed over the wall into the garden. We do that all the time so we can come in through the kitchen. Well, quick as a flash, that Irishwoman is pointin' a twelve-round automatic at Roland's skull."

"Did she hurt him?"

"Nah. But he just about pissed in his pants. Swear to God, Gabriel. Maybe she could wait outside the house during your speech. I don't want her killing anybody tonight."

"Don't worry. We'll be out of here as soon as I'm done speaking."

"And then what?"

"I'm going to ask for some help and we'll see what happens. I want you to be the middleman between me and the people downstairs."

"No problem. I can handle that."

"I'm staying in Camden Market in an underground area called the catacombs. There's a drum shop there run by a man named Winston. He'll know how to find me."

"Sounds like a plan, mate." Jugger nodded solemnly. "Everyone wants to hear you, but give us a couple more minutes. I got to move some people around a bit."

The Free Runner left the garret and climbed back down the narrow staircase. Gabriel remained in the chair, looking out at the little garden in the middle of the square. According to Sebastian, the garden had once been a bombed-out building during World War Two and then a dumping ground for trash and old cars. Gradually, the community had come together, cleaned up the site, and planted a mixture of conventional shrubs and ivy plus more exotic tropical vegetation. There were palm trees and banana plants growing right next to English tea roses. Sebastian was convinced that Bonnington Square was a distinct ecological zone with its own particular climate.

The Free Runners had planted a vegetable garden behind Vine House, and you could see bushes and trees growing on the roof of every building around the square. Although there were thousands of closed-circuit television cameras all over London, the constant desire for a garden showed that the average citizen wanted a refuge that was separate from the Vast Machine. With friends and food and a bottle of wine, even a backyard garden felt large and expansive.

A few minutes later, Jugger knocked twice and opened the door. "You ready?" he asked.

Several Free Runners sat on the staircase and others were squeezed into the hallway. Mother Blessing stood in the living room near a table with a small microphone lying at the center. One of her Irish mercenaries, a tough-looking man with a white scar on the back of his neck, was directly outside the house.

Gabriel picked up the microphone and switched it on. A cord led to a stereo receiver that was attached to different speakers. He breathed deeply and heard the sound coming from out in the hallway.

"When I was in school, we were all handed a big history textbook on the first day of classes. I remember how hard it was to shove it into my backpack every afternoon. Every historical era had a color-coded section, and the teacher encouraged us to believe that—at a certain date—everyone stopped acting medieval and decided they were in the Renaissance.

"Of course, real history isn't like that. Different worldviews and different technologies can exist side by side. When a true innovation appears, most people aren't even aware of its power or implications for their own lives.

"One way to see history is that it's the story of a continual battle: a conflict between individuals with new ideas and those who want to control society. A few of you may have heard rumors about a powerful group of people called the Tabula. The Tabula have guided kings and governments toward their philosophy of control. They want to transform the world into a giant prison where the prisoner always assumes that he's being watched. Eventually each prisoner will accept his condition as reality.

"Some people aren't aware of what's going on. Others choose to be blind. But everyone here is a Free Runner. The buildings that surround us don't intimidate you. We climb the walls and jump the gaps."

Gabriel noticed that Cutter, the head of the Manchester Free Runners, was sitting against the wall with a plaster cast on his broken arm. "I respect all of you, and especially this man, Cutter. A London cab hit him a few weeks ago when we were racing and now he's here with his friends. A true Free Runner won't accept the conventional boundaries and limitations. It's not a 'sport' or a way to get on television. It's a choice we've made in our lives. A way to express what's in our hearts.

"Although some of us have rejected certain aspects of technology, we are all conscious of how the computer has changed the world. This truly is a new historical era: the Age of the Vast Machine. Surveillance cameras and scanners are everywhere. Soon the option of a private life will disappear. All these changes are justified by a pervasive culture of fear. The media is constantly shouting about some new threat to our lives. Our elected leaders encourage this fear as they take away our freedom.

"But Free Runners aren't frightened. Some of us try to live off the Grid. Others make small gestures of rebellion. Tonight I'm asking you for a larger commitment. I believe that the Tabula are planning a decisive step forward in the creation of their electronic prison. This isn't just a few more surveillance cameras or a modification of a scanner program. It's the final evolution of their plan.

"And what is that plan? That's the question. I'm asking you to sort through the rumors and see what's real. I need people who can talk to their friends, explore the Internet—listen to the voices carried by the wind." Gabriel pointed to Sebastian. "This man has designed the first of several underground Web sites. Send your information there and we'll begin to organize resistance.

"Remember that all of you can still make a choice.

You don't need to accept this new system of control and fear. We have the power to say no. We have the right to be free. Thank you."

No one applauded or cheered, but they seemed to support the Traveller as he left the room. People touched Gabriel's hand as he walked past them.

It was cold out on the street. Mother Blessing motioned to Brian, the Irish mercenary who was waiting on the sidewalk. "He's done. Let's go."

They got into the back of a delivery van while Brian slid into the driver's seat. A few seconds later the van was moving slowly, passing through the fog on Langley Lane.

Mother Blessing turned her head and stared at Gabriel. For the first time since he had met the Harlequin, she didn't treat him with complete contempt. "Are you going to make any more speeches?" she asked.

I'm still going to search for my father, Gabriel thought, but he kept that plan to himself. "Maybe. I don't know."

"You remind me of your father," Mother Blessing said. "Before we went to Ireland, I heard him speak a few times to groups in Portugal and Spain."

"Did he ever mention his family?"

"He told me that you and your brother met Thorn when you were little boys."

"And that's it? You guarded my father for several months and he never said anything else?"

Mother Blessing gazed out the window as they took a bridge across the river. "He said that both Harlequins and Travellers were on a long road, and sometimes it was difficult to see the light in the distance."

Camden Market was where Maya, Vicki, and Alice had stepped off the canal boat and entered London. In the Victorian era it had been used as a loading point for the coal and lumber carried on the boats. The warehouses and shipping yards had been converted into a sprawling market filled with little clothing shops and food stalls. It was a place to buy pottery and pastry, antique jewelry and army surplus uniforms.

Brian dropped them off on Chalk Farm Road, and Mother Blessing led Gabriel into the market. The immigrants who ran the food stalls were stacking up chairs and dumping chicken curry into bin bags. A few colored lights left over from Christmas swayed back and forth, but the edges of the market were dark, and rats scurried through the shadows.

Mother Blessing knew the location of every surveillance camera in the area, but occasionally she stopped and used a camera detector—a handheld device about the size of a mobile phone. Powerful diodes in the device emitted infrared light that was invisible to the human eye. The lens of a surveillance camera reflected this narrow-spectrum light so that it glowed like a miniature full moon in the device's viewing port. Gabriel was impressed by how quickly the Irish Harlequin was able to detect a hidden camera and then move out of its range.

The east end of the market was filled with old brick buildings that had once been used as stables for the horses that dragged carts and omnibuses through the streets of London. More old stables were in tunnels called the catacombs that ran beneath the elevated railroad tracks. Mother Blessing led Gabriel through a brick archway into the catacombs and they hurried past locked shops and artists' studios. For twenty feet, the tunnel walls were painted pink. In another area the walls were covered with aluminum foil. Finally, they reached the entrance to Winston Abosa's shop. The West African was sitting on the concrete floor stitching an animal skin to the top of a wooden drum.

Winston got to his feet and nodded to his guests. "Welcome back. I hope the speech was successful."

"Any customers?" Mother Blessing asked.

"No, madam. It was a very quiet evening."

They stepped around the African drums and ebony statues of tribal gods and pregnant women. Winston pushed back a cloth banner advertising a drum festival in Stonehenge, revealing a reinforced steel door set into the brick wall. He unlocked the door, and they entered an apartment of four rooms attached to a single hallway. The front room had a folding cot and two television monitors that showed images of the shop and the entrance to the catacombs. Gabriel continued down the hallway past a small kitchen and a bathroom to a windowless bedroom with a chair, desk, and cast-iron bed. This had been his home for the last three days.

Mother Blessing opened up the kitchen cabinet and took out a bottle of Irish whiskey. Winston followed Gabriel into the bedroom. "Are you hungry, Mr. Gabriel?"

"Not right now, Winston. I'll make some tea and toast later tonight."

"All the restaurants are still open. I could buy some take-out food."

"Thanks. But get what you want. I'm going to lie down for a while."

Winston shut the door, and Gabriel heard him talking to Mother Blessing. He lay down on the bed and gazed up at the single lightbulb that hung from a cord in the middle of the ceiling. The room was chilly and water oozed from a crack in the wall.

The energy Gabriel had felt during the speech had faded away. He realized that he was just like his father at this moment—both bodies were lying in a hidden room, guarded by a Harlequin. But a Traveller didn't have to accept these limitations. Light could search for Light in a parallel world. If he crossed over, he could try to find his father in the First Realm.

Gabriel got up and sat on the edge of the bed, with his hands on his lap and his feet on the concrete floor.

Relax, he told himself. In the first stage, crossing over felt like prayer or meditation. Closing his eyes, he imagined a body of Light within his physical body. He sensed its energy, tracing its outline inside his shoulders, arms, and wrists.

Breathe in. Breathe out. And suddenly, his left hand fell off his lap and flopped down on the mattress like a deadweight. When he opened his eyes, he saw that a ghost arm and hand had broken out of his body. The arm was black space with little points of light like a constellation in the night sky. Concentrating on this other reality, he moved the ghost hand higher, a little higher, and then all at once the Light cracked out of his body like a chrysalis emerging from its cocoon.

25

$\mathcal{S}$tanding on the porch of her two-story clapboard house, Rosaleen Magan watched Captain Thomas Foley stagger down a narrow side street in Portmagee. Her father had emptied five bottles of Guinness during supper, but Rosaleen hadn't complained about his drinking. The captain had helped raise six children, gone out fishing in every sort of weather, and had never started a fight at the village pub. *If he wants another bottle let him have it*, she thought. *It helps him forget about his arthritis.*

She walked into the kitchen and switched on the personal computer in the alcove near the pantry. Her husband was in Limerick for a training class, and her son was working as a cabinet-maker in America. In the summertime, her house was filled with tourists, but in the cold months even the bird-watchers stayed away. Rosaleen preferred the quiet season even though very little happened during the day. Her oldest sister worked for the post office in Dublin. She was always prattling on about the latest movie or a play she saw at the Abbey Theatre. Once she was even rude enough to call Portmagee "a sleepy little village."

Tonight, Rosaleen had enough news for a decent e-mail. There certainly had been some mysterious activities on Skellig Columba, and her father was the only true source of information about the island.

Rosaleen reminded her sister that a year ago an older man named Matthew had gone out to the island with a red-haired Irishwoman who had suddenly become the leader of the Poor Clares. A few days ago, an even more exotic group arrived at Portmagee—a little Chinese girl, a black woman, an American man, and a young woman with a British accent. One day after taking them out to the island, their father was told to transport the so-called abbess and the American man back to the mainland. *Whatever is going on is certainly strange*, Rosaleen typed. *This might not be Dublin, but we do have mysteries in Portmagee.*

Hidden within the computer was a spy worm that had infected millions of computers throughout the world. The worm waited like a tropical snake at the bottom of a dark lagoon. When certain words and names appeared, the program detected the new information, copied it, and then slithered off through the Internet to find its master.

* * *

VICKI FRASER ENJOYED waking up in the dormitory room of the convent's cooking hut. Her face was always cold, but the rest of her body was wrapped within a goose-down quilt. Alice was asleep in the corner and Maya was just a few feet away, her Harlequin sword within reach.

The cooking hut was quiet in the morning. When the sun hit the building at a certain angle, a yellowish-white beam of light came through the slit window and slowly moved across the floor. Vicki thought about Hollis and imagined him lying beside her. His body was covered with scars from all kinds of fights and confrontations, but when she looked into his eyes she saw the gentleness there. Now that they were safe on the island, Vicki had the time to think about him. Hollis was a very good fighter, but she was worried that his confidence would get him into trouble.

Around six o'clock, Sister Joan returned to the hut and began banging kettles around as she brewed tea. The three other nuns arrived half an hour later, and everyone ate breakfast together. A large jar of honey was in the middle of the dining room table. Holding the jar with both hands, Alice liked to pour gooey shapes on the surface of her porridge.

The little girl still refused to talk, but she seemed

to enjoy living on the island. She helped the nuns with their daily tasks, picked flowers and stuffed them into empty marmalade jars, and explored the island with a stick for a Harlequin sword. Once she guided Vicki down a narrow path cut into the side of a cliff. It was a hundred yards straight down to the rocky shore, where waves surged around the rocks.

A little cave was at the end of the path. It had a stone bench covered with moss and a little altar with a Celtic cross. "This looks like a hermit's cave," Vicki said, and Alice seemed pleased with this idea. The two of them sat just outside the cave's narrow opening while the little girl threw pebbles at the horizon.

Alice treated Vicki like an older sister who was in charge of brushing her hair. She adored the nuns, who read her adventure books and baked raisin cakes for her tea. One evening, she even lay on a bench in the chapel with her head on Sister Joan's lap. Maya was in a different category for the little girl; she wasn't Alice's mother, sister, or friend. Sometimes, Vicki watched them glance at each other with an odd sort of understanding. They seemed to share the same feeling of loneliness no matter how many people were in the room.

Twice a day, Maya visited Matthew Corrigan's body in the chamber beneath the supply hut. The rest of the time she kept to herself, following the stone pathway to the dock and looking out at the sea. Vicki didn't dare ask what had happened, but it was clear that Maya had done something that gave Mother Blessing an excuse to take Gabriel and leave Skellig Columba.

On their eighth day on the island, Vicki woke up early in the morning and saw the Harlequin kneeling beside her. "Come downstairs," Maya whispered. "I need to talk to you."

Wrapped in a black shawl, Vicki went downstairs to the dining area, where there was a long table with two benches. Maya had started a peat fire in the stove and it gave off a faint heat. Vicki sat on one of the benches and leaned against the wall. A large candle burned in the middle of the table, and shadows passed across Maya's face when she circled the room.

"Remember when we first arrived in Portmagee and Gabriel and I went to find Captain Foley? After we left his house, we sat down on that bench by the shore, and I swore that I would stand by Gabriel—no matter what happened."

Vicki nodded and spoke softly. "That must have been difficult. You once told me that Harlequins don't like to make promises . . ."

"It wasn't difficult at all. I wanted to say those words—more than anything." Maya approached the candle and stared at the flame. "I made a promise to Gabriel and I intend to keep it."

"What do you mean?"

"I'm going to London to find Gabriel. No one can do a better job of protecting him."

"What about Mother Blessing?"

"She attacked me in the chapel, but that was just to get my attention. I'm not going to let her intimidate me again." With an angry look in her eyes, Maya resumed pacing. "I'll fight her or Linden or anyone else who tries to keep me from Gabriel. Different Harlequins have been ordering me around since I was a child, but those days have passed."

Mother Blessing will kill you, Vicki thought. But she stayed silent. Maya's face seemed to glow with a fierce energy.

"If this promise is important to you, then go to London. Don't worry about Matthew Corrigan. I'll be here if he crosses back over to this world."

"I'm concerned about my obligation, Vicki. I did agree to stay and protect him."

"It's safe on the island," Vicki said. "Even Mother Blessing said that. She was here almost six months and didn't even see a birdwatcher."

"What if something happens?"

"Then I'll solve the problem. I'm just like you, Maya. I'm not a little girl anymore."

Maya stopped pacing and smiled slightly. "Yes. You've changed, too."

"Foley arrives tomorrow morning with the supplies and he can take you back to the mainland. But how are you going to find Gabriel in London?"

"He's probably going to contact the Free Runners.

I've been to their house on the South Bank so I'll go there and speak to Gabriel's friends."

"Take all the money in my knapsack. We can't use it on the island."

"Maya . . ." said a wispy voice, and Vicki was surprised to see Alice Chen standing near the staircase. The child had spoken for the first time since she had come into their lives. Her mouth moved in silence as if she didn't believe that sound could emerge from her throat. Then she spoke again. "Please don't go, Maya. I like you here."

Maya's face became the usual Harlequin mask, but then her mouth softened and she allowed herself to feel an emotion other than anger. Vicki had watched Maya act brave so many times during the last few months. But the bravest moment was now—right now—when she crossed the room and embraced the little girl.

* * *

ONE OF THE British mercenaries who had flown to Ireland with Boone opened the side door to the helicopter's cargo bay. Boone was sitting on a steel bench working on his laptop computer.

"Excuse me, sir. But you wanted to know when Mr. Harkness arrived."

"That's correct. Thank you."

Boone pulled on his jacket and got out of the

helicopter. The two mercenaries and the pilot stood on the tarmac, smoking cigarettes and talking about job offers in Moscow. During the last three hours, everyone had been waiting at a small airfield outside of Killarney. It was late in the afternoon, and the amateur pilots who had practiced their crosswind landings had tied down their planes and driven home. The airfield was in the middle of the Irish countryside, surrounded by fenced-in pasture. Sheep grazed on the north side of the field; dairy cattle were south of the Quonset huts. There was a pleasant smell of cut grass in the air.

A small pickup with a steel shell covering the truck bed was parked about two hundred yards away, directly inside the entrance gate. Mr. Harkness got out of the truck as Boone walked across the tarmac. Boone had met the retired zookeeper in Prague when they had captured, interrogated, and killed Maya's father. The old man had pale skin and bad teeth. He wore a tweed sports coat and a stained regimental tie.

Boone had hired and supervised a great many mercenaries, but Harkness made him uncomfortable. The old man seemed to enjoy handling the splicers. It was his job, of course. But Harkness got excited when he talked about these genetic distortions created by the Brethren's research scientists. He was a man without power who now controlled something that was highly dangerous. Boone always felt as if he were dealing with a beggar who was juggling a live grenade.

"Good evening, Mr. Boone. A pleasure to meet you again." Harkness bobbed his head up and down respectfully.

"Any problems at the Dublin airport?"

"No, sir. All the papers were stamped and signed properly by our friends at the Dublin Zoo. Customs didn't even look in the cages."

"Were there any injuries during transit?"

"Every specimen looks healthy. You want to see for yourself?"

Boone was silent while Harkness opened up the back of the truck's shell. Four plastic cargo containers—the size of airplane dog carriers—were in back. The airholes were covered with a thick wire mesh, but all four boxes emitted a foul odor of urine and rotten food.

"I fed them upon arrival at the airport, but that was all. Hunger is always best for what they might have to do."

Harkness slapped the flat of his hand on the top of a container. A raspy barking noise came from within the box, and the three other splicers answered. The sheep grazing in the nearby field heard the sound. They bleated and ran in the opposite direction.

"Nasty creatures," Harkness said, showing his stained teeth.

"Do they ever fight one another?"

"Not often. These animals are genetically engineered to attack, but they have the same general characteristics of their species. This one in the green carrier is the captain and the other three are his junior officers. You don't attack your leader unless you know you can kill him."

Boone paused and looked straight at Harkness. "And you can handle them?"

"Yes, sir. I've got some heavy pincers in the truck and an electric cattle prod. It shouldn't be a problem."

"What happens after we let them out?"

"Well, Mr. Boone . . ." Harkness looked down at his shoes. "A shotgun is the best tool once they've done their job."

Both men stopped talking when a second helicopter approached from the east. The chopper circled the airfield and then settled onto the grass. Boone left Harkness and walked across the tarmac to the new arrivals. The side door opened, a mercenary lowered a short ladder, and Michael Corrigan appeared in the doorway. "Good afternoon!" he said cheerfully.

Boone still hadn't decided if he should call the Traveller Michael or Mr. Corrigan. He nodded politely. "How was the flight?"

"No problem at all. Are you ready to go, Boone?"

Yes, they were ready. But it bothered Boone that someone other than General Nash could ask that question. "I think we should wait until night," he said. "It's easier to find a target when they're inside a building."

* * *

AFTER A LIGHT supper of lentil soup and crackers, the Poor Clares left the warmth of the cooking hut and went down to the chapel. Alice followed them. Since Maya had left the island, the little girl had resumed her self-imposed silence, but she seemed to enjoy hearing the prayers sung in Latin. Sometimes her lips moved as if she were singing along with the nuns in her mind. *Kyrie eleison. Kyrie eleison. Lord have mercy on us all.*

Vicki stayed behind to wash the dishes. Sometime after they'd gone, she realized that Alice had left her jacket beneath the bench near the front door. The wind had picked up again, blowing from the east, and it would be cold in the chapel. Leaving the dishes in the stone sink, Vicki grabbed the child's jacket and hurried outside.

The island was a closed world. Once you hiked around it a few times, you realized that the only way to break free of this particular reality was to look upward at the heavens. In Los Angeles, a smudged layer of smog concealed most of the stars, but the air was clean above the island. Standing near the cooking hut, Vicki looked up at the sliver of a new moon and the luminous dust of the Milky Way. She could hear the distant cry of a seabird that was answered by another.

Four red lights appeared in the east; they were like twin sets of headlights, drifting through the night sky. *Airplanes*, she thought. *No, it's two helicopters*. Within a few seconds, Vicki realized what was about to happen. She had been at the church compound northwest of Los Angeles when the Tabula had attacked the same way.

Trying not to stumble over the rough chunks of limestone, she hurried down to the lower ledge and entered the boat-shaped chapel. The singing stopped immediately when she slammed open the oak door. Alice stood up and glanced around the narrow room.

"The Tabula are coming in two helicopters," Vicki said. "You need to get out of here and hide."

Sister Maura looked terrified. "Where? In the storage hut with Matthew?"

"Take them to the hermit's cave, Alice. Can you find it in the dark?"

The little girl nodded. She took Sister Joan's hand and pulled the cook toward the doorway.

"What about you, Vicki?"

"I'll join you there. First I need to make sure that the Traveller is safe."

Alice stared at Vicki for few seconds and then she was gone, leading the nuns past the chapel and into the night. Vicki returned to the middle ledge and saw that the helicopters were much closer now—the red safety lights hovering over the island like malevolent spirits. She could hear the dull *thump-thump-thump* of the revolving blades pushing the air.

Inside the storage hut, she lit a candle and pulled up the trapdoor. Vicki almost believed that Matthew Corrigan could sense the approaching danger. Perhaps the Light would return to his body and she would find Gabriel's father sitting up in his tomb. Once the trapdoor was open it took her only a few seconds to climb down the stairs and see that the Traveller was still motionless beneath the thin muslin sheet.

Quickly, she returned upstairs, lowered the trapdoor, and covered it with a plastic cloth. She placed an old outboard motor on the cloth, and then scattered around a few tools as if someone were trying to repair it. "Protect your servant Matthew," she prayed. "Please save him from destruction."

That was all she could do. It was time to join the others in the cave. But when she got outside she saw flashlight beams on the upper ledge and the dark shapes of Tabula mercenaries silhouetted against the stars. Vicki slipped back into the storage hut and shoved the steel crossbar into its holding bracket. She had told Maya that she would protect the Traveller. It was a promise. An obligation. The Harlequin meaning of that word came to her with a terrible force as she pushed a heavy storage container up against the oak door.

More than a hundred years ago, a Harlequin

named Lion of the Temple had been captured, tortured, and murdered alongside the Prophet, Isaac T. Jones. Vicki and a small group within her church believed that they had never repaid this sacrifice. Why had God brought Maya and Gabriel into her life? Why had she ended up on this island, guarding a Traveller? *Debt Not Paid*, she thought. *Debt Not Paid*.

* * *

THREE OF THE beehive huts were empty, but the fourth hut was locked and the mercenaries hadn't been able to force open the door. Before coming to Skellig Columba, Boone had read all the available data on the island and knew that the ancient buildings had heavy stone walls. The walls made it difficult to use an infrared scanner, so Boone's team had brought along a portable backscatter device.

When the two helicopters had touched down on the island, everyone had jumped out with a desire to capture or destroy. Now this aggressive impulse had melted away. The armed men spoke in low voices as their flashlight beams cut across the rocky landscape. Two men came down the slope with the equipment from the helicopter. One part of the backscatter device looked like a refractor telescope on a tripod. It shot X-rays through the target, and a small parabolic dish captured the resulting photons.

Hospital X-ray machines worked on the principle that objects with a greater density absorbed more X-rays than objects with a lesser density. The backscatter device worked because X-ray photons moved in a different way through various kinds of materials. Substances with lower atomic numbers—like human flesh—created a different image than plastic or steel. The citizens living within the Vast Machine didn't realize that backscatter devices were hidden throughout major airports and that security personnel were peering beneath the clothes of passengers.

Michael Corrigan came up from the chapel with two mercenaries. He was wearing a warm-up jacket and running shoes, as if he were going to jog around the island. "No one is in the chapel, Boone. What about this building?"

"We're about to find out." Boone attached his laptop computer to the backscatter receiver, turned on the device, and sat down on a chunk of limestone. Michael and a few other men stood behind them. It took a few seconds for the gray-and-white backscatter image to appear. A woman was inside the storage hut stacking boxes against the door. *It's not one of the Poor Clares*, Boone thought. The backscatter would have displayed a shadowy hint of the nun's robes.

"Take a look," Boone said to Michael. "There's one person in the building. A woman. Right now she's blocking the doorway."

Michael looked angry. "What about my father? You told me that either Gabriel or my father was on this island."

"That was the information I received," Boone said. He rotated the image to check different angles of the room. "This could be Maya. She's the Harlequin who was guarding your brother in New York and—"

"I know who she is," Michael said. "Don't forget, I saw her the night she attacked the research center."

"Perhaps we can question her."

"She'll kill your men and kill herself unless we can force her out of the building. Ask Mr. Harkness to come down with the splicers."

Boone tried not to sound annoyed. "It's not necessary at this point."

"I'll decide what's necessary, Boone. I did some research before Mrs. Brewster and I agreed to this operation. These old buildings have incredibly thick walls. That's why I wanted Mr. Harkness to be part of the team."

* * *

WHEN THE MEDIEVAL monks had piled up stones to construct each building, they had left a few gaps in the upper walls to let out smoke. Many years later, these airholes had been turned into windows on the top floor of the storage hut. The windows were between twelve and sixteen inches in diameter. Even if the men from the helicopter smashed the glass, they wouldn't be able to crawl inside.

Standing in the shadows, Vicki heard the door handle rattle, and someone hammered his fist on the door. Silence. Then there was a loud slamming sound. The oak door vibrated and strained against the heavy steel crossbar, but the brackets were cemented into the walls. Vicki remembered hearing the nuns talk about the Viking raids on the Irish monasteries during the twelfth century. If the monks couldn't flee into the countryside, they would retreat into a stone tower with their gold crosses and jeweled reliquaries. They would pray—and wait—as the Norsemen tried to break in.

Vicki pushed more storage containers over to the door and stacked them up on top of one another. The pounding started again and then stopped. She walked over to the base of the stairs and saw a flashlight beam jabbing through one of the little round windows on the upper floor.

In his letter from Meridian, Mississippi, Isaac Jones had told the faithful to *Look into yourself and find the well that will never go dry. Our hearts overflow with bravery and love* . . .

Just a few months ago, Vicki stood in the Los Angeles airport—a church girl feeling timid and scared as she waited to meet a Harlequin. She had been tested many times since that first moment, but had never run away. Isaac Jones was right. The bravery had always been within her.

A sharp cracking sound came from upstairs as someone shattered a window. Shards of broken glass fell onto the floor. *Can they get in?* Vicki thought. No, only a child could crawl through that opening. She waited for the sound of a gunshot or an explosion. Instead she heard a raspy screech that sounded like a bird being killed.

"God save me. Please, save me . . ." Vicki whispered. She searched the room for a weapon and found two fishing rods, a bag of cement, and an empty fuel can. Frantically, she pushed these useless objects to one side and discovered some garden tools stacked against the wall. At the bottom of the pile was a mud-crusted shovel.

Vicki heard a low grunting sound and retreated into a corner. There was a figure on the staircase—a squat little dwarf with a potbelly and broad shoulders. The dwarf got halfway down the stairs and then turned his face in her direction. That was when she realized that it wasn't a human at all, but some kind of an animal with a dog's black muzzle.

Shrieking and chattering, the animal leaped over the staircase banister and ran toward her. Vicki raised the shovel up to her shoulder. When the animal jumped from the top of a carrying case, she swung her weapon as hard as she could—striking it in the middle of its chest. The animal fell back onto the floor, but it scrabbled to its feet immediately and leaped forward, grabbing her legs with five-fingered hands.

Vicki jabbed the shovel downward and the tip hit the creature's neck. Shrieks filled the room as she began using the shovel like a club, swinging it down again and again. Finally the animal rolled over on its back and bared its teeth. Blood trickled out of its mouth and it moved its arms stiffly. The animal tried to get up, but she kept hitting it with the shovel. Finally, it stopped moving. Dead.

Two of the candles had fallen over and sputtered out. Vicki picked up the only candle still burning and examined her attacker. She was surprised to discover that it was a small baboon with yellowish-brown fur. The monkey had cheek pouches, a long, hairless snout, and powerful arms and legs. Its close-set eyes were still open, and it looked as if the dead creature were glaring at her.

Vicki remembered Hollis talking about the animals that attacked him in his Los Angeles home. This was the same kind of thing. Hollis had called the animals . . . splicers. The baboon's chromosomes had been manipulated and spliced together by the Tabula scientists, creating a genetic hybrid whose only desire was to attack and kill.

The men outside smashed a second upstairs window. Vicki held the shovel with two hands and moved quietly around the room. Her left leg was bleeding from a cut. Blood dripped from the cuffs of her pants, and her shoes smeared it across the floor. For a minute or so nothing happened; then the light from the single candle flickered slightly and three splicers came down the stairs. They stopped, sniffed the air, and the leader made a raspy barking sound.

There were too many of them and they were too strong. Vicki knew that she was going to die. Thoughts appeared in her mind like photographs in an old scrapbook—her mother, school, and friends—so many things that had once seemed so important were already fading away. Her clearest memory was of Hollis, and Vicki felt a deep sadness that she would never see him again. *I love you*, she thought. *Know this forever. My love will never be destroyed.*

The splicers smelled her blood. They leaped off the staircase and came toward her at a furious speed. The animals were shrieking and the sound filled the little room. Their sharp teeth reminded her of wolves. *No chance*, Vicki thought. *No chance at all*. But she raised the shovel and met the attack.

26

Sophia Briggs had told Gabriel that every living thing contained an eternal, indestructible energy called the Light. When people died, their Light returned to the energy that was present throughout the universe. But only Travellers were able to send their Light to different realms and then return to their living bodies.

The six different realms, as Sophia explained it, were parallel worlds separated by a series of barriers made of water, earth, fire, and air. Gabriel had found the different passageways through each barrier when he first learned how to cross over. And now, while his body remained in the back room of a Camden Market drum shop, he felt as if he were floating through space, surrounded by an infinite darkness. Gabriel thought about his father, and he suddenly felt as if he were propelled forward into the unknown, guided by the intensity of his desire to find this one person.

* * *

THE FLOATING SENSATION vanished; he felt wet dirt and sharp pieces of gravel under his hands. Opening his eyes, he saw that he was lying on his back a few feet away from a large river.

He got up quickly and looked around him for any sign of danger. He was standing on a muddy slope littered with wrecked automobiles and rusty pieces of machinery. The blackened ruins of several buildings were twenty feet above him, up on the edge of the riverbank. Gabriel wasn't sure if it was day or night, because the sky was covered with a layer of yellowish-gray clouds that occasionally broke apart to show a lighter shade of ash gray. He had seen clouds like this a few times in Los Angeles when the smoke from a hillside brushfire had combined with air pollution to blot out the sun.

A collapsed bridge was a half mile upriver. It looked as if the structure had been blown up with explosives or bombed from the sky. Brick pilings and two graceful arches remained in the water. They held up twisted girders and the fragment of a road.

Gabriel took a few cautious steps toward the river and tried to remember what Hollis had said back in New York when he was talking to Naz, their guide through the subway tunnels. Hollis and Vicki were always quoting from the letters of Isaac Jones, and

Gabriel hadn't been paying much attention. It was something about the wrong path leading you to a dark river.

Well, Isaac Jones was right about this place, he thought. This particular river was as black as oil except for little bits of dirty white foam floating on the surface. It had a sharp, acidic odor, as if it had been tainted with chemicals. Gabriel knelt and scooped up some of the water in his palm, then flicked it away when his skin began to burn.

Gabriel stood up again and looked around to make sure he was safe. For a moment, he wished he had brought along the talisman sword his father had given him, but Maya had kept it with her. *You don't need a weapon*, he told himself. *You're not here to kill someone*. He would move carefully and try to stay out of sight. Perhaps he would find his father while searching for the passageway back to his own world.

He was fairly sure he had reached the First Realm. In other cultures it was known as the Underworld, Hades, Sheol—hell. The story of Orpheus and Eurydice was a Greek myth taught to schoolchildren, but also showed the experiences of an unnamed Traveller who had once visited this place. It was important not to eat any of the food—even if offered by a powerful leader. And when you finally reached the passageway, you should never look back.

In the confession of Saint Columba translated by Gabriel's father, the Irish saint described hell as a city with human inhabitants. The citizens of hell told Columba about other cities, known by rumor or seen in the distance. Gabriel knew that he could be killed or imprisoned in this place. He decided to stay near the river and walk away from the wrecked bridge. If he reached a barrier or saw something that looked dangerous, he would turn around and follow the river back to this starting place.

The slope was steep and slippery; it took him several minutes to reach the brick shell of a destroyed building. A flickering light came from inside the structure, and he wondered if it was still burning. Cautiously, he peered through the window frame. Instead of a fire, he saw a dark orange flame spurting from what looked like a broken gas pipe. This room had once been a kitchen, but the stove and sink were now covered with soot, and the only furniture was a wooden table propped up with a single leg. Shoes made a scuffling sound. Before he could react, an arm grabbed him from behind while a hand put a blade against his throat.

"Give me your food," a man whispered. The voice had a breathless, hesitant tone, as if the speaker couldn't believe his own words. "Give me all your food and you won't die."

"All right," Gabriel said, starting to turn.

"Don't move! Don't look at me!"

"I'm not trying to look at you," Gabriel said. "My food is down by the bridge. It's hidden in a secret place."

"No one has secrets from *me*," the voice said with a little more confidence. "Take me to the food. Hurry up now."

With the knife still pressed against his neck, Gabriel moved slowly away from the building. When he reached the top of the riverbank, he took a few steps down the slope so that he was slightly lower than his assailant.

Gabriel grabbed the man's wrist, pushing it downward and twisting it to the right. The man shrieked with pain, let go of the knife, and fell forward onto the slope. Gabriel picked up the blade. It was an improvised weapon that looked like a steel bracket that had been sharpened on a stone.

Gabriel stood over an impossibly thin man cowering on the ground. The man had greasy hair and a scraggly black beard. He wore torn pants—rags, almost—and a frayed tweed jacket. The bony fingers of his left hand kept stroking his soiled green necktie, as if this improbable piece of clothing could somehow save his life.

"I do apologize," gasped the thin man. "I shouldn't have done that." He folded his spindly arms across his chest and ducked his head. "Cockroaches don't do such things. Cockroaches shouldn't act like wolves."

Gabriel raised the knife. "You're going to talk to me. Understand? Don't make me use this . . ."

"I understand, sir. Look!" The man raised his grimy hands in the air and stood frozen. "I'm not moving."

"What's your name?"

"My name, sir? Pickering. Yes, it's Pickering. I did have a first name once, but I've forgotten it. Should have written it down." He laughed nervously. "It was Thomas, Theodore—something that started with a T. But Pickering is correct. No question about that. It's always been 'Come here, Pickering. Do this, Pickering.' And I know how to obey, sir. Ask anyone."

"All right, Pickering. So where are we? What's the name of this place?"

Pickering looked surprised that anyone would ask such a question. His eyes darted left and right nervously. "We're on the Island. That's what we call it. The Island."

Gabriel looked up the river at the wrecked bridge. For some reason, he had assumed that he could leave this area and find a safe place to hide. If that was the only bridge—or if all of them were destroyed—then he was trapped on this island until he found a passageway. Was that what had happened to his father? Was he wandering this shadowy world, looking for a way home?

"You must be a visitor, sir." Pickering considered this a moment, then spoke in a high, wheezy rush. "That is . . . I don't mean to imply you're not a wolf, sir. Nothing of the kind! Clearly you're a strong wolf indeed. Not a cockroach. Not at all."

"I'm not sure I know what you mean. I am a visitor.

And I'm searching for another visitor like me—an older man."

"Maybe I could help you," Pickering said. "Yes, of course. I'm just the one to help you." He stood up and smoothed his green necktie. "I've been all over the Island. I've seen everything."

Gabriel thrust the homemade knife into his belt. "If you help me, I'll protect you. I'll be your friend."

Pickering's lips quivered as he whispered to himself, "A friend. Yes, of course. A friend . . ." It sounded as if he were saying the word for the first time.

Something exploded in the city—a dull thumping noise—and Pickering began to scramble back up the slope. "With all due respect, sir—we can't stay here. A patrol is coming. Very unpleasant. Please follow me."

Pickering had called himself a "cockroach," and he moved as quickly as an insect that had just been startled by a bright light. Entering one of the destroyed buildings, he passed through a maze of rooms filled with discarded furniture and piles of rubble. At one point, Gabriel realized that he had just stepped on some bones from a human skeleton. There was no time to figure out what had happened. "Watch your step, sir. But don't stop. We can't stop." And Gabriel followed the thin man through a doorway and onto the street.

He was startled by the light that came from an enormous gas flare that roared up from a crack in the pavement. The orange flame wavered back and forth like a malevolent spirit. Smoke from this fire left a sticky black residue that covered the walls of the surrounding buildings as well as the shell of a smashed taxicab.

Gabriel stopped moving and stood in the middle of the street. Pickering reached the opposite sidewalk. He waggled his hands frantically like a mother coaxing her child forward. "A little faster, my friend. *Please*. A patrol is coming. We need to hide."

"What patrol?" Gabriel asked, but Pickering had already disappeared through a doorway. The Traveller sprinted to catch up with his ragged guide and followed him through empty rooms to another street. He tried to imagine what the city had looked like before its destruction. The white buildings were four or five stories high, with flat roofs and balconies outside many of the windows. A twisted steel awning covered the broken tables of what had once been a sidewalk café. Gabriel had seen cities like this in movies and magazines. It resembled the provincial capital of a tropical country—the sort of place where people went to the beach during the day, then ate supper late in the evening.

Now every window had been smashed, and most of the doors had been ripped off their hinges. Attached by a few bolts, an elaborate iron balcony clung to the side of a building like a living creature trying not to fall into the street. Every wall was covered with graffiti. Gabriel saw numbers, names, and words written in block letters. Crudely drawn arrows pointed toward some unknown destination.

Pickering ducked inside a new building and began to move cautiously. A few times he stopped and listened, not moving until he was certain they were alone. Gabriel followed his guide up a marble staircase and down a hallway to a room where a half-burned mattress was leaning against the wall. Pickering pushed the mattress to one side, revealing a hidden doorway. They entered a room where the two windows were covered with plywood boards. The only light came from a small gas flare burning from a copper pipe that had been ripped out of the wall.

While Pickering pulled the burned mattress back across the doorway, Gabriel looked around the room. It was filled with trash that Pickering had collected during his explorations around the city. There were empty glass bottles, a stack of moldy blankets, a green easy chair with only two legs, and several cracked mirrors. Gabriel thought that the wallpaper was peeling; then he realized that Pickering had pinned up illustrations from a dress pattern book. The women in the faded drawings wore the floor-length skirts and high-necked blouses from a hundred years ago.

"Is this where you live?"

Pickering gazed at his drawings on the wall and spoke without a hint of irony. "I hope you find it comfortable, sir. My home sweet home."

"Have you always lived in this building? Were you born here?"

"What is your name, my friend? Can you tell me? Friends should use names with each other."

"Gabriel."

"Sit down, Gabriel. You are my guest. Please sit down."

Gabriel sat in the easy chair. The green fabric gave off a musty, stale odor. Pickering seemed both nervous and pleased that he had another person in his home. Like a diligent housekeeper, he kept moving around the room, picking up pieces of trash and arranging them in tidy little piles.

"No one was born on the Island. We all just woke up here one morning. We had apartments and clothes and food in our refrigerators. When we pressed a switch, the light went on. When we turned the tap, water came from the faucet. We had jobs, too. On my bedroom dresser, I had keys to a shop a few blocks away from here." Pickering smiled blissfully, almost overcome by the memory. "I was *Mr.* Pickering, a ladies' dressmaker. There were bolts of expensive fabric in my store. I wasn't an ordinary tailor. That's clear."

"But didn't you wonder why you were here?"

"That first morning was a magical time because— for a few hours—everyone thought that they were in a special place. People explored the whole Island, examining the different buildings and the destroyed bridge." For the first time, Gabriel glimpsed a hint of sensitivity and intelligence behind the fear. "That was such a happy day, Gabriel. You can't believe how happy. Because all of us believed that we were in a wonderful place. Some even suggested that we had been transported to heaven."

"But couldn't you remember your parents or your childhood?"

"There are no personal memories earlier than that first day. A few dreams. That's all. Everyone here can write words and add numbers. We can use tools and drive cars. But no one remembers being taught these skills."

"So the city wasn't destroyed that first day?"

"Of course not." Pickering picked up some empty wine bottles and placed them against the wall. "There was electric light. All the cars had gasoline. That afternoon people were talking about organizing a government and repairing the bridge. If you stood on a rooftop, you could see that the Island was in the middle of an enormous river. Another shore was just a few miles away."

"And then what happened?"

"The fighting started that evening—a few men kicking and punching one another while the rest of us watched like children learning a new game. By dawn of the next day, everyone began killing." Pickering looked almost proud of himself. "Even I killed a man who was trying to break into my shop. I used my scissors."

"But why did people destroy their own houses?"

"The city was divided into sectors ruled by different warlords. There were checkpoints and borders and dead zones. This was the Green Sector for a long time. Our warlord was a man named Vinnick until his second in command killed him."

"And how long did the fighting last?"

"There are no calendars on the Island, and all the clocks have been destroyed. People used to count days, but then different groups came up with different numbers and, of course, they fought about who was right. For a while, our Green Sector had a treaty with the Red Sector, but we made a secret alliance and betrayed them to the Blues. There were handguns and rifles in the beginning, and then the bullets were gone and people had to make their own weapons. Finally, the warlords were killed and their armies melted away. Now there is a commissioner who sends out patrols."

"But why couldn't everyone work out some kind of agreement?"

Pickering laughed without thinking, then looked frightened. "I don't mean to offend, sir. My friend Gabriel. Don't be angry. Your question was just . . . unexpected."

"I'm not angry."

"In the time of the warlords, people began to say

that the fighting would go on until a certain number of people had survived. We argued about the number. Was it ninety-nine survivors or thirteen or three? No one knows. But we believe these survivors will find a way to leave this place and the rest of us will be reborn to suffer again."

"So how many people are left?"

"Maybe ten percent of the original population. Some of us are cockroaches. We hide in the walls and beneath the floors—and survive. People who don't hide are called wolves. They walk around the city with their patrols and kill everyone they see."

"And that's why you hide?"

"Yes!" Pickering looked confident. "With all my heart, I can assure you the cockroaches will outlast the wolves."

"Look, I'm not part of this war and I don't want to be on anyone's side. I'm searching for another visitor. That's all."

"I understand, Gabriel." Pickering picked up a cracked bathroom sink and placed it in one corner of the room. "Please accept my hospitality. Stay here while I search for your visitor. Do not risk yourself, my friend. If a patrol finds you, the wolves will kill you in the street."

Before Gabriel could react, Pickering had pushed the burned mattress to one side, slipped through the gap, and then replaced the barrier. Gabriel remained in the easy chair thinking about everything he had seen since he stood up beside the river. The violent souls in this realm would be trapped here forever in an endless cycle of rage and destruction. But there was nothing unusual about hell. His own world had already been given glimpses of its fury.

The gas flare burning from the slender copper pipe seemed to use all the oxygen in the room. Gabriel was sweating and his mouth was dry. He knew that he shouldn't eat food in this place, but he would need to find a source of water.

Gabriel stood up, pushed the mattress away, and left Pickering's hiding place. As he began to explore the building, he realized that it had once been divided up into offices. Desks and chairs, file cabinets and old-fashioned typewriters had been abandoned, and now everything was covered with a fine white dust. Who had worked here? Had they left their apartments that first morning and gone to their jobs with a vague feeling that all this was just an extension of their dreams?

Still searching for water, he found a shattered window and looked down at the street. Two soot-covered automobiles were smashed together, their hoods crumpled up like crushed boxes. Pickering came around the corner, and Gabriel stepped back into the shadows. The thin man stopped and looked over his shoulder as if he were waiting for someone.

A few seconds later, five men appeared. If Pickering called himself a cockroach, then these men were obviously the wolves. They wore an odd assortment of clothes gathered from different sources. A blond man with braided hair wore bush shorts and a black tuxedo jacket with satin lapels. He walked beside a black man wearing a white lab coat. The wolves were armed with homemade weapons—clubs, swords, axes, and knives.

Gabriel left the room immediately, took a wrong turn, and ended up in another suite of deserted offices. By the time he reached the marble staircase, he could hear Pickering's breathless voice coming from the ground floor.

"This way, everyone. This way."

Gabriel continued up the staircase to the third floor. Looking down the stairwell, he saw a flash of orange fire. One of the wolves had just lit a torch crudely made from a table leg wrapped with tar-covered rags.

"I didn't lie to you," Pickering said. "He was here. Look, he's gone upstairs. Can't you see?"

Gabriel realized that he had left footprints in the fine white dust that covered the staircase. The hallway behind him was also covered with dust. No matter where he stepped, the wolves would be able to track him down.

Can't stay here, he thought, and continued up the staircase. The stairs ended on the fifth floor. He passed through a steel fire door hanging from one hinge and found himself on the roof. The yellowish-gray clouds that covered the sky had turned dark and billowy, as if a malignant rain were about to fall. Gazing over the skyline, he could see the shattered bridge and the black line of the river.

Gabriel walked to the low safety wall that ran around the edge of the roof. There was a fifteen-foot gap between where he was standing and the adjacent building. If the jump failed, he would never return to his own world. Would Maya ever see his dead body? Would she press her ear to his chest and realize that his heart had finally stopped beating? He circled the roof once, twice, and returned to his original position. Because of the safety wall, he couldn't run and throw himself forward.

The steel fire door was ripped away and tossed down the stairwell. Pickering and the patrol stepped onto the roof. "See? I told you so!" Pickering said.

Gabriel stepped onto the top of the concrete wall and looked over at the next building. *It's too far*, he thought. *Much too far.*

The wolves raised their weapons and started toward him.

27

Two of the Tabula mercenaries hiked up the slope to the helicopters and returned with a portable electric generator. The generator was placed near the storage hut and attached to a sodium light. Michael glanced upward. The thousands of stars visible in the night sky resembled little chips of ice. It was very cold now, and the moisture from everyone's lungs left a faint haze in the air.

Michael was disappointed that neither Gabriel nor his father was on the island, but the operation wasn't a complete failure. Perhaps the team would find documents or information on a computer that would lead them to a more promising target. Word would get back to Mrs. Brewster that he had brought in the splicers and demanded an aggressive approach to searching the huts. The Brethren liked people who took charge.

He sat down on a slab of limestone and watched Boone give orders to his men. When the backscatter device told them that the person inside the hut was neutralized, a man with an ax attacked the heavy oak door. Boone told the mercenary to stop working when he had chopped a jagged hole about two feet square. A moment later, one of the baboons peered out of the hole like a curious dog. Boone shot the animal in the head.

The two remaining splicers inside the hut began calling to each other. They were clever enough to sense danger and stay away from the hole. The man with the ax resumed his work. Fifteen minutes later he had completely destroyed the door. Boone's men moved cautiously, pushing away storage containers and raising their shotguns before edging inside. Michael heard more shrieks and then gunshots.

One of Boone's men had started a fire in the cooking hut and served mugs of tea to the others. Michael used the cup to warm his cold hands while he waited for more information. Ten minutes later, Boone walked out through the wrecked door. Boone was smiling and moving his body in a confident way, as if he had somehow regained his power. He accepted a cup of tea and strolled over to Michael.

"Is the Harlequin dead?" Michael asked.

"Maya wasn't in the building. It was a young woman from Los Angeles named Victory From Sin Fraser." Boone chuckled. "That name always amused me."

"And she was the only person in the building?"

"Oh, someone else was there. Down in the cellar." Boone hesitated for a few seconds, enjoying the tension in Michael's face. "We just found your father. That is . . . your father's body."

Michael took a flashlight from one of the mercenaries and followed Boone into the storage hut. The floor and walls were splattered with blood, still bright red and glistening. A plastic cloth covered the four dead splicers. A second cloth covered Victory Fraser, but Michael could see the scuffed soles of her shoes.

They climbed down a staircase to a cellar with a gravel floor and passed through a door into a side room. Matthew Corrigan lay on a stone slab with a white muslin cloth over his legs. As Michael looked down at the body, images from the past overwhelmed him with an unexpected force. He remembered his father weeding the garden behind the farmhouse, driving the family's battered pickup truck, and sharpening a carving knife for a Christmas turkey. He remembered his father chopping wood on a winter's day, the snow clinging to his long brown hair as the blade of his ax rose up against the sky. Those childhood days were gone now. Gone forever. But the memories still had the power to move Michael—and that made him angry.

"He's not dead," Boone explained. "I got the medical kit stethoscope and heard a heartbeat. This is how you look when you cross over to another world."

Michael resented Boone's cocky smile and his insinuating tone of voice. "All right, you found him," he said. "Now get out of here."

"For what reason?"

"I don't need a reason. If you want to keep your job, I would recommend you show some respect to a representative of the executive board. Go upstairs and leave me alone."

Boone's mouth became a tight line, but he nodded and left the cellar. Michael could hear the other men walking around the storage hut and pushing boxes against the wall. Holding the flashlight in his left hand, he gazed down at Matthew Corrigan. When Michael was growing up in South Dakota, adults always said that Gabriel looked like their father. Although Matthew's hair was gray and his face was deeply lined, Michael could now see the resemblance. He wondered if there was any truth to the rumor picked up by Tabula computers. Had Gabriel been on this island and had he discovered the body?

"Can you hear me?" Michael asked his father. "Can . . . you . . . hear . . . me?"

No response. He touched his father's throat and pushed hard. For a second, he thought he felt the flutter of a pulse. If he got rid of the flashlight he could squeeze the throat with both hands. Even if your Light was traveling through another realm, your body could die in this world. No one would stop him from killing Matthew. No one would criticize his judgment. Mrs. Brewster would see his action as another demonstration of his loyalty to the cause.

Michael placed the flashlight on the ledge in the wall and stepped closer to his father's body. His breath appeared and then vanished in the cold air. In his entire life, he had never felt so completely focused on the moment. *Do it*, Michael thought. *He ran away fifteen years ago. Now he can disappear forever.*

He reached out again and peeled back his father's eyelid. A blue eye stared back at him with no spark of life in its dark pupil. Michael felt as if he were looking at a dead man—and that was the problem. In one world or another, he wanted to confront his father and force him to admit that he had abandoned his family. Destroying this empty shell meant nothing; it would never provide him with satisfaction.

A memory flashed through his mind of a schoolyard fight back in South Dakota when he was a teenager. After Michael had punched and kicked his opponent, the other boy had fallen to the ground and covered his face with his hands. But that wasn't enough. That wasn't what he was looking for. He wanted complete surrender. Fear.

He retrieved the flashlight and walked upstairs to the blood-covered room where Boone and two mercenaries were waiting. "Load the body into one of the helicopters," Michael told them. "We're taking him off this island."

The wolves waited until Gabriel stepped back onto the roof and then they grabbed him. His arms were forced behind his back, his wrists tied with a length of wire, and his eyes blindfolded with a torn shirt. When the Traveller could no longer defend himself, one of the wolves punched him in the throat. Gabriel fell onto the tar-paper roof and tried to roll up into a ball as the wolves began kicking him in the chest and stomach. He was blind and desperate, gasping for air.

Someone swung a club at the base of his spine, and a wave of pain surged through every part of his body. Gabriel heard voices talking about the school. *Take him to the school.* Hands pulled him to his feet and dragged him down the marble staircase. Out on the street, he kept stumbling and tripping over chunks of rubble. He tried to remember where they were going. Left turn. Right turn. Stop. But the pain made it difficult to think. Finally, he was guided up another staircase and taken into a room with a smooth tile floor. The electric cord was untied and replaced with handcuffs. A shackle was fastened around his neck, and he was chained to a steel ring bolted into the floor.

The Traveller's body was sore, and he could feel dry blood on his face and hands. Images of the river, the shattered bridge, the gas flares burning among the ruined buildings overwhelmed his thoughts. After a while he fell into an uneasy sleep, waking up with a start when he heard the clang of the door swinging open. Hands pulled off his blindfold and he found himself looking at the black man wearing the white lab coat and the man with the braided blond hair. "You can't get out of this building," the blond man told him. "You got no life—unless we give it back to you."

As the wolves took off his shackles, Gabriel glanced around the room. He saw a teacher's desk and an old-fashioned blackboard. A cardboard alphabet had been fastened to the wall, but some of the faded green letters dangled upside down, held by one last remaining pin.

"You're coming with us," the black man said. "The commissioner wants to meet you."

Holding Gabriel's arms, the two wolves pulled him into the hallway. The three-story building had brick walls and small windows covered with shutters.

During some stage of the endless fighting, the wolves had converted the school into a fort, dormitory, storage house, and prison. Who was the commissioner? Gabriel wondered. He had to be bigger and stronger and even more vicious than the men who swaggered down the hallway with clubs and knives hanging from their belts.

They turned a corner, passed through some swinging doors, and stepped into a large room that had once been the school's auditorium. Curving rows of wooden seats faced a stage. A steel pipe ran across the stage and fed gas into an L-shaped fixture that burned with a bright flame. Two benches were placed near the back wall; the wolves sat there like petitioners outside the door of a king.

At the center of the stage was a large table stacked with manila folders and black ledger books. The man sitting behind the table wore a dark blue business suit, a white shirt, and a red bow tie. He was thin and bald and his face radiated self-righteousness. Even from a distance, Gabriel felt like this man knew all the regulations and he was prepared to enforce them in every possible way. There would be no negotiations or concessions. Everyone was guilty—and they would be punished.

Gabriel's two guards stopped halfway down the aisle and waited for the commissioner to conclude his interview with a large man who was holding a gunnysack wet with blood. One of the commissioner's assistants counted the objects inside the sack and then whispered a number.

"Very good." The commissioner's voice was strong and purposeful. "You may receive your food allocation."

The man with the sack left the stage as the commissioner entered a number in a black ledger. Ignoring the other petitioners, the two wolves led Gabriel up a ramp to the stage and forced him to sit on a wooden stool in front of the desk. The commissioner closed his ledger and looked up at this new problem.

"Well, it's our visitor from somewhere else. I've been told that your name is Gabriel. Is that accurate information?"

Gabriel stayed silent until the blond man jabbed him in the back with a club.

"That's correct. And who are you?"

"My predecessors were fond of grandiose and meaningless titles like major general or chief of staff. Indeed, one man called himself president for life. Of course, he lasted only five days. After much thought, I've chosen a more modest title. I'm the commissioner for patrols in this sector of the city."

Gabriel nodded, but stayed silent. The gas flare burning behind him made a hushing sound.

"Visitors from the outside have appeared in the city, but you're the first one I've encountered. So who are you and how did you get here?"

"I'm just like everyone else," Gabriel said. "I

opened my eyes and found myself beside the river."

"I don't believe that." The commissioner of patrols got up from the desk. Gabriel saw that he had a revolver in his belt. He snapped his fingers and one of his assistants hurried over with a second stool. The commissioner sat down close to Gabriel, leaned forward, and whispered.

"Some say that a divine power will rescue the final group of survivors. Of course, it's in my interest to encourage such hopeful fantasies. But it's my belief that we've been condemned to slaughter one another over and over again until the end of time. That means I'm here forever, unless I find a way out."

"Is this the only city in this world?"

"Of course not. Before the sky darkened, you could see other islands farther down the river. But my assumption is that they were only other hells, perhaps with inhabitants from different cultures or different historical eras. But all the islands are the same—a place where souls are condemned to repeat this cycle forever."

"If you let me explore the Island, I could look for a passageway out."

"Yes, you'd like that. Wouldn't you?" The commissioner stood up and snapped his fingers again. "Please bring the special chair."

One of the assistants ran away and returned with an old-fashioned wheelchair—an elaborate construction made of bentwood, a wicker seat, and rubber tires. The handcuffs were removed from Gabriel's wrists. Using nylon rope and lengths of electric cord, the petitioners tied Gabriel's arms and legs to the frame of the chair. The commissioner of patrols watched this process, occasionally telling his men to add a few extra knots.

"You're the leader here," Gabriel said. "So why can't you stop the killing?"

"I can't get rid of the anger and hatred. I can only channel it in various directions. I've survived because I'm able to define our enemies—the degenerate forms of life that must be exterminated. Right now, we're hunting down the cockroaches that conceal themselves in the darkness."

The commissioner walked down the ramp. The blond man followed him, pushing Gabriel in the wheelchair. Once again, they passed down the school's ground-floor hallway. The wolves waiting there lowered their heads slightly when the commissioner of patrols walked past them. If he saw some trace of disloyalty in their eyes, then they would immediately become his enemies.

At the end of the hallway, the commissioner took a key out of his pocket and unlocked a black door. "Stay here," he told the blond man, then pushed Gabriel through the open doorway.

They were in a large room filled with rows of green metal file cabinets. A few of the drawers had been pulled out and the contents dumped on the floor.

Gabriel looked down and saw school grades, test results, and teacher comments. Some of the files were stained with blood.

"All these cabinets contain student files," the commissioner explained. "There are no children on the Island, but when we woke up that first morning this was a real school. There was chalk for the blackboards, paper and pencils, and canned food in the student cafeteria. Little details like that increase the level of cruelty. We didn't just destroy an imaginary city, but a real place with stoplights and ice-cream parlors."

"Is that why you brought me here?"

The commissioner of patrols pushed Gabriel past the file cabinets. Two small gas flares were burning from wall pipes, but the light was almost overcome by the shadows in the room. "There's a reason why I picked this school as my headquarters. All the stories about visitors are connected to this room. There's something special about this particular location, but I haven't been able to discover the secret."

They reached a central work area with tables, trays, and metal chairs. Gabriel was captive in the wheelchair, but he moved his head around, searching for the patch of infinite black space that would provide a passageway back to the Fourth Realm.

"If visitors can travel to this world, then there has to be a way out. Where is it, Gabriel? You have to tell me."

"I don't know."

"That's not an acceptable response. You need to listen to me clearly. At this point, I can see only two possibilities. You're either my only hope for escape, or you're a threat to my survival. I do not have the time, or the inclination, to guess which option is correct." The commissioner drew his revolver and pointed it at Gabriel's head. "There are three bullets in this gun—probably the last three bullets that exist on this island. Don't make me waste one of them killing you."

2-9

Maya was still carrying the snub-nosed revolver she had acquired back in New York. The weapon determined her choice of transportation. Avoiding airports, she used a rural bus, a ferryboat, and a train to travel from Ireland to London. She arrived at Victoria Station in the middle of the night without a clear idea of how to find Gabriel. Before he left Skellig Columba, he had promised to contact the Free Runners, so Maya decided to drop by Vine House on the South Bank. Perhaps Jugger and his friends would know if Gabriel was still in the city.

She crossed the Thames and walked up Langley Lane toward Bonnington Square. The streets were empty at this late hour, but she could see the glow of televisions in darkened rooms. Maya passed some renovated terrace houses and a redbrick school built in the Victorian era that had been transformed into an upscale apartment building. In such surroundings, the Vine House looked like a shabby old man surrounded by well-dressed bankers and barristers.

When Maya reached the six-foot-high stone wall that surrounded the garden at Vine House, she smelled a harsh odor that reminded her of a trash fire. The Harlequin stopped and peered around the corner of the house. No one was on the sidewalk or sitting in the little garden at the center of the square. The neighborhood seemed safe until she noticed two men sitting in a florist's delivery van parked near the end of the block. Maya doubted that anyone had ordered a dozen red roses to be delivered at one o'clock in the morning.

There was no entrance to the back garden from Langley Lane, so she grabbed the top of the stone wall and pulled herself over. The burning smell grew stronger, but she still couldn't see a fire. Light came from a streetlamp and the new moon glowing in the western sky. As quietly as possible, she moved down the garden pathway to the back of the house, found the door unlocked, and eased it open.

Smoke surged out of the open doorway and flowed around her like a flood of foul gray water. Maya stumbled backward, coughing and waving her hands. Vine House was on fire, and the eighteenth-century oak beams and floorboards gave off as much smoke as a coal pit burning underground.

Where were the Free Runners? Had they fled the

house or were they dead? Falling on her hands and knees, Maya crawled into the ground-floor hallway. A door on the left led to the empty kitchen. A door on the right opened to a bedroom with a single electric lamp that gave off a feeble point of light within the darkness.

A man lay in the middle of the room—half on the floor and half on a mattress, as if he were too weary to find his way to bed. Maya grabbed the man's arms and dragged him out the doorway and into the garden. She was coughing hard and her eyes were filled with tears, but she could see that the unconscious man was Gabriel's friend Jugger. Straddling his body, she slapped him hard across the face. Jugger's eyes fluttered open and he started coughing.

"Listen to me!" Maya said. "Is there anyone else in the house?"

"Roland. Sebastian . . ." Jugger began coughing again.

"What happened? Are they dead?"

"Two men came in a van. Guns. Put us on the floor. Gave us injections . . ."

She returned to the house, took a deep breath, and stepped back inside. Crawling like an animal, she moved down the hallway and headed up the narrow staircase. One part of her mind was clear while her lungs struggled to breathe. Killing the Free Runners with guns or knives would have attracted too much attention from the authorities. Instead the Tabula mercenaries had drugged the three men and set fire to the dilapidated house. Now they were watching the front door and the entrance to the garden to make sure no one escaped. The next morning, firemen would find what was left of the bodies in the smoldering ruins. The local council would sell the land to a speculator and the London papers would run the story in the back pages: *Three Die in Illegal Dwelling*.

Maya found Sebastian in an upstairs bedroom, grabbed his arms, and dragged him down the stairs to the garden. When she returned the third time, she could see flames flashing in the darkness, burning the floorboards beneath a parlor chair, reaching up the walls to touch the banisters. There was black smoke at the top of the stairs, and she was completely blind when she reached out and found Roland's body in the garret bedroom. Pull and stop. Pull and stop again. Sight and sound disappeared and she became a small fragment of consciousness passing through the smoke.

Maya burst out the back door, let go of Roland's body, and collapsed on the muddy soil of the garden. After several minutes of coughing and gasping for air, she sat up and rubbed her eyes. Jugger was still conscious, talking with slurred speech about the injections. Maya touched the chests of the two other Free Runners and felt them breathing. Still alive.

She was carrying the gun, but using it would be

dangerous in this neighborhood. Hollis had once explained that there were so many handguns in Los Angeles that New Year's Eve celebrations sounded like a firefight in a war zone. In London, the sound of a gun was an unusual occurrence. If she fired her revolver, half the people living around the square would hear it and immediately call the police.

The house continued to burn, and there was a flash of orange flame as the window curtains in Jugger's bedroom caught fire. Standing up, Maya approached the back door and felt a wave of heat pushing through the cold night air. As her breathing returned to normal, she remembered overhearing a discussion between her father and Mother Blessing about silencers. Gun silencers were illegal in Europe, hard to find and awkward to carry. Sometimes it was easier to improvise a substitute.

Maya searched the backyard and found some overflowing rubbish bins near the wall. She rummaged through the garbage until she discovered an empty two-liter water bottle and a wad of pink rubbery material that looked like carpet padding. Maya stuffed bits of padding into the bottle, then inserted the gun barrel into the opening. An old roll of tape was on the steps near the back door, and she wound it tightly around the gun and the plastic bottle. Jugger was sitting up and staring at her from the other side of the yard.

"What . . . what are you doing?"

"Wake up your friends. We're getting out of here."

Clutching her improvised weapon, she climbed back over the wall, hurried down an alleyway, and approached the back of the delivery van. A side window was rolled halfway down to let out cigarette smoke, and she could hear the two men talking.

"How long do we have to wait?" the driver asked. "I'm getting hungry."

The other man laughed. "Then go back into the house. Some meat cooking there . . ."

Maya stepped up to the driver's window, raised the gun, and fired. The first bullet blew out the bottom of the plastic bottle and cracked through the glass. The gun made a sound like hands clapping—two quick shots, and then silence.

30

An hour before his flight reached Heathrow Airport, Hollis stepped into one of the airplane toilets and changed his clothes in the cramped space. He felt conspicuous returning to his seat wearing a navy blue shirt and pants, but people were groggy from the overnight flight and no one appeared to notice. His old clothes were stuffed into a small bag that would be left on the plane. Everything he needed to enter England undetected was inside a manila envelope that he carried under his arm.

During his last few days in New York, Hollis had received an e-mail from Linden telling him that his work was done and it was time to come to England. The French Harlequin wasn't able to find a merchant ship that would illegally transport Hollis to Europe. It was possible that the Tabula had inserted Hollis's biometric information into the security data bank that fed information to customs officials throughout the world. When Hollis arrived at Heathrow Airport, he might activate a security alert and be detained by the authorities. Linden told Hollis there was another way—an off-the-Grid way—to enter Britain, but that would require some skillful maneuvering at the terminal.

The American Airlines flight landed on time at Heathrow, and the people sitting around Hollis began switching on their cell phones. Security guards watched the passengers carefully as they walked across the tarmac, then were loaded into airport transit buses and taken to terminal four.

Since Hollis wasn't transferring to another flight, he needed to take another bus across the sprawling airport to passport control at terminal one. He went into the men's room for a few minutes, then came back out and mingled with passengers arriving from different flights. Gradually, he was beginning to understand the clever simplicity of Linden's plan. He was no longer surrounded by anyone who knew that he had just arrived from New York. The other passengers were tired and passive and ready to leave the terminal.

He got on another transit bus that was going to terminal one. When the bus was filled with people, he took a bright yellow safety vest out of the envelope and put it on. The blue shirt, pants, and vest made him look exactly like an airport employee. A card dangling around his neck held a fake ID card, but that really wasn't necessary. The drones working at the airport looked only at the surface, searching for quick clues to put each stranger into a category.

When the bus reached terminal one, the other passengers got out and hurried through the electric door. Hollis pretended to talk into his mobile phone as he stood on the narrow sidewalk in the loading area. Then he nodded to the bored security guard sitting inside at a desk, turned, and strolled away. He half expected emergency sirens to go off while police officers ran out waving guns, but no one stopped him. The airport's high-tech security system had been defeated by an eight-dollar reflective vest bought at a bicycle shop in Brooklyn.

* * *

TWENTY MINUTES LATER, Hollis was sitting in a delivery van with Winston Abosa, a plump young man from Nigeria who had a soothing voice and a pleasant manner. Hollis gazed out the window as they drove into London. Although he had traveled through Mexico and Latin America, Hollis had never visited Europe. British roads had lots of roundabouts and zebra-striped pedestrian walkways. Most of the two-story redbrick houses had little gardens in back. Surveillance cameras were everywhere, focusing on the license plates of each passing vehicle.

The new landscape reminded Hollis of a passage from Sparrow's book, *The Way of the Sword*. According to the Japanese Harlequin, a warrior had a big advantage if he was familiar with the city that would be his battleground. When the warrior suddenly had to fight in a new area, it was like waking up in the morning and finding yourself in a different room.

"Did you ever meet Vicki Fraser?" Hollis asked.

"Of course." Winston drove carefully, with both hands on the steering wheel. "I have met all your friends."

"Are they in England? I could never get an answer from my e-mails."

"Miss Fraser, Miss Maya, and the little girl are in Ireland. Mr. Gabriel is . . ." Winston hesitated. "Mr. Gabriel is in London."

"What happened? Why aren't they together?"

"I am just an employee, sir. Mr. Linden and Madam pay me well, and I try not to question their decisions."

"What are you talking about? Who is *Madam*?"

Winston looked tense. "I know nothing, sir. Mr. Linden will answer all your questions."

Winston parked the van near Regent's Canal and led Hollis down back streets to the crowded arcades and courtyards of Camden Market. Following a zigzag route to avoid the cameras, they reached the entrance to the catacombs beneath the elevated railway tracks.

An elderly British woman who had dyed her hair a pinkish-white color sat beside a sign that offered her services as a tarot reader. Winston dropped a ten-pound note on the woman's folding table. As she reached for the money, Hollis saw a small radio device concealed in her right hand. The old woman was the first line of defense against unwelcome visitors.

Winston walked down a tunnel and they entered a shop filled with drums and African statues. There was a banner at one end of the room that concealed a steel door to a hidden apartment. "Tell Mr. Linden I'll be here in the shop," Winston said. "If you want anything, let me know."

Hollis found himself in a hallway that led to four rooms. No one was in the first room, but Linden sat in the kitchen drinking coffee and reading a newspaper. Hollis made a quick evaluation of the French Harlequin. Some of the big men Hollis had fought in Brazil were bullies, eager to use their size against a smaller opponent. Linden weighed at least 250 pounds, but there was nothing swaggering in his appearance or behavior. He was a calm, quiet man whose eyes seemed to notice everything.

"Good morning, Monsieur Wilson. I assume everything was satisfactory at the airport?"

Hollis shrugged. "It took me a while to find the employee exit. After that, it was easy. Winston was parked down the street in the van."

"Would you like some coffee or a cup of tea?"

"I want to see Vicki. Winston said she was in Ireland."

"Please sit down." Linden gestured to the opposite chair. "A great deal has happened in the last ten days."

Hollis put down the manila envelope that had contained his disguise and sat on the chair. Linden got up, plugged in an electric kettle, and measured coffee grounds into a French press. He kept glancing at Hollis as if he were a boxer evaluating a new opponent on the other side of the ring.

"Are you tired from the flight, Monsieur Wilson?"

"I'm okay. This country is just a 'different room.' That's all. I've got to adjust to the changes."

Linden looked surprised. "You've read Sparrow's book?"

"Sure. Is that against the Harlequin rules?"

"Not at all. I had the book translated into French and published by a small press in Paris. Maya's father met Sparrow in Tokyo. And I met his son before he was killed by the Tabula."

"Yeah, I know. Let's talk about that later. When am I going to see Vicki, Maya, and Gabriel? Your e-mail said you'd answer all my questions when I got here."

"Vicki and Maya are on an island off the west coast of Ireland. Maya is guarding Matthew Corrigan."

Hollis laughed and shook his head. "Well, that's a

surprise. So where has Gabriel's father been hiding all these years?"

"It's just his shell—his empty body. Matthew crossed over to the First Realm and something went wrong. He hasn't come back."

"What's the First Realm? I don't know all this stuff."

"L'enfer," Linden said, and then realized that Hollis didn't know French. "The underworld. Hell."

"But Vicki's all right?"

"I'm assuming she is. Mother Blessing, an Irish Harlequin, left a satellite phone with Maya. During the last few days, we've called and called, but no one has answered. Madam was quite annoyed about this. Right now, she's traveling back to the island."

"Maya told me about Mother Blessing. I thought she was dead."

Linden poured boiling water into the French press. "I can assure you that Madam is very much alive."

"And what about Gabriel? Can I see him? Winston said he was in London."

"Mother Blessing brought Gabriel down to London, and then he was lost."

Hollis twisted around in his seat to look at Linden. "What are you talking about?"

"Our Traveller went searching for his father in the First Realm. He's still alive, but he also hasn't returned."

"So where's the body?"

"Why don't you have some coffee first."

"I don't want any goddamn coffee. Where's Gabriel? He's my friend."

Linden shrugged his massive shoulders. "Go down the hallway . . ."

Hollis left the kitchen and walked down the hallway to a shabby little room where Gabriel lay on a bed. The Traveller's body was limp and unresponsive—as if he was trapped within the deepest level of sleep. Sitting on the edge of the bed, Hollis touched the Traveller's hand. Although he knew that Gabriel probably couldn't hear anything, he felt like speaking to him.

"Hey, Gabe. This is your friend Hollis. Don't worry. I'm going to protect you."

"Good. That's exactly what we want." Hollis turned around and saw Linden standing in the doorway. "We'll pay you five hundred pounds a week."

"I'm not a mercenary and don't want to be treated like one. I'll guard Gabriel because he's my friend. But first I need to make sure that Vicki's all right. You got that?"

Hollis had always favored the aggressive approach when someone was trying to order him around, but now he wasn't so sure. Linden bent down and drew a 9mm semiautomatic pistol from an ankle holster. Seeing the gun and the cold expression on the Harlequin's face, Hollis thought he was dead. *This bastard is going to kill me.*

Linden reversed the handgun and offered Hollis the grip. "Do you know how to use this, Monsieur Wilson?"

"Sure." Hollis took the automatic from Linden and hid it beneath his shirt.

"Mother Blessing will reach the island tomorrow. She'll talk to Mademoiselle Fraser and see if she wants to travel to London. I'm sure that you'll see the young lady in a few days."

"Thank you."

"Never thank a Harlequin. I'm not doing this because I like you. We need another fighter and you've arrived at the right time."

* * *

HOLLIS AND WINSTON Abosa walked up Chalk Farm Road. Most of the shops on the street were selling different styles of rebellion: black leather motorcycle pants, vampire Gothic dresses, or T-shirts with obscene messages. Punks with lime green hair and pierced eyebrows huddled in little groups, enjoying the stares of the passing citizens.

They bought cheese, bread, milk, and coffee, and then Winston took Hollis to an unmarked door between a tattoo parlor and a shop that sold fairy wings. A room with a bed and a television was on the second floor. The bathroom and kitchen were down the hall.

"This is where you'll be staying," Winston said. "If you have any questions, I'm at the drum shop all day long."

After Winston left, Hollis sat on the bed and ate some bread and cheese. The smell of curry came from somewhere in the building. Cars honked their horns out on the road. Back in New York he could find a way out, but now the Vast Machine surrounded him. Everything would be all right if he could hold Vicki Fraser and hear her voice. Her love made him feel stronger. Love increased you. It connected you to the Light.

Before he went down the hall to take a shower, he stuck a piece of chewing gum in the gap between the floor and the lower edge of the door. The shower stall had mold around the drain, and the water was luke-warm. When he dressed and returned to his room, he noticed that the gum had been pulled in two.

Placing the soap and towel on the floor, Hollis reached beneath his shirt and pulled out the automatic. He had never killed before, but now it was going to happen. He was sure that the Tabula were waiting for him. They would attack the moment he came through the door.

Holding the gun in his right hand, he inserted the key into the doorknob as quietly as possible. *One*, Hollis counted. *Two*. *Three*. He turned the doorknob, raised the gun, and charged into the room.

Maya stood alone beside the window.

Early the next morning, Maya climbed up onto the roof of the old horse hospital at the center of the Camden Market. The sick horses and the slaughterhouse had vanished at the end of the Victorian era, and now boutique shops selling organic soap and Tibetan prayer rugs occupied the three-story building. No one noticed Maya as she stood next to a creaky weather vane of a galloping horse.

She watched Hollis walk through the market and enter the brick tunnel that led to the catacombs. Linden had spent the night at the drum shop, and Hollis would let her know when the French Harlequin left the secret apartment.

During the last twenty-four hours, she had been continually moving around London. As Vine House burst into flames, she helped Jugger and his friends get out of the back garden. The four of them had found a taxi near Vauxhall Bridge, and the driver had taken them to an empty apartment in Chiswick owned by Roland's brother. The Free Runners were used to living off the Grid, and all of them promised to stay hidden until the authorities stopped investigating the two dead men in the florist's van.

Gabriel had told Jugger he was staying at a drum shop in the Camden Market. Maya assumed that both Linden and Mother Blessing were guarding the Traveller. For the rest of the day, she watched the entrance to the catacombs until Hollis arrived at the shop. Mother Blessing would have killed her for disobedience, but Hollis was a friend. He would arrange everything so she could safely see Gabriel.

She was standing on the roof when Linden came out of the brick tunnel that led to the catacombs. With a sword carrier hanging from his left shoulder, the Harlequin strolled off to have breakfast at a café that overlooked the canal. Hollis came out of the tunnel ten minutes later and waved his arms. All clear.

*　*　*

HOLLIS LED HER past the drums and the African carvings to a cold little room where Gabriel's body lay on the bed. Kneeling on the concrete floor beside the bed, Maya took Gabriel's hand. She knew he was still alive, but she felt like a widow touching her dead husband. Maya had seen the saint's book on Skellig Columba and studied the illuminated paintings of hell. She had no doubt that Gabriel had gone there to search for his father.

All the skills Thorn and the other Harlequins had taught her seemed useless at that moment. There was no one to fight, no guarded castle with stone walls and iron gates. She would make any sacrifice to save Gabriel, but no sacrifice could be made.

The steel door to the apartment squeaked open. Hollis looked surprised. "Is that you, Winston?"

Maya jumped to her feet and drew her gun. Silence. And then Linden appeared in the bedroom doorway. The big man kept his hands in his pockets and smiled slightly. "Are you going to shoot me, Maya? Always remember to aim a bit lower. When people are nervous, they aim too high."

"We didn't know who it was." Maya slid the revolver back in its holster.

"I thought you might come here. Mother Blessing told me you had an *attachement sentimental* to Gabriel Corrigan. When you switched off your satellite phone, I realized you had probably left the island."

"Did you tell her?"

"No. She's going to be angry enough when she shows up on Skellig Columba and finds a Traveller guarded by an American girl and some nuns."

"I had to see him."

"Was it worth it?" Linden straddled the only chair in the room. "He's as lost as his father. There's nothing there but a shell."

"I'm going to save Gabriel," Maya said. "I just need to find a way."

"That's impossible. He's gone. Vanished."

Maya thought before speaking again. "I need to talk to someone who knows as much as possible about the realms. Do you know anyone here in England?"

"It's not our concern, Maya. The rule is, we guard Travellers only in *this* world."

"I don't care about the rules. 'Cultivate Randomness.' Isn't that what Sparrow wrote? Maybe it's time to do something different, because this strategy isn't working."

Hollis spoke for the first time. "She's got a point, Linden. Right now, Michael Corrigan is the only Traveller in this world, and he's working for the Tabula."

"Help me, Linden. Please. All I need is a name."

The French Harlequin stood up and began to leave the room. When he reached the doorway, he stopped and shifted his weight from one foot to the other like a man trying to pick the right pathway on a dark night.

"There are several experts on the realms who live in Europe, but there's only one person we can trust. His name is Simon Lumbroso. He was your father's friend. As far as I know, he's still in Rome."

"My father never had any friends. You know that as well as I do."

"That's the word Thorn used," Linden said. "You should go to Rome and find out for yourself."

Hollis was making a cup of coffee in the hidden apartment when Linden walked in from the drum shop carrying a satellite phone. "I just heard from Mother Blessing. She's on Skellig Columba."

"I bet she wasn't happy when she found out that Maya was gone."

"The conversation was very brief. I told her you had arrived in London and she requested that you come to the island."

"Does she want me to guard Matthew Corrigan's body?"

Linden nodded. "That's a logical conclusion."

"What about Vicki?"

"She didn't mention Mademoiselle Fraser."

Hollis poured a cup of coffee for the French Harlequin and placed it on the kitchen table. "You've got to tell me how to travel to Ireland,

and I'll need a boat to take me to the convent."

"*Madam* said that she wanted you on the island as soon as possible. So ... I've made other arrangements."

* * *

HOLLIS QUICKLY DISCOVERED that "other arrangements" meant chartering a private helicopter to fly to the island. Two hours later, Winston Abosa drove him out to White Waltham—a small airfield with a grass runway near Maidenhead in Berkshire. Carrying a manila envelope filled with cash, Hollis was met in the parking lot by a pilot in his sixties. There was something about the man's appearance—the short haircut and straight-backed posture—that suggested a military background.

"Are you the client going to Ireland?" the pilot asked.

"That's right. I'm—"

"I don't want to know who you are. But I do want to see the money."

* * *

HOLLIS HAD THE feeling that the pilot would have flown Jack the Ripper to a girls' school if there had been enough euros in the envelope. Ten minutes later, the helicopter was in the air and heading west.

The pilot was quiet except for a few terse comments to air traffic controllers. His only expression of personality was revealed in the aggressive way he roared over a line of hills, swooping down a green valley where each field was defined by a stone wall. "You can call me Richard," he said at one point, but he never asked Hollis for his name.

Pushed by an eastern wind, they crossed the Irish Sea and refueled at a small airport near Dublin. As they flew across the countryside, Hollis looked down and saw haystacks, little clusters of homes, and narrow roads that rarely seemed to go in a straight line. When they reached the west coast of Ireland, Richard removed his sunglasses and began glancing at a GPS device in the instrument panel. He stayed low enough to pass a flock of pelicans flying in a V formation. Directly below the birds, waves surged upward and collapsed into white foam.

Finally, the two jagged spires of Skellig Columba came into view. Richard circled the island until he saw a white strip of cloth fluttering from a pole. He hovered over this improvised flag for a minute, and then landed on a patch of flat, rocky ground. When the propeller stopped moving, Hollis could hear wind whistling through a crack in the air vent.

"There's a group of nuns on this island," Hollis said. "I'm sure they'd be glad to give you a cup of tea."

"My instructions were to stay in the helicopter,"

Richard said. "And I've been paid a certain premium to follow those instructions."

"Suit yourself. You might want to hang around for a while. There's an Irishwoman who probably wants to go back to London."

Hollis got out of the helicopter and looked down the rocky slope at the convent. Where's Vicki? he thought. Didn't they tell her I was coming?

Instead of Vicki, he saw Alice running toward the helicopter, followed by a nun and—several yards back—a woman with dark red hair. Alice reached him first and stepped up on a rock so that they would be on the same level. Her hair was tangled and her boots were covered with mud.

"Where's Maya?" Alice asked.

It was the first time Hollis had ever heard her voice. "Maya is in London. She's okay. Nothing to worry about."

Alice jumped off the rock and continued up the slope, followed by a plump nun with a flushed face. The nun nodded at him, and he saw a hint of sadness in her eyes. But then she was gone and he was facing Mother Blessing.

The Irish Harlequin wore black wool pants and a leather jacket. She looked smaller than Hollis had imagined, and had a proud, imperious look on her face. "Welcome to Skellig Columba, Mr. Wilson."

"Thanks for the helicopter ride."

"Did Sister Joan speak to you?"

"No. Was she supposed to?" Hollis looked down the slope. "Where's Vicki? That's who I really came to see."

"Yes. Come along."

Hollis followed the Harlequin down a pathway to the four beehive-shaped huts on the second terrace. He felt as if a car had crashed and he was going to be shown the wreckage.

"Have you ever been punched very hard, Mr. Wilson?"

"Of course. I fought professionally in Brazil."

"And how do you survive that?"

"If you can't avoid someone's fist, you try to move with it. If you just stand there like a stone, you're going to get knocked out."

"Good advice to follow," Mother Blessing said, and she stopped in front of a hut. "Two days ago, the Tabula came to the island with their helicopters. The nuns fled to a cave with the girl, but apparently Miss Fraser stayed here to protect the Traveller."

"So where is she? What happened?"

"This will not be easy, Mr. Wilson. But you may see—if you wish."

Mother Blessing opened the door to the hut, but allowed him to go in first. Hollis entered a cold room where cardboard boxes and plastic storage containers had been pushed against the wall. Something was splattered all over the wooden floor. It took him a few seconds to realize it was dried blood.

Mother Blessing stood behind him. Her voice was as calm and unemotional as if she were talking about the weather. "The Tabula brought splicers with them so they could crawl in through the windows. I'm sure they killed the animals afterward and dropped their bodies into the sea."

She motioned to an object covered by a plastic tarp, and Hollis immediately knew it was Vicki. Moving like a sleepwalker, he shuffled over to the body and pulled back the tarp. Vicki was almost unrecognizable, but teeth marks on her legs and arms showed that animals had killed her.

Hollis stood over the mutilated body, feeling like he had also been destroyed. The left hand was a mass of torn flesh and shattered bone, but Vicki's right hand was untouched. A heart-shaped silver locket lay in the center of her palm, and Hollis recognized the style immediately. Most of the women in the church wore a similar piece of jewelry. If you opened the locket, you discovered a black-and-white photograph of Isaac Jones.

"I removed the locket from her neck," Mother Blessing said. "I thought you might want to see what's inside."

Hollis picked up the locket and pushed his fingernail into the top of the little silver heart. It clicked open. The familiar picture of the Prophet had disappeared, replaced by a piece of white paper. Slowly, he unfolded the paper and smoothed it out on the palm of his hand. Vicki had written seven words with an old-fashioned fountain pen, trying to make each letter perfect: *Hollis Wilson is in my heart—always*.

His shock and pain were shoved aside and replaced by anger so extreme that he felt like howling. No matter what happened, he would hunt down the men who had killed her and destroy them all. He would never rest. Never.

"Have you seen enough?" Mother Blessing asked. "I think it's time to dig a grave." When Hollis didn't answer, she crossed the room and pulled the tarp over the body.

Maya left the drum shop and went to a cybercafé on Chalk Farm Road. Linden said he trusted one expert on the six realms—an Italian named Simon Lumbroso. A quick search of the Internet showed that a man with that name worked as an art appraiser in Rome. Maya wrote down Lumbroso's office address and phone number, but didn't call him. She decided to fly to Rome and meet the person who was supposed to be her father's friend.

After making a plane reservation, she took a taxi to the storage locker she kept in East London and picked up a new set of false identification papers. For her trip to Rome, Maya decided to use the safest option, one of her unused OR-IF passports. OR-IF was an acronym for "origin real, identity false." These passports had been obtained from the government and all the data had been fed into the Vast Machine.

Maya's OR-IF identification had taken years to prepare. When she was nine years old, Thorn had obtained the birth certificates for several dead children. All of their "lives" were tended like fruit trees that needed to be occasionally pruned and watered. On paper, the girls had taken their O-levels and received driver's licenses, started jobs, and applied for credit cards. Maya had kept the documentation current even during the period that she was living on the Grid and trying to act like a citizen.

When the British government introduced biometric ID cards, the physical data embedded in the e-passports had to match each false identity. Maya had bought special contact lenses that would allow her to handle the airport iris scanners, along with the fragile plastic finger shields that would cover her index fingers. Some of her passports had photographs with her regular face, while others displayed photographs taken after facer drugs changed her appearance.

Over the years, she had started to regard each passport as a different aspect of her own personality. Her false passport as Judith Strand made her feel like an ambitious professional woman. The passport she was taking to Italy used the name of a dead girl from Brighton called Rebecca Green. Maya had decided that Rebecca was an artistic type who liked electronic music.

* * *

IT WAS TOO dangerous to take a gun on a plane—even in checked luggage—so Maya left her revolver in the locker and carried Gabriel's talisman sword, along with a stiletto and a throwing knife. All three weapons were hidden inside the steel framework of a folding baby stroller that had been built several years ago by one of her father's Spanish contacts.

From Da Vinci Airport, she took a taxi into Rome. The heart of Rome could be contained within a triangle set beside the Tiber River. At the base of the triangle were the familiar tourist sites of the Forum and the Coliseum. Maya checked into a hotel near the northern tip of the triangle, close to the Piazza del Popolo. She strapped the knives to her arms and walked south past the mausoleum of Emperor Augustus to the cobblestone streets of the old city.

The ground floors of the eighteenth-century buildings had been taken over by tourist restaurants and upscale boutiques. Bored salesgirls wearing tight skirts stood outside the little shops and chattered to boyfriends on their cell phones. Avoiding the surveillance cameras around the Parliament building, she entered the square that contained the Pantheon. The huge brick-and-marble building was built by the Emperor Hadrian to be the temple of all the gods. It had stood at the center of Rome for two thousand years.

Maya passed through the granite columns of the

portico. The nervous energy that came from the groups of tourists and their guides dissipated in the domed space. They whispered as they crossed the marble floor and examined Raphael's tomb. Standing in the middle of the huge temple, Maya tried to come up with a plan. What was she going to say when she met Lumbroso? Could he possibly know some way to rescue Gabriel?

Something passed through the air and she gazed upward at the oculus—the round opening at the top of the dome. A gray dove was trapped inside the temple and was trying to escape. Desperately flapping its wings, the bird rose through the air in a tight spiral. But the oculus was too far away, and the dove always gave up a few yards from freedom. Maya could see that the dove was getting tired. Each new attempt brought another failure and it kept drifting lower— pulled down by the weight of its exhausted body. The bird was so frightened and desperate that all it could do was keep flying, as if the motion itself would provide a solution.

The feeling of certainty that had come to her in London seemed to melt away. Feeling weak and foolish, she left the temple and hurried down the street to the crowds that were boarding buses and trolleys near the Teatro Argentino. Maya circled the ruins at the center of the square and entered the maze of narrow streets that used to be the Jewish ghetto.

The ghetto had once been like East London in the Victorian era—a refuge where fugitives could hide and find allies. Jews had lived in Rome since the second century B.C., but in the sixteenth century they were forced to live inside the walled area near the old fish market. Even the Jewish physicians who treated Italian aristocrats could leave the ghetto only during daytime. Every Sunday, Jewish children were forced to attend a sermon at the Church of Saint Angelo in Pescheria, where a friar told them they were damned to hell. The church was still standing, along with a large white synagogue that looked like a belle epoque museum plucked out of the center of Paris.

Simon Lumbroso lived in a two-story building near the ruins of the Portico of Octavia. His name was on a brass plate near the door along with a description of his services in Italian, German, French, Hebrew, and English: SIMON LUMBROSO/ART APPRAISAL/ CERTIFICATION PROVIDED.

Maya pressed the black button for the doorbell, but no one answered. When she tried again, a man's voice came from the speaker in the wall. "*Buongiorno.*"

"Good afternoon. I'm looking for Mr. Lumbroso."

"And for what reason?" The voice—once warm and friendly—had a sharp, critical tone.

"I'm thinking about buying a certain object and I want to know how old it is."

"I'm looking at you on my video screen and I don't see any statues or paintings."

"It's jewelry. A gold brooch."

"Of course. Beautiful jewelry for *una donna bella*."

The lock buzzed open and Maya entered the building. The ground floor consisted of two connecting rooms that led to an enclosed courtyard. The apartment looked as if the contents of a scientific laboratory and an art gallery had been loaded into a truck and then dumped into the same space. In the front room, Maya saw a spectroscope, a centrifuge, and a microscope on various tables along with bronze statues and old paintings.

She stepped around some antique furniture and entered the back room, where a bearded man in his seventies sat at a workbench examining a piece of parchment with illuminated letters. The man wore black pants, a long-sleeved white shirt, and a black skullcap. Like many Orthodox Jews, he showed the white fringe from his *tallit katan*: a linen garment similar to a poncho worn beneath his shirt.

The man gestured to the page on his workbench. "The parchment is old, probably cut from a Bible, but the inscription is modern. For ink, the medieval monks used soot, crushed seashells—even their own blood. They couldn't drive over to the store and buy products from the petrochemical industry."

"You're Simon Lumbroso?"

"You sound skeptical. I do have business cards, but I keep losing them." Lumbroso slipped on a pair of eyeglasses with thick lenses that magnified his dark brown eyes. "Names are fragile these days. Some people change names like pairs of shoes. And what's your name, signorina?"

"I'm Rebecca Green, from London. I left the brooch back at my hotel, but perhaps I could draw you a sketch that shows you what it looks like."

Lumbroso smiled and shook his head. "I'm afraid I'll need the actual item. If there's a stone, I can remove it and look for a patina in the setting."

"Loan me some paper. Maybe you'll recognize the design."

Looking skeptical, Lumbroso handed her a pad of paper and a felt-tipped pen. "As you wish, signorina."

Quickly, Maya drew the Harlequin lute. She tore off the page and placed it on the workbench. Simon Lumbroso glanced at the oval with the three lines, then turned slightly and studied her face. Maya felt as if she were an art object that had been brought to his house for evaluation. "Yes, of course. I recognize the design. If you allow me, perhaps I could give you some more information."

He walked over to a large safe set against the wall and began to turn the dial. "You said that you were from London. Were your parents born in Great Britain?"

"My mother came from a Sikh family living in Manchester."

"And your father?"

"He was German."

Lumbroso opened the safe and took out a cardboard shoe box filled with over one hundred letters, arranged by date. He placed the box on the workbench and thumbed through its contents. "I can't tell you about the brooch. In fact, I don't think it really exists. But I *do* know something about *your* place of origin."

He opened an envelope, took out a black-and-white photograph, and placed it on the bench. "I think you're the daughter of Dietrich Schöller. At least, that was his name before he became a Harlequin named Thorn."

Maya examined the photograph and was surprised to see herself, at the age of nine, sitting next to her father on a bench in St. James's Park. Someone, perhaps her mother, had taken the shot.

"Where did you get this?"

"Your father has sent letters to me for almost forty years. I have one of your baby pictures if you'd like to see it."

"Harlequins never take photographs unless it's for a fake passport or some kind of identification card. I always stayed home when they took pictures at school."

"Well, your father took some pictures, and then he stored them with me. So where is he, Maya? I was sending letters to a postbox in Prague, but they've all been returned."

"He's dead. Murdered by the Tabula."

Tears for Maya's father—her violent, arrogant father—filled Lumbroso's eyes. He sniffed loudly, found some tissues on the workbench, and blew his nose. "I'm not surprised by this news. Dietrich lived a very dangerous life. But still, his death saddens me greatly. He was my closest friend."

"I don't think you knew my father at all. He never had a friend in his life. He never loved anyone, including my mother."

Lumbroso looked astonished and then sad. He shook his head slowly. "How can you say that? Your father had a great deal of respect for your mother. When she died, he was depressed for a very long time."

"I don't know anything about that, but I do know what happened when I was a little girl. My father trained me to kill people."

"Yes, he turned you into a Harlequin. I'm not going to defend his decision." Lumbroso stood up, went over to a wooden hat stand, and retrieved a black suit coat. "Come with me, Maya. Let's get something to eat. As we Romans would say, 'No story on an empty stomach.'"

Wearing the suit coat and a black fedora, Simon Lumbroso escorted her through the ghetto. The sun had disappeared behind the red tile roofs, but quite a few people were sitting on kitchen chairs out in the street and gossiping while children kicked at a ball. Everyone appeared to know Lumbroso, who greeted his neighbors by touching two fingers to the wide brim of his hat.

"Forty years ago I used to offer tours of this area to foreigners. That was how I met your father. One afternoon, he was the only person who showed up outside the synagogue. Your father was a gentile, of course, but he knew a great deal about Jewish history. He asked intelligent questions, and we had a pleasant time debating various theories. I told him that I had enjoyed practicing my German and that he didn't need to pay me anything."

"That meant my father had an obligation."

Lumbroso smiled. "Yes, that's how a Harlequin would see it. But I didn't realize any of that. At the time, a group of wealthy young men here in Rome had formed a fascist group, and they would come down to the ghetto late at night to beat up Jews. They caught me down by the Tiber—just a few hundred yards from here. It was five against one. And then, suddenly, your father appeared."

"He destroyed them . . ."

"Yes. But it was the way he did it that startled me. He showed no anger while fighting—just this cold, focused aggression and a complete lack of fear. He beat all five men unconscious and would have tossed them into the river to drown if I hadn't pulled him away."

"Now *that* sounds like my father."

"From then on, we began to see each other to

explore the city and eat dinner together. Gradually, Dietrich told me about his life. Although your father came from a Harlequin family, he never saw that as his destiny. As I recall, he studied history at the Free University of Berlin; then he decided to become a painter and moved to Rome. Some young men experiment with drugs or sexuality. For your father, having a friend was just as forbidden. He never had a friend— even when he was a teenager at the *Oberschule*."

They circled the synagogue on Lungotevere and took the Ponte Fabricio footbridge to the small island in the middle of the Tiber. Lumbroso paused in the middle of the bridge, and Maya gazed down at the muddy green water that flowed through Rome.

"When I was growing up, my father told me that friends made you weak."

"Friendship is as necessary as food and water. It took some time, but eventually we became close friends with no secrets between us. I wasn't surprised to learn about the existence of Travellers. There's a mystical branch of Judaism based on the Kabbalah that describes these kinds of revelations. As for the Tabula—you just have to read the newspaper to realize that they exist."

"I can't believe that my father didn't want to be a Harlequin."

"And what's so surprising? That he was human— like the rest of us? I thought he had broken free of his family and that he was going to stay in Rome and paint. Then a Harlequin from Spain showed up and asked for help. And Dietrich gave in. When your father returned to Italy eight months later, he had taken his Harlequin name. Everything was changed—his normal life was over—but a love for Rome remained in his heart. We saw each other occasionally and he would send me letters twice a year. Sometimes the letters included a photograph of you. I watched you grow up and become a young lady."

"He trained me to become a Harlequin," Maya said. "Do you know what that means?"

Lumbroso touched Maya lightly on the shoulder. "Only you can forgive your father. All I can say is that he did love you."

Each lost in their own thoughts, they crossed the bridge and entered the Trastevere neighborhood on the other side of the river. The three- and four-story houses lined narrow streets—some no wider than alleyways. The houses were painted with faded pastel colors, and dark ivy crept up the walls.

Lumbroso led her down one street that ended at a cobblestone square called Piazza Mercanti. It was empty except for a dozen hungry seagulls fighting over the contents of a spilled trash can. The birds screeched at one another like a group of Romans arguing about football.

"Only tourists and invalids eat at such an early hour," Lumbroso said. "But it's a good time for a private conversation." They entered a trattoria that was empty of customers. A waiter with an imposing mustache escorted them to a back table, and Lumbroso ordered a bottle of pinot grigio and a first course of deep-fried cod fillets.

Maya took a sip of wine, but didn't touch the food. Lumbroso's view of her father was different from anything she had ever imagined. Did Thorn really care about her? Was it possible that he had never wanted to become a Harlequin? The implications of these questions were so disturbing that she pushed them from her mind and focused on the reason she had traveled to Rome.

"I didn't come here to talk about my father," she said. "A Harlequin named Linden said you were an expert on the six realms."

Lumbroso smiled as he cut the fish into bite-sized pieces. "A Traveller is the only real expert, but I know a good deal. Meeting your father changed my life. I've had a career in art appraisal, but my real passion has been learning about these different worlds. I have tried to acquire a copy of every book, diary, or letter that has described their complexity."

Keeping her voice low, Maya explained how she found Gabriel in Los Angeles and how they ended up in Europe. Lumbroso put down his fork and listened intently when she told him what they discovered on Skellig Columba.

"I think Gabriel went to find his father in the First

Realm. If he's trapped, is there any way I can bring him back?"

"No," Lumbroso said. "Not without going there yourself."

Both of them stopped talking when the waiter brought out the pasta course, the small semolina dumplings called *gnocchi alla Romana*. Maya wouldn't touch the food, but Lumbroso poured her another glass of wine.

"What do you mean? How is that possible?"

"You must understand that the classical Greeks and Romans did not perceive a rigid separation between our world and other realities. There were Travellers during that time, but the ancients also believed that certain 'doors' existed that allowed anyone to cross over to a different realm."

"So it's like a passageway?"

"I would say it's more like an access point available to any seeker. A modern analogy for this would be the so-called 'wormholes' described in theoretical physics. A wormhole is a shortcut through space and time that allows us to travel faster from one parallel universe to another. Many physicists these days sound like the Delphic oracle—with equations."

Lumbroso picked up a napkin and wiped some tomato sauce from his chin. "Reading ancient texts, it seems clear that many of the sacred places in the classical world, such as Stonehenge, were originally built around an object that provided an access point to other realms. To my knowledge, none of these access points still exist. But the Romans might have left us a guide that will show us where to find one."

Maya put down her glass of wine. "Is it a map?"

"It's much better than that. Maps can be lost or destroyed. This particular guide is hidden beneath the streets of Rome. It's the Horologium Augusti— the sundial created by the Emperor Augustus."

When the waiter came to their table, Lumbroso discussed various options for the next course, finally deciding on veal cooked with fresh sage. When they were alone again, he poured himself another glass of wine.

"The Horologium was not some little sundial found in the back garden. It was the center of Rome—an enormous circle of white travertine inlaid with bronze lines and letters. If you've walked passed the Italian Parliament building in the Piazza di Montecitorio, you've seen the Egyptian obelisk that created the shadow."

"But now the sundial is buried underground?"

"Most of ancient Rome is underground. It could be argued that every city has a ghost city hidden from view. A small portion of the sundial was excavated in the 1970s by German archaeologists—some friends of mine—but they stopped after a year of work. There are still natural springs beneath the streets of Rome, and a stream flows across the surface of the sundial. And there were security problems as well. The carabinieri didn't want the archaeologists digging a passageway that would lead directly to the Parliament building."

"So what does this have to do with finding an access point to another realm?"

"The sundial was more than just a clock and a calendar. It also served as the center of the Roman universe. On the outer rim of the sundial there were arrows pointing to Africa and Gaul, as well as directions to spiritual gates that led to other worlds. As I said, the ancients didn't have our limited view of reality. They would have seen the First Realm as a distant province on the edge of the known world.

"When the German archaeologists finished their project, most of the sundial was covered with dirt and rubble. But that was over thirty years ago, and Rome has experienced several floods since that time. Remember—an underground stream flows through the whole area. I've inspected the site and I'm convinced that a much larger section of the sundial is now exposed to view."

"So why didn't you check it out?" Maya asked.

"Anyone entering this area would have to be flexible, athletic, and"—Lumbroso gestured to his stomach—"a good deal less corpulent. You'd need an oxygen tank and breathing apparatus to go underwater. And you'd need to be brave. This ground is highly unstable."

Both of them were silent for a few minutes. Maya

took a sip of wine. "What if I bought the necessary equipment?"

"The equipment is not the problem. You're my friend's daughter—which means I want to help you—but no one has explored this area since the flooding. I want you to promise that you'll turn around and come back if it looks dangerous."

Maya's first reaction was to say *Harlequins don't promise*, but she had broken that rule with Gabriel.

"I'll try to be careful, Simon. I can't agree to anything more than that."

Lumbroso bunched up his napkin and dropped it on the table. "My stomach doesn't like this idea. That's a bad sign."

"But now I'm famished," Maya said. "So where's the waiter?"

3 4

The next evening Maya met Simon Lumbroso in front of the Pantheon. She had spent the day buying scuba equipment at a dive shop in the western suburbs and had stuffed everything into two canvas bags. Lumbroso had also gone shopping, buying a large battery-powered lantern, the kind of equipment miners carried in caves. He gazed at the tourists eating gelato in the square and smiled.

"The Greek philosopher Diogenes of Sinope wandered around Athens with a lantern looking for an honest man. We're looking for something equally rare, Maya. You need to take a photograph—just one photograph—of the directions that will lead us to another world." He smiled at her. "Are we ready?"

Maya nodded.

Lumbroso led her over to Campo Marzio, a side street near the Parliament building. Halfway down the block, he stopped in front of a doorway between a tearoom and a perfume store.

"Do you have a passkey?" Maya asked.

Lumbroso reached into his suit coat pocket and pulled out a wad of euros. "This is the only passkey you need in Rome."

He knocked loudly and a bald old man wearing rubber boots opened the door. Lumbroso greeted the man politely and shook his hand, paying the bribe without the vulgarity of mentioning money. The bald man let them into a hallway, said something in Italian, and then left the building.

"What did he tell you, Simon?"

" 'Don't be a fool and lock up when you're done.' "

They walked down the hallway to an open court-yard filled with lumber, scaffolding, and empty paint cans. Families had lived in the tenement for hundreds of years, but now the building was empty and the stucco walls were stained from flooding. All the windows were smashed, but iron bars still formed a grid in the window frames. The rusty bars made the building look like an abandoned prison.

Lumbroso pulled open an unlocked door and they climbed down stairs covered with plaster dust. When they reached what appeared to be the building's cellar, Lumbroso switched on the lantern and opened a door labeled with red paint: *PERICOLO—NO ENTRI*.

"There's no electric power from this point on, so

we'll have to use the lantern," Lumbroso explained. "Be very careful where you step."

Holding the lantern low, he moved slowly down a passageway with brick walls. The floor consisted of plywood boards placed over concrete crossbeams. Fifteen feet beyond the doorway, Lumbroso stopped and knelt beside a gap in the floorboards. Maya stood behind him, peered over his shoulder, and saw the Horologium Augusti.

The excavated section of the emperor's sundial had become the floor of a stone-walled cellar about eight feet wide and twenty feet long. Although the sundial was underwater, Maya could see its travertine surface as well as a few bronze lines and Greek letters inlaid in the limestone. The German archaeologists had removed all the rubble, and the room resembled a looted sepulchre. The only modern touch was a steel ladder that ran from the gap in the plywood boards to the floor of the cellar nine feet below.

"You go first," Lumbroso said. "I'll hand you the equipment; then I'll come down with the lantern."

Maya placed the two sacks of equipment on a plywood board and removed her jacket, shoes, and socks. Then she climbed down the ladder to the sundial. The water was cold and about three feet deep. Lumbroso handed Maya the equipment sacks, and she looped the drawstrings around the steps of the ladder so that they hung from opposite sides.

While Simon took off his fedora, suit coat, and

shoes, Maya inspected the cellar. As she moved around the room, little waves sloshed back and forth, breaking against the walls. Over the years, the minerals in the water had transformed the white travertine sundial into slabs of grayish stone; in various places it was pitted, cracked, and stained. The bronze lines and Greek symbols that had been embedded in the limestone had once been a bright gold color that glittered brightly in the Roman sun. The metal had oxidized completely and now the letters were dark green.

"I don't like ladders," Lumbroso said. He put one foot on the top rung as if to test the ladder's strength, and then climbed down slowly with the lantern. Maya walked over to the corner and found a drainage hole in the gray stone wall. The hole was about two feet square and completely underwater. Its bottom edge was flush with the surface of the sundial.

"The water flows out here?"

"Correct. That's where you have to go." Still wearing his long-sleeved white shirt, necktie, and black pants, Lumbroso stood with an odd sort of formality in the water. "Turn back immediately if it gets too difficult to move."

Maya returned to the ladder and took the scuba equipment out of the canvas bags. There was a belt with lead weights, a two-stage air regulator, a diving mask, and an air tank that was a foot long and four inches in diameter. She had also purchased an underwater flashlight and a digital underwater camera—the sort of thing a tourist would use when snorkeling in the Bahamas.

"That air tank looks very small," Lumbroso said.

"It's called a pony tank. You told me that there wasn't a lot of room in the tunnel."

Maya put on the weight belt first, attached one end of the regulator to the pony tank, and slung the camera's plastic lanyard around her neck. The tunnel was so narrow that she would have to hold the tank with one of her arms, pressing it tightly against her body.

"So what am I looking for?"

"You need to take photographs of any Latin or Greek phrases on the outside of the sundial. Some of these phrases will describe cities in the ancient world, while others will describe a spiritual location—an access point."

"And what if the words are covered with rubble?"

"You can brush it away, but don't touch the walls."

Maya pulled on the diving mask and sealed it against her face, then turned on the air and started to breathe with the mouthpiece.

"Good luck," Lumbroso said. "And, please—be careful."

She knelt on the floor and lowered her head beneath the water. Lying flat, she moved toward the opening in the wall. Maya could hear her own breath, the bubbles coming out of the regulator, and a scraping sound from the edge of the pony tank as she dragged it across the limestone floor.

When she reached the opening, she extended her arm and pointed the flashlight into the darkness. Over the years, the flowing water had cut an underground tunnel through the rubble of the past. The walls of the tunnel were an aggregate of stones, Roman brick, and chunks of white marble. It looked fragile, as if everything would crumble, but the real danger was created by the present era. In order to support the collapsing foundation of the building, someone had driven steel rods deep into the ground. The tips of the rods jutted out into the tunnel like the tips of rusty sword blades.

Pushing with her toes, Maya glided down the tunnel. When she looked up at the rubble and the steel rods, she felt as if the weight of Rome were directly over her head. Her body was pressed against the travertine floor of the sundial, but she couldn't find any words set in bronze.

The scuba regulator rasped. Bubbles rose past her face. Inch by inch, she crawled forward until her entire body was in the tunnel. The tunnel was so low and narrow that it was impossible to turn around. In order to return to the cellar room, she would have to push backward with her hands.

Forget about your fear, Thorn told her. *Concentrate on your sword.* Her father never seemed to hesitate about anything. And yet he had spent two years in Rome avoiding his destiny. Maya pushed everything but the tunnel out of her mind and kept moving forward.

She had traveled twelve or fifteen feet when the tunnel took a turn to the right. Passing beneath one of the steel rods, she entered a wider area that looked like an underground cave. The surface of the sundial looked dark in this area, but when she crawled closer she saw that the floor was embedded with bronze words written in both Greek and Latin.

Holding the flashlight with her left hand, Maya grabbed the underwater camera with her right and began taking pictures. Whenever she moved her body, shadows formed or disappeared.

As she crawled forward, the air tank got away from her and touched the side of the tunnel. Some debris was shifted loose from the wall and rolled across the sundial floor. It was nothing, really—just a few black pebbles—but she felt a stab of fear.

More sand and stones fell from the wall. A good-sized rock hit the floor and rolled toward her. She took a few more quick photographs and tried to ease backward, but suddenly a chunk of ceiling collapsed and fell in front of her.

The water was dark with sand. Maya tried to escape, but something was holding her. Fighting panic, she forced her palms flat onto the marble floor and pushed hard. There was an explosion of air bubbles and water rushed into her mouth.

She had cut the regulator tube on one of the metal rods. There was no air to breathe and no way to get out. Her flashlight was lost and she was struggling in total darkness. Maya gripped the mouthpiece with her teeth, reached over her shoulder, and felt for both sections of the severed air hose. The section connected to her mouth was filled with water, but air bubbled through the hose connected to the pony tank. She forced the two sections together and held them in her fist. Air mixed with water started to flow out of the mouthpiece. Maya swallowed the water and sucked the oxygen into her lungs.

With both sections of hose held tightly in her right hand, she pushed back with her left, feeling the gritty sand with her feet. Like a bystander staring at a car accident, her mind disengaged from the situation except to observe calmly and draw conclusions. She was completely blind, and within a minute or so the air tank would be empty. Her only chance was to find the tunnel that led back to the cellar room.

When her feet touched the side of the tunnel, she stopped immediately and slid her body sideways. Maya concentrated on the gritty texture of the fallen rubble. Her life had collapsed into a particle of bone and blood and tissue.

Trying not to cause another cave-in, she crawled backward inch by inch. The regulator made a faint gurgling sound and then her tongue tasted something that reminded her of ashes. She tried to inhale, but nothing filled her lungs. The ruptured hose had bled the tank dry.

Maya extended her arms, pushed backward, and her toes felt the bend in the tunnel. She kept moving and prayed that she wouldn't get caught on the barbs. It felt like her brain was reacting slowly and she wondered if she was about to pass out.

A few seconds later, she felt hands on her ankles. With a swift tug, Lumbroso pulled her out.

"What happened?" he asked. "I saw sand coming out of the tunnel. Are you injured? Are you all right?"

Maya ripped off the face mask, spit out the mouthpiece, and gasped for breath. Her lungs were burning, and it felt as if someone had punched her in the stomach. Lumbroso kept talking to her, but she couldn't answer. She was incapable of speech, and only one thought stayed in her brain: *I'm still alive.*

The underwater camera dangled from its lanyard, and she handed it to him like a precious stone.

* * *

AROUND EIGHT O'CLOCK the next morning, Maya was a customer at an outdoor café in the Piazza San Lorenzo in Lucina. The piazza was less than one hundred yards from the entrance to the deserted building that concealed the sundial. Directly below her feet were layers of the past and secret rivers flowing through the darkness.

If she closed her eyes, she could see herself trapped within the underwater tunnel, but she had no desire to reflect on that moment. She was alive and in this world. Everything that surrounded her seemed both ordinary—and beautiful. She touched the smooth marble top of the table while a young Italian waiter brought her a cup of cappuccino and a peach tart decorated with a sprig of mint. The crust of the tart was light and flaky, and she let the sweet peach filling linger on her tongue. Although her sword case hung from the back of the wrought-iron chair, she had the mad impulse to abandon it and wander around the square like an ordinary woman, entering each shop to sniff the perfume samples and try on silk scarves.

Lumbroso arrived as she finished the pastry. He was wearing his usual dark clothing and carrying a leather portfolio beneath his arm. "*Buongiorno*, Maya. *Come sta?* It is a pleasure to see you this morning." He sat and ordered a cappuccino.

"Last week I saw a tourist ordering a cappuccino at five o'clock in the afternoon. This is Roma, not Starbucks! The waiter was deeply offended. There should be a sign in all trattorias: 'It's Against the Law to Order a Cappuccino after Ten in the Morning.'"

Maya smiled. "What about an espresso?"

"Espresso is appropriate." He opened the portfolio and pulled out a manila folder filled with glossy photographs. "I downloaded the images last night and printed them on photo paper. You did a very good job, Maya. I could read everything quite clearly."

"Did it mention an access point?"

"The sundial combined locations that our modern sensibility would consider 'real,' as well as those places that connected you to another world. Look at this image . . ." He placed a photograph in front of her. "It's written in Latin and refers to *Aegyptus*—the Roman name for Egypt. After the death of Cleopatra, Egypt became part of the Empire. To the right of this Latin inscription are words in Greek."

Lumbroso handed her another photograph and sipped his cappuccino. Maya studied a photograph that showed both Greek and Latin words.

"The inscription uses a word that means 'doorway' or 'portal.'" Lumbroso picked up the photograph and began to translate. "The portal to God was taken from *Ludaea* to *Ta Netjer*—the Land of God."

"In other words, we don't know where the doorway is."

"I disagree. The directions are as clear as one of those guidebooks the tourists carry around Rome. *Ludaea* is the Roman name for the province that included Jerusalem. *Ta Netjer*—the Land of God—was also called *Punt*. It's generally believed to be northern Ethiopia."

Maya shrugged. "I don't understand, Simon. How could a portal—an access point—be portable?"

"Only one famous object was taken from Jerusalem to Ethiopia. It's a 'portal' that, in our modern day, is referred to as the Ark of the Covenant."

"The Ark is just a legend," Maya said. "It's like Atlantis or King Arthur."

Lumbroso leaned forward and spoke in a low voice. "I haven't studied the books about King Arthur, but I do know a great deal about the Ark of the Covenant. It's a chest of acacia wood plated with gold, with a solid-gold cover called a *kapporet*. The Bible even gives us the dimensions of this sacred object. It's about forty-five inches in length and twenty-seven inches in width.

"The Ark was created by the Israelites during the exile in the desert. It had a place of honor in the first temple, built by Solomon. The common assumption was that the Ark contained the Ten Commandments, but I think it's more logical that it's some kind of access point. The Ark was kept in the 'Holy of Holies'—the innermost part of the temple."

"But wasn't it destroyed by the Assyrians?"

"You probably mean the Babylonians." Lumbroso smiled. "The one fact that is consistent in all sources is that the Ark wasn't in the temple when Nebuchadnezzar sacked Jerusalem. The Babylonians made detailed lists of their plunder, but the Ark was never mentioned. The famous Copper Scroll—one of the Dead Sea Scrolls found in 1947—states explicitly that the *Mishkan*, the portable temple for the Ark, was removed from the temple before the invasion.

"A few people think that Josiah hid the Ark somewhere in Israel, but the inscription on the sundial reflects the legend that it was taken to Ethiopia by Menelik the First, the son of Solomon and the Queen of Sheba. The Romans knew that when they wrote the inscription."

"So the Ark is in Africa?"

"It's not exactly a secret, Maya. You can go on the Internet or read a dozen different books. The Ark is currently being kept at the Church of Saint Mary of Zion in the northern Ethiopian city of Axum. It's guarded by a group of Ethiopian priests, and only one priest is allowed to go into the shrine."

"There's one problem with your theory," Maya said. "If the Ark is in Ethiopia, then why hasn't Israel done something about reclaiming it or protecting it?"

"Ahhh, but they have. In 1972, a group of archaeologists from the Israel Museum flew to Ethiopia. They received permission from the Emperor Haile Selassie to examine certain historical artifacts. At the time there was a major drought in the province of Wollo and the emperor was desperate for international aid.

"These archaeologists traveled to the monasteries on Lake Tana and to the city of Axum. But, strangely enough, they never issued a report or any other public statement. Two weeks after their return to Jerusalem, Israel began to send military and humanitarian aid to Ethiopia. This support continued after the emperor's death in 1975. It still continues today." Lumbroso smiled and finished his cappuccino. "The Israelis don't publicize this aid and neither do the Ethiopians. Because, of course, there's no political reason for giving the money—unless you believe in the Ark."

Maya shook her head. "Maybe a few historians have thought up this theory and a few Ethiopian priests want to believe it. But why didn't the Israelis just grab the Ark and take it back to Jerusalem?"

"Because the Ark goes in a temple which no longer exists. The Dome of the Rock currently occupies the site: that's where the Prophet Muhammad ascended into paradise. If the Ark were returned to Jerusalem, then certain fundamentalist groups—both Christian and Jewish—would want to destroy the Dome of the Rock and rebuild the temple. That would start a war that would dwarf any previous conflicts.

"The men and women who lead Israel are devout Jews, but they're also pragmatists. Their objective is the continual survival of the Jewish people—not the start of World War Three. It's best for everyone if the Ark stays in Ethiopia and that people are encouraged to believe that it was destroyed thousands of years ago."

"And what happens if I go to Ethiopia?" Maya asked. "I can't just walk up to this shrine and demand to see the Ark."

"Of course not. That's why I have to go with you. For the last few years, I've bought artifacts from an Ethiopian Jew named Petros Semo. I'll ask him to meet us in Addis Ababa and help us talk to the priests."

"And the Ark is an access point that will take me to the First Realm?"

"Perhaps any of the realms. The texts can't agree on this matter. The general conclusion is that you have to send your spirit first and then follow it. I think that means you have to want to go there—want it with all your heart. We have left both history and science far behind at this point. If you step through this doorway, you abandon our particular reality."

"But will I find Gabriel?"

"I don't know."

"And what if I can't find him? Can I return to this world?"

"I don't know that either, Maya. If you study the classical myths about the underworld, they agree on only one thing—you have to go back the way you came."

Maya looked out at the piazza and the beauty that had captivated her only a few minutes ago. She had promised Gabriel that she would always stand beside him. If she refused to honor her own words, then that moment between them lost its meaning.

"So how do we get to Ethiopia?"

Lumbroso stuffed the photographs back into their envelope. "First—we order another cappuccino." He nodded to the waiter, and then pointed to their empty cups.

35

It was early spring in south England. When Michael stepped out onto the third-floor balcony of Wellspring Manor he could see that pale green leaves were beginning to appear on the beech trees that covered the surrounding hills. Directly below him, the guests at the afternoon party were leaving the house and wandering through the rose garden. White-jacketed waiters were serving glasses of sparkling wine and canapés, while a quartet of musicians played *The Four Seasons*. Although it had rained yesterday afternoon, this Sunday was so clear and warm that the sky looked vaguely artificial—a blue silk tent set up to shelter the party.

Wellspring was another property owned by the Evergreen Foundation. While the first two floors were dedicated to public activities, the top floor was a private suite guarded by the security staff. Michael had been living at the manor house for the last eight days. During this time, Mrs. Brewster had fully explained both the public and private goals of the Young World Leaders Program. The army colonels and police officials who were sampling the bite-sized crab cakes in the rose garden were visiting England to learn how to defeat terrorism. During three days of seminars, they learned about Internet monitoring, surveillance cameras, RFID chips, and total inform-ation systems.

The garden party was the culmination of this learn-ing process. The leaders would meet corporate representatives who were eager to establish this new technology in underdeveloped nations. Each leader was given a special leather folder to hold the business cards handed out after the first glass of wine.

Leaning over the edge of the balcony, Michael watched Mrs. Brewster move through the crowd. Her turquoise blue skirt and jacket stood out among the somber business suits and olive green military uniforms. From a distance, she appeared to be a catalyst molecule dropped into a beaker filled with different chemicals. As she met and talked and parted with a kiss, she formed new connections between the young leaders and those who wanted to serve them.

He left the balcony, passed through some French doors, and walked into what had once been a master bedroom. Now his father lay on an operating table in the center of the room. White plaster Cupids gazed down on him from the ceiling. Matthew Corrigan's head was shaved and sensors had been inserted into his brain. The body's heartbeat and temperature were continually monitored. One of the neurologists had announced that the lost Traveller was as "dead as you can be and still be alive."

It bothered Michael that he kept returning to his room to see the motionless body on the table. He felt like a boxer who had backed his opponent into one corner of the ring. It looked like the fight was over, but somehow his father had sidestepped and danced away from him.

"So here's the famous Matthew Corrigan," said a familiar voice.

Michael made a half turn and saw Kennard Nash standing in the doorway. Nash wore a blue business suit with an Evergreen Foundation pin on the lapel.

"Hello, General. I thought you were still on Dark Island."

"I was in New York last night, but I always show up for the final ceremony of the Young World Leaders Program. Besides, I wanted to inspect Mr. Boone's recent acquisition . . ." Nash strolled over to the table and studied Matthew Corrigan.

"This is really your father?"

"Yes."

The general extended his index finger and poked at Matthew's face. "I must admit, I'm a little disappointed. I thought he was going to be a more impressive-looking individual."

"If he were still active, he could have caused significant resistance to the Shadow Program in Berlin."

"But that's not going to happen, is it?" Nash sneered at Michael, making no effort to hide his contempt. "I realize that you've manipulated the executive board and made them frightened of a lifeless body on a table. As far as I'm concerned, Travellers have stopped being a relevant factor. That includes you—and your brother."

"You should speak to Mrs. Brewster. I think I'm helping the Brethren achieve our goals."

"I've heard about your various suggestions and I'm not impressed. Mrs. Brewster has always been a firm believer in our cause, but I think she's done great damage by allowing you to travel around Europe and spout a lot of nonsense."

"You were the first person to introduce me to the executive board, General."

"That's a mistake that will soon be corrected. It's time you went back to the research center, Michael. Or perhaps you could just join your father in a different realm. I mean, that's what Travellers are compelled to do. Correct? You're genetic freaks. Just like our splicers."

The French doors were still open, and Michael listened as the string quartet glided toward a soothing conclusion. A few seconds later, there was a slight squeal of audio feedback and then Mrs. Brewster's voice boomed out of a portable speaker.

"Wel-come," she said, pronouncing the word with two distinct syllables. "It's a beautiful day and a fitting conclusion to this three-day symposium of the Young World Leaders Program. I have been inspired—no, not just inspired—I have been genuinely moved by the comments I've heard in the garden today . . ."

"Sounds like Mrs. Brewster is about to begin her little speech." Nash thrust his hands in his pockets and headed for the doorway. "You coming along?"

"That's not necessary."

"No, of course not. You aren't really one of us. Are you?"

General Nash swaggered away while Michael remained behind with his father's body. The threat from Nash was quite real, but Michael felt calm at that moment. He had no intention of returning to a guarded room, nor was he planning to float off to another realm. There was still time for some maneuvering. He had already formed an alliance with Mrs. Brewster. Now he had to get other members of the Brethren on his side. Michael found it easy to talk to anyone these days. Since he could see the subtle, split-second changes in each person's expression, he could adjust his words to guide them in the right direction.

"So why didn't you do that?" he asked his father. "Get some money. Get some power. Get anything. Instead you made us hide . . ."

Michael waited for an answer, but his father

remained silent. Turning away from the body, Michael left the room and returned to the balcony. Mrs. Brewster was still giving her speech.

"All of you are true idealists," Mrs. Brewster said. "And I salute you for your strength and wisdom. You have rejected the foolish slogans of those who advocate the so-called 'virtue' of freedom. And freedom for whom? For criminals and terrorists? The decent hard-working people in this world want order, not rhetoric. They are desperate for strong leadership. I thank God that all of you are ready to answer this challenge. During the next year, a European country will take the first step toward an orderly control of their population. The success of this program will inspire governments everywhere."

Mrs. Brewster raised her wineglass. "I offer a toast to peace and stability."

There was a respectful murmur from the crowd. All over the rose garden, other glasses flashed in the sunlight.

36

Leaving Alice on the island with the nuns, Hollis and Mother Blessing returned to London. Hollis had been in the city for only twenty-four hours, but he had already come up with a plan. One of the Free Runners, a college student named Sebastian, had fled to his parents' house in South England, but Jugger and Roland weren't going anywhere. Jugger spent an hour pacing around a two-room apartment in Chiswick making speeches against the Tabula and waving his hands. Roland sat on a wooden stool, hunched forward with his hands on his knees. When Hollis asked what he was thinking, the Yorkshireman spoke in a low, menacing voice. "They're gonna pay for what they did."

At six, Hollis went back to the drum shop to guard Gabriel. Jugger showed up four hours later and wandered around the cluttered room inspecting the African statues and tapping his fingers on the drums.

"This place is something," he said. "Like a bloody trip to the Congo."

As it got close to midnight the Free Runner began to get nervous. He kept eating chocolate bars and his head jerked around whenever he heard a noise.

"Do they know I'm coming?"

"No," Hollis said.

"Why not?"

"There's no reason to be frightened. Just tell them what you told me."

"I'm not frightened." Jugger stood up straight and sucked in his stomach. "I just don't like that Irishwoman. She'd kill you if you coughed on her."

The dead-bolt lock clicked softly, then Linden and Mother Blessing were in the shop. Neither Harlequin seemed pleased to see Jugger. Instinctively, Mother Blessing crossed the room and guarded the entrance to the hidden apartment where Gabriel's body lay in the darkness.

"It appears that you have a new friend in London, Mr. Wilson. But I don't recall making the introduction," Mother Blessing said.

"Maya saved Jugger and his friends when she came back to London. She told me where they were hiding. As you know, Gabriel gave a speech to the Free Runners. He asked them to find out what the Tabula were planning."

"And that's why those men tried to kill us," Jugger said. "I guess people talked too much on their mobiles or sent some gossip through the Internet. But we got some crucial information before they burned down the house."

Mother Blessing looked skeptical. "I doubt that someone like you knows anything crucial."

"The Tabula have a public face called the Evergreen Foundation," Jugger said. "They do genetic research and bring foreign policemen here to England so they can learn how to track people on the Internet."

"We know all about the Young World Leaders Program," Mother Blessing said. "It's been going on for several years."

Jugger stepped between a zebra-skin drum and a wooden statue of a rain god. "Our friends in Berlin say that the Evergreen Foundation has been testing a beta version of a computer program called Shadow. They use data from RFID chips and surveillance cameras to track every person in the city. If it works in Berlin, they're going to roll it out to all of Germany and then the rest of Europe."

Linden glanced at Mother Blessing. "Berlin is a good location for them. That's where they currently have their computer center."

"And we know where the center is," Jugger said. "A Free Runner named Tristan found the building. It's in an area that used to be the dead zone for the Berlin Wall."

"That's all we need to know at this point. Thanks

for coming tonight, Jugger." Hollis opened the entrance door to the shop. "I'll be in touch with you."

"You know where to find me." Jugger sauntered over to the doorway. "There's just one thing I want to know—is Gabriel all right?"

"No need to worry," Linden said. "He's being protected."

"I don't doubt that. Just be aware that the Free Runners are still talking about him. He made us feel that there was a little bit of hope."

Jugger left the shop and the three of them were alone together. Mother Blessing shifted her sword case and crossed the room. "He might tell his friends about this place. That means we have to move the Traveller."

"Is that all you're going to say?" Hollis asked. "Aren't we going to do anything about his information?"

"What happens in Berlin is not our concern."

"If the Shadow Program works, every government in the world is going to end up using it."

"The technology is inevitable," Mother Blessing said.

Hollis concentrated on the silver locket hanging from his neck and an ice-cold anger changed the tone of his voice. "You can think whatever you want—run around the world with your goddamn sword—but I'm not going to let the Tabula win."

"I want obedience from you, Mr. Wilson. Not initiative. Blind obedience and mindless bravery."

"Is that why you brought me to see Vicki's body?" Hollis asked. "You wanted to turn me into a perfect little soldier?"

Mother Blessing smiled coldly. "I guess it didn't work."

"I want to destroy the people who killed Vicki. But I've got my own way of doing things."

"You don't know the history of the Tabula and the Harlequins. This conflict has been going on for thousands of years."

"And look what's happened. You Harlequins are so wrapped up in the past—all your little traditions—that you've lost the war."

Linden sat down on a bench. "I don't think we're entirely defeated. But we are at a turning point. It's time we did something."

Mother Blessing spun around and faced the other Harlequin. Although her face was a rigid mask, her dark green eyes were intense and focused. "So now you're on Mr. Wilson's side?"

"I'm not on anyone's side, but it's time to face the enemy. The Tabula don't fear us anymore, madam. We've been hiding for a long time."

Mother Blessing touched her sword case as she moved around the cluttered room. Hollis felt as if she wanted to kill someone just to prove that she was alive. "Do you have a proposal?" she asked Hollis.

"I want to travel to Berlin, contact the Free Runners there, and destroy the Shadow Program."

"And you're going to do this alone?"

"Looks that way."

"You'll fail completely—unless a Harlequin is with you. Any successful plan will require my participation."

"And what if I don't want you to come along?" Hollis asked.

"You don't have a choice, Mr. Wilson. What you're telling us is that you want to be an ally, not a mercenary. All right, I'll accept that change of status. But even allies require supervision."

Hollis let a few seconds pass, and then he nodded his head. Mother Blessing relaxed slightly and smiled at Linden. "I can't imagine why Mr. Wilson wouldn't want to go to Berlin with me. I'm just a pleasant middle-aged Irishwoman . . ."

"*Oui, madame. Une femme Irlandaise* . . . with a very sharp sword."

At random intervals, the man with the blond braids and the black man wearing the white lab coat would remove Gabriel from his cell and drag him downstairs to the school gymnasium. The long, narrow room still had bleachers on one side and a wooden floor with red stripes painted on the edge. Instead of basketball and badminton, the room was used for the torture of prisoners.

There were no new forms of torture in hell. All of the techniques used to inflict pain, fear, and humiliation had already been used in Gabriel's world. At some earlier time, the wolves had learned about the four barriers that separated their own realm from the others; their particular system of torture corresponded to the barriers of air, fire, water, and earth.

For the interrogation inspired by air, Gabriel's wrists were tied to a rope and his arms twisted behind his back. The rope was attached to a basketball hoop;

then he was pulled upward so that he was dangling a few inches off the ground. "Are you flying?" the men asked. "Why don't you fly a little more." Then someone would push him, and Gabriel would swing back and forth while his arms were almost pulled from their sockets.

For fire, metal rods were heated up in a gas flare and then pressed against his skin. For water, his head was pushed deep into a tub of water and released only when he had sucked water into his lungs.

The "earth" interrogation was particularly frightening. One day, he was blindfolded and dragged out of his cell to a patch of dirt behind the school. Someone had placed a straight-backed chair at the bottom of a deep pit in the ground. Gabriel was strapped to the chair and then—slowly—his interrogators began to bury him alive.

The cold dirt surrounded his feet first, and then moved up past his legs, waist, and chest. Occasionally, the two wolves stopped and asked the same questions: *Where is the passageway? How do we find it? Who knows a way out of this place?* Finally the dirt reached Gabriel's face. He was completely covered, each breath drawing dirt into his nostrils, before the two men dug him out.

During each of these ordeals, Gabriel wondered if his father had also been captured. Maybe another group on the Island was holding him prisoner or maybe Matthew had finally found the passageway home. Gabriel tried to figure out what lesson his father had learned from this place. It wasn't surprising to discover that hatred and anger had a persistent power, but compassion still survived within his heart.

Gabriel refused to eat the scraps of food brought to his cell, and the hungry guards gobbled down anything left in the bowl. Gradually, he became frail and weak, but his memories of Maya remained. He could see the intense grace of her body as they practiced together in the loft back in New York. He could remember the sadness in her eyes and the way her skin felt against his when they made love in the chapel. These moments were gone—lost forever—but sometimes they seemed more real than anything around him.

* * *

THE BLOND MAN called himself Mr. Dewitt, and the black man was Mr. Lewis. They were enormously proud of their names, as if having a name suggested both an elaborate past and a possible future. Perhaps because of the lab coat, Lewis had a quiet, serious manner. Dewitt was like a big boy in a schoolyard. Sometimes, when the two men were dragging their prisoner through the hallways, Dewitt would tell a joke and laugh. Both wolves were terrified of the commissioner of patrols, who held the power of life and death in this section of the city.

Time passed and, once again, he was brought back down to the gymnasium, where the tub of water was waiting for him. The men tied Gabriel's wrists in front of him with a length of rope, and he suddenly glanced up at them.

"Do you think it's right to do this?"

Both men looked surprised—as if they had never heard this question before. They glanced at each other, and then Lewis shook his head. "There's no right or wrong on this island."

"What did your parents teach you when you were children?"

"Nobody grew up here," Dewitt growled.

"Were there any books in the school library? A philosophy book or a religious book—like the Bible?"

Both men glanced at each other as if they shared a secret; then Lewis reached into the outside pocket of the lab coat and pulled out a loose-leaf school notebook filled with stained sheets of paper.

"This is what we call a Bible," he explained. "After the fighting started, certain people realized that they were going to be killed. Before they died, they wrote books describing where weapons were stored and how to destroy their enemies."

"It's kind of a textbook explaining how to be powerful next time around," Dewitt explained. "People hide Bibles around the city so that they can find them at the beginning of the next cycle. Have you seen the words and the numbers painted on the walls? Most of the numbers are clues about finding Bibles and caches of weapons."

"Of course, some people are really smart," Lewis said. "They write false Bibles that deliberately give the wrong advice." Cautiously, he offered the book to Gabriel. "Maybe you could tell us if this is a false Bible."

Gabriel accepted the notebook and opened the cover. Each page was scrawled with instructions on how to find weapons and where to establish defensive positions. Some pages were filled with meandering explanations about why hell existed and who was supposed to live there.

Gabriel handed the notebook back to Lewis. "I can't tell you if it's real or not."

"Yeah," Dewitt muttered. "Nobody knows anything."

"There's only one rule around here," Lewis said. "You do what's good for yourself."

"You better rethink your strategy," Gabriel said. "Eventually, you'll be executed by the commissioner of patrols. He's going to make sure that he's the last person alive."

Dewitt scrunched up his face like a small boy. "Okay. So maybe that's true. But there's nothing we can do about it."

"We could help each other. If I discovered a door out of here, you two could leave with me."

"You could do that?" Lewis asked.

"I just have to find the passageway. The commissioner said that most of the legends involve the room where they keep the school files."

The wolves glanced at each other. Their fear of the commissioner almost overwhelmed their desire to escape.

"Maybe . . . maybe I could take you there for a quick view," Dewitt said.

"If you're getting off the Island, then I'm leaving, too," Lewis said. "Let's do it now. Everyone is out of the building, doing a sweep for cockroaches . . ."

The two men untied Gabriel's wrists and helped him stand up. They held his arms tightly as they left the gymnasium and hurried down an empty hallway to the file room. The wolves appeared cautious and frightened as they opened the door and pulled him inside.

The file room hadn't changed since his last visit. The only light came from the small flares burning from broken pipes. Although Gabriel was in pain, he felt alert. There was something in this room. A way out. He glanced over his shoulder and saw that Dewitt and Lewis were watching him as if he were a magician about to perform a spectacular trick.

Slowly, he shuffled down the outside aisle past the metal file cabinets. When he and Michael were little boys they used to play a game with their mother on rainy days. She would hide a small object somewhere in the house and they would search for it while she occasionally told them they were "cold" or "warm." Down one aisle. Up another. There was something near the work area at the center of the room. *Warm*, he thought. *Warmer. No, now you're going the wrong way.*

Suddenly, the door to the file room burst open. Before Lewis and Dewitt could react, a group of armed men ran down the aisles.

"Take their weapons," a voice said. "Don't let them get away." The men grabbed the two traitors as the commissioner appeared, holding his gun.

Hollis gazed out the window of the Eurostar train as it raced down a gradient and entered the tunnel that ran beneath the English Channel. The first-class train car resembled the cabin of a passenger plane. A French steward pushed a trolley down the aisle, serving a breakfast of croissants, orange juice, and champagne.

Mother Blessing sat beside him wearing a gray business suit and eyeglasses. Her unruly red hair was pinned back in a neat bun. As she read coded e-mail on her laptop computer, she looked like an investment banker on her way to meet a client in Paris.

Hollis had been impressed by the efficient way the Irish Harlequin had organized their trip to Berlin. Within forty-eight hours of the meeting at Winston Abosa's drum shop, Hollis had been provided with business clothes, a forged ID, and documentation for his new identity as a film distribution executive based in London.

The train emerged from the tunnel and headed east through France. Mother Blessing switched off her computer and ordered a glass of champagne from the steward. There was something about her imperious manner that made people lower their heads when they served her. "Is there anything else I can bring you, madam?" the steward asked in a soothing voice. "I noticed that you didn't eat breakfast . . ."

"You've done your job adequately," Mother Blessing said. "We don't need anything more from you." Holding the napkin-wrapped bottle of champagne, the steward retreated back down the aisle.

For the first time since they had left London, Mother Blessing turned her head toward Hollis and acknowledged the fact that another human being was sitting next to her. A few weeks ago, he might have smiled and tried to charm this difficult woman, but everything had changed. His anger about Vicki's death was so powerful and unrelenting that sometimes it felt as if a malevolent spirit had taken over his body.

The Irish Harlequin removed the gold chain hanging from her neck. It held a black plastic device about the size of a stubby pencil. "Take this, Mr. Wilson. It's a flash drive. If we're able to get into the Tabula computer center, it's your job to attach this to a USB outlet. You don't even have to touch a keyboard.

The drive is programmed to download automatically."

"What's stored on this?"

"Ever heard of a banshee? It's a creature that wails outside a house in Ireland before someone dies. Well, this is the Banshee Virus. It destroys not only all the data on a mainframe computer, but the computer itself."

"Where'd you get it? From some hacker?"

"The authorities like to blame computer viruses on seventeen-year-old boys, but they know quite well that the most powerful viruses come from government research teams or criminal groups. I bought this particular virus from former IRA soldiers living in London. They specialize in extortion attempts on gambling Web sites."

Hollis placed the chain around his neck and tucked the flash drive under his shirt next to Vicki's silver locket. "And what if this virus gets out onto the Internet?"

"That's highly improbable. It's designed for a self-contained system."

"But it could happen?"

"Many unpleasant things can happen in this world. It's not my problem."

"Are all Harlequins as self-centered as you?"

Mother Blessing removed her glasses and gave Hollis a hard, critical look. "I'm not self-centered, Mr. Wilson. I concentrate on a few goals and discard everything else."

"Have you always acted this way?"

"I don't need to explain myself to you."

"I'm just trying to understand why somebody becomes a Harlequin."

"I suppose I could have quit and run away, but the life suits me. Harlequins have broken free of the petty annoyances of day-to-day life. We don't worry about dry rot in the basement or this month's credit card bill. We have no lovers to upset because we don't come home on time, or friends who feel put out because we don't return their calls. Aside from our swords, we have no attachment to any object. Even our names aren't important. As I get older, I have to force myself to remember the current name on my passport."

"And that makes you happy?"

"'Happy' is such an overused word it's almost lost its meaning. Happiness exists, of course, but it's a moment that passes. If you accept the idea that most Travellers cause positive change in this world, then a Harlequin's life has *meaning*. We defend the right of humanity to grow and evolve."

"You defend the future?"

"Yes. That's a good way to put it." Mother Blessing finished the champagne and placed her glass on the folding table. As she appraised Hollis, he sensed a perceptive mind working behind her harsh persona. "Does that life interest you? Harlequins usually come from certain families, but sometimes we accept outsiders."

"I don't give a damn about the Harlequins. I just want to make the Tabula suffer for what they did to Vicki."

"As you wish, Mr. Wilson. But I warn you from my own experience: some hungers can never be satisfied."

* * *

THEY REACHED THE Gare du Nord train station by ten o'clock in the morning and took a taxi to the northeast suburb of Clichy-sous-Bois. The area was dominated by public housing projects—huge gray buildings that loomed over side streets crammed with video stores and butcher shops. The blackened shells of burned-out cars were everywhere, and the only bright colors in the neighborhood came from bedsheets and baby clothes drying on clotheslines. Their French driver locked the doors of the cab as they glided past women in chadors and sullen groups of young men wearing hooded sweatshirts.

Mother Blessing ordered the driver to let them off at a bus stop, then led Hollis down a cobblestone street to an Arabic bookshop. The storeowner accepted an envelope of cash without saying a word and handed Mother Blessing a key. She went out the back door of the shop and used the key to unlock the padlock holding a steel garage door. Inside the garage was a late-model Mercedes-Benz. Every detail had been handled. There was fuel in the gas tank, water bottles in the cup holders, and a key in the ignition.

"What about the car's registration?"

"It's owned by a shell corporation with an address in Zurich."

"And weapons?"

"They should be in the back."

Mother Blessing opened the trunk and took out a cardboard shipping box that contained her Harlequin sword and a black canvas bag. She placed her laptop computer in the bag and Hollis saw that it held bolt cutters, lock picks, and a small canister of liquid nitrogen for disabling infrared motion detectors. Two aluminum suitcases had also been left in the trunk. They contained a Belgian-made submachine gun and two 9mm automatics with holsters.

"Where did you get this stuff?"

"Weapons are always available. It's like a cattle auction in Kerry. You find a seller and haggle over the price."

Mother Blessing went to the bathroom and returned wearing black wool pants and a sweater. She opened the equipment bag and took out an electric-powered screwdriver. "I'm going to disable the car's black box. It's connected to the air bag."

"Why? Isn't that supposed to record information about accidents?"

"That was the original intention." The Harlequin

opened the driver's front door and lay down on the seat. She began to unscrew the plastic panel beneath the car's steering wheel. "At first, Event Data Recorders were just for accidents, and then car rental companies began to use electronic monitoring to identify drivers who were speeding. These days, all new vehicles have attached the black box to the GPS device. Not only do they know the location of your car, but they can tell if you're accelerating, using the brakes, or wearing your seat belt."

"How did they get away with this?"

Mother Blessing pried off the panel, exposing the car's air bag system. "If privacy had a gravestone it might read: 'Don't Worry. This Was for Your Own Good.'"

* * *

THEY TURNED ONTO the A2 highway and drove across the French border into Belgium. While Mother Blessing concentrated on the road, Hollis attached a satellite phone to the computer and contacted Jugger in London. Jugger had received another message from some Free Runners in Berlin. Once Hollis and Mother Blessing reached the city, they were supposed to meet these people at an apartment building on Auguststrasse.

"Did he give us any names?" Mother Blessing asked.

"Two Free Runners named Tristan and Kröte."

Mother Blessing smiled. "Kröte is the German word for toad."

"It's just his nickname. That's all. I mean—come on—you're called Mother Blessing."

"That wasn't my choice. I grew up in a family of six children. My uncle was a Harlequin and my family picked me to carry on the tradition. My brothers and sisters became citizens with jobs and families. I learned how to kill people."

"Are you angry about that?"

"Sometimes you talk like a psychologist, Mr. Wilson. Is that an American affectation? If I were you, I wouldn't waste time worrying about childhood. We're living in the present, stumbling toward the future."

* * *

WHEN THEY CROSSED into Germany, Hollis took the steering wheel. He was startled to discover that there was no speed limit on the Autobahn. The Mercedes was going 160 kilometers an hour and other cars raced past them. After hours of driving, signs appeared for Dortmund, Bielefeld, Magdeburg, and finally—Berlin. Hollis took exit seven to Kaiserdamm, and a few minutes later they were cruising down Sophie-Charlotten-Strasse. It was close to midnight. Glass and steel skyscrapers glowed with light, but very few people were out.

They parked the car on a side street and took their weapons out of the trunk. Both of them concealed a 9mm automatic beneath their clothing. Mother Blessing slid her Harlequin sword into a metal tube with a shoulder strap while Hollis unloaded the submachine gun and placed it in the equipment bag.

Hollis wondered if he was going to die tonight. He felt empty inside, detached from his own life. Perhaps that was what Mother Blessing had seen in him; he was cold enough to become a Harlequin. It was a chance to defend the future, but Harlequins were always going to be hunted. No friends. No lovers. No wonder Maya's eyes had shown such loneliness and pain.

The address on Auguststrasse turned out to be a shabby five-story building. On the ground floor was Ballhaus Mitte, a working-class dance hall now taken over by a restaurant and nightclub. There was a line of young Germans waiting to get inside. They smoked cigarettes and watched as one couple kissed passionately. When the door was opened everyone was hit with a sound wave of harsh electronic music.

"We're going to 4B," Mother Blessing said.

Hollis checked his watch. "We're an hour early."

"It's always best to be early. If you don't know your contact, never show up when you promised."

Hollis followed her into the building and up a

staircase. Apparently, the wiring was being replaced throughout the building, because the walls were ripped open and plaster dust covered the floor. The music coming from the nightclub began to fade and then it disappeared.

When they reached the fourth floor, Mother Blessing motioned with the palm of her hand. *Be quiet. Get ready.* Hollis touched the doorknob for apartment 4B and realized that it wasn't locked. He glanced over his shoulder. Mother Blessing had drawn her automatic and was holding it close to her chest. When he opened the door, the Harlequin charged into an empty room.

The apartment was filled with cast-off furniture. There was a couch with no legs, two old mattresses, and some mismatched tables and chairs. Every wall in the apartment was decorated with printed photographs of Free Runners performing cartwheels in the air, backward somersaults, and running cat leaps from one building to another. It looked as if the young men and women in the photographs were free of the laws of gravity.

"Now what?" Hollis asked.

"Now we wait." Mother Blessing slid the gun back into her shoulder holster and sat down on a kitchen chair.

At exactly one o'clock in the morning, someone climbed down the facade of the Ballhaus. Hollis saw two legs dangling in the air just outside the window, and then the climber's left foot found an ornamental cornice. He reached the ledge outside, pulled up the window, and jumped into the room. The climber was about seventeen years old. He wore torn jeans and a hooded sweatshirt. His long black hair was braided to resemble dreadlocks, and he had geometric tattoos on the backs of his hands.

A few seconds later, another pair of legs dangled above the window frame. The second Free Runner was a boy about eleven or twelve years old. He had a mass of curly brown hair that made him look like a feral child raised in the forest. A digital recording device was clipped to his belt, and earphones covered each ear.

After the boy entered the room, his older friend bowed. There was a certain exaggerated quality in his movements; he was like an actor who was always conscious of his audience.

"*Guten Abend*. Welcome to Berlin."

"I'm not impressed with your climbing," Mother Blessing said. "Next time you can use the stairs."

"I thought this was a quick way to show—what is the English word—our 'credentials.' We are from the Spandau crew of Free Runners. I'm Tristan and this is my cousin, Kröte."

The curly-haired boy was bobbing his head up and down to whatever music was in his download file. Suddenly, he noticed that everyone was staring at him. Looking shy, he retreated to the window. Hollis wondered if Kröte was going to return to the ledge and escape.

"Does he speak English?" Hollis asked.

"Just a few words." He turned to his cousin. "Kröte! Speak English!"

"Multidimensional," the boy whispered.

"*Sehr gut!*" Tristan smiled proudly. "He learned that on the Internet."

"And is that how you heard about the Shadow Program?"

"No. It was from the Free Runner community. Our friend Ingrid was working for a company called Personal Customer. I guess she was good at her job, because a man named Lars Reichhardt asked her to work for his division. Each person on the team was given a small job and told not to share information with their colleagues. Two weeks ago, Ingrid got access to another part of the system and found out about the Shadow Program. Then we got the e-mail from the British Free Runners."

"Hollis and I need to get into the computer center," Mother Blessing said. "Can you help us?"

"Of course!" Tristan extended his hands as if he were offering them a gift. "We'll take you all the way."

"Do we have to climb up walls?" Mother Blessing asked. "I didn't bring any ropes."

"Ropes are not necessary. We're going beneath the streets. During World War Two, thousands of bombs fell on Berlin, but Hitler was safe in his bunker. Most of the bunkers and tunnels are still there. Kröte has been exploring the system since he was nine years old."

"I guess you guys don't have time for school," Hollis said.

"We go to school—sometimes. The girls are there, and I like to play football."

* * *

THE FOUR OF them left Ballhaus a few minutes later and crossed the river. Kröte was carrying a nylon backpack that contained his equipment for going underground. Looking like a wild-haired Boy Scout, he kept darting ahead of his cousin.

After walking down a wide avenue that bordered the Tiergarten, they reached the Memorial to the Murdered Jews of Europe. The Holocaust memorial was a large, sloping grid covered with concrete slabs of different heights. Hollis thought they looked like thousands of gray coffins. Tristan explained that the antigraffiti chemical painted on the slabs was provided by an affiliate of the company that had manufactured the Zyklon-B used in the death chambers.

"For war, they made poison gas. For peace, they fight taggers." Tristan shrugged. "It's all part of the Vast Machine."

A row of souvenir shops and cafés was directly

across the street from the memorial. The building looked like a flimsy structure created with plywood and a few pieces of glass. Kröte ran past a Dunkin' Donuts shop and disappeared around the corner of the building. They found the boy unlocking a padlock on a steel hatch cover set flush to the concrete.

"Where'd you get the key?" Mother Blessing asked.

"We cut the city lock a year ago and put on a substitute."

Kröte opened his knapsack and took out three flashlights. For his own use, he slipped on a headlamp with a high-intensity lightbulb.

They pulled open the hatch and hurried down a steel ladder. Hollis climbed with one hand on the rungs while he held the equipment bag to his chest. They reached a maintenance tunnel filled with communications cables, and Kröte unfastened another padlock on an unmarked steel door.

"Why hasn't anybody noticed that you changed the locks?" Hollis asked.

"Nobody official wants to enter this place—just explorers like us. It's dark and scary down here. It's *altes Deutschland*. The past."

One by one, they passed through the doorway to a corridor with a concrete floor. Now they were directly below the memorial, standing in the bunker used by Joseph Goebbels and his staff during the bombing raids. Hollis had been expecting something a bit more impressive—dust-covered office furniture and a Nazi banner hanging on the wall. Instead, their little pool of light illuminated concrete-block walls coated with a grayish-white paint and the words *Rauchen Verboten*. No smoking.

"The paint is fluorescent. After all these years, it still works."

Kröte paced slowly down the corridor with his light beam focused on the wall. "*Licht*," he said in a faint voice.

Tristan told Hollis and Mother Blessing to turn off their flashlights. In the dark they saw that Kröte's movements had created a bright green line on the wall that glowed for three or four seconds before fading.

They switched on the flashlights again and continued through the bunker. In one room there was an old bed frame, stripped of its mattress. Another room looked like a small clinic, with a white examination table and an empty glass cabinet.

"The Russians raped the women of Berlin and looted almost everything," Tristan said. "They stayed away from only one place in this bunker. Maybe they were too lazy or it was too horrible to see."

"What are you talking about?" Mother Blessing asked.

"Thousands of Germans killed themselves when the Russians arrived. And where did they do it? In the toilet. It was one of the few places where you could be alone."

Kröte was standing beside an open doorway with the word *Waschraum* painted on the wall. Arrows pointed in two directions: *Männer* and *Frauen*. "The bones are still in the toilet stalls," Tristan announced. "You can see them—if you're not frightened."

Mother Blessing shook her head. "A waste of time."

But Hollis was compelled to follow the boy up three steps and through a door that led to the women's washroom. The two light beams revealed a row of wooden toilet cabinets. Their doors were closed, and Hollis felt as if they concealed the remains of more than one suicide. Kröte took a few steps forward and pointed. Near the end of the room one of the wooden doors was slightly open. A mummified hand, looking like a black claw, pushed through the gap. Hollis felt as if he had been guided into the land of the dead. His entire body shivered and he hurried back to the main corridor.

"Did you see the hand?"

"Yeah. I saw it."

"And all Berlin is built on top of this," Tristan said. "Built on the dead."

"I don't give a damn," Mother Blessing snapped. "Let's go."

At the end of the corridor was another steel hatch, but this one was unlocked. Tristan grabbed the handle and pulled it open. "Now we enter the old sewage system. Because this area was near the wall, both East and West Germany left it alone."

They climbed beneath the bunker into a drainage pipe about eight feet in diameter. Water trickled along the floor of the pipe. Their flashlights touched the surface and made it gleam. Salt stalactites came down from the top of the pipe like pieces of white string. There were white mushrooms and a strange-looking fungus that resembled yellowish globs of fat. Splashing through the water, Kröte guided them forward. When he reached a juncture and turned to wait, the light jiggled like a firefly.

Eventually they reached a much smaller pipe that emptied into the larger system. Kröte began chattering in German to his cousin, pointing at the pipe and gesturing with his hands.

"This is it. Crawl about ten meters down the drain and force your way in."

"What are you talking about?" Mother Blessing glared at Tristan. "You promised to take us all the way."

"We're not going into a Tabula computer center," Tristan said. "It's too dangerous."

"The real danger is in front of you, young man. I dislike people who don't deliver what they promise . . ."

"But we're doing you a favor!"

"That's your interpretation, not mine. All I know is that you accepted an *obligation*."

The coldness in the Harlequin's eyes and the precise way she spoke were intimidating. Tristan stopped dancing around, frozen in the middle of the tunnel. Kröte glanced at his cousin and looked frightened.

Hollis stepped forward. "Let me go in first. I'll check things out."

"I will wait for ten minutes, Mr. Wilson. If you're not back, there will be consequences."

39

Hollis crawled through the horizontal pipe toward a distant patch of light. The pipe was narrow and his hands touched a slimy liquid that felt like motor oil mixed with water. Quickly, he reached a steel drainage grate set in a frame at the top of the pipe. The light from the room above him was divided into little squares by the grate, and he lay directly beneath a grid of lines.

He bent his head so that his chin was touching his chest, and then he came up so that his upper back was in contact with the grate. The steel rectangle was about three inches thick and very heavy, but his legs were strong and the grate didn't appear to be bolted in place. Hollis pushed upward until the rectangle broke out of its frame. He raised his hands and shifted the grate a few inches to the right. When a four-inch gap appeared, he changed his position and pushed the grate sideways across the floor.

Hollis pulled himself out of the drainage pipe and immediately drew his handgun. He found himself in an underground corridor lined with electric cable and water pipes. When nothing happened, he returned to the drainage pipe and crawled back to Mother Blessing and the two Free Runners.

"This pipe takes us to a maintenance area. It looks like a safe entry point. There's no one there."

Tristan looked relieved. "You see?" he asked Mother Blessing. "Everything is perfect."

"I doubt that," she said, and handed the equipment bag to Hollis.

"Can we go?"

"Thank you," Hollis said. "And be careful."

Tristan had regained some of his confidence. He bowed from the waist, and Kröte gave Hollis a big smile. "Good luck from the Spandau Free Runners!"

* * *

HOLLIS DRAGGED THE equipment bag down the pipe with Mother Blessing a few yards behind him. When they were both standing in the maintenance corridor, the Harlequin pressed her mouth against his ear. "Speak softly," she whispered. "They could have voice sensors."

They moved cautiously down the corridor to a heavy steel door with a slot for a key card. Mother Blessing placed the equipment bag on the floor and unzipped it. She took out the submachine gun and something that looked like a credit card fastened to a thin electric cable. The Harlequin attached the cable to her laptop computer, typed a command on the keyboard, and inserted the card in the door slot.

They both watched the computer screen as six blue squares appeared on the screen. It took about a minute to place a three-digit number in the first square, but then the process went faster. About four minutes later, all six squares were filled and the lock clicked open.

"Do we go in?" Hollis whispered.

"Not yet. We can't avoid surveillance cameras, so we'll have to use a shielder." She picked up something that looked like a small video camera. "Carry this on your shoulder. When I open the door, press the silver button."

As Mother Blessing repacked the equipment bag, Hollis placed the shielder device on his right shoulder and aimed it forward.

"Ready?"

Holding the submachine gun, Mother Blessing eased the door open. Hollis stepped into the doorway, saw a surveillance camera, and pressed the button of the shielder as if he were taking a video. An infrared beam was projected down the corridor. The beam struck the retroreflective lens of a surveillance camera and the infrared light was bounced back to the source. Once the position of the camera was determined, a green laser beam was automatically aimed at the camera lens.

"Don't stand here," Mother Blessing said. "Start moving."

"What about the surveillance camera?"

"The laser takes care of that. If a security guard is watching his monitor, all he'll see is a flash of light on the screen."

They hurried down the corridor and turned the corner. Once again, the shielder detected a new camera and a laser beam hit the center of the lens. A second door was at the end of the corridor, which led to an emergency staircase. They followed the staircase upward to the landing and paused again.

"You ready?" Mother Blessing asked.

Hollis nodded. "Keep going."

"I spent too many months sitting around on that wretched island," Mother Blessing said. "This is much more entertaining."

She pushed open the door and they entered a basement room filled with machines and communications equipment. A white walkway on the floor led to a reception desk where a security guard was eating a sandwich wrapped in wax paper.

"Stay here," Mother Blessing said to Hollis. She handed him the submachine gun, stepped out of the shadows, and walked briskly toward the reception area. "Don't worry! Everything is going to be all right! Did you get the phone call?"

Still holding the sandwich, the guard shook his head. "What phone call?"

The Irish Harlequin drew the automatic from beneath her jacket and fired. The bullet hit the guard in the middle of his chest and knocked him out of his chair. Mother Blessing didn't break her stride. She slipped the handgun back in the holster, stepped around the desk, and approached a steel door.

Hollis caught up with the Harlequin. "There's no door handle."

"It's electronically activated." Mother Blessing scrutinized a small steel box attached to the wall near the door. "This is a palm vein scanner that uses infrared light. Even if we had known about this, it would be difficult to create a bio dupe. Most veins aren't visible beneath the skin."

"So what are we going to do?"

"When you're trying to overcome security barriers, the choices are either low-tech or very high-tech."

Mother Blessing took the submachine gun from Hollis, removed a spare ammunition clip from the equipment bag, and slid the clip between her belt and waistband. The Harlequin pointed her weapon at the door and motioned Hollis to step aside. "Get ready. We're going low."

She fired the submachine gun. Pieces of metal and wood spun through the air as bullets cut a jagged hole through the left edge of the door. As Mother Blessing snapped the spare clip into her weapon, Hollis shoved his hand through the hole and pulled hard. Metal scraped against metal and the door lurched open.

He rushed into the room and found himself staring at a glass tower at least three stories high. Layers of piled-up computer hardware were inside the tower, and their blinking lights were reflected on the glass like miniature fireworks. The whole structure looked both beautiful and mysterious—as if an alien space-ship had suddenly materialized inside the building.

A large monitor hung on the wall about twenty feet away from the tower. It showed an image of Berlin from some location outside the building, a duplicate world where computer-generated figures strolled through a city square. Two frightened computer technicians stood at a control panel directly below the monitor. They were motionless for a few seconds, and then the younger man hit a button on the panel and darted across the room.

Mother Blessing drew her handgun, paused for a second, and shot the fugitive in the leg. As the tech-nician sprawled across the floor, an emergency light started flashing and the computer-generated voice came from a wall speaker.

"Verlassen Sie das Gebäude. Verlassen Sie—"

Looking annoyed, Mother Blessing put a bullet in the speaker. "We don't *want* to leave the building," she said. "We're having such a lovely time."

The wounded man lay on his side, clutching his leg

and screaming. Mother Blessing approached her target and stood over his body. "Stay quiet and be glad you're alive. I don't like people who set off alarms."

The wounded man ignored her. He shouted for a doctor and began to roll back and forth.

"I asked you to stay quiet," Mother Blessing said. "That's a simple request."

She waited a few seconds to see if the wounded man was going to obey her. When he kept shouting, she shot him in the head and walked over to the control panel. The surviving technician was a slender man in his thirties with short black hair and a bony face. He was breathing so quickly that Hollis thought he might faint.

"And what's your name?" Mother Blessing asked.

"Gunther Lindemann."

"Good evening, Mr. Lindemann. What we want is access to a USB outlet for a flash drive."

"Not . . . not here," Lindemann said. "But there are three outlets inside the tower."

"Okay. Let's take a tour."

Lindemann led them over to a sliding door on one side of the tower. Hollis could see that the walls of the tower were six inches thick. Each glass panel was held in place by an outer steel frame. Another palm vein scanner was mounted on the wall. Lindemann slid his hand into the box and the door clicked open.

Cold air surrounded them as they entered the sterile environment. Quickly, Hollis walked over to a workstation with a computer, keyboard, and monitor. He removed the gold chain holding the flash drive, then snapped the drive into an access port.

A message scrolled across the monitor screen in four languages: UNKNOWN VIRUS DETECTED. RISK— HIGH. The screen went blank for a moment and then a red square appeared containing ninety little squares. Only one of the boxes was a solid red color, and it flashed on and off as if a single cancer cell had appeared in a healthy body.

Mother Blessing turned to Lindemann. "How many guards are in the building?"

"Please don't—"

She interrupted him. "Just answer my question."

"One guard is at the desk outside and two are upstairs. The off-duty guards live in an apartment across the street. They'll be here any moment."

"Then I should probably be ready to greet them." She turned to Hollis. "Let me know when we're done."

Mother Blessing led Lindemann out the door while Hollis remained at the workstation. A second red square started flashing, and Hollis wondered what kind of battle was going on inside the computer. As he waited, he thought about Vicki. What would she say if she were standing beside him right now? The death of the guard and the computer technician would have bothered her deeply. *Seed to sapling*. She had always used that phrase. Anything done with hatred had the potential to grow and block the Light.

He glanced back at the monitor. The two red squares glowed brightly and now the virus began to double itself every ten seconds. All the other lights on the terminal started to flash, and a warning siren went off somewhere in the tower. In less than a minute the virus had conquered the machine. The workstation monitor was a solid red color, and then the screen went completely black.

Hollis ran out of the tower and found Lindemann lying face-down on the floor. Mother Blessing stood ten feet away from the technician, pointing the submachine gun at the entrance.

"That's it. Let's go."

She turned toward Lindemann with the same cold look in her eyes.

"Don't waste your time killing him," Hollis said. "Let's get out of here."

"As you wish," Mother Blessing said as if she had just spared an insect. "This one can tell the Tabula that I'm no longer hiding on an island."

They returned to the basement. As they retraced their steps around the equipment stacks, the room lit up with a sudden explosion of gunfire. Hollis and Mother Blessing threw themselves on the floor behind an emergency power generator. Bullets from different angles cut into the heating ducts overhead.

The firing stopped. Hollis heard the click and snap of ammunition clips being loaded into assault rifles. Someone shouted in German, and all the ceiling lights in the basement were turned off.

Hollis and Mother Blessing lay next to each other on the concrete. A small amount of light came from the glowing red switches on the power generator. Hollis could see the dark shape of Mother Blessing's body as she sat up and grabbed the equipment bag.

"The stairs are a hundred feet away," Hollis whispered. "Let's run for it."

"They turned off the lights," Mother Blessing said. "That means they probably have infrared devices. We're blind, and they can see."

"So what do you want to do?" Hollis asked. "Stand here and fight?"

"Make me cold," the Harlequin said, and she gave Hollis the flashlight and a small metal canister. It took him a few seconds to realize that it was the liquid nitrogen they had brought along to disable motion detectors.

"You want me to spray this on you?"

"Not on the skin. Spray my clothes and hair. I'll be too cold to be seen."

Hollis switched on the flashlight and held it in his hand so that light leaked through the gaps between his fingers. Mother Blessing lay on her stomach, and Hollis sprayed the liquid nitrogen on her pants, boots, and jacket. When she turned over on her back, he tried not to spray her hands and eyes. The canister made a faint sputtering sound when it was empty.

The Harlequin sat up and her lips trembled. He

touched her upper arm and felt a burning coldness. "Do you want the submachine gun?" he asked.

"No. The muzzle flash would show my location. I'll carry the sword."

"But how are you going to find them?"

"Use your senses, Mr. Wilson. They're frightened, so they'll be breathing hard and firing at shadows. Most of the time, your enemy defeats himself."

"What can I do?"

"Give me five seconds, then start firing on the right."

She moved to the left and disappeared into the shadows. Hollis stood up and fired the submachine gun until the clip was empty. The mercenaries returned fire—from three points on the left side of the room. A second later, he heard a man screaming, and then more gunfire.

Hollis drew the semiautomatic pistol, then pulled back and released the slide mechanism, forcing a round into the firing chamber. He heard an ammunition clip being loaded into a rifle and ran toward the sound. Light came from the open elevator at the end of the room, and he fired at a dark shape standing beside one of the machines.

Another burst of firing. And then silence. Hollis switched on the flashlight and found a dead man lying six feet in front of him. Cautiously, he moved across the basement and almost tripped over another body near the air-conditioning unit. The mercenary's right arm had been separated from his shoulder.

Hollis swept the flashlight beam across the room and spotted another dead man near the far wall and a fourth body near the elevator. A crumpled figure was a few feet away, and when Hollis ran forward he saw it was Mother Blessing. The Harlequin had been shot in the chest and her sweater was soaked with blood. She still gripped the handle of her sword as if it could save her life.

"He got lucky," she said. "A random shot." Mother Blessing's voice had lost its usual harshness, and it sounded as if she were trying to catch her breath. "It seems right that death comes from randomness."

"You're not going to die," Hollis said. "I'm going to get you out of this place."

Her head rolled toward him. "Don't be foolish. Take this." Mother Blessing extended her hand and forced him to accept the sword. "Make sure you pick the right Harlequin name, Mr. Wilson. My mother chose my name. I've always hated it."

Hollis placed the sword on the ground and reached down to pick her up. With her remaining strength, Mother Blessing pushed him away.

"I was a beautiful child. Everyone said so." Her speech became slurred as blood trickled from her mouth. "A beautiful little girl . . ."

4o

When she was eighteen, Maya was sent to Nigeria to retrieve the contents of a safe-deposit box kept at a bank in downtown Lagos. A dead British Harlequin named Greenman had left a packet of diamonds there, and Thorn needed the money.

There was a power failure at the Lagos airport, and none of the conveyer belts was working. It started to rain as she was waiting for her luggage. Dirty water poured through holes in the ceiling. After paying bribes to everyone wearing a uniform, Maya entered the airport's main lobby and was surrounded by a crowd of Nigerians. Taxi drivers fought for her suitcase, screaming and waving their fists. As Maya pushed toward the exit, she felt someone tugging at her purse. An eight-year-old thief was trying to cut the leather strap, and she had to twist a knife out of his hand.

* * *

IT WAS A different experience to fly into Bole International Airport in Ethiopia. Maya and Lumbroso arrived about an hour before dawn. The terminal was clean and quiet, and the passport officials kept saying *tenastëllën*—an Amharic word that meant "May you be given health."

"Ethiopia is a conservative country," Simon Lumbroso explained. "Don't raise your voice and always be polite. Ethiopians usually call one another by their first names. For men, it is respectful to add *Ato*—which means 'Mister.' Because you're un-married you'll be called *Weyzerit* Maya."

"How do they treat women in this culture?"

"Women vote, run businesses, and attend the university in Addis. You're a *faranji*—a foreigner—so you're in a special category." Lumbroso glanced at Maya's travel clothes and nodded with approval. She was wearing loose linen pants and a long-sleeved white shirt. "You're dressed modestly, and that's important. It's considered vulgar for women to display bare shoulders or knees."

They passed through customs to the welcome area, where Petros Semo was waiting for them. The Ethiopian was a small, delicate man with dark brown eyes. Lumbroso towered over his old friend. They shook hands for almost a minute as they spoke Hebrew to each other.

"Welcome to my country," Petros said to Maya. "I've hired a Land Rover for our journey to Axum."

"Did you talk to the church officials?" Lumbroso asked.

"Of course, *Ato* Simon. All the priests know me quite well."

"Does this mean that I can see the Ark?" Maya asked.

"I can't promise that. In Ethiopia we say *Egziabher Kale*—if God wills it."

They left the terminal and got into a white Land Rover that still showed the emblem of a Norwegian aid organization. Maya sat up front with Petros while Lumbroso took the backseat. Before leaving Rome, Maya had sent Gabriel's Japanese sword to Addis Ababa. The weapon was still in its shipping container, and Petros handed the cardboard box to Maya as if it were a bomb.

"Forgive me for asking, *Weyzerit* Maya. Is this your weapon?"

"It's a talisman sword forged in thirteenth-century Japan. It's said that a Traveller can take talisman objects into different realms. I don't know about the rest of us."

"I think you are the first *Tekelakai* to be in Ethiopia for many years. A *Tekelakai* is the defender of a prophet. We used to have many of these people in Ethiopia, but they were hunted down and killed during our political troubles."

In order to reach the northern road they had to pass through Addis Ababa—Ethiopia's largest city. It was early in the morning, but the streets were already clogged with blue-and-white taxi vans, pickup trucks, and yellow public buses covered with dust. Addis had a core of modern hotels and government buildings surrounded by thousands of two-room houses with sheet-metal roofs.

The main streets were like rivers fed by dirt roads and muddy pathways. Along the sidewalk, the Ethiopians had put up brightly painted booths that sold everything from raw meat to pirated Hollywood movies. Most of the men on the street wore Western clothes. They carried an umbrella or a short walking staff called a *dula*. The women wore sandals, full skirts, and white shawls wrapped tightly around the upper body.

On the edge of the city, the Land Rover had to force its way through herds of goats being driven into the city for slaughter. The goats were only a prelude to more encounters with animals—random chickens, sheep, and slow-moving groups of humpbacked African cows. Whenever the Land Rover slowed down, the children standing beside the road could see that two foreigners were inside the vehicle. Little boys with shaven heads and skinny legs would run beside the vehicle for a mile or more laughing and waving and shouting, "You! You!" in English.

Simon Lumbroso leaned back in his seat and

grinned. "I think it's safe to say that we've stepped out of the Vast Machine."

After passing through low hills covered with eucalyptus trees, they followed a dirt road north though a rocky highland landscape. The seasonal rains had fallen a few months earlier, but the grass was still a yellowish green with patches of white and purple Meskel flowers. About forty miles from the capital they passed a house surrounded by women dressed in white. A high-pitched wailing came through the open doorway, and Petros explained that Death was inside the building. Three villages down the road, Death appeared again: the Land Rover came around a curve and almost hit a funeral procession. Wrapped in shawls, men and women carried a black coffin that appeared to float above them like a boat on a white sea.

The Ethiopian priests in the villages wore cotton togas called *shammas*, and their heads were covered with large cotton caps that reminded Maya of the fur hats worn in Moscow. A priest holding a black umbrella with gold fringe was standing at the beginning of the zigzag road that led down a gorge to the Blue Nile. Petros stopped and handed the priest some money so that the old man would pray for their safe journey.

They descended into the gorge, the Land Rover's wheels just inches away from the edge of the road. Maya looked out the side window and saw only clouds and sky. It felt as if they had two wheels on the road and two wheels riding on air.

"How much did you pay the priest?" Lumbroso asked.

"Not much. Fifty birr."

"Next time, give him a hundred," Lumbroso muttered as Petros negotiated another switchback.

They crossed the metal bridge that spanned the Nile and drove out of the gorge. Now the landscape was dominated by cactus and desert vegetation. Goats still blocked the road, but they also passed a line of camels with wooden carrying frames lashed to their humps. Lumbroso fell asleep in the backseat, his fedora mashed up against the window. He slept through the potholes and the loose stones that rattled up inside the wheel wells, the vultures outlined against the blue sky, and the dust-covered trailer trucks that groaned their way up each new hill.

Maya rolled down the side window to get some fresh air. "I'm carrying both euros and American dollars," she told Petros. "What if I gave the priests a gift? Would that push things forward?"

"Money can solve a great many problems," he answered. "But this discussion concerns the Ark of the Covenant. The Ark is a very important object for the Ethiopian people. The priests would never allow a bribe to influence their decision."

"What about you, Petros? Do you think the Ark is real?"

"It has a power. That's all I can say."

"Does the Israeli government think it's real?"

"Most of the Ethiopian Jews are now in Israel. There's no advantage for the Israelis to give foreign aid to this country, but the aid still continues." Petros smiled slightly. "That's a curious fact to consider."

"Legend says that the Ark was taken to Africa by the son of King Solomon and the Queen of Sheba."

Petros nodded. "Another theory is that it was removed from Jerusalem when King Manasseh brought an idol into Solomon's temple. Some scholars believe that the Ark was first taken to the Jewish settlement on Elephantine Island in the Upper Nile River. Hundreds of years later, when the Egyptians attacked the settlement, it was removed to an island in the middle of Lake Tana."

"And now it's in Axum?"

"Yes, it's kept in a special sanctuary. Only one priest is allowed to approach the Ark, and he does that once a year."

"So why would they give me permission to go inside?"

"As I told you at the airport, we have a long tradition of warriors defending Travellers. The priests can understand this idea, but you present a difficult problem."

"Because I'm a foreigner?"

Petros looked embarrassed. "Because you're a

woman. There hasn't been a woman *Tekelakai* for three or four hundred years."

* * *

IT BEGAN TO rain as they drove across the mountains into northern Ethiopia. The road passed through a bleak landscape, bare of any vegetation except for some terraced farm plots and a few eucalyptus trees planted as a windbreak. The houses, schools, and police stations were all built with chunks of yellow sandstone. Stones were piled on the sheet-metal roofs, and stone walls ran up the hillside in a useless effort to stop erosion.

Maya kept the sword on her lap and stared out the window. In this area, the only points of interest were other human beings. In one village all the men wore blue rain boots. In another village, a three-year-old girl stood by a drainage ditch holding an egg between her thumb and forefinger. It was Friday and the farmers were heading toward the open-air market. Umbrellas bobbed up and down like an army of different-colored mushrooms marching up the hill.

It was evening when they reached the ancient city of Axum. The rain had stopped falling, but a light mist lingered in the air. Petros looked tense and worried. He kept glancing at Maya and Lumbroso. "Everyone get ready. The priests have been told that we're coming."

"What's going to happen?" Lumbroso asked.

"I'll do the talking at first. Maya should carry her sword to show she is a *Tekelakai*, but they might kill her if she takes it from the scabbard. Remember, these priests will die to protect the Ark. You can't force your way into the sanctuary."

The church compound in the center of the city mingled garish modern architecture with the gray stone outer walls of the Church of Saint Mary of Zion. Petros drove the Land Rover into a central courtyard and everyone got out. They stood in the mist waiting for something to happen as storm clouds passed overhead.

"There . . ." Petros whispered. "The Ark is there." Maya looked to the left and saw a cube-shaped concrete building with an Ethiopian cross on the roof. Steel shutters and iron bars covered the narrow windows, and the door was covered with a red plastic tarp.

Suddenly, Ethiopian priests began to come out of the various buildings. They wore different-colored cloaks over their white robes and a wide variety of head coverings. Most of the priests were old and very skinny. But there were also three younger men carrying assault rifles who stood guard around the Land Rover like the three points of a triangle.

After about a dozen priests had appeared, a side door opened on the Mary of Zion church, and an old man came out wearing spotless white robes and a skullcap. Clutching a *dula* with a carved handle, he took one slow step and then another. His sandals made a faint shuffling sound on the flagstone pathway.

"This is the *Tebaki*," Petros explained. "The Ark's guardian. He is the only person allowed into the sanctuary."

When the guardian was about twenty feet from the Land Rover, he stopped and motioned with his hand. Petros approached the old man, bowed three times, and then launched into a passionate oration in Amharic. Occasionally, he gestured at Maya as if he were reciting a long list of her virtues. Petros's speech lasted about ten minutes. When it was over, his face was covered with sweat. The priests waited for the guardian to say something. The old man's head trembled as if he were considering the matter; then he spoke for a short time in Amharic.

Petros hurried back to Maya. "This is good," he whispered. "Very promising. An old monk on Lake Tana has been saying that a powerful *Tekelakai* is coming to Ethiopia."

"A woman or a man?" Maya asked.

"A man—perhaps—but there is some disagreement. The guardian will consider your request. He wants you to say something."

"Tell me what to do, Petros."

"Explain why you should be allowed into the sanctuary."

What am I supposed to say? Maya wondered. *I'm probably going to insult their traditions and get shot.* Keeping her hands away from the sword, she took a few steps forward. As she bowed to the guardian, she remembered the phrase Petros had used back at the airport.

"*Egziabher Kale,*" she said in Amharic. *If God wills it.* Then she bowed again and returned to her place next to the Land Rover.

Petros's shoulders relaxed as if a disaster had just been avoided. Simon Lumbroso was standing behind Maya, and she heard him chuckle. "*Brava,*" he said softly.

The guardian stood quietly for a moment, considering her words, and then he said something to Petros. Still clutching his walking staff, he turned and shuffled back to the main church followed by the other priests. Only the three young men with the assault rifles remained.

"What just happened?" Maya asked.

"They're not going to kill us."

"Well, that's an accomplishment," Lumbroso said.

"This is Ethiopia, so there must be a long conversation," Petros said. "The guardian will make the decision, but he will hear everyone's opinion on this matter."

"What do we do now, Petros?"

"Let's get some dinner and rest. We'll come back late tonight and find out if you're allowed inside."

* * *

MAYA DIDN'T WANT to eat at a hotel where they might encounter tourists, so Petros drove to a bar and restaurant outside the city. After dinner, the place began to get crowded and two musicians stepped onto a small stage. One man carried a drum while his friend had a single-string instrument called a *masinko* that was played with a curved bow like a violin. They performed a few songs, but no one paid attention until a little boy led a blind woman into the room.

The woman had a massive body and long hair. She wore a white dress with a full skirt and several copper and silver necklaces. Sitting on a chair in the middle of the stage, she spread her legs slightly as if anchoring herself to the ground. Then she picked up a microphone and began to sing in a powerful voice that reached every part of the room.

"This is a praise singer. A very famous person here in the north," Petros explained. "If you pay her, she'll sing something nice about you."

The drummer kept the beat going as he circulated through the crowd. He would accept money from a customer, learn a few things about him, and then return to the stage, where he whispered the information into the blind woman's ear. Without missing a beat, she would sing about the honored man—lyrics that caused the man's friends to laugh and pound the table with their hands.

After an hour of this entertainment, the band took a short break and the drummer approached Petros. "Perhaps we could sing for you and your friends."

"That's not necessary."

"No, wait," Maya said when the drummer began to walk away. As a Harlequin, she had lived a secret life under a series of false names. If she died, there would be no memorial to mark her passing. "My name is Maya," she told the drummer, and handed him a wad of Ethiopian currency. "Perhaps your friend could make up a song for me."

The drummer whispered in the blind woman's ear and then returned to their table. "I am very sorry. Please excuse me. But she wants to speak to you."

While people ordered more drinks and the bar girls wandered around looking for lonely men, Maya stepped onto the stage and sat on a folding chair. The drummer knelt beside the two women and translated as the singer pushed her thumb against Maya's wrist like a doctor taking her pulse.

"Are you married?" the singer asked.

"No."

"Where is your love?"

"I'm searching for him."

"Is the journey difficult?"

"Yes. Very difficult."

"I know this. I can feel this. You must cross the dark river." The singer touched Maya's ears, lips, and eyelids. "May the saints protect you from what you must hear and taste and see."

The woman began singing without a microphone as Maya returned to the table. Surprised, the *masinko* player hurried back to the stage. The song for Maya was different from the praises that had been given earlier in the evening. The words came sad and slow and deep. The bar girls stopped laughing; the drinkers put down their beers. Even the waiters paused in the middle of the room, money still clutched in their hands.

And then, just as suddenly as it started, the song was over, and everything was the same as before. Petros's eyes glistened with tears, but he turned away so that Maya couldn't see him. He threw some money on the table and spoke in a harsh voice. "Come on. It's time to get out of here." Maya didn't ask him for a translation. For once in her life, she had been given her own song. That was enough.

* * *

IT WAS ALMOST one o'clock in the morning when they returned to the compound and parked in the court-yard. Most of the area was filled with shadows, and they stood under the only light. Wearing his black suit and necktie, Simon Lumbroso looked somber as he stared at the sanctuary. Petros, the smaller man, seemed nervous. He ignored the sanctuary and watched the church.

This time, everything happened much faster. First the young men appeared with their rifles; then the church door opened and the guardian came out, followed by the other priests. Everyone appeared very solemn, and it was impossible to predict the old man's decision.

The guardian stopped on the pathway and raised his head as Petros approached him. Maya was expecting a special ceremony—some kind of proclamation—but the guardian simply tapped his walking staff on the ground and said a few words in Amharic. Petros bowed and hurried back to the Land Rover.

"The saints have smiled on us. He has decided that you are a *Tekelakai*. You have permission to enter the sanctuary."

Maya slung the talisman sword over her shoulder and followed the guardian to the sanctuary. A priest with a kerosene lantern unlocked the outer gate, and they went inside to the fenced-in area. The guardian's face was a mask without emotion, but it was clear that he felt pain whenever he moved his body. He climbed one step to the front door of the sanctuary, stopped to compose himself, and then took another step forward.

"Only *Weyzerit* Maya and the *Tebaki* will go inside the sanctuary," Petros said. "Everyone else stays here."

"Thank you for your help, Petros."

"It was an honor to meet you, Maya. Good luck with your journey."

Maya was going to offer her hand to Simon Lumbroso, but the Roman stepped forward and embraced her. This was the most difficult moment of all. Some small part of her wanted to stay within that circumference of comfort and safety.

"Thank you, Simon."

"You're as brave as your father. I know he'd be proud of you."

A priest lifted up the red plastic tarp, and the guardian unlocked the door to the sanctuary. The old man placed the key ring inside his robes and accepted the kerosene lantern. He grunted a few words in Amharic and gestured to Maya. *Follow me.*

The door was opened very slowly until there was a two-foot gap. The guardian and Maya slipped into the building and the door was shut behind them. She found herself in an anteroom about twelve feet square. The only light in the room came from the lantern. It swung back and forth as the guardian shuffled across the concrete floor to a second door. Maya looked around her and saw that the history of the Ark had been painted on the walls. Israelites with the skin color of Ethiopians followed the Ark during the long journey through the Sinai desert. The Ark was carried into battle against the Philistines and stored within Solomon's temple.

Now the second door was open, and she

accompanied the guardian into a much larger room. The Ark had been placed in the middle of the room and was covered with an embroidered cloth. Twelve earthenware pots surrounded it, their lids sealed with wax. Maya remembered Petros explaining that this consecrated water was removed once a year and given to women who were unable to conceive.

The priest kept glancing at Maya as if he expected her to do something violent. He placed the lantern on the floor, walked over to the Ark, and removed the cloth. The Ark was a wooden box completely covered with gold leaf. It stood up to her knees and was about four feet long. There were poles on both sides held by rings, and the gold figures of two cherubim were kneeling on the lid. These angelic beings had the bodies of men and the heads and wings of eagles. Their wings glowed brightly in the lantern light.

Maya approached the Ark and knelt before it. She gripped the two cherubim, removed the lid, and placed it on the embroidered cloth. *Be careful*, she told herself. *No reason to move quickly*. Leaning forward, she looked inside the Ark and found nothing but the acacia-wood interior. *It's nothing*, she thought. *A complete fraud*. This wasn't an access point to another realm—just an old wooden box protected by superstition.

Feeling angry and disappointed, she glanced back at the guardian. He leaned on his walking staff and smiled at her foolishness. Once again, she looked inside the Ark and saw a tiny black spot near the bottom edge. *Is that a burn mark?* she wondered. *An imperfection in the wood?* As she watched, the black spot grew larger—to the size of the British penny—and began to float across the surface of the wood.

The spot appeared to be immensely deep, a patch of dark space without limit. When the spot grew to the size of a dinner plate she reached into the Ark and touched the darkness. The tips of her fingers completely disappeared. Startled, she jerked her hand back. Still in this world. Still alive.

When the access point stopped moving, she forgot about the guardian and the other priests, forgot about everything but Gabriel. If she reached forward, could she find him?

Maya steadied herself, and then forced her right arm into the darkness. This time, she felt something—a painful coldness that caused a tingling sensation. She pushed her left arm in and the pain startled her. She suddenly felt as if she were being knocked over by an enormous wave, dragged out to sea by a powerful current. Her body wavered and then surged forward into nothingness. Maya wanted to say Gabriel's name, but that was impossible. She was in darkness now. And no sound came from her mouth.

It was raining hard when Boone reached Chippewa Bay on the Saint Lawrence River. When he stood at the edge of the dock, he could barely see the castle on Dark Island. Boone had been on the island only a few times. Recently, it had been the site of the meeting where Nash had presented the Shadow Program to the executive board. Boone had expected to be in Berlin right now, looking for the criminals who had destroyed the computer center, but the board had insisted that he travel to the island. Although the job was going to be unpleasant, he had to follow orders.

When the two mercenaries finally arrived, Boone told the ferryboat captain to head across the river. Sitting in the boat cabin, he tried to evaluate the men who were going to help him kill someone. Both mercenaries were recent immigrants from Romania who were somehow related to each other. They had long names with too many vowels, and Boone didn't think it necessary to learn the correct pronunciation. As far as he was concerned, the smaller Romanian was Able and the larger man was Baker. The two men sat on the left side of the cabin and braced their feet against the floor of the boat. Able was the talkative one, and he babbled nervously in Romanian while Baker nodded every few seconds to show that he was listening.

Waves rose up from the river and splashed against the bow. Raindrops struck the fiberglass roof of the cabin and made a sound that reminded Boone of fingers drumming on a tabletop. The boat's two windshield wipers clicked back and forth as a sheet of water flowed across the glass. The Canadian boat captain kept adjusting his radio as the pilots of the container ships announced their position along the seaway. "We're half a mile starboard," a voice kept saying. "Can you see us? Over . . ."

Boone touched the front of his parka and felt two hard lumps hidden beneath the waterproof fabric. The vial of CS-toxin was in his left shirt pocket. In his right pocket was the black plastic case that contained the syringe. Boone hated to touch people, especially when they were dying, but the syringe demanded some degree of physical contact.

* * *

WHEN THEY REACHED Dark Island, the captain cut power and allowed the ferryboat to drift up against the dock. The head of island security, an ex-police officer named Farrington, came out to greet them. He grabbed the bowline and looped it around a stanchion as Boone stepped out of the boat.

"Where's the rest of the staff?" Boone asked.

"They're having lunch in the kitchen."

"What about Nash and his guests?"

"General Nash, Mr. Corrigan, and Mrs. Brewster are all upstairs in the morning room."

"Keep the staff in the kitchen for the next twenty minutes. I need to present some important data. We don't want anyone walking into the room and eavesdropping on the conversation."

"I understand, sir."

They hurried through the sloping tunnel that went from the shore to the ground level of the castle. Boone transferred the syringe case and the toxin to his pants pocket while the two mercenaries removed their damp overcoats. Both men wore black suits and neckties, as if they were back in Romania attending a village funeral. The soles of their leather shoes made a scuffling sound on the grand staircase.

The oak door was closed, and Boone hesitated for a few seconds. He could hear the Romanians breathing and scratching themselves. They were probably wondering why he stopped. Boone smoothed down his wet hair, stood up straight, and led them into the morning room.

General Nash, Michael, and Mrs. Brewster sat at one end of a long table. They had finished their bowls of tomato soup and Nash was holding a platter of sandwiches.

"What are you doing here?" Nash asked.

"I received instructions from the executive board."

"I'm the head of the board and I know nothing about it."

Mrs. Brewster took the platter from Nash and placed it in the middle of the table. "I called a second teleconference, Kennard."

Nash looked surprised. "When?"

"Quite early this morning—when you were still asleep. The Brethren weren't happy with your refusal to resign."

"And why should I resign? What happened yesterday in Berlin has nothing to do with me. Blame it on the Germans or blame it on Boone—he's the one in charge of security."

"You're the head of the organization, but you won't accept responsibility," Michael said. "Don't forget the attack a few months ago when we lost the quantum computer."

"What do you mean, we? You're not a member of the executive board."

"He is now," Mrs. Brewster said.

General Nash glared at Boone. "Don't forget who

hired you, Mr. Boone. I'm in charge of this organization and I'm giving you a direct order. I want you to
escort these two down to the basement and lock them
up. I'll call a meeting of the Brethren as soon as
possible."

"You're not listening, Kennard." Mrs. Brewster
sounded like a schoolteacher who had suddenly lost
patience with a stubborn pupil. "The board has met this
morning and voted. It's unanimous. As of today, you are
no longer executive director. There's no negotiation
about this. Accept your emeritus position and you'll be
given a stipend and perhaps an office somewhere."

"Do you realize who you're talking to?" Nash asked.
"I can get the president of the United States on the
phone. The president—and three prime ministers."

"And that's exactly what we don't want," Mrs.
Brewster said. "This is an internal matter. Not something to discuss with our various allies."

If Nash had remained seated, Boone might have
allowed him to continue talking. Instead the general
pushed back his chair as if he were going to run into
the library and call the White House. Michael
glanced at Boone. It was time to follow orders.

Boone nodded to the mercenaries. The two men
grabbed Nash's arms and pinned them to the table.

"Are you crazy? Let go of me!"

"I want one thing to be clear," Mrs. Brewster said.
"I've always considered you to be a friend, Kennard.
But remember—all of us answer to a higher goal."

Boone stepped behind Nash's chair, opened the plastic case, and took out the syringe. The toxin was in a glass container about the size of a pill vial. He forced the needle through the safety seal and filled the syringe with the clear liquid. Kennard Nash glanced over his shoulder and saw what was about to happen. Shouting obscenities, he struggled to get away. Dishes and silverware fell onto the floor, and a soup bowl cracked in two.

"Calm down," Boone murmured. "Have a little dignity." He jabbed the needle into Nash's neck just above the spine and injected the toxin. Nash collapsed. His head hit the table and spit drooled out of his mouth.

Boone looked up at his new masters. "It only takes two or three seconds. He's dead."

"A sudden heart attack," Mrs. Brewster said. "How very sad. General Kennard Nash was a servant to his nation. Missed by his friends."

The two Romanians were still holding Nash's arms as if he might come back to life and jump out the window. "Go back to the boat and wait," Boone told them. "I'm done with you."

"Yes, sir." Able adjusted his black necktie, bowed his head, and he and Baker left the room.

"When will you call the police?" Michael asked.

"In five or ten minutes."

"And how long will it take them to travel to the island?"

"About two hours. There will be no trace of the toxin by the time they get here."

"Dump him on the floor and rip open his shirt," Michael said. "Make it look like we were trying to save him."

"Yes, sir."

"I think I'd like a drop of whiskey," Mrs. Brewster said. She and Michael stood up and walked over to the side door that led to the library. "Oh, Mr. Boone. One more thing . . ."

"Ma'am?"

"We need a higher level of efficiency in all our endeavors. General Nash didn't understand that. I hope you do."

"I understand," Boone said, and then he was alone with the dead man. He pulled back the chair, pushed the body to the right, and it fell onto the floor with a thump. Crouching down, Boone ripped open the general's blue shirt. A pearl button flew through the air.

First he would call the police, and then he would wash his hands. He wanted hot water, strong soap, and paper towels. Boone walked over to the window and looked out over the trees at the Saint Lawrence Seaway. The rainstorm and the low clouds colored the water dark silver. And the waves rose up and collapsed as the river flowed eastward to the sea.

Maya passed through darkness so absolute that her body seemed to disappear. Time continued, but she had no point of reference, no way to judge if this moment lasted a few minutes or a few years. She existed only as a spark of consciousness, a succession of thoughts unified by her desire to find Gabriel.

* * *

SHE OPENED HER mouth and it was filled with water. Maya had no idea where she was now, but water surrounded her and there didn't seem to be a way to the surface. Desperately, she flailed her arms and legs, then controlled her panic. As her body screamed for oxygen, she relaxed and let the bubble of air held in her lungs pull her body upward. When she felt certain about the right direction, she kicked hard with her legs and emerged from the top of a wave.

Breathing deeply, she floated on her back and looked up at a yellowish-gray sky. The water around her was black with patches of white foam. It smelled like battery acid, and her skin and eyes began to burn. She was in a river with a current that was pushing her sideways. If she changed position and bobbed up and down, she could see a riverbank. There were buildings in the distance and points of orange light that looked like flames.

Maya closed her eyes and began to swim toward land. The scabbard strap was slung around her neck and she could feel the sword moving slightly. When she stopped to adjust the strap she realized that the riverbank was even farther away. The current was too strong here. Like an abandoned rowboat, she was spinning around aimlessly.

Looking in the direction of the current, she could see the distant outline of a shattered bridge. Instead of fighting the river, she turned slightly and swam toward the stone arches anchored in the water. Both the current and her own strength propelled her forward until she slammed against the rough gray stone. Maya held on for a minute or so, then swam over to a second arch. The current wasn't as powerful at this point, and she walked through shallow water to the shore.

Can't stay here, she thought. *Too exposed*. She

scrambled up the bank of the river into a patch of
dead trees. Fallen leaves crunched softly beneath her
shoes. Some of the trees had already fallen, but
others were leaning against one another like silent
survivors.

About a hundred yards from the river, she
crouched down and tried to adjust to her new
surroundings. This dark forest was not a fantasy or a
dream. She could reach out and touch the dry stalk of
grass in front of her. She could smell something burning and hear a distant roaring sound. Her body sensed
danger, but—no, it was more than that. This was a
world dominated by anger and a desire to destroy.

Maya stood up and moved cautiously through the
trees. She found a gravel pathway and followed it to a
white marble bench and a park fountain filled with
fallen leaves. These two objects seemed so out of
place in the dead forest that she wondered if they
were put there to mock the person who found them.
The fountain suggested a genteel European park with
old men reading newspapers and nannies pushing
perambulators.

The pathway ended at a redbrick building with all
the windows smashed and the doors ripped off their
hinges. Maya shifted her sword so that she was ready
for combat. She walked inside, passed through the
empty rooms, and peered out the window. Four men
were out on the road that ran past the abandoned
park. They wore boots or mismatched shoes and a

motley collection of clothes. All of them were armed with homemade weapons—knives, clubs, and spears.

When the men reached the far end of the park, a second group appeared. Maya expected a fight, but the two groups greeted each other and headed off in the same direction—away from the river. Maya decided to follow them. She stayed off the streets and passed through the ruins of the city, stopping occasionally to glance through a shattered window. Darkness concealed her movements, and she stayed away from the gas flares burning from broken pipes. Most of these flares were small and sputtering, but a few larger ones were twisting columns of fire. The flares left black soot on the walls and the smell of burned rubber filled the air.

She got lost in a half-destroyed office building. When she found her way to an alley, she saw a crowd of men forming near a gas flare down the street. Hoping no one would see her, she dashed across the street to an apartment complex with oily water flowing like a stream through the concrete hallways. Maya climbed up the staircase to the third floor and peered through a hole in the wall.

About two hundred armed men had gathered in the central courtyard of a U-shaped building. Names were carved into the building's facade. PLATO. ARISTOTLE. GALILEO. DANTE. SHAKESPEARE. She wondered if the building had once been a school, but it was difficult to believe that children had ever lived in this place.

A white man with braided hair and a black man wearing a torn lab coat stood on chairs beneath a wooden frame that served as a crude gallows. Their hands were tied behind their backs, and ropes were around their necks. The crowd milled around these two prisoners, laughing at them and jabbing them with knives. Suddenly, someone shouted a command and a separate contingent marched out of the school. A man wearing a blue suit led this group. Directly behind him, a bodyguard pushed a young man tied to the frame of an old-fashioned wheelchair. Gabriel. She had found her Traveller.

The man in the blue suit climbed onto the roof of an abandoned car. He stood with his left hand in his pocket while his right hand jabbed and gestured at each word that came out of his mouth.

"As the commissioner of patrols, I've guided you and defended your liberties. Under my leadership, we have hunted down the cockroaches that set fires and steal our food. When this sector is finally rid of these parasites, then we will march on the other sectors and take over the Island."

The mob cheered, and several men thrust their weapons in the air. Maya stared at Gabriel, trying to see if he was conscious. A line of dried blood ran from his nose down to his neck. His eyes were closed.

"As you know, we have captured this visitor from

the outside world. Through rigorous interrogation, I
have increased my knowledge of our situation. My
goal is to find a way for all of us to leave this island
together. Unfortunately, spies and traitors have
sabotaged my plans. These two prisoners made a
secret alliance with the visitor. They betrayed you and
tried to find their own private means of escape.
Should we allow this? Should we let them run away if
we remain captive in this city?"

"No!" shouted the crowd.

"As commissioner of patrols I have sentenced these
traitors to—"

"Death!"

The commissioner moved his fingers as if a fly had
landed on his hand. One of his followers kicked out
the stools, and the two prisoners were strangled to
death, jerking at the ends of the ropes while the
others mocked them. When the prisoners finally
stopped moving, the leader raised his palms and ·
quieted the crowd.

"Be alert, my wolves. Watch those around you. All
the traitors have not yet been discovered—and
destroyed."

Although the man in the blue suit was supposed to
be in control of the wolves, he kept jerking his head
around as if he expected to be attacked. When he
climbed off the car, he hurried back into the school
with Gabriel and the bodyguards.

Maya remained in her hiding place as the crowd

dispersed in different directions. The patrols had been unified at the moment of execution, but now everyone glanced at one another with a certain degree of wariness. The two prisoners were left hanging from the ropes, and the last patrol in the area stayed around long enough to steal the dead men's shoes.

When everyone was finally gone, Maya crossed the empty street to the building next to the school. Some kind of bomb had exploded, and the staircase was reduced to a metal frame with a few crossbeams. Climbing with her hands and feet, Maya reached the top floor, and then jumped across a three-foot gap to the roof of the school.

When she entered the third-floor hallway, she found a skinny man with a beard chained to a radiator. He had a green silk tie around his neck, the knot pulled so tight that it looked like a noose.

The man looked unconscious, but Maya crouched beside him and jabbed his chest with the handle of her sword. He opened his eyes and smiled. "Are you a woman? You appear to be a woman. I'm Pickering, the ladies' tailor."

"I'm looking for the man in the wheelchair. Where did they—"

"That's Gabriel. Everyone wants to talk to the visitor."

"So where can I find him?"

"Downstairs—in the old auditorium."

"How many guards?"

"There are twelve or more in the building, but only a few in the auditorium. The commissioner of patrols doesn't trust his own wolves."

"Can you guide me?"

Pickering shook his head. "I'm sorry. The legs won't move."

Maya nodded and began to walk away. "Remember my name," the man said. "I'm Mr. Pickering. Gabriel's *friend*."

Standing at the top of the stairs, she breathed evenly and prepared herself for a long, continuous attack. Both her father and Mother Blessing had always made the distinction between observing and perceiving an enemy. Most citizens spent their lives passively observing what went on about them. In combat, you had to use all your senses and focus on your opponent, anticipating their next move.

Maya took the first flight of stairs slowly, like a student who didn't want to go back to class. Then she heard someone moving below her and she picked up speed, taking the steps two at a time. One of the commissioner's bodyguards was trudging upward and she caught him by surprise, driving the point of her blade through a gap in his ribs. A few seconds later, she reached the ground-floor hallway and ran toward two more wolves. She slashed the first guard in the neck, ducked a blow from a club, and stabbed the second wolf in the belly.

Clutching her sword, she ran into the auditorium.

One of the wolves was near the front of the room. She stabbed him and leaped onto the stage. The commissioner of patrols was getting up from his desk and reaching for his revolver. Before he could aim, Maya swung the sword downward and chopped off his hand. The commissioner screamed, but she brought the blade up hard and silenced his voice forever.

She turned. And there was Gabriel in the wheelchair. He opened his eyes when she cut the ropes off his arms. "Are you all right?" she asked. "Can you stand up?"

As Gabriel opened his mouth to speak, a creaking sound came from the back of the auditorium. Four armed men had entered the room, and more followed a few seconds later. Six wolves faced her. Seven. Eight. Nine.

73

Gabriel got up from the wheelchair and took a few clumsy steps toward the men. "What about the food?" he asked. "Now that the commissioner is dead, you can have all the food that you want. The storage room is on the other side of the courtyard."

The wolves glanced at one another. Maya thought they might attack, but then the man standing closest to the exit slipped out of the auditorium. Everyone lowered their weapons and hurried after him.

Gabriel reached out and touched Maya's arm, then smiled as if they were back in the Chinatown loft. "Are you really here, Maya? Or maybe I'm just having another dream . . ."

"It's not a dream. I'm here. I found you."

Maya placed her sword back in its sheath and embraced him. She could tell that he had lost weight. His body was fragile and weak.

"We can't stay here," Gabriel said. "Once they divide up the food, they'll come looking for us."

"So they're like human beings back in our world? They can get hungry and thirsty?"

"And they can die."

Maya nodded. "I saw the execution in front of the building."

"These people can't remember their past," Gabriel said. "They have no memories of love or hope or any other kind of happiness."

Gabriel put his arm around her shoulder, and Maya helped him out of the auditorium. Out in the hallway, they stumbled past the two men she had killed.

"How did you get here? You're not a Traveller."

"I used an access point."

"What does that mean?"

Maya told him about the sundial of the Emperor Augustus and her journey to Ethiopia with Simon Lumbroso. She decided not to mention that the Tabula had attacked Vine House and almost killed his Free Runner friends. There was a time for these revelations, but not now—when they had to escape.

Gabriel opened a door to a room filled with rows of green file cabinets. A musty smell reminded Maya of old books rotting in a cellar. The only light came from two gas flares burning from pipes that had been ripped out of the walls.

"This doesn't look safe," Maya said. "We should get out of the building."

"There's no place to hide on this island. We have to find the passageway back to our world."

"But that could be anywhere."

"The commissioner of patrols said that the legends about Travellers were always connected to this room. The passageway is here. I can feel it."

Gabriel grabbed a metal table and pushed it against the door. He seemed to gain strength as he found boxes and chairs and piled them on the table. For weeks, Maya had fantasized about this moment—when she and Gabriel would be together in this strange world. But what would happen now? When Simon Lumbroso first told her about the access points he had stressed, *You have to go back the way you came*. Maya never considered the possibility that her only way back would be lost within the dark river. Could she leave with Gabriel, or would she be trapped in this place?

When Gabriel finished blocking the door, he hurried past the cabinets to a workstation in the middle of the room. Suddenly, he stopped and stared at a bookshelf pushed against the wall.

"See that black line? It might be something."

He grabbed an armful of ledger books and tossed them onto the worktable. Then he pushed the bookshelf sideways, exposing a wall. The Traveller smiled at Maya like a math student who had just solved a difficult equation.

"Our way home . . ."

"What do you mean, Gabriel?"

"Right here. This is the passageway." He outlined the shape with his index finger. "Can you see it?"

Maya leaned forward and saw nothing but cracked plaster. She knew at that moment—knew without words—that she was going to lose him. Quickly, she stepped back into the shadows so that he couldn't read her face. "Yes," she lied. "I see something."

A thumping noise came from the entrance to the file room. The wolves had opened the door a few inches, and now they were throwing their bodies against it—forcing back the barricade.

The Traveller grabbed her hand and held it tightly. "Don't be frightened, Maya. We're going to cross over together."

"Something could go wrong. We might lose each other."

"We'll always be connected," Gabriel said. "I promise, no matter what happens, we will be together."

He took a few steps forward, and then she watched his body pass through the plaster as if it were a water-fall with a cave hidden behind it. He pulled her along: *Come with me, my love.* But her hand struck the hard surface of the wall and Gabriel's fingers slipped away.

With one final shove, the wolves forced open the door. Gabriel's barricade slipped sideways and every-thing hit the floor. Maya hurried away from the workstation and stepped between two rows of file cabinets. She could hear deep breathing and whispered voices. A warrior would have picked a familiar battleground, but these men had allowed anger to influence their choices.

She waited for five heartbeats and then came out into the side aisle. A man was standing about twenty feet away from her holding a steel pole with a knife blade lashed to one end. Maya returned to her previous spot between the two rows of cabinets as a second man with a spear came around the corner.

Her hands moved without thought or form. Running forward, she aimed the sword at the man's eyes, then flicked her wrists and knocked the spear blade downward. She stepped on the blade, holding it to the floor, and jabbed upward, stabbing her opponent in the chest.

The dead man fell backward, but he had already perished within her mind. She pulled out two drawers and used them as steps to climb onto the top of the cabinet. Maya was in a three-foot space between the cabinet and the ceiling, watching the first attacker move cautiously down the aisle. Time slowed down. She felt as if she were observing everything through two eyeholes in a mask.

When the spearman reached his companion, she jumped behind him and slashed down the length of his backbone. Now one body lay on top of the other and the room was quiet.

* * *

MAYA LEFT THE school and walked down the street to a twisted stop sign. A hundred yards away, an enormous gas flare trembled like a candle flame near an open window. She turned in a slow circle and surveyed her new world. It no longer made a difference whether she went to the left or to the right. The wolves roamed through every part of the island. Occasionally, she might find a hiding place, but this would be only an interlude in an endless battle.

Two men carrying clubs and knives appeared at the end of the street. "Over here!" they shouted. "She's right here! We found her!" A few seconds later, three other men joined them. They circled the gas flare and stood in front of the light.

Standing alone, Maya understood the full meaning of her choice. She would be trapped in this realm of anger and hate until she was destroyed. *Damned by the flesh*. Yes, that was true. But had she also been saved?

Maya remembered what Gabriel had told her about these men—they had no memory of the past. But she could still recall her life in the Fourth Realm. It was a world of great beauty, but it was also filled with glittering distractions and false gods. What was real? What gave life meaning? At the point of death, everything was lost except love. It could sustain you, heal you, make you whole.

The five men were talking to one another, organizing a plan of attack. Maya drew her sword and swung it around so that the light from the flare was reflected on the blade. "Come on!" she shouted. "I'm ready for you! Come toward me!"

When the men didn't move, she stood up straight, gripping her sword with both hands and concentrating her power in her lower legs. *Saved by the blood*, Maya thought.

She took a deep breath and ran toward the wolves as her shadow passed across the broken surface of the street.

THE END